CRAVING

By

Kristina Meister

JournalStone
San Francisco

JournalStone books may be ordered through booksellers or by contacting:

JournalStone
199 State Street
San Mateo, CA 94401
www.journalstone.com

ISBN: 978-1-936564-51-4 (sc)
ISBN: 978-1-936564-56-9 (ebook)

Library of Congress Control Number:

Printed in the United States of America
JournalStone rev. date: October 12, 2012

Cover Design: Denise Daniel
Cover Art: Philip Renne

Edited By: Elizabeth Reuter

Check out these titles from JournalStone:

That Which Should Not Be
Brett J. Talley

The Demon of Renaissance Drive
Elizabeth Reuter

Cemetery Club
JG Faherty

Jokers Club
Gregory Bastianelli

Women Scorned
Angela Alsaleem

Shaman's Blood
Anne C. Petty

The Pentacle Pendant
Stephen M. DeBock

Pazuzu's Girl
Rachel Coles

ENDORSEMENTS

ACKNOWLEDGEMENTS

For my sister, Carla
Who asks all the right questions

CHAPTER
1

I looked into the two-way mirror and suspected that someone was in the adjoining room staring back at me just as critically. My dark hair was stringy, my brown eyes, bloodshot, and my skin, sallow. I hadn't brushed my teeth in almost two days and I still wore the same baggy sweater, loose-fitting jeans, and ridiculous hair scrunchie as I had when I got the call. I looked horrible; finally the outside reflected the inside.

"I'm sorry for your loss."

Thus far that day, I'd easily heard those words more than all the other times in my life put together, which was saying a lot. Was it my face? Did it welcome sympathy? Even if it had, who were they to assume they could make me feel any better? I wished they would just shut the hell up and stop trying to empathize. It was insulting.

Papers were shuffled behind me. It was as if he wanted to be compassionate, but had a job to do. "The Medical Examiner hasn't given us his findings yet. It will be a day or two, as homicides are given priority. However, there were a few things that seemed out of place and I wanted to run them by you, if you're alright to go on."

I nodded, though I was not really listening. *Eva is dead,* I kept thinking, over and over, just to feel the emptiness of my foot dangling over the cliff's edge and know the fall was real.

It made sense that I was left. After all, she was the sensitive one, while I was older, more responsible. I was the sister that got things done. I wasn't allowed to feel afraid or alone. If they had questions, then I had to suck it up and answer them, because Eva expected it from me.

"You're going to ask me if she was suicidal," I said, sitting down, and he seemed surprised at how calm I sounded.

He had a weathered, thin face with eyes that looked as if they spent a great deal of time reading tiny letters or staring at grainy photos. They narrowed into mere slits as he frowned. "Did she have a history of depression?"

"My sister," I began, cutting across his familiar and comfortable groove, "was in love with the idea of wasting away."

I had tried to keep the disdain from my voice, but he was trained in hearing those subtle inflections. "What does that mean?"

I shook my head and tried to think of how to explain it to an outsider. My chest felt so tight I couldn't breathe, which only made the hollow of my stomach seem cavernous.

"You have to understand, we lost our parents when I had just graduated from high school. It was the year she started junior high. She was vulnerable and when . . . she just turned inward." I pushed my hair behind my ears and massaged my face. "I don't know why. She just became a different person. I took her to people, my aunt took her to people, and over time, she improved, but it was always there, just beneath the surface."

"Was she ever on any medication?" he asked while scribbling notes.

"No. She wouldn't have taken it if it had been prescribed."

He blinked his droopy eyes, his graying brows drawn together. "Did you two have a falling out?"

"When I got married, she moved away," but that wasn't true, because I had pushed her away and would never get her back, "and we sort of . . . grew apart," but that wasn't true either, because I had wanted an escape to a normal life where I wasn't yet a mother.

"When was the last time you spoke to her?"

It hit me then: the vivid memory of her voice, a sound I'd never hear again. My sleeve was soaking wet. He pushed a box of Kleenex toward me.

"Take your time," he allowed, though it was obvious that the more time he spent with me, the less time he had.

"No. I'm fine," I declared, more to myself than him. "She called me last week."

"How did she sound?"

I hid my face behind a tissue and squeezed my eyes shut.

"Do you remember what Dad used to say about heaven?"

"She . . . she didn't usually make sense, she was kind of, all over the place, you know?"

He nodded.

I looked at my hands, at the tan line around my ring finger. Now I had nothing. I was free from all my responsibilities. For the life of me, I wanted them all back.

"She finally had a good job and . . . I thought this time . . . I thought she'd . . ." my voice disappeared somewhere in my sob.

He comforted me with an impersonal smile and a touch to my shoulder. "What did you talk about, specifically?"

"We reminisced . . . about our parents."

"Did she sound upset?"

"She was always upset," and my voice came back with a lurch. I was the responsible one, so why was I sitting there letting this man treat me as if I was a child? "Look, she's dead. It would seem that things are rather simple. Didn't she leave a note?"

He looked at me speculatively and removed his hand from me as if he felt something there, but wasn't sure he knew what it was. "Not that we found."

Finally, I thought, *something I can grasp.*

"My sister always wrote things down. She had a whole set of journals. She blogged for God's sake! You're telling me that though she's always transcribed every factor of her life, she didn't detail her own death?"

"Now you understand why I wanted to speak to you," he said, leaning back. "We searched her place and I didn't find anything. I thought she might have called instead."

"My sister used to send me hand-written letters . . . with penmanship and everything. She single-handedly kept stationery stores afloat," I persisted.

"Her neighbors said they heard voices coming from her apartment. They also said she was into some strange stuff. Do you know anything about that?"

I tried to remember her face, but the only image of her that came to mind was clipped from a different tragedy. She was standing off by herself, silent, her black dress and French braid in perfect order, like she was a doll in a box. She was staring at the wreathed picture of our parents, a look on her face that was so distant, she seemed catatonic. That was the last time I knew what she was feeling. After that, we handled our grief differently.

I braced myself. "No. Define 'strange'."

"Several tenants said they saw 'colorful' looking people coming and going from her apartment, 'punks', and one said they saw her arguing with a man in the alley where the dumpster is located, two days before her death."

It was odd, thinking of her as an adult that did adult things like hang out in alleys or have loud conversations with strange men, but she was all grown up, or rather, she had been.

"Is that all?"

"There were, what appeared to be, needle marks on her arm," he tried to clarify gently, "and some other marks that might have been self-inflicted."

"Drugs?" And that image just didn't seem to make any sense. If there was one thing my sister was, it was clear-headed about wanting to be melancholic.

"We are doing a tox panel on her, when that comes back, we'll know for sure."

"What about the other marks, the self-inflicted ones?"

He closed his file folder and seemed to be debating what he should and should not say. "They circled her wrist, almost as if she had been wearing hand cuffs, but they were clean incisions, like she tried to cut off her own hand."

I felt my face contorting into a sickened expression. "Cut off her own hand?" I repeated.

"They were antemortem, partially healed, which is why the M.E. is doing a more detailed examination."

"So now you're going to ask me if she was in a cult."

He pursed his lips and stared fixedly at my pupils. "Why do you say that?"

"Masochism, needles, depression, bad poetry; plus the only detergent she buys is Woolite Dark. I don't know anything about it, but honestly, she's the type that could have been."

He drew a line under something in his notebook.

"When can I see her?"

He began chewing his lip, trying to find the least hurtful way to tell me that I shouldn't see her in whatever condition she was in.

"I don't care what she looks like. I need to see her," I insisted.

He closed the notebook with a sigh. "It's probably better if you remember her the way she was."

"That's the problem. I can't remember her face. I haven't seen her . . . in a while. I need to see her, please." However I'd seemed to him before, I tried to emphasize it.

He looked as if he might relent. "Let's finish up here and then I can arrange it."

I gave in with a nod.

Until I saw her and touched her cold skin, I wouldn't believe it. And even though it wasn't her anymore, it was important to see the shell and know that the soul had left it behind as proof. I needed that, just like I'd needed it with our parents.

CHAPTER 2

There was a weird kind of separation. It was just a body, in pieces, and though I still thought of her as alive, that person that had cried in my arms was not the thing lying on the metal table. That person was gone.

I don't know where it came from, but the sob shook me and the blinds fell shut. The detective touched me, but there was no comfort in it. In embarrassment, he opened the door and went inside the office. I heard them talking about my sister, "the deceased," they called her. Then he came out.

"Mrs. Caldwell," he began and something in his tone was almost ominous.

"Caldwell is my ex-husband's name."

"Ms. Pierce, then. It will probably be a few days until we can be certain that she . . . um."

"Threw *herself* off the roof."

It was the moment when a door slams on angry words or the metallic crunch around one wrong turn. It was final and could so easily have been avoided, if I'd simply reached out to her one final time. If only I had been more patient.

"Yes, but the tox panel has returned and your sister was not under the influence when she died, which is a bit unusual, though not unheard of."

I nodded. "So why does she have needle marks?"

"We don't know for sure but our investigation will continue until we're certain. Her . . . uh . . . body," he said with hesitation, "will be released to whatever funeral home you request and her personal effects will pass to you as next of kin, after the investigation no longer requires them as evidence."

I took a deep breath. "Thank you."

His face scrunched up again and he seemed to shuffle without moving. It was obvious to me he had been doing this a long while and slowly was tiring of being the one to give miserable people bad news on the worst days of their lives. He looked worn out, and because thinking about him helped me forget her, I wondered why he did it if it tore him down. It was either dedication or hopelessness.

"Have you . . . made arrangements?" he asked.

I smeared my face. "No, but I will."

"Where will you be staying if I need to speak to you?"

"Uh," and before I could think up an answer, the obvious one presented itself, "I was hoping I could stay in her apartment, unless that interferes with the investigation."

He shook his head. "She died across town from her apartment and as I said, we've already taken a look. There's really no reason for us to keep you out. It might even help us. I'll sign out her keys. May I visit?"

"Absolutely. I'll cooperate in full."

I shook his hand and caught a glimpse of the holstered weapon within his coat.

"Try and get some sleep," he said by way of parting.

The rest was a blur for me. I don't remember getting into the rental car, nor listening to the GPS lead me to what remained of my sister in its cold feminine voice, but I do recall her front door on the fourth floor of her building, how it reflected the dingy light from the grimy hallway window.

There was no color there, bad lighting, peeling paint, traces of a life deteriorating that someone should have cared about. How many of her neighbors passed her in the hallway or laundry room and asked themselves, "Who loves her?" I was that person and I had failed.

I unlocked her door and stepped through. It felt so sweetly torturous; I thought I might faint. I thought of star-crossed lovers passing in the street and never seeing each other. I thought of a child born into the world motherless. Bittersweet, I thought, stepping foot into her life without her there to guide me, closest to her when we were farthest apart.

I'm sorry.

I looked around blankly. It was a tiny one-bedroom. The living room had a kitchenette in the corner and several IKEA bookshelves filled with leather bound volumes. There was a yoga exercise ball, a yellow happy face beanbag chair, and a cheap folding TV tray. The curtains on the window could have been there for years, untouched; they hung stiffly and blocked all but a little light creeping in at the edges. A tasteless beaded curtain from her grade school years divided her bedroom from the main room and beyond it, was a bed piled with blankets. The place had not been dusted in ages, dirty dishes were in the sink, and a pile of laundry was sitting by the door.

"Honestly . . . couldn't even leave me with an empty sink before you jumped off a fucking building," I whispered, and it felt good to be angry.

For a few moments, I was disgusted with her miserable life. I hated that I felt obliged to help her, that I had needed her to be alive. How could I have thought I had failed her? Why hadn't the thought that she might be failing me ever crossed her ungrateful, selfish mind before she smeared it onto a sidewalk?

"God damn you."

I dropped my suitcase and slid down the wall. I cried for myself more than her. I cried out of frustration. She had always been this way, doing these things to me, and now that it was over, I was mourning her and felt stupid for it. It wasn't as if I had chosen to be related to her, so why did it hurt so much to no longer have her around?

Because I'm all alone now.

I cried until I had squeezed every last drop from my heart, and when I had finally reached that state of ambiguous stillness, the light had vanished from the edges of the curtains.

I ached all over. Standing made my whole body spasm, but I searched for cleaning products and went to work. I splashed my hands in septic water and scrubbed dishes with fervor. I made her bed. I dusted her book shelves. I opened the windows and cleaned every last pane. In the absence of her self-consciousness, her ennui, I scoured her inner sanctum and left it sparkling and entirely not hers. Looking at it, I felt sick with emptiness.

The smiling face of the beanbag looked up at me and I vowed to one day find the man who had propagated that iconic image and punch him in his grinning pie hole. It was not comfortable to sit in, pressed my spine into an unnatural curve, but I was willing to do anything that brought the stable ground closer to me without the aid of gravity.

My fingers stroked the spines of her books and over time, I noticed a pattern. None of the volumes had titles; they were simply bound in monochromatic leather, each shelf in a separate color. I drew one out and opened it. It cracked in protest, but split in half in my lap. Every page was of a different type of paper, as if she'd scavenged all that she could and had them independently bound, but even that hadn't been good enough. Tiny scraps were glued inside, doodles were drawn on receipts, and even a few cocktail napkins containing little phrases were stuffed in like bookmarks.

On a piece of legal paper, I found her beautiful handwriting in a purple sharpie below a scribble she had swirled into being.

"The soul is chipped, the days are hammers. They find my weak spaces and pry. They look at me with nails and sharp tools. They chisel me raw. What am I now? They say, 'You are beautiful. You are perfect, faceted and sparkling.' But my beauty was my filth, my roughened splendor, my mystery. They stole it from me to

make themselves richer and now, thousands strong, they smile as I reflect them. But my soul is a black stone, an obsidian mirror, and when they tire of deceiving themselves, they will see the darkness of their crude refinement. They will scry and find no future. I am a gateway to nothingness."

The book slipped from my hands. I closed my eyes and tried to block it out, but it was no use. The memory was going to fight its way out whether I liked it or not.

"Do you remember what Dad used to say about heaven?"

"No," I had said, knowing what she meant, but wanting her to just shut up about it. I was tired of her constant search for moral support and rescue. Who rescued me? No one, that's who.

"He used to say that heaven was the greatest place you could imagine. Don't you remember?" She sounded hurt, but at the time, I didn't care how badly I stung her. I didn't want to talk of suffering eventually ending in bliss, because to me, at that time, it felt endless. Perhaps it was wrong of me, but I was tired.

I had been sitting at my kitchen table, phone squished uncomfortably between ear and shoulder, trying to soap the wedding ring off my finger for once and for all, and somehow everything else had shrunk in comparison with that final, frantic task.

"You know, Ev, I don't. I don't remember a thing about it, and to be honest, that's the dumbest thing I've ever heard, because no matter how good your heaven is, I'm pretty fucking sure I can imagine better."

"I know," she had said softly, *"It's different for every person and it changes. That's the point. When we were kids, it was a room full of candy with no adults, but now I wonder what it is."*

"A place where Brad Pitt tells me how beautiful I am and insists on killing Howard for me," I had joked, just to stifle her.

Her throat scratched in the hollows of my ear, *"I just don't think perfection or happiness are really enough anymore."*

"You've never been happy. How would you know?" I lashed back. I didn't want to talk about meaning. Meaning was having your husband dump you after years because he'd impregnated a stripper. Had she asked me about my pain? No. She had just called to free-speak indie poetry at me, and I didn't want to hear it. I had real problems she would never understand.

"You don't believe it," she whispered.

"No, I don't. Why do you always feel it necessary to remind me that the memories I have of them are marred by ridiculous childhood stories? Why do you always have to make me feel like I'm not living up to their standards? Any faith I

may have had in omniscient deities died the moment I realized that people see what they want, until they go blind."

"Lily, I . . ." she began.

"Can it."

She sighed and seemed to halt what she was about to say. It was a moment I would never get back. Whatever she wanted to tell me, I would never know.

"It doesn't exist, Lily, I know," she had said with surprising clarity, *"but that's just it. It's a direction. It's meant to keep us alive. You can find hope all the time without stuff like that, but I needed it, and you always knew it. I have to say this to you, because you're the strongest person I've ever met."*

I had snorted.

I thought back on it and was ashamed that I had not asked what she meant, had not accepted her compliment and found something to say back. I had just been too upset.

"I'm not going to cheer you up. I'm not going to convince you to put down the knife. I just can't handle it anymore, Ev. Do it yourself and leave me alone."

She hadn't responded for a long time while I twisted and pulled at that damn golden band, my fingers cramped and my skin raw. I don't know what she was thinking, and I wasn't even listening to the silence.

"Everything means something, you know," she whispered. *"Even if you don't want to accept what it means, it means something. There is no such thing as nothing."*

"What are you talking about?"

"I know you hate me. I've always known."

"I don't hate you," I had growled at her defensively, knowing she was right and dismayed that I'd been transparent.

"You do, and it doesn't matter, because it all means something. I'm not supposed to live. I'll die and when I do, you're fated to wonder why, because you don't have faith in anything. You're fated to always rescue me, because you're just that tough."

"What?"

She had laughed strangely, like it was all not quite a joke, and for a moment, in my kitchen, I had known that she was crazy.

"Ev, you're not doing something stupid are you?"

"Demons, angels, villains . . . vampires," then she laughed again and I realized that something was not the same as it had always been, *"they don't stand a chance."*

Then she hung up.

Had she been cutting herself when she called me, sitting in her kitchenette, carving a band around her arm while I was contemplating hacking off my left ring finger? Why had I chosen those words, 'put down the knife'? Where had my strength been then? Why hadn't she put more faith in it, if she was such a believer?

I took a shaky breath and picked the book back up. On the inside of a large sheet of drawing paper that had been bound folded in half, I found a sketch of a man. It was only lines, hatch marks that formed a shape seated in a cross-legged position, hands joined in his lap as if in meditation. It reminded me of the ghost story books she had collected as a child, eerie in its smeared, yet accurate, grotesquery. Below the drawing was a smudged charcoal paragraph.

"It's a wall that stretches upward, constantly tipping over me like a wave. I see far from beneath it, but it rolls over and I'm blind again. I breathe in dust and drown. I am buried in a fat, breathing, sweating animal that churns as it eats me whole. I sink into its flesh and am incorporated. When I open my eyes again, I see the horizon through the gaze of a universe."

A piece of me wondered what had inspired her ramblings. Did she have a brain like a waterwheel constantly churning out thoughts she found lovely enough to scrawl on any handy bit of paper? For a few minutes, I flipped through the pages, watching them crack and slide against each other, wondering why she had never been diagnosed with hypergraphia.

The phone rang. The sound was so sudden that I dropped the book and mistook my heartbeat for someone pounding at the door. I had to look around to find the handset, half-buried by the pile of clothing. It warned me of a low battery as I hit the button.

"Hello?"

"This is Detective Matthew Unger. I'm calling for Ms. Pierce."

"It's me."

"How are you?" he asked and it sounded more perfunctory than heart-felt, which probably had something to do with how much sleep he had gotten.

"I'd be great if my sister wasn't dead."

His beleaguered mind did a systems-check and I could feel him kicking himself. "Of course, that sounded bad. I'm sorry. I was just checking in to make sure you made it okay. Are you busy?" which was just cop-speak for "are you too fucked up to talk to me?", and the answer was yes, but as Eva had said, I was curious to a fault.

"Have you learned something new? That was fast."

The phone beeped again. Unger's voice was withdrawn and a bit fatigued. "Your sister made a complaint a few months ago."

"Complaint? Like a police report?"

I heard a car alarm from his side of the connection and realized he was on a cell phone. "Yes. She claimed that she had a stalker, someone who would follow her to and from work. She didn't go into detail, and it could not be substantiated. They wrote it off as a . . . false complaint."

Great, I thought, *just fucking great. She had a stalker and I'm staying at her house.*

"Do you know anything about who it might have been?"

"No, I'm sorry," I said.

"Given her state of mind, it may have just been . . ."

I pinched the bridge of my nose and grew even more frustrated by his roughened chivalry. Fate had a sense of irony, to hand me a gentleman, now of all times, when it could have made my life a lot easier and been consistent. "Paranoia?"

There was a more insistent beep, as if the phone had a personality and was whining for food. "Yes. Please make sure to lock your doors and windows, just in case. I'll let you know if anything pans out."

"I appreciate it."

"Call me if you need anything."

"Okay. Bye."

I set the phone in its recharging cradle on the TV tray. The clothes were there beside me, and it looked as if they were the contents of her entire closet waiting to be laundered. I picked up a blouse and brought it to my face. Chanel, like always, ever since my mother had bought her a bottle for Christmas and she'd fancied herself an adult. Tomorrow I would have to start going through it all, washing the clothes, picking which things I would keep and which I would give away.

I would not sell a single piece of it.

The phone rang again and I nearly ripped the cord out of the wall and threw it out the window in recoil, but just stared at it instead. After a few rings, I heard her voice, but it was not the almost shy voice it had been. It sounded strained to my ears.

"This is Eva Pierce. I screen my calls. Leave a number."

Then there was the beep.

I listened. First, a scraping sound, like a hand over the mouthpiece. Then there was the hiss of a sensitive mic picking up ambient noise.

I reached for the loudspeaker button, prepared to tell whoever it was to piss off, but another sound stopped me: footsteps and the lonely wail of a car alarm.

I jabbed the button.

"Detective Unger?" I called, thinking he had perhaps pocket-dialed me by accident.

There was the rhythmic chafe of breathing and then, "Lilith."

No one called me Lilith. I had strictly forbidden it after the jokes my teenaged friends had made about *Cheers*. The voice was one I didn't recognize. It sounded like the forced whisper of an emphysema sufferer. For some reason, a tingle shot from my sacrum to my skull.

I picked the phone off of the cradle and pressed it to my ear. "Who is this?"

I heard more footsteps, what sounded like a conversation taking place somewhere in the background.

If eardrums could expand like pupils, mine were fully dilated. Scratching and jiggling became as loud as canons. When the phone beeped again, explaining to me in not so many words that it was about to shut itself off, I nearly went deaf.

"Hello?"

"Oh, Hell," I heard and recognized the voice as Unger's, though it was muffled.

"Hello," I repeated, hoping he'd hear the sounds of my tiny shout and get the hint, but he just kept on talking to himself.

Suddenly, the raspy voice returned at full volume. "Everything means something," it said.

The phone trilled angrily and went dead in my hand.

I stared at it and put it back on the charger. When it came back to life, I hit the loudspeaker button and dialed the number from Detective Unger's business card, but before it got to the third ring, a new, harassed beep told me that there was someone else ringing in. Huffing, I tapped the flash button thinking that if Unger answered while I dealt with the other caller, it would be fitting payback.

What came from the other line was the sound of a cell phone ringing in chorus with a car alarm. It went on for some time, until silence intruded.

"The detective is unreachable," said the raspy voice.

CHAPTER 3

The next day, I went to the police station. I had spent most of the night trying to call Unger back, only to leave about a hundred useless and rambling messages in various states of discontinuity. I had even dialed 9-1-1, but hung up, thinking they would probably know before I would. I thought sure I would find the station in a shambles with men in bad suits running back and forth shouting incomprehensible codes or taking phone calls off a tip line. I thought I would find them huddled in tight knit groups with sallow, glazed faces mourning the loss of one of their fellows.

Everyone was exactly where they had been the day before, doing what they always did, including Detective Unger.

I watched him for a while from the front desk. I'm not sure why, I just had to. What was going on? I was positive I had heard him being accosted by the same someone who had called to taunt me, to let me know that they had gotten to my sister and to the man investigating her supposed suicide. Why else say what they said?

"Everything means something."

But there he was, drinking a cup of coffee from a black mug, reading something in a file, and frowning expertly. He was a cop, through and through, had probably been one for most of his long life. He seemed the type of guy who smoked like a chimney, drank Jack straight, remembered the face of every victim, and could voice over a *film noir* without batting an eyelash. I felt trapped inside a screenplay.

It took me a while to build up the courage to speak to him; after all, I had nearly stalked the man. I stood there like a fool, even though the lady at the desk kept trying to welcome me with her gaze, and thought about the excuses I would make. When I had picked one that wasn't too lame, I stepped out of the cover of the silk tree and smiled at her.

"I'm here to see Detective Unger about my sister's case."

She nodded. Guessing it was a welcome, I strode boldly up to his desk, still gross, unshowered, and wearing the shapeless sack of clothing.

"Detective?"

He glanced up, blinked, and then offered me the chair beside his desk.

"I'm sorry to have called you so many times. I thought for sure I had heard something happen to you and right before then I got a weird phone call."

He frowned again.

"I thought it might be related to the case," I kept blabbing, though he looked more and more confused as the moments passed, "and I wanted to run it by you. He knew my name and everything. When I couldn't reach you I was worried so . . ."

"Um."

That was all, but it felt like a sledgehammer. I realized then, that what I saw in his face wasn't confusion about my freakish interest in his safety; it was confusion about my identity.

My heart sped up.

"I'm . . . sorry if I know you, but I can't place you," he said in gruff perplexity.

I gave a hard swallow. "I'm Lilith Pierce. We spoke yesterday about my sister."

"Your sister?"

Something was wrong. This was not how it was supposed to happen. I was there all day. I had come directly from the airport and spent hours in his company, but this man for some reason, had no idea who I was.

"Eva Pierce. She . . . she threw herself off a building. I was here . . . talking to you about it." I know there was that whisper in my voice, that softened tone that tells others that the speaker should be considered as worthy of medication.

He stared at me and clearly, I saw a reflection of myself altered in the funhouse mirror of his warped memory.

In that catering, condescending way, he smiled and apologized yet again. "I'm afraid I'm not on any cases like that, ma'am."

"How can you not be on the case? How do you explain the fact that I know your name, that I called your phone, that *you* called *me*?"

A spark of life flickered. "I have two phones, maybe someone . . ."

I jumped up from my chair, though I'm not sure what I meant to do. "No! It *was* you! We talked here! Here! Yesterday!"

He started up slowly, his hand out in front of him as if I might hit him or bolt for the door. Then I realized how I seemed, disheveled, distraught, clutching my purse like a delusional old woman. I forced myself to relax, to uncurl my hands and stand tall.

"I was here all day yesterday. Ask her, she's the one that signed me in!" I demanded and pointed to the lady at the desk.

Everyone was looking at me, at Unger, at each other. This was a defining moment, the period of about thirty seconds wherein I was free to be whatever I was. After that, I was either credible, or a nutcase, so I held onto it for dear life, seeing everything in slow motion.

Unger looked at the woman over my shoulder. "Was she here yesterday, Cynthia?"

Cynthia shook her head in amazement.

"I didn't see her," one of the detectives volunteered.

Unger frowned even deeper and crooked his fingers under his chin. He was staring at me as if he wanted to believe me and that gave me enough courage to plead with my gaze.

"Anyone else see her?"

Glances were exchanged. I took a deep breath and glowered at them defiantly.

"We got a call," said a second detective quietly. "We were gone."

I had lost my patience. "Look, I don't get what you're trying to pull, but I want to know where my sister is! I want her body back, right now!"

The woman from the desk was closing in on my six. I could hear her squeaky ergonomic shoes. She put what was supposed to be a comforting hand on my shoulder. "What's your sister's name, dear?"

"Eva Pierce! I visited her in the morgue yesterday!"

"And how did she pass, dear?"

"She jumped off the Old River Motel!" I nearly shrieked. "I already said that!"

Everyone stood still, gave me space. The hand recoiled from me, but ever so slowly came to rest on my shoulder again.

"I'll check the records for you, dear. I'm sure we have not misplaced her. I'll call right now, see?" and she reached for the phone, a look in her face and a tone in her voice that was the tried and true recourse of a baffled grief counselor. It was the tone my ex-husband used when he had already worked me into a frenzy, the one that said "By talking this way to you, I'm demonstrating superiority."

She dialed an extension and spoke in an almost silent whisper. "Doctor, we have a situation here. Have you . . ."

"Ms. Pierce," Unger said, reaching out. "Won't you sit down while we sort this out?"

I glared at him, smoothed back my hair and glanced away haughtily. "I'm fine standing, thanks."

After a few minutes, Cynthia hung up the phone. The click echoed into a long silence.

"Well?" I barked.

"Did you receive a call from someone, dear?"

"My name is Lilith Pierce. Call me 'dear' one more time, I dare you. Where is my sister!?"

"Calm down," Unger soothed, and for it nearly received a black eye. "How did you find out that your sister passed away?"

"I didn't fly all the way from California for my health!"

"I understand that, ma'am," he said, trying not to shout at me. He turned a dark eye on Cynthia instead, "What did he say?"

"She was brought in this morning."

"What?!" we all said at once.

"The clerk said she was brought in two hours ago, suspected suicide. They were just going to call . . . her next of kin."

My heart stopped beating. In that one instant, not only was I free, I was free-falling. My mind lost the faculty of forming the simplest of queries. This was impossible. This was unacceptable.

They were experiencing something similar, but for them it was an odd clerical error and I was a basket case.

I think it was my knees that went, but when people say that, what they really mean is that the whole leg sort of slackens, like I was instantly a paraplegic. They caught me, inexpertly, and I fell without a complaint. Sitting on the hard ground, I looked at their shiny shoes and wondered what was going on.

"Who's the lead on it?" he asked around.

"Mitchell and Thomas. They dropped by on their way to lunch, but it was a pretty definite suicide. Apparently, there were witnesses. I can call them now if you want and have Thomas email . . ."

"God damn it, yes! Tell them I'll take over and figure out what the hell is going on."

Had it all been a dream? Was I so mentally overwhelmed that I had mixed up the ride from the airport with the ride from her house that had happened two days later?

Then I thought of the plane ticket. Opening my bag without a moment's hesitation, I rummaged for it, and produced it. Unger took it from my shaking fingers and read the time stamp on the luggage tag.

"She flew in today. She was on a plane when . . ."

His voice sounded odd, like he was in a car and being carried away from me at an incredible rate of speed.

I woke up on the ground, a wet paper towel on my head, someone shining a light in my eyes. I sat up, finally understanding how important it was to breathe on a regular basis.

"Where is she?" I gasped.

"You can't see her, dear," Cynthia said. "She's too badly hurt."

"Right now," I raged. "I want to see her *right now*!"

They pulled me upright and Unger took only enough time to give his coworkers a vengeful look, as if they had somehow caused it.

"I'll take her," he said, and helped me to my feet.

It was the same as it had been the day before, the same journey to the bowels of the building, the same grey hallway, the same dusty blinds. A heated conversation was going on inside the room. I spent the time staring into space, wondering if I had lost my mind.

When he came back, he seemed a bit frazzled. The shades were jostled.

"Are you sure this is what you want? She's . . . she hasn't been cleaned or . . ."

"Now!" I hissed.

He gave a final sigh of concern and tapped the glass.

The blinds went up.

There she was, for certain, inside a dark rubber bag, still wearing a pin-stripe suit and pink blouse. Her head was at an odd angle and was slightly misshapen. Blood had congealed at the back of it. She was pale, a mottled, darkish tide-line surrounding her ears and the back of her neck. One of her earrings was gone, and even though it was covered, her right leg was obviously broken.

My God, I thought, *I was only a few minutes too late. I could have saved her!*

I think he saw it in my face. The blinds dropped.

"I'm sorry for your loss."

I turned to look at him, my touchstone to reality. It was obvious he was a good man.

"You already said that," I breathed.

He managed a hard swallow. "Did I?"

"I just talked to her," I murmured vaguely, glancing around. "She had an argument in an alley. Make sure you look closely at her arm. I don't know where they came from. May I have her keys?"

I don't think he knew what to make of me, really. I was speaking in riddles, but in his eyes, I was either the worst criminal in the history of assassinations, or I was a psychic. Either way, he apparently had enough faith in his ability to decode it eventually.

He pulled out one of his cell phones and spoke briefly with someone about the search of Eva's apartment. Evidently, his coworkers had been and gone, finding nothing to lead them to believe her death was anything beyond self-perpetrated. He hung up, and in a few moments had retrieved the keys from the evidence clerk. As I walked away, he scribbled notes, following close behind me. He didn't leave my side until I got to the rental car.

"Ms. Pierce?"

I froze with the key in the lock.

"Did you really . . . see me?"

"I wouldn't make something like that up."

"I can see that. I don't know what's going on. I . . . I've seen some strange things . . . nothing like this . . . I promise you, I'll do my absolute best."

I could hear the sincerity in his voice, peeking through the disbelief. "Thank you."

"Do you have a cell number?"

"No."

"Then, I assume you can be reached at her home?"

I nodded, prepared to leave, but as I stared at myself in the window reflection, I knew there was more to be said. "She didn't commit suicide."

"How can you be sure?"

"I . . ." but how could I say it? I knew because some wacked out shit was happening to me, her dearest sister, her caretaker, the one who'd practically raised her. I was having some kind of weird psychic break and that was how I knew? "It just doesn't make any sense," I finished.

He touched my arm, and this time, he really meant it. Funny, how one unordinary thing could snap a person out of their routine.

"I'll call you when I have something."

I glanced at his elbow. "She had a stalker. I've spoken to him. He has a raspy voice."

But had I, or had it been a needle-sharp lie amongst a haystack of truth?

He said nothing and handed me a card. "Are you alright to drive?"

I shot an acidic look at his face. "I got on a plane in a delusional state. Obviously I am."

"I'm sorry, I really don't know . . ."

I opened the door, got in and pulled away before he could say anything else.

* * *

I went straight to her apartment without directions and was not the least bit surprised to find it looked exactly as I remembered it. The only difference was that I had never been there. The dishes reeked from the sink, the bed was still unmade, and the phone was in the pile of clothes, slowly dying.

I picked it up by the antennae with thumb and forefinger, aware that even as I treated it like an offender, it was not responsible for anything. As I set it in the cradle and stared at the sleek darkness of its pod-like construction, I knew why I hated it. It was an obelisk, an icon of an open line of communication that had tediously broken down. It was the natural course of a relationship with so many stops and misconceptions, but it was our fault for letting it get to that point.

My finger hit the answering machine button.

"This is Eva Pierce. I screen my calls. Leave a number." There was no recording of my call from the stranger.

"What happened?" I whispered.

Had it really been a vision? I thought back to the notification call, to the first time I'd heard Unger's voice, but it had never happened. When I focused hard on it, all I could recall was the feeling, not the place, not the moment, not even the phone in my hand. Maybe that was normal, but I had a feeling it wasn't. So what happened to the time? What day was it really? What was going on?

I looked around. This time, I saw no reason to impose order on her decay. I just left it, stood in the center of it and looked around, trying to feel it as she had. It was either a symptom or a cause of her mental state, and that was just how I had to look at it, until she made more sense.

The color-coded journals called to me from their rows so antithetical to the rest of the home. I reached for one that was level with my eye and turned it over and over in my hand. Simple bindings concealing so much chaos, devoid of symbol or explanation; they were all I had left, but they were unreadable. The page I turned to had a date on it, and to my horror I realized the date was a recent one, only two weeks old.

"You were there again tonight. My Mad maudlin. When I look at you I don't see those other things. I see me in my purest form, looking back. I see what I might be, not what I am. That's why I'm afraid. What is that? Is it selfish? Is it evil to be selfish? How can it be? Because I find that I want . . . desperately, to live for something other than myself. I want to live for wind and rain, for terror and peace,

for falling. I want to live. You teach me that so simply, but I have never been a good student. Perhaps you knew, all along."

My diaphragm contracted so violently, I thought I might vomit.

"Oh, Ev," I sighed, and in a fitful attempt to stay apart from that dreadful blackness I could see in front of myself, I set the book down. As it left my fingers, my energy simply stayed with it. It anchored my soul away from me and I felt more tired than I had ever been. I went to her bedroom, unburied the mattress, and in misery, pressed my face into her pillow.

I don't know how long I slept, but I was troubled by nightmares, jumbles of the awful things I'd felt or seen, the things that truly confused me. I awoke with such a sharpened mind that I could have cut a man in half with a glance.

Hadn't she said it? She was fated to die and I to seek the truth. I sat up and took a deep breath. It was time to make sense of things.

What, if any part of my vision was real? Had the entire dream occurred in the car, waiting in the parking lot, or on the plane? Was it rational, stemming from exhaustion or . . . but that was too crazy to think about. It just made no sense. But how else had I gotten the particulars so accurate? How had I known what would happen to her? What did it mean?

Everything means something.

I balled my hands into fists and squeezed my skull between them. An insistent headache was building behind my eyes.

"Okay, so . . ." I said to the room, "I don't really know anything, right?"

The last echoes of my voice mocked me.

"If everything in the vision was false, then I don't know anything. I can't do anything. But if even *one* part was true," I thought of her leap from the building, "doesn't that mean that it's at least probable that the rest might also be true?"

I don't know what I expected. It wasn't as if she seemed to have enough of an attachment to her home to visit it in the after-state, whatever that may be, if anything.

I sniffed and tried to keep the tears from falling, "Where do I start, Eva?"

The phone trilled and I jumped. Nearly leaping from the bed, I rushed to it and hit the button as if tackling her off the roof's edge.

"Hello?!"

For a moment, no one spoke. I think my fervor caught them off guard. Then a throat cleared and I knew who it was.

"Detective."

He gave a startled snort, realized how improper it was, and ended with another cough. "Ms. Pierce."

"Yeah, I know, kinda intense that I can do that right?" I quipped, instantly livid that I had, for one brief moment, believed Eva's pronouncement. Not everything meant something. It all just happened. Sometimes things meant something to someone, but lots of things went unnoticed and never meant anything to anyone.

"It . . . it does make me . . . uncomfortable."

"My sister's dead, try it from my perspective."

"I'm sorry."

"I really hate it when you do that," I sighed. The headache was intensifying.

"Huh? Do what?"

"When you apologize. You're not very good at it."

"That's what my Lieutenant says," he lamented.

"I'm over it," I declared. "Please, don't treat me like a victim. Say what you called to say."

He paused to take a breath and let it out slowly. No doubt, he talked to quite a few people in that way, balancing dexterity with nuance and falling short of either. But if he wasn't good at dealing with survivors, he had to be good for something, or they wouldn't have kept him around. Hopefully that something was turning over rocks and shaking trees.

"I'm sorry if I seemed to be *handling* you. I just . . ."

"I know, lots of emotions, empathy training, blah blah."

"Are you sure you're alright?"

"Yes," I snarled.

"Okay," he said soothingly in a tone that reminded me of my father. "I was calling to let you know that you were right. She had some very odd circular marks on her wrist, as if she . . ."

"Yes, I know."

"Right," he hesitated, "and she did make a complaint."

"Mmmhmm."

"But seeing as how I've got a head start thanks to your . . ."

"Don't say it," I warned.

It sounded like he was tapping a pencil on his desk. "Yeah, well, I was able to do a little research. I tracked down her employer and spoke to him."

Ah, here it is, I thought, *a starting point.*

"He said that she was a diligent person, never late, never talkative, serious, but didn't seem to be suicidal. In fact, he said that she went out a lot."

"Went out?" I laughed. "On what planet? My sister didn't go *out*."

He cleared his throat again.

"Unger, don't. I've known you longer than you've known me. I know when you're holding back. Full disclosure."

This time, he really did chuckle. Perhaps it was morticians' humor, but I almost felt like chuckling too. Anything to lift this painful ache from my chest.

"Maybe your sister was turning into someone you didn't know that well."

"And maybe the sky isn't blue. She's been the same since our parents died. That's why it's called a chronic condition. She wouldn't suddenly get over it."

"True, but not impossible. Maybe the job was helping her focus on something else and her coworkers were pulling her out of depression. Her boss said she came in to work a few times a bit 'depleted'," he persisted.

I traced the spines of her journals with my fingers. "What is she, a bank account?"

"Hung over," he translated.

"Also not possible," I insisted. "My sister would *never* touch alcohol. Our parents were killed by a drunk driver. Substance abuse was something I almost wish she *had* been into. It would have made it a lot easier to figure out what was wrong with her."

He sighed and I heard the creak of a chair as he leaned back. "Well, I'm still interviewing her coworkers."

I couldn't help it. Bitterness was welling up in me. Other people were experiencing her in a new life apart from me, viewing her in a way I would never get to see her. She existed outside of what I thought of as *our* misery, but I never had. I felt betrayed.

"What did they have to say about the marks on her wrist, that she was cutting her losses?" I spat out.

"You're reading my mind again," he warned helpfully. "They said that she told them she got her arm stuck in her garbage disposal."

I thought back to my vision-quest and glanced at the sink. "She doesn't have one."

"I see."

"Nor does she have any bloody knives, circular saws, or wood-carving tools, in case you want to know."

I could hear his little sounds of acquiescence. "Well, then I'll have to figure out who her friends were and how the marks got there."

"Could the . . ."

"Nope, not hand cuffs."

"That's what you said last time, so I wasn't going to ask about that. I was going to ask about the needle marks. I know she didn't have anything in her system."

He made a soft noise of surprise in his throat at the revelation of my complete knowledge, but he should have known better. "Sorry. We're not sure. One of three things: something harmless went in, something went in that degraded in the body, or finally, that something went out. She could have given blood or plasma lately, but I doubt it. No one would have taken her blood with a cut like that on her wrist."

"So you're saying that she could have been drugged several days before her death and then cut, but if that happened, what would they have used? Pretty much any opiate or over-the-counter drug that induces drowsiness stays in the body a day or so. I mean, Diphenhydramine Hydrochloride wacks me out for at least twenty four hours, which means its half-life has got to be about that long. Which means that it would have been at least *detected* two days later. For that matter, why cut her up and then let her go? That's not very rational."

Unger paused, "What did you say you did for a living?"

"I'm a housewife. I read a lot of detective fiction."

"Listen, I've got some cold cases, if you want to lay your hands on a few files and divine some new leads, now that you have a calling."

Frowning, I cleared *my* throat. "Isn't that remark slightly inappropriate?"

The uncomfortably diligent Unger reappeared instantly. The chair squeaked out an apology before he could get his voice to work.

"I'm kidding, Detective. It's fine to make jokes, I'm an expert in black humor. Just add some hard details in here or there, okay? All I have are her diaries and I'm just awash, walking around in her head. I feel like I'm going nuts."

"You're telling me," he murmured.

"Is there anything I can do?"

"As hard as it may be," he said apologetically, "read her diaries and let me know if anything probative appears."

"Great," I said unenthusiastically.

"Don't worry, I'll find something, but if I don't . . ."

"I know, don't assume she wasn't insane."

"Ms. Pierce," he offered gently, "no matter how detailed it was, grieving in your head for a few days doesn't count."

I sat there for a few moments, wanting to shout at him, ask him how he dared assume I would *ever* be over it, but I couldn't. He was right. The reason people like him existed was so that people like me didn't get so emotionally involved that they missed some obvious detail. Like the fact that the person had always been a wreck.

"I know, but I've at least got a head start. Thanks."

He said good bye. I hit the button. The phone dropped to the floor and I stared at it. Faced with the prospect of reading her thoughts mapped out in thousands of inks, I cowered, and the line of communication slipped away yet again.

If everything meant something, then every word, troubled synonym, and tortured metaphor would stick to my open mind and fill me up. I would lose myself. Why? To find her?

"You're already gone," I said.

CHAPTER 4

Going through her papers was like rummaging through an office building dumpster. Receipts were scattered through her desk and kitchen drawers, a few statements lay about unopened, and a W-2 was holding a place in one of her journals. I had done this once before with the help of the executor of my parents' wills. I knew exactly how it all went.

I looked at the balances of her bills, made a list of what I would need, and after a long shower and some more businesslike clothing, I made my way to the bank. For the first time, I was glad I had been her cosigner. Her debts in college would fall back on me to solve, but it was perhaps very good planning. Ever since she'd gotten her new job, it seemed as if all her money was handled through automatic channels and because she didn't need financial support, I had sort of viewed our relationship as complete, like a business deal. Now I had to tie up all the loose ends.

God, I'm a bitch.

As I drove, I wondered if she had set up automatic payments so that she would never be reminded of how little she had. I could see the costs of her funeral, the settling of her estate and hoped she had some kind of savings in the account.

I waited in the highly polished room of marble, where even the bulletproof glass looked decorative, and when I could be waited on by a banker, I made my way to her desk. She was wearing a tan skirt suit and had her blond hair in a French twist. I envied her pale, chemically preserved beauty, reminded of all the girls I had always hated.

"So, Ms.?" she coaxed with a smile.

"Pierce."

"Ms. Pierce, you have an account with us?" The glint in her eye was hoping I would ask for a loan or the newest debt management refinancing.

I was almost delighting in the way I was about to make her feel, that horrible sense of confusion over what to say mingled with the aversion to approaching someone else's hopelessness. Lilith Pierce, picking right back at the cheerleaders who had tormented her in high school.

It's not her fault.

"I cosigned an account with my sister when she went to college. I'm afraid she's passed away."

Her face, like any good people-person's, sank. "I'm very sorry."

I forced a smile. "I need to settle her affairs. I'd like an account balance, as well as her overdraft credit card frozen."

Her fingers flew to the keyboard and as expected, she forgot my plight all too willingly, "I'll need you to swipe your ATM card and enter the pin."

As I did it, my stoicism failed. My pin number - her birthday. My eyes dripped as I punched blindly at the colored keys. The machine beeped and very kindly, the lady pushed a box of tissue toward me, before carrying on with her routine. While she typed, the sounds of a room as soft as a library, but sharp as a train station, faded together as I tried to regain my composure.

"Ms. Pierce?" she asked, and a waver in her voice seemed slightly worried.

"Yes? What?"

She wrote something down on a slip of paper and slid it across the desk to me. "This is the current account balance. Your sister had no other accounts with us and I've notified the credit bureaus. It's a complimentary service for our customers."

I took the paper, glanced at it, and nearly shouted in surprise. "*Four hundred thousand* dollars?"

The teller blinked. "Is that wrong?"

My mouth hung open for several moments. "Well, I don't know . . . she . . . she had a good job, but . . . I didn't think it was *that* good."

"Would you like to see an account history?"

"Yes, please."

After several minutes, she got up and went to a printer. When she came back, a stack of papers listed regular deposits each week for the last nine or ten months, each of about ten thousand dollars.

I leaned forward and examined them closely, but it was all codes and numbers to me. "Were these checks?"

"Transfers," she said quietly.

"From whom?"

Her face lost all emotion. "It's just an account number."

I looked at her, feeling the slow build of frustration. "Can't you tell who it belongs to?"

She shook her pale head and gave an apologetic smile carved out of wax. "Will you want to transfer the funds to another account or make a withdrawal?"

The tone in her voice clearly said she did not recommend me taking out much, and for her manager's sake I shook my head.

"I'll keep the account," I put a hand to my temple, still lost in the shock of it, "but is there some kind of paperwork I need to fill out?"

"No, you're a cosigner, so you've always had a right to this money, and since it's under the state limit, I don't think you'll have to file probate."

I gave a sigh of relief and then realized that I had nothing to be relieved about. If anything, I should be outraged. I, through saving pennies, working two jobs, sacrificing any chance of a family outside her, putting in hours of work on her applications and her loan papers, had gotten her through grade school and into college. I had even loaned her several thousand dollars the first year to make it easy on her as she transitioned. She had always sworn to pay me back, but even when she had nearly half a million dollars in the bank, she hadn't done so. If anything, I should be righteously pissed.

"We'll ask you to bring in a copy of her death certificate for our records, though."

Then it hit me; of course she hadn't bothered to pay me back. She never intended to live and I was her next of kin. She was paying me back with exorbitant interest.

In that moment, I nearly snapped my ATM card in half.

"May I help you with anything else?"

"Her bills . . ."

"Are on automatic payment plans."

"I'll be terminating the services soon. Will I need to do anything to stop the payments?"

She was getting tired of me and the mortality I represented, it was obvious from the drawn look on her face. "No, it's all done by computer."

I got to my feet, a bit dazed. "Thanks. I'll bring that certificate in as soon as they finish with her."

"You're welcome. Again, I'm sorry."

Without an answer, I walked back out to the parking lot and to the car. When I got there, I stared up at the sun roof for several minutes, breathing deeply. In some sick way I was relieved that I wasn't going to have to buy her a casket myself. That was, until a dark thought found its way into my head.

Before I knew what I was doing, I was up and walking back into the bank. Banker Barbie was with another customer, but she smiled at me as I walked past her to the courtesy phone.

"Unger."

I took a deep breath, "This is Lilith Pierce."

He paused. "I had a feeling . . ."

"I've found something odd."

"Oh?"

I squeezed my eyes shut and for some reason could picture him sipping his coffee from that black mug. "I know you have to wait for . . . warrants or whatever for bank records right? Well, I'll help you there. She had over four hundred thousand dollars in her checking."

He was silent.

"Regular deposits from a private numbered account. Every week. I was a cosigner, but it was just so she could get an account. I never checked in on it, until now."

"And you suspect that a records keeper wouldn't have access to that kind of money without . . . oh . . . leverage?"

"It would be a motive, right?" I pushed.

"Hmm," he said ambiguously.

I sat down at the chair and leaned into the voice shield. "You said you spoke to her boss."

"I did."

"What did he seem like to you?"

I could hear him thinking; his little gaps and soft murmurs under his breath told me everything. "A sleaze. I think I know where you're going with this. Are you sure that's the only wealthy man she might know?"

"It's a perfect place to start," I nearly whined, knowing I sounded too excited, "if you think it's worth it."

He gave a chuckle, "Do *you* think it's a good idea. I mean you're the psy. . ."

"Don't, Unger, I swear."

He deferred in a hiss. "I'll check it out."

"I want to be there." I don't know why I said it. It was just me, nosy and exactly the cat to die from it.

The throat grumbled. "Not allowed."

"Come on! I'm level-headed, and like you said, I'm the . . ."

"I *didn't* say it, if you recall."

I shrugged and realized he couldn't hear a shrug.

"Well . . . They've had me going through cold files, since my partner went on maternity leave and I'm soon to be put out to pasture. I'm what they like to call a meddler . . . I'm sort of the only one who thinks there might be a case here," he murmured softly, "so I'm on it on my free time, if you catch my drift."

With a sigh, I knew why. It didn't help that one crazy woman showed up days too soon for the death announcement of another crazy woman. Because of me, there was an investigation, but because of me, there was no case. I hid my face in my hand.

He whispered an apology into my private silence.

"Don't be. I get it."

I waited, listening to him debate with himself the shit-storm he'd endure and whether or not it was worth it to make me feel better. I hoped he was a big enough fan of the X-files to at least take an interest in me. Eventually, he clucked his tongue.

"Alright."

In triumph, I bowed my head. "When and where?"

He gave me an address that I scribbled down hastily on the back of the balance slip.

"Can you find it?"

"Yes."

"Half an hour."

"I'll be there," I said. Then I hung up the phone and drifted past the security guard. Outside, I meandered to the ATM, put in the card and pin and looked at the numbers for myself. It was not a dream. The numbers were as clear as plasma. I was rich, but if it was blood money, it would all go to charity. I took out a hundred dollars and went back to my car.

I didn't bother to wait, but drove across town to the corporate headquarters of the company called AMRTA. In the shadow of the gleaming tower of slanting angles, I watched as people went in and out. I tried to recall everything she had said about her job, but like her schooling and all the other aspects of her personal life, I had never really listened. I had done my duty and didn't think that with all that I had done, I needed to do anything else. I couldn't even recall her major in college; though, I knew there was some kind of literature or book connection.

Sifting through echoes, I remembered her telling me it was the job of a lifetime and that she was amazed that they'd given it to her, but beyond that, nothing. Regrettably, all I could clearly see from the call announcing her employment was the glass I had thrown at the wall, right after I had hung up on her for telling me that Howard and I should never have gotten together in the first place. At the time, I had felt righteous, since a child like her had no place giving me advice.

I wondered if she had forgiven me as she stood on the edge looking down.

A knock on my window startled me from my brooding. Unger's face smiled in at me tensely. I got out and tried to look pulled together.

"Are you sure you want to do this?"

I nodded.

"You're not going to fly off the handle again, are you?"

"I've never flown off the handle. I have no idea why that happened."

He gave me a skeptical glance.

"Unger, I know you think I'm a grieving family member, but it's not like that. We weren't close. I never knew her, that's obvious. This isn't about vengeance. My best behavior," I attested, with my hand in the air.

He looked away. "Then if you do this, you're not her sister. You're my associate."

"Do I get a fake name?"

He glanced at me with a raised eyebrow, "Only because I'm afraid of you."

I couldn't help but smile. "Then I'll go by Cassandra Blake. It sounds professional-ish."

He was already heading to the door and I followed behind him swiftly. "Let me do the talking." Suddenly he stopped and turned around. "You can't ever tell anyone I let this happen."

I sighed and put my hand on his shoulder. "If you didn't, I'd be here on my own."

He frowned and gave a decisive nod. "Let's go then," he said, but I could tell from his tone that this was just a courtesy for a grieving woman, which didn't matter to me in the slightest.

I trotted behind him. "So, what's this company all about?"

"Well, their mission statement is hardly explanatory. As far as I can tell from my research, they're into all sorts of things, from pharmaceuticals to real estate."

"What's the acronym stand for?"

"I wondered the same thing," he shook his head, "but it's not an acronym. It's a Sanskrit word."

"Meaning what?"

"The nectar of immortality," he said with a confused shrug.

CHAPTER 5

As soon as we passed through the doors, something in my stomach twisted uncomfortably. There was nothing specific, but the sterile severity of the place stunned me.

It was almost as if we had fallen into a postmodern pit of ergonomics and efficiency. I looked at Unger, but he seemed focused on what he was doing and gave no sign that he felt it too. With an uneasy touch, I put it out of my mind and tried to look as if I did this sort of thing all the time.

The reception desk was a massive stone structure directly in the center of a granite echo chamber. The immense windows that made up the north-facing wall were tinted, so that the entire scene had an aura of man beating materials into a sterile kind of submission. A bank of elevators shone behind the security guard's head in a vicious silver beam, but dinged cheerfully. Clones in every kind of suit moved around, like ichor in the fat, hardened, corporate arteries, their leather shoes clicking impatiently.

It set my teeth on edge.

"What's with the security?"

"I've been told they contract with the government too," Unger whispered.

He walked up to the desk and laid his badge on it. "I'm Detective Unger," he said to the waiting official. "This is my associate, Ms. Blake. I've talked with Mr. Moksha once before. Some questions have come up and I'd like to speak to him again."

The man looked at me and I looked back, as blank as a sheet of paper and probably just as pale.

"Regarding?"

"A murder investigation."

His head snapped from my breasts to Unger's face and the hand reached for the phone concealed beneath the desk. "Wait just a moment."Unger took a few steps back and pretended to be killing time. Turning his back to the man, he shoved his hands in his pockets and blinked in my direction.

"Moksha's a strange guy, kind of, eccentric, I guess is the word."

I gave a subtle nod. "I thought 'sleaze' was the word."

"Yeah well, sometimes they're synonyms."

"Ah."

"I don't want you to *do* anything. You're just here to watch him react, to *see* his face and *know* who he is."

Something in the way he said it caught my ear. I frowned. "Unger, you know that I'm not usually psychic, right?"

"Yeah, but don't put up a wall, you know? Let it happen, if it has to."

"Are you sure about that?" I gaped. "You *want* me to pass out again?"

"You better not."

"Well, *I* know I'm perfectly rational, but . . . there're probably quite a few people that while grieving, don't exactly make sound, rational decisions . . . or stay in this astral plain, ehem." I wanted him to have ample opportunity to back out, given what he was jeopardizing.

His face shifted into a smile, but his eyes kept their jaded crispness.

"I mean, I'm not going to blame him and hatch a plot to do him in, but surely . . ."

He turned to face me fully and for the first time, I knew that this man could be trusted. His eyes, though bloodshot and circled in dark rings, seemed to look into me and understand.

"There's something to *you*," he murmured, "even if there's no case."

At the desk, the guard was whispering furiously, glancing at us every few seconds, and I felt an almost eerie sense of urgency.

"What?"

He shook his head in bemusement. "I don't know. Maybe it's just a feeling, but . . . I feel like we've known each other a long time." His eyes immediately went wide and the mouth worked a few times. "I'm sorry if that came out sounding forward, but I meant it in a . . ."

I put my hand on his elbow. "I feel the same way; I however, have a reason to."

"I didn't know your sister, but if this will make you feel better, I feel like I have to do it. Maybe it's the credential I need to tell the story, I guess." He looked away, ran a rough hand through his thinning hair, and sighed self-consciously. "I'll probably be fired for sure."

I felt the tug of the guard's interest and caught his wave with my eye. "You can go up. He's cancelled his meeting."

Unger's brows drew together in that quintessential cop-sign for powerful interest. "Well, I'll have to thank him for that."

"Anything for the authorities," the man said with a smile, apparently oblivious that it sounded scornful. He set two visitors' badges on the counter and we clipped them to our shirts.

We made our way to the elevator and were interred inside its metal body for what seemed like an eternity, as it traveled up the shaft. Not even its music calmed me. Unconsciously, my feet shifted, I put my arms around myself and felt goose bumps, and for some reason, felt as if I was being watched. I looked up at the security camera and narrowed my eyes at the guard who was probably looking down my blouse even then.

"You feeling okay?" Unger asked casually, so casually it sounded anything but. I knew what he really meant. He meant to ask if I was going to collapse in a prophetic seizure.

"Yes. This place just gives me the creeps."

"Why?"

"I don't know," I replied with a shake of my head. "Just a gut thing; isn't that what you detectives say? Something about it is freaking me out."

He turned and leaned against the rail. "It's to be expected. It's where your sister spent her days. You're dealing with a very stressful thing. You have to let time close the wound."

I nodded, but didn't feel like healing. The more I thought about it, the less her death made any sense. Even if it had been her choice, there had to be a reason why it was now, and not back in high school when she'd been at her worst.

Everything means something.

I closed my eyes until the final ding and the scraping of the door announced us.

Positioned on the top floor, this office was decidedly modern, but also quite comfortable and lacking the entrance's severity. Clean lines, bright contrasting colors, acrylic, wood laminate, art, and a sense of fun. The secretary facing us appeared cheerful and my foreboding seemed to slip away. Within seconds, I was certain my cover was complete, that I was an actress of the first order, and that whoever Mr. Moksha was, he would absolutely delight at meeting me and answering my questions; then, I remembered the look on the guard's face, his furious conversation, and knew it was all some kind of illusion.

Before we could even speak to the set of white teeth in front of us, a large door in the wooden wall opened and a man came toward us. He wore an impeccable suit of white linen and a red shirt, was well-tanned, and greeted Unger with a curious smile that lit up his whole face.

"Detective Matthew Unger! So you've thought of more things to ask me?"

He wagged Unger's hand up and down in both of his, grinning as the surprised detective tried to state his case. But even as Moksha smiled, he was *watching*. Then his eyes slid to mine by way of the sleeve of my silk blouse, and for a moment I felt my face flush.

"Who is this?" he said in an appreciative voice of the softest tenor.

"My associate, Ms. Blake," Unger said, but as Moksha passed him to gather my thin fingers in his strangely warm hands, my cohort began to frown almost protectively.

Something in Moksha's smile was canine. "Ms. Blake," he murmured as if he wanted to remember the name forever. "Welcome. What do you do for the department? You're not a detective, surely?" He tilted his head over his shoulder at Unger, but his greedy eyes never left my face. "You're much too lovely."

I am not an unattractive woman. I have what my mother always called a "regal" face, which I took to mean the kind of face you'd want a dominatrix to have. I have always tried very hard to keep my posture tall, dress for success, and at any cost, maintain the upper hand. Years of fighting peoples' impressions, I'm sure, but though I was stern, it did not necessarily intimidate men. I had been known to receive advances.

However, I was never a creature of sensual appetites, one of the oft lamented "irreconcilable differences", and I had a way of giving pick-up-liners the cold shoulder, that made certain I left every bar completely sober. This man, though, disarmed and disgusted me in a thoroughly new way.

The longer his hand stayed on me, the more my skin crawled, and as I looked into his dark brown eyes, set in that sun-kissed face, I began to feel nauseus The sharpness I saw there was stifling. He was struggling to appraise me from the inside out, and as he gripped my hand, I worried he would have a full accounting in a matter of moments. But before my vision could darken, he released me and stepped back, still smiling almost sardonically.

"Isn't it a bit fifties to assume a pretty woman can't be intelligent too?" I threatened with a sweet smile.

"She's a forensic specialist," Unger intervened.

Moksha nodded, but didn't turn away. My skin burned. It seemed his eyes widened a bit.

"In what?" he replied in curt civility.

"Records," Unger said uncomfortably. "Would you mind if we went into your office?"

The spell seemed to break then, and finally, the caster turned away. I breathed a deep sigh of relief, but before I could compose myself, was being left outside. Whatever the intensity of that examination, it seemed in a moment, Moksha had lost interest. He was in the door and seated at his desk so quickly, I barely had time to look around before I was forced to pay attention again.

Just as the floor contrasted from the lobby, this office differed from all that I had seen thus far from AMRTA. Deep reds, dark woods, foreign sculptures from a mixture of tribal backgrounds, thick fabrics, and even a fireplace; it could have been cut from a castle, if not for the oddly bright lighting. I looked up, and instead of a chandelier, found a ceiling of glass and the noonday sun.

"So what may I do for you, Detective?" He didn't wait to hear an answer, but instead, snapped his cuffs and folded his hands on the desk. "I told you all I really know about Eva Pierce. I didn't know her that well."

Unger opened his notebook. "Yes, I know, but recently, we've discovered a few new details that spark some interest."

Moksha's face did not change. Even an honest man's would have moved, made some kind of expression, but he seemed to have turned to ambivalent stone.

"It appears that Ms. Pierce was making a considerable amount of money."

"I should think so," Moksha replied smoothly, yet somehow managed to barely move a muscle. "We're very generous to our employees. After all, they're our lifeblood."

It almost seemed like a joke, and in its flippancy I saw a lie. He was too composed, too refined and practiced.

There had to be a way that I could force something from him without jeopardizing our little illusion. I took a seat in a soft red chair and crossed my legs, satisfied that his eyes followed the path of one white knee moving over the other.

"What exactly did she do here?" Unger asked quietly, proving himself a very observant man, his askance nearly burning a hole in my arm.

"She was our chief record-keeper, as I'm sure I told you before," Moksha replied, once again tracing my lines to find my face. For once, I was glad to make use of the supposed "feminine wiles".

"What exactly does that mean?"

Moksha finally relaxed a little, though it was the relaxation of a giant cat just before it leapt out at some unsuspecting prey. He was unabashedly smiling at me, objectifying me that easily.

Record-keeper, my ass.

Eva was so much my opposite, it was almost uncanny; light and sentimental where I was dark and uncompromising, withdrawn and uncertain where I was intrusive and focused. Her girlish looks, her curly, light hair, her expressive mouth and eyes, there was no way a man of taste would pass her up. Vulnerability was her charm and her weakness. It may have even killed her.

"It means that she kept our records, of course."

Some part of me chilled. I leaned forward just enough to tempt him to glance at my cleavage. His eyes hardened a bit. He was avoiding answering the obvious question, even as he was enjoying my company. It should have been an even trade, and I was feeling more annoyed with each passing moment.

"How *well* do you usually treat your employees," I interrupted, "give us a number."

His head slowly tilted, and I was so lost in his subtle astonishment, that I did not even try to see what my words had done to Unger's train of thought.

"We follow competitive hiring practices. Sometimes we pay more than we should, but it is worth every penny."

"How much was she making here?" I pressed as pleasantly as I could, while attempting to maintain the advantage.

He leaned back and nearly laughed at me. Stopping himself just in time, he reached out and touched the intercom on his desk. "Katherine, will you photocopy Eva Pierce's personnel file and all our records concerning her pay, if you please?" He let the button go, not even glancing at the machine or the door to make certain the girl had received her instructions. He was confidently stripping me with his eyes and getting away with it.

"What was the nature of your relationship with Ms. Pierce," Unger let fly and without a single beat skipped, Moksha replied.

"Professional. She was a very efficient and organized person. I believe that she loved her file room. I almost think she might have found the records to be her friends." He seemed to think that amusing, but why, I couldn't say.

"I just find it odd that the CEO of a company would know the head of records," Unger continued stoically. "I also find it strange that when I asked to talk to the people who might know about her work, I was referred only to you. Can you explain that?"

He didn't even bother to say "of course", it was written on his self-assured face. "When we hired her, I made certain I was hiring someone whom I could rely upon for the type of comprehensive research I required. We acquire a few odd antiques here and there, something she specialized in, and off and on, we needed a polyglot for confidential reasons."

"Odd antiques?" I frowned, never having recalled that Eva had a love for the past. "What kind of antiques? And what languages specifically?"

The eyes gave a slow blink. "I'm afraid I can't go into any more detail. Suffices to say," he shrugged slightly, "she was also very charming, intelligent, and easy to like or want to know better."

"I'm sure," I murmured.

His smile suddenly swept off his face without a sign and I was left in the cold light of the sun, alone.

"I'm not sure what you're insinuating. Eva Pierce was a colleague, a valued employee. I have no need to acquire women here. I can do that in much more intimate settings."

I was shunned, and couldn't have cared less. "Then you have no idea why she'd be receiving ten thousand dollars a week for the last year or so, or who might have given it to her?"

He scowled for an instant and slowly shook his head. "Perhaps she was embezzling; I'll have our accountants check on it."

Before I could retort, Unger's stern rejoinder put me back in mind of our scenario. "You mentioned that she went out a lot. How would you know that?"

"Exhaustion in meetings, old eye makeup, frequent headaches," Moksha said with a derisive smile.

"But she never mentioned who her friends were."

He sighed and spun in his chair until he could get to his feet, obviously bored with us. "Try around the water cooler." The corner of his mouth gave a snide twitch. "I have postponed a meeting; are we finished?"

"No," I interjected. Before he could escape or stand at the door in polite dismissal, I rose and stood in front of him. "Why would she jump off *that* building, why not here, a place she knew?"

He crossed his arms, and with his face out of Unger's view slowly began to sneer almost cruelly. A cloud moved across the sun, streaming down from right above us. The outlines slid over his features like leaches. For a moment, he had no shadow, and all his darkness was on his face.

"Perhaps she knew better than to make a mess for me," he said emotionlessly. "Katherine will see you out."

CHAPTER 6

We were rushed from the building and a thick file was dropped in Unger's hands. Beside the car, I finally lost my temper and caught his elbow.

"What the hell?" I demanded. "He all but admitted that he hated her guts! What if he's the reason she jumped?"

He looked at me, and though his eyes said that he was in complete agreement, it was clear that there was nothing he could do about it. "Corporations like this have vicious public relations policies. They all walk a fine line between countless insider trading rules or environmental agreements and criminality. If we start knocking down walls asking questions for one suicide, then they'll have my badge."

I glared at him.

"Ms. Pierce," he sighed and looked around, "I wanted to help give you some answers, but the truth is, I don't think there are any. I'll go through this file, but I'm not sure we're going to find anything."

I knew he was right. The logical part of my brain was sure that he would find nothing but a sterling employment record, decent pay, and not a trace of embezzlement. Eva predicted her death because she knew what she was going to do and I was just grieving. I knew it, but I still couldn't let it be.

"Unger . . . Matthew, there has to be something. She wouldn't just *do this.* She had to have a reason. She had to feel like there was nothing else. Otherwise there's no point!"

He tossed the folder into his back seat and put his hand on my shoulder. "Ms. Pierce, sometimes people don't have a point, and that's the point."

While I stood there refusing to cry in his presence, he got into his car and drove away. After he was gone, I stared at the entrance to the lot in dejection, until the town car pulled in and parked in front of the entrance. As I stood behind my car and watched, Moksha swept out of the building, a look of harassed outrage on his face. He got into the back of the car and it pulled out of the lot in a considerable hurry.

I got in and pulled out behind it. Maybe I wasn't a detective, but I'd yelled at enough detective movies to know how a tail worked. Two cars back, not too aggressive or safe, I drove like someone who had somewhere to be. Never mind that I wasn't sure where the somewhere actually was.

I thought they might take him to the airport, to jump into a private jet, or to his opulent, high-rise condo, or something equally rich and spectacular, but instead the sleek car made its way across the city toward the river. I slowed down, and when the car pulled from the busy avenue into a narrow access street between two warehouses, I pulled over and put it in park.

"Where is he going?"

I sat there for a few moments, debating. I ticked reasons off on my fingers, wished I had binoculars, a camera, or a trench coat, and finally, pounded the steering wheel in frustration. Making up my mind, I ran across the street and stood behind a dumpster, trying to ignore the wretched smell. The town car sat idling in front of a metal doorway that stood open. Above the door was a darkened neon sign that I could not quite read.

A night club?

For fifteen minutes, I waited behind the putrid dumpster, sure that whatever Moksha was doing, it would only take him a few minutes, or the car would have been parked. Just as I was regretting my choice of shoe and promising to never again consume any kind of meat product, Moksha exited the building with a woman in a blue silk dress. They seemed to be arguing, though I couldn't hear anything that was said. He stood very close to her, his dark eyes pummeling hers with questions. His lips barely moved, though he looked fierce, like he might lean forward and tear out her throat with his teeth. For a moment, I pitied her, until he pushed past her and she turned.

She was beautiful, with luminous, pale skin, long, auburn hair in a wavy, forties style, and it was clear that if he had struck her, she would have fought right back. Her majestic face glared after him and as he pulled away in his fancy car, she crossed her arms and tilted up her chin. In her eyes was the pure, unadulterated disgust of a duchess.

Moksha with his rich corporation, his flagrant disrespect, and a smile that oozed nouveau riche, for some reason couldn't hold a candle to her imperial, nonchalant elegance. She leaned against the door frame, slowly blinking her false eyelashes, until her glance found me.

My heart jumped. I had to make a choice. Sensible, happily-married-to-a-cheating-loser Lilith would have pretended to be looking for something in the dumpster that she might have accidentally dropped while pulling a double shift in the meat packing plant, or whatever, but pretend-forensic specialist, Cassandra Blake, already had one stiletto heal knee-deep in the proverbial mire. I stepped out, and as the car pulled past me, dark reflections smoothing over its tinted windows, I gave it a stoic glance, as if I had backup waiting, and walked toward the entrance.

I didn't turn around, though I could feel myself being watched. Moksha knew he'd led me there. He knew I was about to question the woman. He knew he was under investigation. The car seemed to hesitate, but as I reached the door, it pulled out and disappeared. The woman looked after it in contempt, and though I thought she'd vanish inside and lock the door, she waited for me to find her, almost as if proving a point to the sleaze inside the car.

My mind went over the things they always said in cop shows.

"Hello, ma'am," I began, "my name is Cassandra Blake."

Close up, she looked like a porcelain statue, a marble sculpture wearing lipstick, and her face never changed, even as her emerald green eyes rolled to follow me.

I had to be careful about what I said. As angry as I was about Unger refusing to do anything else, I didn't want to get him fired. If this woman and Moksha compared notes, a few well-treated lawyers might make a few well-timed calls.

"Is this a night club?"

One manicured fingernail, painted to match the dress, uncurled and pointed upward at the sign. But the writing was still unintelligible, and not because I was at an angle. It was a symbol and I didn't know what it meant. I looked at her and it was clear that those who didn't know, would never know.

"Strange place for it, isn't it, next to a meat packing plant?"

She shrugged one shapely shoulder.

"Do you know a young lady by the name of Eva Pierce?"

She slid away from the door and took a step forward. The dress slinked around her narrow hips and at her ankle, a few crystals clinked together atop her expensive-looking sandals.

"I did."

It was too late to retreat, even though I was beginning to feel more than anxiety. Beyond her was a rectangle of darkness, where anything could be lurking.

"Past tense," I noted quietly. "Did Moksha tell you?"

She smiled, a lush red mouth exposing incandescent teeth. "It was only a matter of time, really."

"Before he'd tell you?"

She shook her head in a slow, deliberate way, "Before she did it."

I swallowed the lump in my throat, but my voice still sounded choked. "Committed suicide, you mean?"

Her arms unwrapped; long thin appendages that looked like the branches of a gray birch tree. A thick, heavy gold bracelet dropped to her wrist and shimmered in the sunlight.

"How well did you know her?"

She smiled again and for some reason, I felt threatened.

"Better than anyone," she said with a laugh in her voice.

My heart skipped a beat. "Did she tell you she wanted to die?"

But my charade was wearing thin. The woman took a step back as her smile reverted into the stern line. "Credentials?"

I stared into her knowing eyes as the adrenalin flooded my body, and shared an understanding with the mind behind them. A penciled eyebrow arched playfully as she stepped backward through the door and slowly pushed it shut. The last thing I saw of her was a green eye and the curl of a red lip.

"Go home, sister dear."

* * *

At the apartment, I spent almost ten minutes on hold while Unger extricated himself from his real business to come speak to me. When he answered, I could already hear the polite withdrawal in his voice.

"Ms. Pierce . . ."

"I know!" I took a deep breath and before he could interrupt me, I pushed ahead. "Just hear me out! After you drove away, Moksha came out of the building and drove to a warehouse by the river."

"You followed him?" Unger almost shouted.

"What else was I supposed to do, just let him walk away when he told us he had a meeting?"

I heard the change of background noise as he covered the mouth of the phone and dropped his voice into it, "You were supposed to do nothing! You told me that you wouldn't fly off the handle! I trusted you!"

"I know! Okay, I'm sorry! I just . . . he looked upset and after what he said about her, I wanted to see if . . . just let me finish, please?"

I could picture him pinching the bridge of his nose, or leaning his head on his hands in frustration. I heard a few papers shuffled.

"I know that what you're going through is tough, Ms. Pierce. I know you're looking for answers or connections, but doing crazy stuff will only get you hurt. You just have to accept that sometimes people lose hope."

"You can find hope all the time without stuff like that, but I needed it, and you always knew it."

But a person couldn't find hope for someone after they were already dead. He was right, I realized. I wasn't doing this for her. I was doing it to assuage my own guilt. It wouldn't work, because the only thing that would do that for me was to hear her say that she forgave me, and that was something that would never happen.

"You're . . . right. I'm sorry, but I think I've just caused you some trouble and I . . . thought you should know, since I won't ever see you again after all this is settled."

He sighed. He was probably recalling that people in desperate situations with no one else to cling to, would reach for the only person that seemed stable, and that to friendless, family-less me, he was that person. I had no right to demand it from him, but it was part of his job description.

"What happened?"

I told him about the club, that Moksha had to have seen me, the questions I had asked the woman in the blue dress. "She knew who I was, Unger, even though I gave her the fake name. I don't know if it means anything, but I thought at least, it might mean that Moksha knew we were lying. I didn't want that to come back and bite you."

He listened in silence and when I finished, took a few moments to think about it before he cleared his throat. "I appreciate that."

I hesitated. That wasn't what I had really felt. What I had really wanted to know was if he thought it was significant that the man who said he didn't know Eva, knew exactly where she might have been spending her free time, or knew the woman who said she was Eva's closest friend. It didn't surprise me that the woman knew me, Eva carried a picture of us in her wallet and if they were friends, she might have seen it, but it did bother me that she hadn't been more forthcoming.

It was obvious that she had no loyalty to Moksha, yet she had told me nothing. Perhaps she wasn't able, perhaps she was a victim of Moksha's too. What I wanted was Unger's badge and the authority to compel her to speak, but I realized then that I would not have it.

"Ms. Pierce."

"Yes?"

"If you promise to drop it and let me handle it, I'll go to the club and speak to the woman you saw."

My chest seemed to open finally and I could breathe. Sitting in the happy face, I finally allowed my shape to conform to its cushy insides.

"I just want to know why he lied, if it was because I was standing there."

I heard him massage his five o'clock shadow. "So would I. Promise me that you'll let me do the legwork."

"I promise. I'm sorry. I knew I was fucking it up, I just . . . when she saw me standing there, I had to."

"It's alright. You've just gone through something horrible, in a way most people don't usually have to suffer it."

"So we're back to that, are we?"

He attempted a chuckle. "It was pretty crazy; cut me some slack here."

For some reason, I could tell it was going to come to an end, and the knowledge that I was depending on him too much did nothing to make me agree to set down the phone. In a last ditch effort to keep his companionship, I segued into another topic with all the expertise of a drunken tugboat captain.

"I don't know the city, do you have any ideas on funeral homes . . ."

"There's Park's over on Grand. That's where the county sends . . ." he stopped and like the good psychic I was becoming, I knew what he was about to say.

"The people who die without family."

"I'm sorry, but it's a good place."

"It's okay."

"The M.E. says he'll be finished with the post by tomorrow. I was going to call you."

My eyes were blurring and there were tears in my throat as I tried to laugh, "Yeah well, you know me."

"I'll have it released to Park's then. There'll be paperwork."

"Thanks."

"Get some sleep," he advised gently. "You need to put all of this in perspective, to see that all things come to an end."

"Unger," I whispered, "do you believe that . . . that everything means something?"

"To somebody, I guess. Are you talking about fate?"

"I don't know what I'm talking about," I mumbled. "Again, I'm sorry. If anyone gets upset with you, just tell them I'm crazy."

"Wouldn't help."

"Yeah, probably not."

"Good evening," he finished.

I didn't bother to say anything back. I just put the phone down and felt the structure of my life erode from beneath my feet. It wasn't a real foundation. I had built it out of wild conjecture and fear. I wanted it all to make sense, just like she said it would. The lack of control was miserable, especially for someone who polished their silver and was too organized to have a junk drawer.

Instead, I got up, got out the chemicals, and began to scrub.

* * *

I wanted rain. I wanted it to be like the movies, where there are slick black streets, rolling clouds of moody fog, umbrellas like seal skin, and a somber parade beneath a weeping sky.

It was seventy-five degrees and a bit muggy. The sun was forcing me to wear a pair of her sunglasses.

I thought there might be someone from her work, Moksha, or the woman from the night club, but no one came. I thought maybe she'd have a friend she'd kept from me because of the multi-purpose criticism I had in my back pocket like a Swiss army knife, but no. I thought even Unger might come, but I could feel him detaching himself from the grieving family and wondered if I'd ever hear from him again.

Instead of the crowd I'd wanted, it was just me, two ever-efficient grave-diggers, and a man from the funeral home.

The casket was pearlescent. I picked it because as soon as I saw it I thought of the tiny grain of ugly, annoying sand, mulled over and gnawed until it became something priceless, trapped inside a horribly plain shell.

There were no flowers. I didn't need any symbols, those were for people who didn't accept reality or were searching for meaning in something that was pointless.

"Would you like to say a few words, ma'am?"

I looked up at the man, thin and just the type of person who knew when to disappear. "No, thank you. Saying it now will only make me feel less responsible, but it won't change anything."

He stared at me, but not in a confused way. I'm sure, as a man who was constantly comforting others he had seen a full spectrum of grief. Sobbing, saying farewell, raging at the universe were all old hat to me. I probably was as unmoved by it as he was, and I think he understood that.

"Shall I say a prayer?"

"No."

Thankfully, he didn't apologize or insist that something be done to commemorate the event. He smiled sympathetically and walked slowly back to the hearse.

"You can do it now."

I watched them lower it in with their mechanized pulley. I gathered that they didn't get many people who stayed to watch them work after enduring such defeat. They kept glancing at me, probably wondering if I'd throw myself onto the casket like Hamlet to take her into my arms once again. It reached the bottom with a soft, hollow sound and graciously, they walked away.

I looked at it, set in its shell, and felt nothing. The longer I looked, the less painful it became. It was an ending, just like the divorce. I almost felt relief and for that, I hated myself. They say that that's what shock feels like, but I was pretty damn sure I'd had time to get over shock.

"Empty handed, I entered the world. Barefoot, I leave it," said a voice.

Something in the way he said it kept me from seeking him out. She was most important at that moment. Like whispering an "Amen" at the end of a prayer or bowing the head at shame, I stood and waited for a reckoning.

"My coming, my going . . . two simple happenings that became entangled."

I wanted to know more. A man who could come to think of all the pieces of his life as things that meant nothing to anyone but him, was a man whose life was interesting. That was the trick really. What made someone else sad was nothing to me, but that sadness was equal to any I would suffer. No one got away clean, so why acknowledge any of it? Life was just a blur bookended by two things a man would never remember about himself.

I looked up finally.

He stood where her headstone would eventually be, a book open in his hand. He wasn't wearing black, but somehow that didn't matter. His face had the smooth planes and high lines of Persian extraction, but his skin was no darker than a cup of tea with milk and had a golden hue in the sunlight. Thick, dark hair smoothed into a ponytail; long, heavy lashes that hid his eyes from me; full lips that respected me enough not to smile in empathy no matter how badly the mind behind them wanted to.

"Excuse me?" I said lamely.

He closed the book and his fingers captivated my attention, but even as I marveled at how attracted I was, and why on earth I could be thinking of something like that at a time like this, I knew a certain amount of embarrassment. He was handsome, yes, but it was not the looks that mattered. It was the calm way that he stood. It was the graceful way he both came near to me and yet kept his distance from my thoughts.

He could not be a man constantly surrounded by death or the miseries of others, but had to be someone living behind a big wall, listening to hymns, reading metaphysics. He had a presence, and though I'd always heard people talk about that kind of thing, I had never before felt it.

In a moment of disquiet, I could have sworn I knew him, but I was positive that if I had ever seen someone like him, I would have remembered it clearly. It felt strange to be so enthralled, just that quickly.

His eyes lifted with the corners of his mouth. They were blue like the sky and gave him an exotic look. "A Japanese poem, written by a Zen master at the moment of his death."

His arm moved away from his body casually and the book landed on top of Eva's casket. Then, he turned and started for the large, iron gate to the cemetery, walking as if he really had no reason to be going anywhere in particular. Something about that demeanor made me think that he might not mind if I admitted not wanting to be alone for once.

"Excuse me?" I called after him, cringing that I hadn't put my years of crossword puzzles to better use.

What was a five letter word, beginning with "I", for an incredibly stupid individual who tripped over her own thoughts as they rolled off her tongue?

"Did you know my sister?"

To my amazement, though, he turned and strangely, even though he seemed relaxed, the glance over the shoulder did not come off as austere. He looked at me for a while as if he had to be sure I could even understand him when he spoke.

"Did you?"

Taken aback that he could be callous while seeming so genteel, I stared after him blankly as he walked toward the street. One of my chief regrets in my life thus far was temper, but even though I tried to manage it, it somehow always took hold of my spine and operated my limbs like a remote control car. I chased after him, forgetting all about the pearl in the ground.

"Excuse me?" I asked angrily, and to my credit, it *did* come out sounding different from all the other times.

He stopped in his tracks and the proximity warning in my mind beeped until my anger management issue got fed up and stormed off. I came to an abrupt, lurching halt and waited to see what he'd do.

"It's all there, you know," he said with a sigh. "Every answer you've ever wanted, but sometimes it's the reason for asking that is the most questionable thing."

I couldn't say it a fourth time, I was sure that was far too many, so I settled for, "What?"

"The only way you'll see the answer, is if you already know what's important to you."

"A lot of things are important to me," I defended, and instantly heard my words in a petulant voice.

He shook his head slightly. "Do you love the sadness you feel, to protect it so viciously?"

I scowled at his back. "Everything that meant anything to me is dead. How about you let me grieve in peace?"

He turned around completely and once again, looked through me.

"You had her within reach for so long and never once asked how she felt, what she knew, who meant the most to her. Now she is gone forever. You do not grieve for her, but for the lost chance."

His honesty cut through me to the core. For some reason, I felt insanely angry that anyone could question my devotion to her, even as I was there cleaning up her final mess.

"She hated everything, thought that the world was out to get her, and only cared about herself! She was the guilty one" I shouted at him, a *real* total stranger, who probably hadn't even met Eva and was just being nice in some twisted way.

"You speak so of someone you loved?"

And then it hit me. I *did* hate her, not for leaving me, but for making me do the heavy lifting, for relying on me to be the person I was. I was mad at her when she had given up everything. What the hell was wrong with me?

"What is this?" I said under my breath, but somehow, he heard me. "What the hell is wrong with me?"

He smiled and passed through the gate to continue on his way. "'Coming, all is clear, no doubt about it. Going, all is clear, without a doubt. What, then, is "all"?'"

CHAPTER 7

I thought about the stranger's words for the rest of the day. It kept repeating in my mind, overlapping what Unger had said about accepting that everything ended eventually. It wasn't about why I was asking; it couldn't be. I *knew* why I was asking, and even if it was a shitty reason, I *already knew*. Yes, it was because *I* felt badly, but so what? Should I feel badly about that too? Should I hate myself because hindsight was twenty-twenty, or should I simply seek out the truth that made me comfortable?

If there was someone else to blame, then it couldn't be my fault and I wasn't the horrible sister I'd never set out to be.

It wasn't her home, her life, or her misdeeds that I was haunting anymore. I was taking them over and soon, they would bear my mark. Or leave their mark on me.

I sat in the happy face, staring at her book cases: four rows of black, one row of blue, two volumes of green, and a long row of fat, red tomes. There had to be a significant reason they were divided, but there was nothing to distinguish them from each other except their bindings.

Never judge a book by its cover.

I pulled out the black book I had gone through before and flipped through its patchwork pages. Her feelings, long essays on the meaning of life, sketches, and even a few song lyrics crowded there. I set it down and picked out one of the green books. This was entirely different. It contained numbers in columns and rows like a ledger, but what the numbers meant was not indicated in any kind of legend. Some had obvious markers like "lb" or "$", but there were no totals, or any kind of averaging. Confused, I set it aside and went for the last blue volume. Lists, dates and locations, it was an appointment book. I flipped to the last entry and promptly dropped the volume to the floor as if stung.

"August 9th

Top of the Old River Motel
Good bye, Lily."

My vision darkened as I looked at the words in their fat, red pen strokes.

"Bye, Ev," I whispered.

My fingers shot out for the last red volume and felt around blindly. I could see nothing through the water-distortion of my tears. The book was heavy, and when I dropped to my knees and lay it on the floor, it almost refused to open. I turned the pages as if looking for an emergency phone number, until I realized that the blurry images there were neat and tidy, unlike anything else I had seen from her. Row after row, stanzas like poems, but none of it made any sense. It rhymed in some places, had a definite rhythm, but some of the words were gibberish and not a single line was a complete sentence. It was the same all the way through, until I found the symbol.

Scrawled in the same red sharpie as her appointment with Death, was the neon sign from above the night club door.

तृष्णा

I looked at it closely for some time, trying to pick out what language it might be. It looked as if it was some kind of Middle Eastern dialect. Then there was a mental spark that had to find a place to burn. I looked around the room blankly and recalled that my sister had no computer.

I grabbed the four books I had pulled from the shelves and threw them into a backpack I found in her closet. Running at full speed, I raced down the stairs to the street and jumped into my car. After the push of a button on its dash, now thankful they had been out of plain old Hondas, I barked orders at the friendly lady who happened to pick up my signal.

"Directions to an Internet Café."

She helpfully stuffed them into an electronic envelope and before long I was driving through dark streets toward an answer. When I had paid the exorbitant fee and logged onto a terminal, I rifled through servers until I found what I was looking for, a dictionary of Sanskrit, but when I had found it, didn't know where to start. I couldn't search by symbol on the paperweight I was using and I couldn't go by the Sanskrit word itself, because I couldn't actually read it. Annoyed, I went through the lists of words, just looking for anything in particular. Letter by letter, I searched, muttering to myself as I scrolled, but when I came to "M", everything changed.

"Moksha," I read aloud, "liberation from Samsara, the cycle of death and rebirth." With an aggravated hiss, I sat back. "That arrogant, stuck up prick."

I wondered if it was his real name. He certainly didn't look like he was someone who might speak Sanskrit; after all, as the webpage told me, it was the root language of the Indian dialects and an ancient cousin of Latin.

I reached into the pack and pulled out the red volume. On the marked page, I examined the stanzas. It had to be some kind of code, but I didn't know anything about codes. I could connect one or two of the words together by counting every fifth word, or second word, but nothing made complete thoughts all the way through.

All too quickly, the time ticked by and before I could stop it, the computer logged off.

The punk sitting at the counter eyed me from behind his square glasses, until at last, I felt uncomfortable and began gathering my things together. Still a little shaky from my adrenalin high, I made to lift the heavy volume and accidentally knocked it to the floor. Cursing, I dropped to pick it up by the back cover, but froze when I saw a watermark.

"You wanna buy more time?" he asked when I got to the counter. The way he spat it at me clearly told me that if I did, he'd slit my throat with his lip stud, so I shook my head and smiled sweetly.

"Do you know where this place is?"

He leaned over the book. "Armchair Philosopher?"

Given that my finger was pointing at the words, I felt I didn't need to be any more specific, but he stared at me until I nodded.

Annoyed, he turned to his computer and spoke to it in the clicks and clatters that always seemed the mechanical equivalent of whistling.

The printer kicked into life and hummed out a map.

"There," he grunted. "Ten cents for the copy."

"You're kidding."

He stared.

"Fine!" Digging through the bag, I found my wallet and handed him the dime. "Thanks!"

"Come again," he dismissed.

Shaking my head, I dashed out to the car and nearly killed five college kids with linked arms standing idly in the crosswalk. It was getting late; the night creatures were rolling out of bed, fluffing their hair, digging for shirts that didn't smell like ass, and preparing themselves for the usual business of a Friday night: attempting to fornicate. That's what single people did, after all.

I parked across the street and approached the storefront slowly. It wasn't what I'd expected. I had pictured a hole in the wall on a side street, but this was in the middle of the charming downtown's cultural center, right next to a GAP, and across from a Bath & Body. It was made up to look old, like a saloon crossed with a Victorian gentleman's club.

Behind the glass, comfortable couches and armchairs sat around little round tables in nooks made to look like living room or library corners. The walls were lined with a vast collection of books and the coffee bar looked like it had been ripped from a saloon. A few people sat, using laptops, chatting, or reading. Curious, I walked in and was greeted by a bell hung over my head.

At the bar, I did the dance of the impatient customer until a haggard man in a white button-up shirt and black suspenders decided to wait on me. At the edge of his rolled up sleeve, I spotted the black outline of what appeared to be a military tattoo.

Not going to ask him to put tiny marshmallows on it, I thought, *it might be code for something.*

I put the book on the counter and showed him the watermark.

"Did this book come from here?" I asked amiably enough, but as I looked up, noted the startled expression on his face. Vaguely, I wondered if it was directed at me or the fact that I couldn't compare the watermark to the sign on the front door, but it wasn't my fault. The place didn't *look* like a bookstore.

He jerked a thumb to the back of the shop.

Feeling out of place, I looked around. "I'll have . . . a . . . whatever's most popular," I said in an overly cheerful voice, though I could have kicked myself for being such a spaz.

He turned away from me almost gratefully and went to work without a sound. While I looked, but didn't look, at his gaunt face in the bar mirror, he clamped his jaw shut and refused to look back. Taking the hint, I wandered down the long bar until it curved out its end. Beyond it were several more seating nooks, the ubiquitous books, and what seemed to be a dutch door, split in half, its upper part open to another room.

Feeling like a kid about to look through the glass of the confectionery and find out where the fudge came from, I put my hands on the tiny counter and tried to see in the low light. Volumes were piled high in stacks, some with covers and some without. Machines of unknown use lined the walls, a swatch booklet lay open on the work table, and a single silver stool glinted.

A book bindery.

Eva hadn't bought the volumes there; she'd had them *created* out of her scraps of paper and discarded notebooks. But no one was manning the counter. I would have to come back earlier in the day.

Distraught, I ambled back to nearest reading nook and looked over the titles. Reference books, history books, and various fictions, none of it organized, and all covers torn or well-loved. It was as if the person who ran the bindery drew a distinction between the outside world and their own books, which needed no covers to tempt them.

I collapsed into the fluffy chair and laid the red book on the table, turned to the symbol. In the light from the green library lamp, it almost looked fresh.

"Trishna," he murmured.

I only pulled myself from my own world because something in me was still capable of salivating to the bell of social obligation and thought it had been addressed by a name that was not its own. I looked up, about to tell the poor man that I was not his blind date, but found a white coffee cup and saucer directly in front of my gaze. It clattered as I took it and clumsily set it down.

"Thanks." I reached into my bag for the wallet. "You didn't have to bring it to me."

I lifted the bill up to his hand, and long, caramel-colored fingers waved it aside. I looked up to the face and instantly recognized it.

He smiled at me warmly. "You found me."

It was the man from the cemetery. While I stared at him in shock, he sat down in the chair across from me, gracefully leaned back, and crossed his long legs.

"You?" I said, feeling my mouth drop open.

He nodded slowly. "The most popular."

I glanced at the cup. "What?"

"Cappuccino. It's what you ordered, yes?"

I blinked. "So you *did* know her!"

"Of course," he said happily. "Though I am sure they would appreciate the sentiment, I don't often attend the funerals of those I have not met."

"You . . ." I looked back at the half-door, "you bound her journals?"

"That is why you're here, isn't it?"

I nodded and with a shaking hand, picked the cup back up to sip, if only to do something with my mouth beside catch flies. I watched him over its rim and he looked back without a single hint of discomfiture or nervousness.

Finally, I managed to piece a few words together. "So she came here a lot?"

"Often."

"How did you know about her funeral? I didn't announce it."

He said nothing. After a moment or two, I realized he wasn't planning on answering the question. At first, I wanted to rave at him, demand an answer, but as I stared at him, I realized that I already knew the answer and he was waiting to hear me say it.

"She was suicidal."

He tilted his head and for the first time, looked away.

"I always knew she was troubled, but I thought . . ." I mumbled. "I thought she was past the worst of it."

He looked at me again. "And perhaps it had nothing to do with sorrow."

I set down the cup, confused. "Then you talked to her?"

"Yes."

"And she didn't seem depressed?"

"If anything, she was focused."

"On killing herself?" I raised my voice.

He shrugged and I could see his sympathy.

I calmed myself. "Did you meet her here?"

His head gave a slow shake. "We met in the park. She was writing in a spiral notebook she bought at the local drugstore."

That sounded like her. The image took me back to her childhood, when I would look up from my toys on the back lawn and find her in a tree, her legs dangling as she drew pictures of birds.

"We live in the information age," he continued, glancing at the bookshelves near our circle of yellow light. "Inundated with words, even in our breakfast cereal. Any person, anywhere can write their thoughts, and instantly they are mine. No one takes the time anymore to think about what it all means."

"It's just noise," I grumbled and took another sip.

His eyes found mine again and locked them into a gravitational pull of the greatest force. "'Every word written is a victory against death'; it isn't noise, but because we cannot filter it, it sounds like noise."

"I'm sorry," I said with my hand up. "I just meant that it feels overwhelming."

He smiled and it was that same smile from the cemetery. "No you didn't. You are nothing if not pessimistic, and you meant what you said, but that is fine."

Absolved, but feeling as if that was a different type of crime, I sat mute, uncertain what could possibly be said to that.

He uncrossed his legs and leaned forward, putting his elbows on his knees and meshing his fingers in the air between us. Without intending to, I fantasized about placing my hands over his and smoothing my fingertips over the details I found there.

"History is composed of major events and in some cases a few characters, because humans cannot recall all those tiny moments in between. In that immense context, Einstein's letters, the drawings of an old man from Florence, even John Hancock's John Hancock are all priceless, but by themselves, without any significance granted by history, a lone man's words are simply discarded as noise. They are sounds not zeitgeist, but the only thing that makes them less valuable is either that we as his fellow men find others who represent those things more perfectly or can only listen to so much of the same before we shut our ears. Such attitudes breed reckless disregard and though it is easy to become overwhelmed, we should fight that at any cost."

I began to see his point. If a person could float in the sea of knowledge and not drown, if they could be universally accepting and receptive, then every word *was* important, and though he seemed to be just that sort of person, I was most definitely not. I needed filtering. For me, it all needed some kind of vast organization, and just thinking about the Herculean effort of such a task, sent my OCD to twitching.

"Your sister told me I sounded like a librarian, but I gave her my card and told her to give her own words the respect they deserved. A few days later, she called me and brought me her first shoebox."

Without meaning to, I laughed and was pleased to see him smile.

"Now she has brought me you," he said with a wave.

When I didn't say anything out of mild embarrassment, his head tilted drastically and his blue eyes sparkled in play.

"You need to hear someone say it, don't you?"

I wasn't sure what he meant, but his soft voice was almost mesmerizing. I knew he knew what *he* meant, and that it was probably completely accurate.

"They all say they knew her, but you need to hear someone say that they knew the same Eva *you* knew. Isn't that right, Lilith?"

I froze, and as I stared at him with eyes as big as saucers, he smiled back calmly.

"You need to know you were right, that you saw her clearly, but why?"

My eyes faltered, fell to his shoes, stuttered around the rug on the floor. I shook my head, because in that moment, my voice had vanished.

"Your parents, Howard, and now her," he whispered.

Frantically, I looked up at his face and was trapped in his fixed gaze. I felt like I was falling into those sky-colored eyes; my heart sped up, the coffee burned in my stomach, and I lost feeling in my legs.

"Your world is chaotic, filled with shattered possibilities."

Tears welled in my eyes and spilled down my cheeks.

"You spend all your time organizing, don't you? Mending the parts of yourself that crash to the ground by learning what can be pushed away without any personal sacrifice. You simplify it to preserve your own sanity. Isn't that true?"

My hand flew to my mouth and drops began to tickle the back of it. He watched me cry for a great while, but did not offer to comfort me, and why should he? It was exactly as he had said. It was my wayward method of compensating for things outside my control, and because of that, when I recalled her words, something in my soul had grasped for them with such tenacity that I could not let go.

Everything means something.

He stretched out an arm and pointed to the book. "Trishna," he repeated.

"Trishna?" I looked after his finger and found the red symbol. "What does that mean?"

He sat back in the chair. "It is a Sanskrit word."

"For what?"

"Craving. Things perceived to be valuable that only end up robbing us of what matters."

For long moments, I frowned at him, wondering if that was all there was.

"There's a night club by the river . . ." I began, but he was already shaking his head.

"Don't, Lilith. You *will* regret it."

"Why?" I demanded, suddenly absurdly angry that he would insert himself into my quest. If that was how I grieved, who was he to say otherwise? "Something's not right about her boss, and this woman at the club knew who I was. If anyone can tell me about her, then I have to talk to them."

"For what purpose?" he asked softly.

"Didn't we just discuss that? I need to have the key, the filter. I need to be able to see her words the way she wanted me to see them."

He looked at me with *real* concern. "How do you know that you don't already see them the way she intended?"

"If that were true, I wouldn't have found this."

He sighed in apparent disappointment. "Her words speak for themselves and anyone reading them would see her clearly. What you are seeking is the context that would make you feel better. You're creating a fiction that turns her death into a mystery you can solve."

"No, it's here," I insisted. I dug through the bag and produced the blue journal, opened it to the last page, set it on the red volume and handed them off to him. He considered them distantly, and passed them back without a word.

"She wrote that the day she killed herself. I've looked through these books, and nowhere was there a red sharpie anywhere inside them. It's a hidden message. She wasn't just some suffering girl, she was someone else with a secret life."

"So you don't want your sister back, you want to expose her as a different person, someone unknown to you who has gone away. Will it make grieving easier, do you think?"

I denied it with a fierce shake of my head though his words had the ring of profound truth. As smeared and adamant as I was, I needed him to look past it and see the real me. I needed someone, *anyone* to hear my words as more than noise, and he just happened to be the man who enjoyed listening.

"You said that every word meant something if a person could listen. Well, I want to listen. I realize now that I never knew her and I never listened. I don't want a *specific* context, an outcome I understand. I'm ready to accept *anything* that will help me know."

"Know what?"

I heaved a sigh and it slipped out of me, as selfish as it had sounded in my head, but the greatest piece of honesty I had ever conceived. "The part of *me* that's gone now."

That confession seemed to impress him, "A very astute observation. You are a sister, no more. Your duty to her is finished."

"No, it isn't," I said quietly. "I owe her."

"How could you?" His expression was the very picture of compassion as he gazed at me. "You were exactly what you needed to be. She always spoke very highly of you."

"Without reason." I denied, hiding my face in my hands. "I could have done more."

To my surprise, he reached out and touched the top of my head ever so gently. "Love is not a tallying of favors, it is a limitless supply given freely."

"So I'll give."

"You love her because she is dead, not because she was alive?" he whispered.

"I love her, because she loved me."

"Therefore, whatever she was, do you really suppose she would want to cause you harm or distress?"

"She killed herself didn't she?"

He seemed to ponder me. His hand slipped from my head as I looked up. After a few moments, he bowed his head. "You believe she was pointing you toward the night club?"

"Yes!" I replied a little louder than necessary.

His arms folded in and his right hand curled up around his beautiful bottom lip. The sapphire eyes watched me attentively, as if committing me to memory, and slowly the expression in them changed from interest to seemingly uncharacteristic concern.

"This is dangerous, Lilith," he replied softly. "You walk in a cavern filled with loose rock. Cry out any louder and you'll be buried alive."

"I can take care of myself."

"It is true that a man with many weapons may survive many situations, but what if a fight is unnecessary. Is he prepared for peace? You are out of your element here."

It was ominous and as understanding and pleasantly analytical as he'd been, I was aggravated. I stood up and held the red volume out at him almost accusingly. "Do you know what these words mean?"

He shrugged sadly.

"Then you aren't going to help me?"

He looked up at me, and in a single blink, had forgotten me. "I don't believe there is any help I am able to provide," he murmured, and looked away.

"Fine." I tossed the five dollar bill onto the table. "Thanks for the coffee."

CHAPTER 8

After a hasty mall visit to buy clubbing clothes that covered as much of my body as I could manage, I downsized my life to fit into a jeweled clutch, and stuffed some cash and my ID in my bra. As I parked my car down the street from Club Trishna, I had to wade through the droves of people wandering like zombies toward the smell of flesh. A long line had formed under the neon sign, lights glowed from the high, industrial windows, and a deep thumping sound hammered the ground beneath my slingbacks.

As I looked around, wondering if I fit in entirely, I spotted a girl with similar attire, laughing with her friends as she waited in line, and breathed a sigh of relief. My personal shopper had done well. At the door, the bouncer looked at my ID, which he enjoyed watching me fish out, took my money, and stamped my wrist with a glowing ankh as if the rubber block was a prod.

Amused and a little giddy, I stepped inside.

What had been darkness during the bright light of day, revealed itself in the intense red, purple, and blue lighting. If I had been blind, I was sure I'd never be able to find my way, for the music was so loud, echo-location would have been impossible. The foyer funneled visitors to the bar like unwilling cattle. In the spirit of the night, I filled up a space there until a bartender in black approached me.

Most of our conversation took place in shouts, lip reading, and repetitions of the word "what". It was my mistake to come to a bar without a drink already chosen. I could tell the other cows were desperate to slake their thirsts and that I was creating a road block. Finally, I told him to give me whatever was most popular, and again wished there was a handy blunt object I could use to knock some sense into myself.

After a few minutes of mixing little elements behind the bar, he lifted up a fluted glass filled with a liquid of deepest crimson.

"What is it?" I shouted.

His lips moved.

"What?"

"Blood!" he shouted back. "Twelve dollars."

I know my painted eyes were suddenly huge, but he ignored it. I handed him fifteen, stepped away from the bar, and was immediately absorbed by human bodies.

I waded through, pushing out toward the dance floor that *had* to exist. It opened before me suddenly like Niagara Falls. Unexpectedly, I was in a barrel, being shoved over the edge, drink in hand. Trying to get away from the rapids of unsympathetic dancers, I found a staircase up to what seemed to be a balcony. By the time I made it to the banister, I was so exhausted I could have curled up into a ball right there, if not for the bass thumping like a massive heartbeat.

For some reason, the stairs were much darker and quieter. I took a few moments to gather myself, leaning against the wall.

"Why here, Ev, of all places? It's so . . . tacky."

Without realizing it, I tipped the glass up to my lips and sipped the concoction. It was thick, just like blood, but it tasted like cherries and strawberries, and bit back with the kick of some kind of fizz.

First it was the nectar of immortality, then a name that meant freedom from reincarnation, a club called "Craving" that stamped people with the cliché of the Egyptian undead, and now I was drinking "blood".

Right.

I rolled my eyes.

Someone pushed past me in the dark. I turned to apologize and move out of the way, but a strong hand took hold of my elbow.

"Wha . . ."

"Ms. Pierce?"

I couldn't see his face clearly in the dark, but it wasn't who I wanted it to be in this land of strangeness and shallow verisimilitude. "Yes?"

"If you'll come with me."

"What? What are you talking about?" I demanded as he escorted me up the stairs. "I'm not doing anything wrong!"

At the top of the stairs, the atmosphere changed. Cubicles like diner booths draped in lush fabrics and set with candles ran along the sides of a smaller dance floor, and softer, more flowing music played. A second bar lit in blue and made to look like ice, lay directly ahead. It was as if a Bedouin camp got set up on Greenland. My guide pulled me past it all to a black door, opened it, and despite my objections, propelled me through it, then shut it behind me.

I was enclosed in pitch darkness for a few moments and was momentarily terrified. My eyes began to adjust, however, and I realized that the room wasn't really that dark, I was just in some type of hallway, draped with black velvet. Around the bend, behind the icy bar's back wall, candles flickered. It was a large room with a few scattered ottomans and chaise lounges. A grand piano sat in the center, lit from above like a stage.

I was tempted to laugh at the whole business. I was trapped inside one of those dime-a-dozen novels about teenage girls who fought or fell for vampires.

"They don't stand a chance."

She couldn't have been serious, sending me to a place like this! Then I looked at the glass in my hand and rolled my eyes again.

"You came, after all."

I looked up. Seated at the piano was the woman in blue, but now she was wearing black, high-waisted slacks, a green blouse, and lace gloves. Her hair was parted on the side and pinned behind her ear by a black, feathered clip. Her smile was just as riveting, and just as haughty.

"I wondered if you would."

I walked toward her hesitantly, trying to figure out if I was as comfortable in this skin as she was in hers.

"You look lovely."

Frowning, I put my hand on the body of the piano and set my glass down. "I've looked through her appointment journal. She came here almost every other day, though she didn't call it by name."

The woman turned and put her fingers to the keys. Her playing was beautiful with a kind of hard precision that mimicked emotion.

The notes trailed away. "Yes," she murmured, "I was never very good."

I said nothing, because something in how she said it told me that she wasn't the type of person to require anything from me, least of all compliments.

"Do you have a Sanskrit name too? Because it's really starting to feel like a joke," I blurted out.

I was worried she would turn her sharp glare onto me, but she tilted back her head and laughed merrily. It rang out like the tinkling of bells, with a great deal more feeling than her music.

"No, my dear. My name is Ursula." She held out her hand.

I hesitated to shake it, but when I did, found it to be cold and stiff.

"Lilith."

"Yes, I know."

"So I gathered." She got up from the piano and walked to one of the divans. A few seconds saw her reclining elegantly. I picked up my beverage and sat across from her on the soft white fabric of an ottoman. "Did Detective Unger come by?"

"Yes, and asked me the same questions you are about to ask," she said with a sweetness that was almost false.

A bit uneasy, I decided not to beat around the bush. "What can you tell me about her?"

"Be more specific, there's a great deal, as I said," Ursula laughed, fingering the necklace of black crystals around her throat, but the laugh had changed. It was a bit more perfunctory, a sedative in place of what I really sought.

"Did she . . . come to see you?"

She nodded almost as if she couldn't care less. "We had good times, ah, but the poor girl, she was so far gone."

Her light tone bothered me. "Gone?"

"Mmm. By the time she came here, it was already too late. There was nothing I could say, her mind was already made up, but oh . . . you have no idea what I'm talking about, have you?"

I looked at her smiling, masklike face, and wasn't sure what I could possibly say.

"If you stay, you'll know," she hinted mischievously, and reached out to touch my hand.

"Stay?" I prodded, looking at her long, sharp nails. "For what?"

Her smile transformed to a garish grin. I pulled away and got to my feet. I don't know why. Something in me revolted. I backed away, pulling her upward as if with an invisible cord.

"You really should stay, my dear. I mean, you *do* want the answers, don't you?"

I continued to take tiny steps toward the door, but suddenly collided with a form in the dark. He caught me and held my upper arms firmly. I struggled to pull away, until she got close enough to touch me and ran her finger down my neck, past my pulse point.

"Don't be afraid, dear. No one wants to hurt you." She laughed. "Just have a seat and watch."

"Why did my sister come here?" I growled.

But her infuriating smile stayed in place. "Because she could be herself."

"What?" I demanded.

The door behind us opened, and in a moment, Ursula forgot me. With a wave, she had me deposited onto one of the settees in the corner of the room. I was tempted to upend my sticky, red drink onto her white furniture, but ignored the impulse, barely.

People began to find their way in and as near as I could tell, they were of varying types and social groups. A few among them had obviously used fake ID's. They sat twittering with their friends, already red-faced and overly gesticular. A few of the swankier, womanizing types chatted here and there, and if not for my bodyguard, I imagine several of them would have come toward me. Everyone gathered as if Ursula, seated again at her piano, would suddenly break into song.

Without anything better to do, I sipped my drink. I couldn't taste the alcohol, but I could sure feel it. It was a crafty potion, and I was positive that over half the room had already had at least one.

At last, the door shut and the music from outside was cut off. The chatter died down slowly and finally at Ursula's charming wave, transformed into silence.

"Welcome," she greeted with a coy smile.

Everyone said their hellos and she accepted them with poise. A few well-placed waves here and there told me that she had seen some of these faces before. Her hands found the ivories and after a few meandering strokes, she coaxed out a slow jazz melody.

"Who among us tonight has been here before?" she sang out, her head tilted to expose her long white neck.

As I looked around, I saw that most of them had been there before. They stood around, their hands in the air, giggling and winking at each other flirtatiously.

Ursula freed up a hand to wave at everyone dramatically. "And how many have no idea what's about to happen?"

A few raised their hands nervously.

Ursula giggled and it sent a spasm through the gathering.

"Well, won't you be surprised? Come here my little virgins," she beckoned. Slowly, because of their friends' cajoling or the assurances that nothing bad would happen, they began to line up in the center of the room. Ursula stood up and as if inspecting them, walked along the line, touching them, one by one.

I looked around. The expression on her face was changing, but no one seemed to catch it. It was as if she were the pied piper and they her willing followers. They were grinning more and more madly, while she, at the heart of it, was distant and hungry looking. Suddenly disturbed, I put the glass on the floor and wrapped my arms around myself in apprehension.

She stopped in front of a girl standing at the end of the line. The poor thing was dreadfully nervous, and it was obvious she was in the same boat as me, but had a painful lack of experience with alcohol. She was tilting where she stood, fighting for control of her eyes, and would have tripped over her own dizziness if not for the man standing next to her in line.

"This one's too intoxicated," she declared, and before anyone could say or do anything, my bodyguard and several of the other invisible security guards had swept the girl and her disappointed friends from the party.

The room once again entirely hers, Ursula stood before the man who now occupied the end and smiled playfully.

"Pick a secret. Not just any secret, mind you, but a deep, dark, painful secret."

The man laughed and looked around at the others. "Come on, really?"

She nodded and put her hand on his chest. "Everyone here has done it."

Along the walls, they confirmed it with shouts and nods. "Okay," he acquiesced, turning back to her. "Got one."

"No, no," she scolded, "not good enough. Give me a truly despicable one, ah yes . . . that's the one."

He frowned in puzzlement.

Her green eyes narrowed almost cruelly as she stroked his chest.

"This game is called 'Tell the Truth'. The rules are simple. Tell the truth or face the consequences." Her gaze roamed the circle of onlookers and for a moment, stopped on me. "Now Derrick," she said to the man gently, "tell the truth. Tell everyone your secret."

It was as if his expression just slid off his face. His complexion paled, and for a moment, as he looked into her eyes, he knew it was not a game. The longer he took to reply, the larger her smile grew, until he looked like he might vomit in response to her eagerness.

"Tell the truth, Derrick, my dear," she insisted quietly.

Like jackals salivating after a wounded wildebeest, the spectators leered.

"I . . . I once . . . robbed a house," he managed finally.

But she was already shaking her head as if saddened by his dishonesty. "Liar," she whispered, and as if suddenly brought to life, the room began to hoot and howl. "You have one chance to survive to the next round, Derrick."

He took a deep breath and looked around as Ursula passed to the next victim.

"Fetch me a secret, my dear," she hissed at the young girl. Uncertain and anxious, the girl looked at Derrick, and quickly learned that she did not want to play.

"I don't . . ."

"What?" the host said loudly as if hurt by the suggestion. "You came to the party; it is *rude* to not play the games. Come now," she snarled viciously, "a secret!"

The girl shivered beneath the stare and finally looked at her shoes.

Ursula's sinister mouth split wide.

"Now speak it," she commanded.

The girl was on the point of tears when a chant started. To my left and right people were shouting, demanding the girl play the game.

Ursula's hand went up, and the voices faded.

"Tiffany," she warned, "tell the truth."

"I . . ." the meek voice shivered, "my . . . my father . . ." she shook her head, but Ursula was merciless. She reached out and took hold of the girl's wrist, and with a hard glint in her eye, made sure that Tiffany knew conscientious objectors would never live it down. "My father . . ." the girl finally continued, all the while yanking on her own arm in desperation ". . . raped me."

I sucked in breath and looked around the room, sure that statement would shut them up, that they'd feel terrible for making her confess such a thing, but they were all cheering, smiling, carrying on as if it was hilarious.

"Now, Derrick, is your chance. Look into Tiffany's pretty, tear-stained face and tell us . . . is she lying?"

Derrick, again on the spot, ran his fingers through his hair and barely glanced at the unfortunate girl beside him. "Yeah, she's lying."

"Ohhh," Ursula sighed grandly, "I'm afraid you are wrong. Alas Derrick, you have failed. You cannot be genuine, nor can you tell another human's verity. You are banished from the game," and Derrick was swept away, pulled to the corner at my left and, for lack of a better word, imprisoned on a divan, just as I had been. Feeling badly for him, I turned and tried to encourage him with a gaze, but he was looking after Tiffany in utter despondency.

Ursula turned back to the line of contestants and stepped from Tiffany to the girl beside her. This girl, not quite drunk or modest enough, seemed ready to tell her secret with pride. She had her hands on her hips and was smiling arrogantly.

"Have your secret, my dear?" Ursula prodded, and in her eyes, I saw that whatever the girl had decided to share, would not be what came out. In the wake of that gaze, the girl faltered a bit, and as Ursula shook her head, the bravery melted completely. "My, you have so many, Ashley . . . but that one will do. Yes, that one."

The girl refused, but with saccharine sweetness, Ursula put a hand on her shoulder and directed her to the crowd of hateful enemies. Beside her,

Tiffany was weeping softly into her hands, raped again in full view of the public. At last, Ashley recovered her nerve and with a great sigh, let it go.

"I poisoned my ex-boyfriend. He . . . he got sick."

The corners of Ursula's mouth stretched yet again and I knew what she was about to declare.

"Liiiiaaar!"

The girl's face paled, for the interrogator had gotten her right; it did not shake her though, as evidently, her strategy was to out-lie everyone else. The man beside her was made to admit he was a serial rapist, and when Tiffany gasped in horror and cowered, Ashley shouted out that he was telling the truth and was saved from dismissal.

By the end of the round, I was thoroughly disgusted, but knew that I could not leave. I was chained, not just by the strong men or the ridicule of the crowd, but by morbid fascination. I felt slightly sick, but my heart pounded as each person was called upon a second time.

"Tell the truth," Ursula ordered, and being sweet and innocent, I could see that Ashley's strategy would never work for Tiffany. There was no way she could afford to lie because there was no way she could tell who was lying. She attempted it though, and her falsehood was too extravagant, which made me wonder what her real secret was. When the second girl was interrogated, Tiffany failed to see through it, and was dismissed.

In the end, there were two liars facing each other in all out war, determined not to share, and to call out the other, but Ursula threw in another twist.

"The game is called 'Tell the Truth'," she admonished, "and you have played it well, but the only way to win, is to confess. Tell the truth. The first person to lie to me is finished."

Both players were horror-struck. To the tune of laughter and catcalls, they were examined and their secrets chosen.

Ursula stood before the girl and crossed her arms.

I could see the poor thing's chest heaving. "I . . . When I was in high school, I had sex with my chemistry teacher to get an 'A'," she nearly shouted.

With a calm nod, Ursula stepped before the man. "Your turn, Todd."

He gulped in a few breaths and planted his feet. "I hit a kid on a bike with my car. I drove away and didn't call the cops."

It was Ashley's turn yet again. Ursula stepped before her sternly and chose her secret. In that moment, I wondered how it was done. Was it a subtle change in eye movement, temperature, pulse? Was Ursula a human lie detector?

"I had sex with my half-brother," she confessed.

It moved to Todd, and I could see it. He was about to lie. He didn't care what the consequences were, because he wasn't going to confess whatever it was she wanted him to say.

"I shot my brother's dog," he lied. The auburn head gave a sad shake, and to a rush of sound, the beautiful referee declared the girl the winner. Todd was escorted to the corner.

"I humbly thank all of you for playing our little game," she said, by way of a grand closing. "For those who would like to play again, please step forward."

And so it went, for hours. They never seemed to tire of it, and each time a winner was selected, they were allowed to sit on the banked seating along the back wall and squirm in half-darkness. It was an ingenious torture device; success was a hollow victory, for really, the only way to truly win, was to have nothing of which to be ashamed. Even if a person didn't play, they were reminded of the disgrace somewhere in their life. What boggled me, was that people came back, seemed addicted, and I wondered if they went out and committed offenses just to have another secret. Impressed with the sick cleverness of it, I watched the host, trying to discover her scam.

At last, it came down to the finals, where liar faced liar, and in the end, told the truth with frantic satisfaction. By the end, a man who had declared himself everything from a murderer to a sadist, but had never once been truthful, took the game with ten straight confessions, and revealed himself to be just as vile as his falsehoods. Ursula took his hand and held it up for the audience and after he had taken his bows, she sat him at her piano.

"And now, my little shriven dears, it is time for you to depart. In Michael here, I have found my winner, and he will receive his reward. Come back with more secrets, my dears. Come back and work harder next time, for if you can see clearly enough, you might just win the prize."

"What is the prize?" someone shouted.

I was beginning to wonder that myself. Was it money, or something equally grand? Certainly it had to be, to make such quick work of secrets that would destroy a man should they be leaked to the outside world.

"Well, you'll just have to play, my dears, but I can assure you, it's the prize of a lifetime."

She had such a charisma to her, that with only a few words and gestures, she had crowned herself in their eyes, and with fawning glances and forlorn faces, they drifted out the door, taking the shaken losers with them. I wondered if any of them would come back, but was fairly certain they would.

"I've been playing a long time for this," the winner grinned up at Ursula, who slowly sank into his lap seductively. He was in his mid-forties, but was obviously still passing himself off as thirty. He wore a close-fitting shirt with a paisley pattern and dark jeans. His thick fingers pawed up her back eagerly, pulling her toward him, until she was straddling him and the piano bench, and had his lip in her mouth. Then he spotted me.

"Is she part of the prize?" he asked with a laugh.

Ursula cast a dark look back at me and shook her head. "Her? No. She's a witness."

"To what?"

The woman laughed, at first like a woman, but all too quickly like a banshee. She laughed until he was looking at her in awkward disquiet and then her voice trembled to a halt.

She tipped herself forward in his arms and touched her nose to his.

"To *my* secret, silly," and before I could do anything, she had toppled him backward onto the piano bench. As I jumped up, something glittered in her hand. I realized too late that the jeweled buckle to her belt was some kind of weapon. Her hand dropped and he let out a single shout that came to a gurgling crescendo. She threw herself over him and like a wild animal, began growling and tearing with her hands. At first too stunned to move, I stood there, but as real blood began to pool on the floor, my adrenalin got the better of me.

I turned to the door and found the way open. In a mad dash, I reached the foyer, just in time to hear her shriek out in wicked laughter. I spun back and she was on her feet, facing me, her entire upper body covered in gore.

I hurled myself at the door and tumbled through it. On the other side, former contestants still gathered, laughing and patting each other on the back. I rammed through them at top speed. A few shouted after me, but there was no way in hell I would apologize. I had reached the bottom of the stairs before the signs of pursuit reached me.

They were moving through the crowd on the dance floor, black suits turned in my direction, shoving people aside. I looked around desperately for an exit and had no choice but to go back through the cattle press to the beacon of the green exit sign. Furiously, I elbowed and kicked my way through the people, and was close enough to feel relief, when someone fought back. A drunken girl caught my fist in her stomach and responded by grabbing hold of my hair.

I managed to turn my head while her boyfriend tried to pull us apart, and caught sight of one of them. A girl a few feet away was hurled back, and as he reached for me, I screamed out in rage and dropped my stiletto heel right unto the bitch's metatarsals. While she shrieked and bled in the bouncer's way, I tore from her hands and slammed into the exit door. The alarm blared, but it was barely louder than the music, as I made my way down the alley. They hit the door right after me, running faster than I was. In desperation, I made for my car, but I knew I would never make it in those shoes.

Suddenly one heel stuck in the metal street grating, and I went down harder than a linebacker. I landed on my knees and rolled over, tried to get up, and found that I couldn't. Sobbing, I tugged at the shoes, trying to get them off so that I could get away, but as I looked up, they were right on top of me. I threw my arms up to protect myself, but to my surprise, nothing happened.

Lowering my shaking hands, I sat in the gutter, a bloody, filthy wreck, and they just stood there looking around. Terrified they had but to confirm their orders, I screamed for help, and before I knew what was happening, warm arms encircled me from behind. A skein of long, dark hair dropped into the crook of my neck. He pulled me to my feet and steadied me. With my heart slamming so loudly, I could barely hear myself think, I pushed back, trying to crawl into my savior for safety. In a frenzy, I looked up at his face and to my further astonishment, found it completely composed.

It was the armchair philosopher, and he was holding my pursuers at bay with a tranquil stare.

"We . . . we have to go now!" I cried. "Please!"

He blinked down at me with a distantly curious look, as if he had happened upon the scene and couldn't fathom what was going on, but when he saw the panic in my face, his eyes transformed into little chunks of cobalt. In a second, flat, he had hooked his elbow beneath my damaged legs and was walking away with me in his arms.

Over his shoulder, I could see the security guards, their faces screwed up in rage, pacing in place and shouting into their radios, like panthers roaring behind cage bars.

"Go faster!" I begged, but he shushed me gently. "They'll follow us!" I insisted in a half-insane voice. I pulled back from his shoulder and looked him in the eyes, my hands on his face. His skin was incredibly smooth. "They'll follow me!"

"They're not going to follow you," he breathed, and I could see knowledge there. He was certain, and even though that certainty had nothing to do with reality, it made me feel worlds better.

"Where's your car?"

I gasped and reached for my chest, wriggling in his arms like an infant. He set me down gently out of sight of the pursuers, and limping in a circle, I dug the keys out of my purse, somehow still hooked around my bicep, its metal chain undamaged. With quaking fingers, I pressed the alarm button, cursing and begging it to please work. After a few seconds a set of headlights blinked and we found the car.

I was already tottering toward it when he scooped me up yet again and carried me to the passenger side. Without a second thought or any hint of fatigue, he pulled open the door, placed me in the seat, and belted me in. He got in on the other side, took the keys from my trembling grasp and pulled away with tires spinning just fast enough to placate me with a screech.

While my heart did its best to escape my chest, my mind touched gingerly on what I had seen, and when I realized I had just witnessed a woman tear a man to pieces with her bare hands, I put my head between my knees and cried so hard, I thought I might just suffocate myself.

CHAPTER 9

He pulled behind his shop into a tiny parking lot and came around to my side of the car. Still shaking, I frantically unbuckled my seatbelt.

"We can't stay here! They saw you! They'll find me!"

He carefully bent down, and with gentle fingers, eased my bruised ankles across the floor mat. "They're not going to look for you. Trust me. Arms around."

I looked at him, dazed and completely unable to form ideas that made sense in the context. "I'm heavy."

He had that look again, that strange expression of detached admiration, like I was an adorable child who belonged to someone else. For some reason, it soothed my frazzled nerves.

"You're not heavy," he said with a compassionate smile. "Arms!"

I reached out and wrapped my arms around his neck. Slowly, he lifted me out of the car and carried me inside. We entered at the back of the bindery, where a storage room butted up beside a staircase.

"Do you live here?" I said quietly in his ear.

"Yes." His apartment was more like a studio. The kitchen and living area was one long room of the same dimensions as the coffee shop. There were only a few pieces of furniture, and not a single decoration. No photos or personal belongings, just more books and strangely enough, several candle stands. He carried me into the bathroom, a stark white, subway-tiled room with a claw foot tub and pedestal sink, and put me down on the toilet.

"I'll be right back," he soothed, but no matter how comforting he was, I couldn't bear the thought of being alone.

I grabbed his wrists and shook my head wildly. He disentangled himself and cupped my face in his hands, staring into my eyes for as long as it took me to understand that he was not leaving me for good.

"Just a moment?"

Shivering, I nodded. While he did whatever it was, I took scattered stock of my person to keep from feeling adrift. My shoes were gone. My beautiful new blouse torn and smeared with grease and whatever had congealed on the ground from the packing plant. My pencil skirt was ripped at the seam in several places. My knees were completely skinned and bloody. A single gash ran down the side of my right shin. I was covered in forming bruises, my hands were scratched up, and my feet looked as if I'd walked across a bed of broken glass. I reached in my purse and managed to drop everything on the floor while attempting to open my compact. My makeup was smeared like a kabuki performer with hay fever. Bits of trash clung to my overly gelled curls. All in all, I was a sorry mess and it didn't help that I was shaking like a leaf.

He returned with a chair, a first aid kit, and a box of Epsom salts. I was tenderly transferred to the chair and the hot water was turned on in the tub. He lifted my feet up and put them into the rising tide that instantly turned a pinkish brown. As he sprinkled the salt into the water, the overwhelming cold began to leach from me, until I stopped shivering and felt numbness take over.

"This is a bad cut," he murmured, ladling water with his hands onto my shin. "I'm not sure yet if you need stitches."

I shook my head. I don't know why, but I couldn't speak yet. Not even the sting of the salt or the careful prodding of his fingers had any effect on my anesthetized body.

He glanced up at me. "You have glass in your feet and knees. It will take me a while to get it cleaned out."

I closed my eyes. In the darkness, with the rushing of the water, I saw it all again; the way he cried out, her ravenous eyes, the ring of blood around her lips and the chunks of flesh stuck to her fingernails. My hands went to my face and I shuddered.

Something warm was wrapped around me. I looked up to see him sitting on the edge of the tub, facing me. He was reaching for my face and I had caught him. Instead of hesitating or looking embarrassed, he finished the gesture and seemed to take a long, deep breath.

"Talk about it when you are ready," he whispered, "and not before. I can wait."

But suddenly the rational side of my mind kicked in, and as if appalled with the fact that it had been ignored, did so with a vengeance. I snatched his hand from the air and clamped my fingers around it in a way that must have been painful to him, though he said nothing.

"No! We have to call the police! I have to call Unger! My god, we have to do something right now!"

His dark brows drew closer together. "Take a deep breath, Lilith," he commanded and his voice was so strong that I couldn't disobey. "What happened?"

"She . . . Ursula, she . . ." but I couldn't match words, those precise little things, to such images. It just didn't seem to do the memory justice.

His hands were back around my face, forcing me to look at him. "What did she do? Is someone hurt?"

"Someone . . . someone's dead!" I shouted, and it was like a release. I sobbed and settled my hands in the crooks of his elbows. "She tore his throat out! He was bleeding everywhere! They were going to kill me!"

There was pressure behind his touch, telling me to stay focused on the present and not fall into fear for things gone by. "Are you sure he's dead?"

"There was so much blood!" My voice crumbled into dust, my dry mouth sticking to itself. I tipped forward and instead of letting me pitch into the water, he propped me up with his shoulder and held me.

There were no more tears in me, but somehow, I still managed to cry. Never in my life had I seen something so horrible. I was no stranger to ends, dead bodies, black clothes, soft-spoken well-wishes that never turned into actions, but spurting veins and monstrous insanity were new to me. What kind of person could do such a thing, and why for the love of all that was sacred, would Eva be mixed up with them?

Finally, I had an answer, finally, I understood, and in one final quake, I lost that hatred for her. Perhaps it had happened to her exactly as it had happened to me and she had jumped to free herself from a world that had turned her into an accessory to crimes unimaginable.

"If he's dead, there's nothing we can do," my rescuer said quietly.

"I have to call Unger; he'll know what to do! He will!" I pulled away and tried to convince him with my raccoon eyes, but something in his expression told me that I was missing some key facts. "What? What is it?"

"I don't think he'd believe you, Lilith."

Caught off guard, I shook my head. "Of course he would! There was blood! Didn't you hear me? They'll find the blood!"

He was already shaking his head almost imperceptibly. "If this is something that woman does often, it will be completely gone by the time any help could arrive."

"So what?" I demanded irately. "We just ignore the fact that a man is dead?!"

"If you rely upon Unger," he warned, "not only will the man be forgotten, but you'll find yourself in a position to do absolutely nothing about it."

"What are you talking about?!" I found myself shouting. My fist pummeled his chest, but it had no effect on him. A man strong enough to toss me over his shoulder, surely it was a useless gesture, but he understood and let me go, crossed his arms and continued to advise me with his gaze.

I had ignored his advice once before, and as he had said, I regretted it almost more than I regretted taking the later flight. Gripping the edges of the chair, I stared into the bathtub.

"What do you mean?"

"Detective Unger was here today."

I blinked at him stupidly. "Here?"

He nodded. "He wanted to know how close I was to your sister."

I frowned, even though my face felt as if it was made of rubber. "How did he find you?"

"He's been following you."

My mouth fell open.

"I told him exactly what I told you, until he started asking about your mental state, if psychological problems ran in your family, if you might do something to hurt yourself . . . or someone else." His face tipped forward, as if with the point of his nose, he could direct my mind to the reality of the situation.

I tried to give Unger the benefit of the doubt. My vision gave me details about him that he didn't possess about me, and indeed, colored any positive impression I might have made. Despite the unexplainable prescience, I was jeopardizing an investigation with rash decisions, so of course he'd want to be sure I was a solid individual. As a serious police officer, he *should* be investigating me.

I think my savior could read it on my face, see me handing Unger my trust. He continued to shake his head. "Then he asked if you and she had ever fought, if Eva had ever mentioned your money troubles to me."

"Money troubles?" I gasped. "What is he talking about? Sure I'm paying my bills alone, but I get alimony!"

Son of a bitch! How could he be thinking I was involved? I was on the plane when she jumped. If I had really been in on something, if I had really paid someone to kill my sister, wouldn't I have at least been smart enough to wait for a phone call before I jumped on a fucking redeye? My temper was beginning to stoke back to life, and even though I had little energy for it, it was warm to the touch.

"Is he stupid? Bastard!"

The stranger went back to cleaning my wounds, averting his eyes from my betrayal.

"I can't believe I trusted him!"

"You can see why calling the police is probably unwise, especially if the people looking for you have any kind of influence. A mad woman suffering from grief is an easy person to blame." He palpated my feet. It stung and I twitched. Tweezers were pulled from the kit and he began to pluck the slivers of glass from me.

"So what should I do?" I sat back in the chair, at a loss. "I mean I know it sounds crazy, but I know what I saw! Something has to be done! She said they did it all the time! She said it was her secret." I shook my head in disbelief. "How do I stop her?"

He didn't seem to be listening. His eyes were narrowed and focused on my knees. Pieces of gravel clinked into the basin.

"But you're right," I continued. "There's no way I could make it sound sane." I pushed my scratched palms to my forehead as if trying to impress on my brain that it needed to function or would pay the price. "How did she do that trick?"

"What trick?" he urged.

"It was like she could read their thoughts. That was the game. She knew their secrets and made them confess. The winner . . ."

He stopped what he was doing and looked at me emotionlessly, as if freezing in the face of an unknowable predator.

"I know, crazy huh?"

"About as crazy as seeing the future," he hinted, his brows twitching upward ever so slightly.

"He told you about that, huh?"

He said nothing. Another piece of glass fell onto the towel in his lap.

"I am so confused," I admitted, and it felt good to be saying it to someone. "I *feel* like I'm going nuts."

"It is when we know a thing that we confine a thing. Confusion, therefore, is the sanest position to take."

As he continued to pick at my wounds, I watched him, feeling as if I was not good enough to be sitting there. Compared to his serenity, his economy of sound, his slow, deliberate movements that spoke of absolute certainty, I was a frenetic wet hen.

I had a moment of pause; as an individual, I had my own priorities, my own ideas of what it meant to be effective, but so did he, and in that moment, I realized that his were much better. He was worried about the person he could help. He was worried about keeping me safe, not what the cops would think, what would change my sister's memory, or what would provide "justice' to someone who was already dead. What had I done to deserve his consideration?

"Now she has brought me you."

Thanks, Ev.

He glanced up. Determined to mimic his example, I smiled and refused to be self-conscious. "Thank you for helping me."

"Would you thank the ground for existing beneath your feet?"

Bemused and mildly separated from my own body, I shook my head. "Maybe, if I thought about it more. Maybe . . . if I thought it cared."

He scooped some water up to my open skin and rinsed out the dirt. "Don't thank me. I lose nothing."

"It's nice, all the same."

He frowned at my cut again, as if he couldn't decide to be concerned or convivial. "I think if I bandage it well enough, it should be fine."

"It hurts."

He smiled. "It will." He got up and unstopped the tub and after the drain had slurped up every trace of my roll in the gutter, he refilled it. He spilled in a few drops from a brown glass bottle, and the smell of lavender wafted in the air. A soft white towel and robe were lain across the toilet and to my surprise, a pair of fluffy white socks appeared.

"You're prepared," I marveled.

"One never knows when a damsel in distress might trip into their lap," he said with a sympathetic chuckle. He pulled a bottle of baby oil from the cabinet and set it on the sink. "For your makeup."

I nodded, impressed despite my exertion.

"Take a bath," he comforted, "try to ground yourself in the physical. Ignore what you saw. You'll have time to think about it when your body is safe."

I stared at him, and tried not to blush. "Something occurs to me," I confessed almost silently.

His head tilted as it had in the coffee shop downstairs. "What?"

"I have no idea what your name is, and I feel like an ungrateful idiot."

He grinned and it was the first time I had ever seen him smile fully. It was absolutely magnetic and lit up both his face and my dark insides. I felt as if I was already healed, like getting over it all would be so easy.

"Arthur," he revealed.

"Like the king of Camelot? Do the rescue thing often?"

He shrugged and the moment of levity passed. With a supportive nod, he pulled the door closed. "I'll be right outside if you need anything."

I sat there for a while. As disgusting as I felt, I wanted to preserve the evidence. If Eva was sure I was the one to solve the mystery and expose the truth, then I had better start living up to the expectation. There was no room to freak out, lose my nerve. I clutched angrily at my elbows, pissed off that I had allowed myself to be terrorized. I should have done something. I should have stood up for that guy. I should have kicked at least one of those security guards in the balls. Where was all my self-defense training from those stupid afternoon classes that had given my husband a timeslot to ruin our marriage?

Getting into the tub was a process of tugging, feeling ineffectual, and trusting gravity to be my friend for once. After about fifteen minutes, my clothes were carefully folded on the floor and I had somehow managed to slide into the tub with minimal whale-splash.

The soreness was setting in, my body rebelling against my terrible treatment and the absence of the natural drugs that had kept it going. I took the bar of soap to my skin in rage, massaged suds through my crispy hair, and lay in the water like a dead fish.

Floating there, his advice made sense. I couldn't ignore my physical body; forcing it to do more than it could, or pushing it to work outside of the realm of its experience was foolish. If I was clever enough, my mind would figure out what I lacked, but since it was a part of my body, I had to take care of that first and foremost.

The man at the club was dead after all, nor was he a man that I should want to save. Ursula was already a criminal, and though I was sure valuable evidence was being washed away even as I scrubbed myself clean, something had to remain. There was no way she could cover the truth forever.

Blood will out.

I closed my eyes and focused on my breathing, pushed the oxygen I collected into my toes, and pulled all the toxins and horrible byproducts of fearing for my life to my lungs to be expelled. I could feel my body slowing, coming to an uneasy acceptance of the demands I had to it, and as it reached a truce with my brain, notions formed. Connections drew themselves, and eventually my body had to struggle yet again.

I fought to get out of the tub, but there was no way it was going to allow me that freedom. I huffed in frustration and there was a soft knock on the door.

"Are you alright, Lilith?"

"Yeah . . . I just can't," I tugged on the edge again futilely, "get out!"

"Do you want me to help you?" and there was no eagerness in it, none of the masculine irreverence I might have expected from another human, but then again, I was very quickly becoming accustomed to Arthur's incredibly sensitive and understanding deportment. Trying to appreciate normal men again would be like trying to chug beer after sipping port, which made the thought of accepting his help that much more intriguing.

"Could you? I mean I know we're practically strangers, but . . ."

The door was already opening. He dropped beside the tub and politely kept his eyes glued to mine. "Arms."

I hooked them around his neck and hid my face in his collar. He smelled wonderful, like soap and incense, and the soft fabric of his shirt tickled me. Certain I was already a bright shade of pink, I tried not to look at him, until I realized that nervousness was just built on an assumption that he saw anything he might like. For all I knew, he could be gay. After all, at no time had I felt that appraisal that inevitably took place in any and all male/female relationships.

Heedless of the water, he stuck his arm in and caught my legs again. Dripping, I was lifted out and deposited on the chair, where I sat shivering until the towel found me. Even though he fluffed my skin helpfully, the gooseflesh remained until the robe was wrapped around me and the towel draped over my head like a veil. He knelt at my feet and began putting Band-Aids on the little nicks and scrapes. My leg was wrapped in gauze and medical tape, and my knees were coated with a thin layer of Neosporin, before the socks were slid onto my feet like the glass slipper from the fairy tale.

To someone else, they were tiny gestures, but to someone who couldn't have gotten her husband to take out the garbage if she taped it to his ass, they were monumental and rekindled the faith that had died with my parents.

I couldn't thank him again. He would make that face that people made when they didn't want their generosity revealed, like they wanted the mystery of their craft to go unexplained. He would only accept an individual returned to her natural state, so as he helped me to my feet and guided me to his bedroom, I dropped my theory in his lap.

"My sister had a lot of money in her bank account."

He said nothing, but was in no way ignoring me. He pulled some sheets from the linen closet and ushered me through the door. He intended me to stay there, and I was too tired to protest. I just followed, hobbling behind him willingly.

"I don't know how that woman did what she did, but what if . . . this sounds nuts, but what if my sister got hired by Moksha . . ."

Arthur halted and raised an eyebrow in my direction. "Moksha?"

I gave a nervous chuckle, "Yeah, I know, right?"

He absolved the man of any misdeed with a fatherly shake of his dark head. "If he chose the name, then he is more aware of his failings than we could ever be."

I lifted my brows in surprise. "I don't know about that, but he sure fails at being suave."

"I am glad he at least tried."

I yawned. It was the bed's fault. It was the "bed" bed, the one from dictionary photos; brass frame, wider than a twin, white and crisp as he draped it. "So what if she was hired by him to keep their records, right, and they realized that she was a really fantastic researcher? I mean that's what he told me, that she was excellent at doing the in-depth research that he needed, finding facts and that kind of thing."

Arthur nodded and removed the dirty pillowcases.

"What if, while she was working there, he realized that he could use her skills in a different way?"

He considered it, hugging the pillow beneath his chin. "I see."

"Yeah, like," I picked up the blanket and unfolded it. He promptly took it from me. I looked after it in mild amusement at his chivalry. "What if that's how he gets ahead? What if he brings them to Ursula's club and she does . . . whatever it is that she does . . . and then my sister writes it down, organizes it, researches it, and comes up with a truth, right? A truth that Moksha can use to further his aims? They both get a cut and everyone's happy. Maybe Moksha even bought Ursula that property, I mean, Unger said they were into real estate."

"And the wicked witch stays in her tower as long as she is given a healthy supply of fresh young men?" he queried.

"Right. I mean that's the story behind the club's name, right?"

"And Eva's conscience pushed her over the edge?"

"Yeah," I murmured, suddenly self-conscious in the spotlight of his even-handed thinking.

"But before she ended it, she somehow managed to point you in the right direction, just so that you could avenge their wrongful deaths in a way she could not."

The more he talked in that ridiculously mature tone, the more hesitant I became. He had to know I needed his support; he was training me to accept him and trust him completely. The pessimistic part of me wondered if he would do like all the other opportunistic bastards had, and go for the treasure right away.

"Yeah," I said defiantly, "maybe!"

He looked at me as he smoothed out the comforter and there was not a single trace of mockery. "It will be difficult to prove. It's a tidy theory, though, and makes use of all the facts in evidence."

"Context right? You're trying to say that there might be some facts I haven't yet discovered."

He gave a slow blink. "Who can say, but I believe your assessments of the characters are sound."

My ire cooled instantly. "Then you think Moksha sounds like the kind of guy who would use Ursula to get information?"

He came around the end of the bed and folded back the covers, "If you were greedy and had someone with that kind of power, would you make use of it?" He pointed at the turn down.

"Then you believe me? You don't think I'm making it up?"

The lips twitched as if he longed to smile. "Are you?"

"No."

"Then if I am your friend, I must believe you."

"You don't have trouble trusting me? I mean I thought Unger was my friend until . . ."

"You have yet to make demands or threaten my safety," he pointed out. "Now sleep."

"You're going to tell me that there's nothing I can do about it, right?" I asked, collapsing onto the bed to stare up at him in dismay.

But he shook his head. "There are several things that you can do, but I'm telling you not to do those things in your mind over and over. Sleep first, then fight injustice."

"Are you making fun of me?" I said in a muted whine, even though I knew he wasn't.

He put his hands on his knees and leveled the space between our gazes. "Not in the least, but I am insisting that you rest."

I narrowed my eyes, and for a moment considered that I was back in the first grade, throwing pencils at the boy I liked. "Did you ever think that maybe some people in this world get more out of being pushed than they do out of being patched up and patted on the head?"

He stood up and patted my head. "You are not one of those people."

I watched him go in consternation, upset that he had gotten so accurate a picture of me in his mind. I was plucky, strong-willed, a fighter, and that's what I wanted people to see, probably so that they knew they couldn't hurt me even if they wanted to. How could he know that I was any more complicated than I presented myself?

Tell the truth.

"I'm really just barely keeping my head above water," I whispered.

CHAPTER 10

I must have passed out directly, but had no idea how long I'd been asleep when I opened my eyes. It was still dark, but I felt refreshed, or rather, I felt as if I'd slept a very long while. I sat up in the bed and rubbed my eyes. I was still wrapped up in the terrycloth robe and fluffy white socks. I tested my feet carefully, but to my surprise, they were fine.

"He's a miracle worker."

I opened the door quietly in case he was sleeping on the sofa and wandered down the hall. My clothes were no longer on the bathroom floor and in a momentary jolt of panic, I hoped that Arthur had been kind enough to at least bag them carefully. Then I remembered that he was a saint and smiled.

I snuck toward the kitchen, where a vague glow was beckoning, and wondered if he was the sort to have lunchmeat in his refrigerator, or if he was a non-violent vegetarian.

To my surprise, he was sitting at his desk against the left wall, surrounded by flickering candles, looking through the pages of one of Eva's red books with such focus, I almost forgot to be confused.

"Where did you get that? Did she leave one here?"

He sat back, but didn't turn. "Do you feel better?"

"Yes. Where are my clothes? I want to make sure that they stay preserved, in case . . . I don't know, in case Unger pulls his head out of his ass."

Finally, he turned and looked at me, but something about his face didn't seem right. He was staring at me, not critically, but certainly with more attentiveness than I felt like enduring.

"What?" I said with a nervous smile. "How long did I sleep?"

He said nothing and it made me incredibly uneasy. I was waiting for some soft-spoken universal truth, but he just sat there, exploring my face in concern.

"Sit down," he instructed quietly, and pointed to a wooden chair beside the desk.

That was what people always said to someone when they had horrible news to reveal, and before I could do anything about it, my heart was racing. I sat down, but even then, his expression didn't change. He turned his chair to face me and leaned forward until his hand could touch mine.

"What do you remember about yesterday?" he asked.

Perturbed, I considered refusing to say anything. What was he playing at, making me relive those things when I needed to be moving forward?

"What are you talking about?" I said with a sniff.

"Humor me," he replied.

"I went to the club, Ursula killed a man, I got hurt, and you rescued me, what else is there? I really don't want to talk about this now!"

He sighed heavily and leaned back. My eyes flicked between his face and the book and a sinking feeling began to drain my body of energy.

I covered my mouth in expectation.

He put his hands out as if to stop me from blurting out any kind of denials or defensive accusations. "Where were you hurt?"

In a flurry of movement, I pushed the robe away from my torn knees and found nothing but unblemished skin. With a weak sound, I frantically took off the socks and discovered why my feet had seemed stable. There were no cuts, no gashes, no telltale signs of glass slivers. I crumpled, my face landing on my perfect knees, and sobbed like a gibbering infant.

"What's . . . happening to me?" I panted.

His hand rested on the back of my head as before, and his fingers massaged my scalp in comfort. "You passed out as soon as you stood up," he explained, "after we talked downstairs."

My mind was a confusion of dates and events. If it had all been another dream, then he didn't know me, there was no fealty of dire necessity, and most importantly, the man from the club was still alive. I sat up suddenly, and instead of pulling away, his hand slid down the side of my face to cup my chin.

"What time is it? What day?"

He combed through my hair and pushed it from my crazed face. "Saturday, but only just."

"Then he's still alive," I insisted. "I've got time, this time! I can do something!"

I knew he had to be confused, but he didn't look it. He was frowning, but not at me. It was as if he was piecing together what I had seen from the few hints I gave, and like scattered breadcrumbs, he found his way to my knowledge.

"You want to prevent a death."

"Yes!"

"I see."

"You don't sound enthusiastic," I admonished.

"If you were hurt last time, what's to stop it from happening again?"

I pushed his hands away. "I know what's going to happen! Look, I know none of this makes sense to you, I get it, but I don't have time to explain!"

"I thought you had plenty of time, this time."

"I do, I mean . . ." I hesitated. If it was early on Saturday, then I had a full day to rally his support. I took a moment, knowing he wouldn't demand anything from me as I focused for a few moments on my own breathing.

"This has happened before," I confessed. "With my sister, I came before she was actually dead. I saw it all before it happened."

He nodded and my heart soared that he seemed completely willing to consider my ability, just as willingly as he had been in my dream.

"It's going to cause me problems, I know. Unger, Detective Unger has already got my name on a short list of . . . oh my god!"

"What?"

"He's been following me." I jumped up, but he pulled me back down. "He's coming here."

"When?"

"I don't know, you didn't say."

"Lilith," he murmured, and his voice sounded so worried for my safety that I couldn't help but be enamored. I stopped struggling to rise, let his hands hold mine, and allowed him to look me over. Afraid he was going to suggest I go back to bed, I set my jaw, but he only appeared to want to make certain I wasn't about to do a flying leap off his roof.

"I'm fine," I whispered. "I don't have any control over it. I'm not even sure if I believe it, but I know it worked once, and if it saves a life, I have to trust it."

His fingers covered the backs of my hands and his thumbs stroked the center of my palms. "Lilith, what's my name?"

I blinked, perplexed for as long as it took me to realign timelines in my mind. It was proof, and he had been smart enough to look for it. "Arthur," I declared earnestly.

With a sorrowful look on his face, he sat back. The fingers slid from me and were concealed by his elbows as he tucked his arms close to his body.

Uncertain, I shook my head. "Did I get it wrong?"

"No," he soothed, "but that's what concerns me."

With a sigh of relief, I looked around his impersonal home. "Why? Aren't you the one who said power of that sort should be used?"

He cleared his throat in mild accusation. "Were those my *exact* words?"

"Well," I blushed, "not *exactly.* It was a hypothetical question, actually."

"Mmm." He looked at Eva's book. "And this Ursula person, tell me about her."

I did, in as much detail as possible, watching his features dance over my revelations with smoothness that was so encouraging, I almost began to have pride in my own accomplishment. He listened without a hint of judgment and after I had finished, he mulled it over in placid consideration, eyes closed.

"Do you think it's some kind of cult?" I wondered aloud. "All this Sanskrit and stuff . . ."

One of his azure eyes opened and looked at me stoically. "Sanskrit is a language."

"I know, but maybe they're like those Wiccan guys who think they're practicing an ancient religion when no one has any idea what the Druids actually did, since they didn't exactly keep files. Who knows, maybe they have a comet to catch!"

"Sanskrit is a part of the Hindu and Buddhist tradition," he murmured.

"Look, are you trying to call me a jerk, or are you trying to educate me?" I grumbled.

He opened the other eye. "If you feel either might be true, then perhaps you have no business declaring anything."

I gasped. I was offended, until it occurred to me that he'd never once insulted me. It was almost humorous and when I smiled, his eyes slid shut in confidence that I took his meaning.

"Do you speak it?" I said, trying to look less like an ass and more like a woman he might take an interest in. "Sanskrit, I mean."

His eyes stayed shut. "It's a dead language."

"Then how did you know how to pronounce it?"

"It is the foundation of many tongues, including the many Pali languages, and through that association, a comprehension can be formed."

I closed my robe tidily and tried to make myself look like a woman, not a wench, though I did it with mild skepticism. Even if he was too polite to say anything, there was no way he wouldn't notice the transformation and wonder why I had waited for him to close his eyes to do it.

"Are you like, some kind of genius?" I stalled, trying to work a few knots from my hair. "Do you just sit around all day reading the books you work on?"

"Ignorance is the source of improper conduct. I read as many of them as possible. What I find inside them often influences how I choose to present them to the world," he said quietly, his hands joined behind a head that was tilted to the ceiling. "If I have freedom to choose, that is."

"How did you get started doing this? I mean, I'd think it was a dead profession, given how many people are functionally illiterate these days."

"You say it as if that makes them less able than you," he chided.

"Doesn't it?" I replied honestly.

"No one can live life without acquiring some knowledge. They receive their information in different ways, and those forms have their own caretakers. To those who still read, I am a guardian, and the number of readers does not diminish the significance of that."

"And when you're not guarding priceless written treasures, you are sermonizing on the nature of the universe," I chuckled. "A noble profession, Arthur."

He smiled. It was *that* smile, and it made my insides warm enough to melt.

"What kind of credentials do you have to have to do this?"

"One needs credentials to have opinions?"

"The books, Arthur," I said with a smile.

"None, but to do it well, you have to have the skill. Training in book arts doesn't hurt."

"Where did you go to school?" Free from his perusal, I frowned and shook my head at myself. What was I doing? I was involved in a life and death struggle, and I was sitting there making small talk. I really needed to reassess my priorities. Howard had undone the list that had been on my fridge, and now without those helpful little reminders, I was completely discombobulated.

Before I could compose myself completely, he opened his eyes and got up. "I didn't," he said, "go to school, and yet I contribute to society."

"I'm sorry," I watched him walk to the kitchen in meek dismay. I had been enjoying the proximity. "I didn't mean to suggest . . ."

"You didn't." He opened the refrigerator and removed a loaf of bread. "I was just drawing an illustration. A man's origins do not determine his quality, nor do his experiences determine his capacity for knowledge. If this is true, then why do we ever attempt to judge him by either?"

"I suppose, because they're convenient definitions."

"And humans are creatures of convenience?" he hinted with a tilt of his head. A package of lunchmeat was produced from a drawer and moments later, condiments joined the sandwich fixings on the counter. "All evidence to the contrary. As much as they try to convince themselves that they are simplifying their lives, they insist on making things more complicated. I have seen the iPhone and though I confess it is quite remarkable, I cannot fathom why I would need to be able to determine which song is playing wherever it is that I am. I feel that soon, there will be no mysteries left, and I wonder what we will do with our tenacity then."

I laughed, feeling the irony of that in my bones. There I was, trying to solve my life by getting into more trouble than ever before. I was making use of the incredibly fortuitous and amazing predictive abilities to try and simplify the whole world down to a series of events that could be avoided, in favor of what? What would I do when I solved it, simplified it, organized everything into neat packages? What did I have to go back to?

Not a damn thing.

I joined him and opened the mayonnaise, happy he was wise enough to simplify me. "Is that why you don't have any personal items in your house? No computer, no television, not even a radio?"

He pointed at me with the butter knife, and a twinkle in his eye. "Do your possessions make you feel any better about your existence?"

I shrugged, after all, I wasn't exactly using them. Living out of a suitcase did have its advantages. I hadn't even wondered about the pilot light in my water heater once.

"I get the whole monastic lifestyle, but really, what's wrong with a few things to call your own?"

He shrugged back, "They end up owning me."

"What about your books? What if the shop burned down? Wouldn't you be upset?"

"It would last only as long as it took me to find a new hobby. I would go somewhere else, do something else."

I couldn't believe it, but then again, it was him. "Wouldn't you be sad, or miss it?"

He glanced at me and smooshed the two halves of the sandwich together. "As you pointed out, I have very little to miss." The sandwich was put onto a plate and slid in front of me.

I looked at it in amusement. Whether in dream or reality, he somehow always managed to give me exactly what I needed to stand, question just enough of me to help me evolve, and sharpen my thoughts just enough to excise my own misgivings. And I'd only just met him.

"I know this is going to sound odd, but on the scale of things, probably not *as* odd as some of the other things that have come out of my mouth since we met."

He leaned against the counter and waited, smile already in place.

I picked up the sandwich and took a bite, chewed it, and swallowed before giving him any reason to step away from my side.

"Where on earth did you come from, and how long would it take me to get there?"

There it was again, two in one day. Triumphantly, I grinned back and happily took another bite as he chuckled. I watched him, wondering if he would try to answer, and even though I knew it would never happen, wanted to know if he could blush.

"Why would you need to go anywhere?" he replied, and with one finger, poked the smooth part of my forehead. For some reason, my spine shivered and it triggered a happy sigh.

"Does that count as an invitation?"

"You're here aren't you? Eat your sandwich, Lilith, and go back to bed. We have plenty of time, especially if you keep reading tomorrow's newspapers."

"What about you?" I asked, before I considered that there was an invitation in my words that I had not meant to be so obvious. I set the sandwich down and gestured blindly at the sofa, "Are you going to sleep? Or do they just doze on your planet?"

"I'll be fine, but you are exhausted."

"No I'm not," I lied. "I just took a long nap!"

"In which you lived through a full day and an attempt on your life. Go back to bed."

I pouted, but he was immune. Instantly, I was thrown back to my youngest days, when my father would make me my midnight snack and carry me to bed, patting my back while I made singsong noises. He would smile and shake his head while I asked interminable questions about why children were made to go to bed before their parents. I would insist that we have a "Waking Contest", which always ended in my happy failure. It had been a long time since I had thought of those days.

My skin warmed.

"Would you believe me," I said quietly, "if I said I didn't want to be by myself?"

I think he heard the catch in my voice. Without a sound, he took hold of my hand and plate and escorted me back to the bedroom. He tucked me in and sat beside me while I ate, and slowly petted my forehead as I tried to find dreams that weren't so foreboding.

"Arthur?"

"Hmm?"

"You remind me of my dad," I said quietly into my pillow.

"Is that a good thing?"

"Yes."

The weight of his body adjusted, slid down so that his arm could wrap around me. "Past *and* future; do you ever spend any time in the present?"

"Some of us don't have much of a present."

"And that is the root of the problem," he whispered in my ear. "No wonder your visions are so bleak."

I settled into his arms and felt completely safe. "Do you think I'm going crazy? Or is this something I should take seriously?"

"I take insanity very seriously, regardless."

I chuckled. "Good point, but really, should I be worried?"

"The problem with the future is that it has not yet been decided. Keep dealing in possibilities and you'll very quickly lose sight of what is happening right now. Then you will have no choice but to believe in fate." His lips were right next to my ear and as he inhaled, he sucked at my nerves.

"I like *this* now," I mumbled sleepily, "this now is good."

His laugh was low and almost silent. "If you were still in dreamland, you'd have missed it."

"All the more reason to stay awake."

His finger tapped my forehead, this time in moderate reprimand. "Go to sleep. I will be here when you open your eyes," he replied, and as if he were a hypnotist, I obeyed.

CHAPTER 11

I stared at his sleeping face, careful to keep my hair from tickling it as I leaned over him. He was truly the most attractive man I had ever encountered, and in a way that I only just realized was my ideal. I had never met anyone that made me feel humble and happy at the same time. If he had been the one teaching my math classes in college, I probably would never have given up on my dream of becoming a doctor.

I wondered if Eva had seen him the same way, if when he'd given her his card, she'd gone home and counted the moments until she could see him again. I wondered if she knew how I would think of him, if we ever crossed paths. She couldn't have, or she wouldn't have ever jumped. So perhaps for her, he was something else. If that was true, then perhaps he was amazing *only* for me, and if that was the case, then maybe I was just as unique to him.

Don't get ahead of yourself, I thought. *He barely knows you.*

And yet, I felt more myself than ever, which was a strange thing to consider, since I was thirty-five and still had no idea who I was supposed to be.

I tipped forward, certain he would not protest, and kissed the smoothness between his eyebrows. My Aikido sensei called it the "third eye", the sharpest point of the self. I hoped that while his blue eyes were closed, I would still be in his thoughts.

Stupid, hero-worshipping girl.

I pulled back to find him looking at me calmly.

"Uh . . . I . . ." I stammered.

"Were greeting me?"

"Um . . . yeah right." I sat up, radiating enough heat from my face to melt a glacier. "Sorry if I bothered you."

He sat up, "You are the one who seems bothered."

I chuckled and tried to pass it off with a wave. "I just didn't expect you to open your eyes.""Isn't the purpose of a greeting to initiate contact?" his arm curved around my head and poked me in the forehead. "It would be rude not to open my eyes. Are you hungry?"

Rubbing my forehead, I shrugged. "I could sure use some of that coffee."

He opened the wardrobe and set the stack of my folded clothes on the end of the bed. "I'll go down and get you some food. Take a shower and get ready to tell me the story again from beginning to end, with all the detail you can recall."

I gave him a sly glance. "I never could summarize."

He smirked. "Then I will be sure to ask pointed questions."

He left the apartment and I could hear the stairs creak as he descended. While he was gone, I took a quick shower and as I pulled my t-shirt over my head, realized he had had my clothes laundered.

"Seriously, people like him don't exist."

I wondered what his story was, if he had done or experienced something horrible enough to push him into such a careful and insightful life, or if he had sprung from his mother's womb that way; the quiet boy in class, the child who rescued baby birds, the teenager who made friends with everyone, the young man who traveled the world doing good deeds. Where was his family? Did he have siblings? Why a coffee shop?

As I came out of the bathroom in a daze of romantic reflections, I heard a voice garbled by the mechanical erosion of a loudspeaker, and in one moment, my blood ran cold.

"I can check," it rasped, grating off my neuronal insulation.

I slipped down the hallway, and concealed myself behind the wall, disgusted with myself and everything else for conflicting reasons.

"It won't do any good. She'll want to go there herself," Arthur replied quietly.

"It's dangerous."

I closed my eyes and listened carefully. It was definitely the voice from the phone call in my first vision, the voice of Eva's stalker.

"She is determined and I will not stand in the way of what she believes is right."

"But that place is . . ." the voice grumbled in defiance.

Arthur made a soft sound of disapproval in his throat. "It is a private hell, and if she is willing to tread through it to save another, I am willing to follow."

There was a pause and while I tried not to breathe too loudly, I wondered if he was speaking of me, of Club Trishna, and if he was, why he was talking to the man I had thought attacked Unger.

"It's just as dangerous for you."

I heard the swish of pages being turned. "I will be careful."

The gruff voice mumbled something unintelligible.

"Your affection is appreciated and returned, Sam," Arthur said with a smile in his voice.

"So what are we going to do about *him*?"

Arthur chuckled. "He's been sitting out there all night. Surely he's tired and hungry. Send out some coffee and a cinnamon roll."

"He'll come in," Sam replied, as if that were a bad thing.

"Sam, we are not a fortress."

Sam grumbled again, but said he would do it. I heard a click and knew the conversation had ended. In the silence, I tried to make sense of it. Was Sam a bad person? He couldn't be if he was concerned about Arthur, for even with the association, my opinion of my constant hero had not diminished. If anything, I respected him more for being so incredibly judicious in his dealings with the man who at least had it in him to injure a police officer. Most importantly, though: who was the lucky recipient of the cinnamon roll?

"It seems that your future is coming true," Arthur said into the empty room. "Detective Unger has been staking out the shop, since you came in, but never left. No doubt he has added another name to his list."

Caught eavesdropping, I stepped out from behind the wall sheepishly, but Arthur was sitting at his desk, several books open and receiving his undivided attention.

"I'm sorry," I offered, for all the crimes against him that I had perpetrated.

He shook his head. "None of it was your doing, except of course, spying on me."

"I wasn't . . . I mean," I looked at the kitchen counter. A tray with a cup of coffee and a cinnamon roll waited for me. More gifts to make me feel inadequate. The least I could do was tell the truth. "I recognized Sam's voice."

He turned suddenly and without looking for me, latched his eyes onto my face. "Unusual, since he rarely speaks."

"He's the man in the suspenders at the coffee bar."

Arthur smiled. "The manager."

"I heard his voice in my first vision."

His eyes stayed on me and picked apart my thoughts with that unerring precision that would have made my skin crawl, if not for the tenderness and sympathy I saw there.

"I will assume that the context was bad, since you were suspicious enough to hesitate."

I nodded, my hands clasped in front of me. The last thing I wanted to do was make him question the trustworthiness of his employees, but I had made a decision to rely upon the visions.

"Sam would never hurt anyone," he professed, and while I might have been skeptical of another person's avowal in like circumstances, I had no choice but to believe his. "Think carefully about what you remember," he counseled, "and ask yourself if there is room for misunderstanding."

"And if there isn't any room? He called me while I was calling Unger and I heard Unger's phone ringing in the background, right after I heard someone jump him."

Arthur turned away. "'Someone' is a very loose term."

It was true, but the likelihood of Sam happening upon Unger's phone right after it had been dropped was very small unless he could see the future too.

"I will remind you that what you saw was only a possible future," he said quietly. "The Sam I know is very kind."

It hadn't seemed that way to me when I had encountered him in the shop. He had appeared withdrawn and nervous, but what could I say? Arthur was the type of person it was impossible to question. In fact, I could never imagine him being wrong, and if he ever had been, it must have been a very strange sight indeed.

I decided to let it go and maneuvered so that I could glance over his shoulder. What I saw on the pages was unreadable. It seemed there were books of mathematical equations and several texts in various languages.

"Arthur?" I said quietly.

"Yes?"

"How many languages do you speak?"

"As many as I need to."

I glanced at his face. His eyes were sliding from book to book, without a discernible rhythm. "You're not very forthcoming, are you?"

The eyes found me. "You are a solver of mysteries, Lilith. Would you be half so interested in me if I revealed myself to you?"

For a moment, I couldn't interpret what he said. There was no tone to it, no context. I couldn't believe he would spurn me when he'd so easily accepted my affection earlier, but I wasn't sure what he meant.

He gave a catlike blink. "You *are* interested in me. You would have gone, otherwise."

"True," I said ambivalently.

"Since you are a woman of discerning taste, that interest is a compliment that I appreciate, and am hesitant to destroy by seeming less *awesome*."

The laugh spasmed out of me before I even knew I found what he said funny. "Discerning taste? Have you been listening at all? I have *no* taste." He frowned and my hands flew up. "I didn't mean it like that! I meant that I . . . I don't know. I'm giving up." I heaved a sigh and walked toward the window.

"Whatever questions you have," he said, "I will answer."

"Cryptically," I shot back.

"I will tell you whatever will make you happiest."

"Meaning you'll deceive me if I might not like what you say?"

"Meaning that I will give you more mysteries to solve."

As I parted the curtains, I grumbled as Sam had done.

His laugh was soft. "When you are free from graver concerns and can be happy with the finer points, then perhaps we will discuss them."

"Hmm," I intoned. He was right, I was interested, but it wasn't pure interest. Part of me wanted a distraction that I somehow knew he'd never be willingly.

I blinked in the light. Unger was sitting in his car, directly across the street, looking as stressed out and pensive as usual. As a girl in a red polo shirt delivered the coffee and pastry curbside, a thought came to me.

"How did you know that he was Detective Unger?"

Arthur's head tilted. "Were you expecting any other stalkers to drop by today?"

The words reminded me of Eva's complaint. If Sam wasn't the stalker, who was? Or maybe he was the stalker, but wasn't really a stalker, just got mistaken for one. I sighed in frustration.

"Not really."

Arthur stood up just as Unger's car door opened. As the detective crossed the street and opened the door beneath my feet, Arthur patted my head.

"You have lost faith in me."

I turned and glared up at him flirtatiously. "No, I'm just constantly impressed by your deductive reasoning."

"Elementary, my dear Lilith," he sighed. "We can't pretend you aren't here, so should I greet the detective, or will you do the honors?"

"I need to stay out of this."

His laughter surprised me. "She says to the man who told her the very same thing."

With a playful punch, I pushed him toward the door. "I just want to watch him for once. If it's possible, mention the man at the club," I instructed. "I want to hear his reaction."

At the door, Arthur turned and eyed me. "You'll be spying again? That's very dishonest."

I reached up and poked his forehead. "He's sitting in a coffee shop. He has no expectation of privacy. How is that dishonest?"

Touching his face gingerly, he led the way down the stairs. I waited at the landing until I heard the Dutch door open and Unger's voice introduce itself. It was a busy day; shoppers and business people were traipsing in and out, clattering dishes, chatting loudly, and so it was not surprising that a few moments later, I heard the top half of the door shut and lock into place.

He's trying to make you feel *dishonest.* No, there were no half-truths with Arthur and I marveled at how quickly he was teaching me to interact with him.

"Yes, Detective, I've been expecting you."

"Oh? How's that?" I heard the little notebook flip open and the pen click into the ready position.

Arthur said nothing. There must have been an expression on his handsome face, because a few seconds later, Unger made an annoyed groan.

"Don't tell me, she pulled the Great Karnak again?"

I barely suppressed my snort. In the juxtaposition of the two men, I came to see exactly how unbalanced the scales were. Unger was good, but not good enough to tell that Arthur was not the type of person to get obscure references to Johnny Carson.

"The Egyptian Temple?" Arthur murmured in confusion.

"The psychic, Karnak!" Unger blurted out in incredulity. "Never mind. Not important."

I heard the metal stool scrape across the floor.

"How do you know Ms. Pierce?"

"Which one?"

"Take your pick," Unger said sardonically.

"Eva Pierce was a repeat customer and friend. Her sister and I met at her funeral. I was the only guest."

Unger shifted in embarrassment. "So you two started hanging out?"

"She came here yesterday by chance. That was the second time we met. She passed out in my shop and I let her stay upstairs. Whatever she saw in her vision frightened her."

Unger, still feeling badly about his absence from the formal goodbye, did not bite back as harshly as I anticipated. "You believe her then?"

"She knew my name. I never told her."

"You could be mistaken."

"I'm not. I only give my name to people who will need to call me, Detective. She knew it and I am now glad that she does."

Unger persisted, ever the rational cop. "Then maybe her sister wrote it down and she saw it."

"This is a book bindery, Detective. What do you imagine it is that I do here? If she'd written it down, I would have seen it and known how *she* might have seen it."

"Remind me to never bring my diaries here," Unger muttered.

"If you'd like your notes preserved with confidentiality, I could manage it, though I confess I find the concept of *justice* to be indecipherable," Arthur offered, and again I tried not to chuckle at how well he could read people. The job was Unger's life and it brought the detective's lack of depth to the forefront to be examined closely.

"No thanks. I'd rather not have them to look at when I retire."

"A man like you could never retire," Arthur insisted in his softest voice.

An understanding of some kind was reached in the awkward moment of silence.

"So you read her journals then?"

"Eva wanted me to. She needed someone to see her, but have no stake in her life."

"What does that mean?"

"Tell me, Detective, does every victim you encounter want your sympathy?"

Unger paused. "No."

"Eva was too sensitive to allow anyone to look at her thoughts, but someone had to see or she would be a non-person. You can understand that, I trust."

"Yes . . . I suppose." I could hear him shuffle his feet. "What did Lilith see in her vision?" he finally asked, as if he didn't want to, but had no choice.

My opinion of him was evolving rather quickly; once he had been the one stake tying my hot air to the ground, then he was a nail in my sister's coffin, but now I could see he was a square peg in a round world. He was a nice man with a difficult job that he probably did very well, when he wasn't dealing with the extraordinary.

Arthur sighed. "Why don't you ask her yourself? Though, I can understand if she'd refuse to speak to you, since in her vision you seemed to be suspicious of her."

"Has she told you anything about the circumstances?" Unger demanded a bit defensively. "Her sister had a lot of money and though she had access, it wasn't hers to do with as she pleased without her sister out of the way."

My mouth fell open. With all the fabulous suspects that existed, he was going for me, when not two days before he had insisted it was a suicide. I was the one who had tried to convince him of wrongdoing in the first place!

"I can assure you, Detective, money is the last thing Lilith Pierce cares about right now and the bank records will prove it," Arthur defended. "Many people claim to love their siblings, but what they feel is the pull of relation. They are alike in some part and it is expected that they will support one another, but that doesn't mean that there is affection. Eva Pierce was more than that to Lilith."

My mouth shut. I closed my eyes and leaned against the wall.

"What do you mean?"

"Lilith sacrificed her happiness for Eva, and even though it didn't work out as she planned it to, even though there was some resentment there, even though they had their differences, each knew what the other felt." His voice lifted and I knew he was speaking to me, tucked in concealment, trying desperately not to cry. "Lilith wanted her sister to succeed and regretted that she wasn't able to give more, that her stamina gave out. Eva knew she was a disappointment and regretted that Lilith had felt so protective of her. Each wanted the other to live for herself and it is a sad irony that neither did."

Then I knew I didn't just value Arthur, I respected him immensely and would have followed him anywhere.

"What are you saying?"

"I am saying that Eva killed herself and left the money as a gift."

"And why should I believe you? For all I know, you argued with Eva about the money, pushed her off a roof, and the two of you are upstairs celebrating. For all I know the vision stuff is a hoax."

Arthur was silent for some time. If it had been me to speak next, I know I would have had some kind of spiteful retort, but like any lover of art, I wanted to watch the master put Unger in his place so gently that the man appreciated the correction.

"There is not a single person," he said softly, "that will tell you Eva was harmed. She took her own life and right now, Lilith is mourning what she perceives to be her own failure to prevent it." He said nothing about the affront. True to form, he let it slide, forgiven, and put Unger again in his debt. "You should be asking yourself, not 'what happened to Eva?', but 'why would Eva do it, when everything else was turning out so well?'."

"How long have you been a detective?" Unger countered.

"How long has it been since you recalled that humans feel things to a distraction? Rational thought is not important in such times and often what they do and say makes no sense to any of us."

Both men were silent and I could imagine the battle of glances that was taking place; Unger would attack and push forward, but never gain any ground. Arthur had no ground to take. Eventually Unger would be sapped for energy and give up, and Arthur would take his hand and call him a friend.

After a while, Unger took a deep breath and gave a huff of surrender.

"What did she see?"

"A murder."

"I can't dispatch uniforms on a premonition."

I was sure Arthur was shrugging. "If she goes tonight, a man will die at Club Trishna, by the river. Of this I am certain."

"Because she knew your name?"

"The same way she knew yours. Tell me it does not make an impression."

Unger coughed. "Where is she?"

I stepped into the doorway. "Right here, Unger, and you're lucky Arthur's teaching me composure."

CHAPTER 12

He stared at me. "You realize what you're telling me sounds completely . . ." I gave him a wry look. "Of course you do," Unger finished and swiped his hand over his unshaven face.

I have to stop it," I declared.

Arthur's eyes were closed and he was turned away from me slightly, but already I could tell when he did not agree with me, his aura was that strong.

"What, Arthur? Say it."

Unger glanced at him, a look of unsettled trepidation on his face.

"Ursula did what she did to frighten you. If you do not go, there is no proof she will do anything. But if you *do* go, she is certain to strike."

I crossed my arms in rebelliousness. "Yeah, and trees falling in the forest don't make sounds unless I'm there to hear them, but so what?"

He made a tiny noise of disapproval. "If she is capable of doing what you suggest and you walk into the room with her, there is nothing to stop her from seeing your vision as clearly as you did."

"Well good! Then she'll know I get away in the end!"

"And will stop you."

"And so I'll run the other way!"

He leaned forward in an emotion as close to annoyance as I had ever seen from him. "You are forgetting that she will have seen this conversation as well. If she is empathic, then you have no chance against her. There is nothing that can be done."

I clamped my lips shut, but glared at him until his face relaxed.

"You are too stubborn."

"It's worked so far," I said blithely.

He looked away. Unger moved uncomfortably and raised an eyebrow. "I can't go in as a cop. There's no probable cause, no warrant. All I can do is go in as a civilian and stand around like an idiot."

I held up my hands. "Maybe that will scare her!" "A woman who eats men alive in a nightclub is not deterred by the presence of one police officer, especially if she has hostages," Arthur said to himself.

"Then what should we do?" I stood up and tried to intimidate him. It happened naturally, without my awareness, but when he looked at me with the expression of a saddened angel, I wilted.

"You should not confront her. You should make a plan to assess her and prevent her movements without seeming to do so."

"Which she will read if I set one foot in the room!"

"Then do not set foot in it."

"You're overlooking the most obvious part of the whole trick," Unger warned.

I looked at him in question.

"She touched them. She put her hand on each person she read, even you."

I thought back, but while that fit every one of the contestants, I realized that her words to me had seemed to answer my thoughts before I had even managed to shake her hand. No, for whatever reason, that didn't work for me. I said as much to him.

He massaged his chin and brooded. "Then all we have to do is put someone else in the room who can keep their distance from her."

"But like Arthur said, she's not going to do anything, unless I'm there too."

Arthur sighed and opened the Dutch door. "You are making a great many assumptions."

I looked at him in disbelief. "Yeah, well, you're talking to a woman who saw a mind-reader in her psychic vision of the future. We love assumptions here. We're all about them."

What was wrong with me? Was I angry with him for protecting me? Was it the stubbornness? As he gazed at me in that unshakeable placidity, I came to understand that I was testing him. I was trying to sound out his depths like a sailor staring into an unfathomable ocean. It was a petty way to do that and I saw that knowledge in his eyes.

"I'm sorry," I apologized immediately. "You know what I'm feeling, Arthur, tell me what I can do that will take that away."

He closed his eyes in thought and upon opening them, looked to Sam, watching from his place behind the bar. At the beckon, Sam slid out and shut the door after himself.

"If you must go, Sam will go with you. Unger and I can wait at either entrance."

The bartender assented with a sallow nod and a fidget in my direction, but Unger was scowling at his shoes.

"There's protocol for this kind of thing."

"If you do not wish to be involved, then we will do it alone," Arthur murmured, "though I am almost positive that you cannot, in good conscience, do such a thing."

Unger tilted his head in a kind of nod.

"Then we will do everything exactly as it was done. Lilith will go shopping as she did." He reached out suddenly and tapped Unger's hunched shoulder. At the man's look, he smiled. "And you will sleep."

He looked as if he might protest, until Sam and I supported the unofficial leader with blinks and insistent stares. "Okay, fine, but you," he pointed at me, "will buy a cell phone, and you," he pointed in Arthur's direction, unable to even look at the man, "will go with her when she shops. Who knows, those people could be watching her."

Sam stepped forward as if to volunteer instead, but a tiny movement of Arthur's hand stayed him. "That is a wonderful idea."

There were a few seconds of pause. The host glanced around and tilted his head. "What is it that they say in sports when the team is sent back out to the field?"

I choked on the giggle that leapt into my throat at the thought of explaining to Arthur that "sports" was not in fact, a single event, but a category, and that many games that fit into the category did not involve fields.

Unger shot another incredulous look at Arthur's shoes. "Break?" he hazarded.

"Yes!" Arthur put his hands together and instead of looking like an indignant coach, seemed more like a glowing piece of iconography. "Break!"

We parted company, Unger and Sam mumbling to each other in the universal language of the dissatisfied guardian, Arthur as serene as ever, and me just happy to have him to myself again. He folded his long legs into my car and somehow managed to make its borrowed interior look high-end. We drove to the mall as I had done in my dream, fought traffic, and jockeyed for a parking space without a single growl from my internal lion of road rage.

As we walked past shops, he strolled along with veiled eyes, taking in his surroundings in an amused detachment that turned heads. Packs of diversion-seeking teenage girls giggled as he walked by, shooting me with envious looks, and for some reason, the toddler standing in front of us on the escalator found Arthur's smile quite entertaining. Like a fool, I was incredibly jealous, when I realized that he was watching me and had never once looked away. While the escalator carried us upward, I began to warm beneath the gaze until I had once again devolved into a child.

"I'm not buying the same clothes."

He smiled.

"Those shoes were death traps and that skirt was a nightmare."

His brows ticked upward.

"You don't know what I'm talking about, but let's just say that even though the purse worked, I'm definitely angling toward a utility belt this time."

It unfolded before my eyes like the sun shining through clouds, and while his dazzling smile remained, a giggle of girls passing us on their downward trek performed a marvelous rendition of the chorus of "Don't look" harmonized with comments about temperature.

His eyes flicked in their direction and they were painted red with bliss, before he gave me back the attention I craved. I leaned toward him, ashamed that I was staking territory and that he was allowing me to.

"That was for you, you know."

His arm slid up the moving banister till his fingers could tap the back of my hand.

"They think you're gorgeous. They want you to look back at them."

His eyes were tracing my features ever so carefully, "Desire is the cause of suffering."

I think my mouth dropped open in shock. "Did you just insult them with Zen?"

The smile graced his face again. "I disappointed them, but to look back would be worse."

We stepped off and walked across the busy tributary of flowing humans to the next escalator. Again I turned to face him, sure I was probably humiliating myself.

"Can I be incredibly personal with you?"

He chuckled, but didn't look away. "Only if you promise to stop prefacing every piece of honesty with a disclaimer."

"Done," I agreed and steeled myself. "There are things . . . that a woman comes to anticipate from a man."

The lady in front of me stepped up to the next stair.

Arthur nodded in encouragement.

I lowered my voice. "It's hard to read you, because . . ." I looked around helplessly, "because you don't se*em* like a normal man."

We stepped off and wandered slowly around the promenade like two friends walking through the park. In front of a promising store, I halted and folded my arms across the balcony railing, trying to find the most thoughtful way to ask him the question that was roasting my insides.

"You're like a hermit," I blurted out, immediately mortified. "I mean . . . are you, like, oblivious, or is it just . . ."

To my shock, he laughed.

Of course he knows what I'm going to say. God, I'm stupid. It wasn't as if I had a particularly stony face.

"Don't laugh at me, please?"

He apologized with a shake of his head, though he continued to chuckle. "But it's so funny, how you always say things without saying them!"

"Alright, so I'll be blunt. You turn it off, right?" What I was saying was confusing even to me. I was a fourteen year old trying to ask out that one untouchable senior who always smiled at me, but because of the unfortunate circumstances of his popularity, I was certain would never be able to confess his affections to me. It was absurd and at my age, I should have outgrown it. Howard had never made me feel so light-headed, so giddy. I had no idea who Arthur was, or even what his last name might be, but if people could have intense one night stands, then why couldn't I be sure he was a catch?

"Do you do it on purpose? Do you have to work at it, ignoring *it*, I mean?"

He looked down over the heads of the people below, remarkably, without confusion. "Never have I heard chastity discussed in such unproductive words."

"Ha ha! Well, help me out here!" I laughed. "I'm a bumbling housewife. Supplement my vocabulary."

He turned and leaned back, his elbows on the rail, his eyes staring up at the skylight. He looked like a child, innocent and mischievous all at once. "At the risk of sounding repetitive, desire is the cause of suffering, and suffering causes one to lose clarity."

"That's very important to you, clarity?"

He nodded slowly and found me again. "Right perception breeds right action."

"So you *are* a Buddhist?"

He seemed to be smirking, but it could have been the light. "Definitions exclude information, and doing that can lead to ignorance."

I propped my head on my hand. "*Cryyyyyyptic,*" I protested.

"I try to keep my mind open to how the world truly functions and find value in all things that exist."

"So . . . reincarnation or do you believe in heaven?" I asked without thinking and before I knew what had happened, I heard her voice again on that night, asking me if I remembered what dad had always said. I had to swallow before another breath could pass my lips.

He thought over my words for a while and with a knowing glance made me feel better. "To believe in an afterlife, you have to believe that death is an end that precedes a beginning. To believe in reincarnation, you must accept that the variety of the universe is finite and must recycle. I am not sure I believe in either, nor do I think that my beliefs would ever make a difference in how it actually takes place."

"Then you don't think it ends, but you don't think it continues?"

He touched my face, turned it to his and stared directly into my eyes with sharp intent. "Can you conceive of a road that leads nowhere?"

I blinked. Of course I could.

"Who built it?" he whispered, but even over the noise, I could hear him clearly.

"Wha . . .?"

"How far does it go?"

"I . . ."

"Does it ever get there?"

I shook my head in a moment of dumbfounded perplexity.

"Then why can you imagine it?"

My vision blurred as I stared into space, trying to see the road that went nowhere, that seemed to exist, but could not. She had walked away from me. My parents had let go of my hands. They were all swallowed up by fog, wandering too far for me to follow, but we were never walking to begin with, and they would never be able to leave.

"Belief is irrelevant."

His fingers slid from my face.

For a moment, it felt like she was just within my reach again, like I could pick up the phone and call her. It hurt, but in a way, it felt better. My shallow breathing slowed. I sorted foreground from background and looked into his eyes.

"I'm sort of glad you don't date. The Zen thing is a definite mood-killer."

He grinned and gestured at the shop. Reminded of our task, I let it swallow me up and belch with the dance beats of pop music. I went straight for the slacks and managed to find a black, long-sleeved top that looked as if it had been inspired by the Israeli Musad, but tailored to fit Tyra Banks. I watched him from the line, leaning against the banister, soaking up the sun like a happy plant, ogled conspicuously by every herbivore that happened to be stampeding by.

Some girls had taken up residence in a nearby seating area of stone benches, and as I walked back out to meet Arthur, I noted with amusement that it was the same group that had passed us on the escalator. While they subtly tried to watch him, I tapped him on the shoulder and held up my ensemble.

He nodded in endorsement. "It's very *ninja*."

I dropped my arms and shook my head. "You know ninja, but not the Great Karnak?"

He shrugged. "So now do we look for non-lethal shoes or try and find a utility belt that holds lipstick?"

"Shoes," I confirmed. I pointed at the girls with a glance. "You have a fan club."

Without looking, he forgave them with a smile.

"Should I tell them it won't do any good to lust after you?" I was hinting, trying to get him to disagree with me, say something that would leave room for anything to grow between us. "I could tell them that bit about suffering."

"Why embarrass them for finding a few moments of contentment?"

For an instant, I thought he was serious and the misunderstanding only made it easier to laugh. "You almost sounded arrogant."

"I apologize," he said playfully. "Don't lose confidence in me. I try to be better every day."

Shaking with silent mirth, I planted my elbow beside his arm and inclined close. "They just want to wait and see if you'll kiss me. It's a girl thing. They don't know that sex is the root of evil."

His expression of humorous disagreement said that he knew I was joking, but wanted to make sure there were no false impressions. "I never said that, Lilith."

"I know. But obviously it has something to do with clouding your clarity, and I get it."

His brows drew closer together and I immediately wanted to make him feel better about my faculties.

"When I was little, like six or so, I asked my mom about sex. You know what she told me?"

Arthur settled against the rail contentedly and attached his eyes to my face with sleepy interest.

"She said that there were lots of types of love." I leaned my head atop my arms and looked away from him. "She said that sex was what happened when two people loved each other so much that the only way they could express it was to try and become the same person. That's poetic, right?"

He nodded in my periphery.

"I thought so too. It stuck with me. I saw my folks, the way they loved each other, knew that it could happen, and wanted the same thing for myself. I went through my whole young life thinking that, even when all that horrible stuff happened. I knew it had to be true. So when the first stable guy came along, I tried to find it with him. It was unfair of me, I realize now." It was true, for even as the words left my mouth, they became real. I was forgiving Howard and instantly felt lighter. "I lay in his arms the first time and tried not to cry, because it didn't feel the way it was supposed to. I never wanted it again and that's why he tried to find that with someone else."

I turned to see what my revelation had done to him and found his eyes closed.

"So I get it. Those kids, they still think it's a fairy tale, but someday they'll be able to see the truth . . ."

He prodded me on with a nod.

"I know desire is the cause of suffering," I sighed, "but if I hadn't suffered, I wouldn't be here, talking to you."

His eyes opened, unbelievably careful with the confession I had shoved out of myself almost vindictively, just to be unburdened.

"I was married once," he divulged.

Stunned, I kept my eyes focused on the far side of the divide. "Was it that kind of marriage?"

His voice had gone blank. "It was something of a convenient arrangement."

"No wonder you feel as you do."

His head shook. "I cared for her, enough that I could not tie her down. There were other things . . . greater concerns than only her happiness."

I knew we couldn't talk about it anymore. It was something that was still too raw for me to try and cover over, even with the healing balm of his fondness. Flirting with him was a joy, but while exposing myself to him, I was learning how vulnerable I really was. It was unfair of me to make him the ear for all my problems and expect him to reciprocate, and it was unfair of me to expect him to invest his emotions in a broken soul.

I turned to give him an understanding smile, but was interrupted when his lips contacted my forehead. The shiver went from his mouth to my mid-back and returned again.

Slowly, he pulled away. "As poetic as were your mother's words, they only spoke for her. Unconditional, blissful love can have as many forms of expression as there are people in this world to feel it."

Without a sound, I took his hand and as casually, he wrapped mine around his arm. We walked to the nearest shoe store like a couple, the tender moment like a respite from the rapids of the mall. I separated from him unwillingly, but found a pair of rubber-soled ballet slippers that received his seal of approval in the form of a confused index finger pointed at the bow on the toe.

"An interesting contrast to your metal zipper pockets."

Before he could ask me about the rack of neon curly shoelaces that were not meant to tie, I herded him toward an accessory store, happier than I had ever been.

"Explain to me why you need an espionage *outfit*," he murmured in my ear as I looked for the heaviest bracelets and rings I could find.

"To be fashionable while kicking ass."

"We're not going to vanquish Medusa, Lilith," he rebuked with a grin, "you do not need a mirrored shield."

I reached past a girl standing in front of one of the racks and snatched a silver bracelet covered in turquoise stones. She looked up at me and for a moment, surprised. I gave her a friendly smile and turned back to him.

"I realize that, but there's no reason I can't be prepared."

"Agreed," he said, his eyes following the girl as she tried to escape our bizarre conversation, "my issue is the 'fashionable' aspect. What purpose does it serve?"

"It's a disguise, Arthur," I said and rolled my eyes.

"Then there were *many* ninja at the club?"

I laughed and put my items on the counter.

"No, but when you walk into Rome not wearing a toga, people tend to wonder." The cashier was grinning, trying not to laugh as she made my change.

"I should think they would care more about the nudity than the choice of attire. Though it *was* Rome, and they didn't really care about nudity."

Harassed, I shook my head and led him to the door, where he halted and pointed out a bracelet of metal spikes. I was about to ask him why he was suddenly such a comedian, when his hand shot out. Without turning around, he took hold of the arm of the young girl we had bothered, as she tried to exit the store. There was no hint of an explanation as he walked her past me and toward the wall, and for some reason, she did not protest.

I was going to demand to know what he was doing, when he stopped and put his face directly in front of hers. Her eyes were wide and I could see the pulse in her neck as it thumped in fear. Her gaze flicked to me, but I had learned to trust her captor implicitly and could offer no camaraderie.

"What you did," he whispered when she looked at him again, "was dishonest."

She froze, every muscle alert and stiff, and suddenly I understood. The baggy sweater, the glance over her shoulder, the willingness to let him pull her aside; she had been shoplifting. Her face fell, but I knew what she was feeling. Trying to look away from his eyes was impossible if he did not allow it. She swallowed.

"It may not hurt the woman working there or the business itself, indeed, no one else might ever find out," he asserted, his hand resting on her shoulder heavily, "but you would know. What is your name?"

"A . . . Anna," she said between gasps that were dangerously close to sobs.

"Anna," he repeated, making the name sound like a prayer. "Anna, as easy as it is to do, it is fifty times harder to undo."

"Are . . . are you a cop?"

He shook his head and without a second thought, released her, turned around, and gently steered me away. I looked back. Like a boulder in a river, she stood, staring after Arthur as if her soul had stuck to his hand. I knew that feeling too; it was what he'd made me feel in the cemetery. As I took his hand, I tried to explain that to her with my eyes and a heartening smile.

"You didn't eat your breakfast," he said. "Do you want something now, while we have time?"

A traffic jam pressed him behind me and his fingers, laced with mine, sat on my shoulder. Without knowing why, I blushed.

Was I as bad off as that girl?

"Sure."

We walked to the food court, oasis of the commercial free-for-all, and while he positioned himself nonchalantly at a table, I waited in line at a sandwich shop. Plastic tray in hand, I juggled its contents, set it atop the condiments bar and tried to keep from upending it into my bags. A helpful hand deposited some napkins in front of me just as I reached for them. I looked up to thank the person and found her, eyes still recovering from the shock of his compelling presence.

Sympathetic, I raised my eyebrows. "Anna?"

She couldn't be older than thirteen. Her hair was pulled back, her clothes had the unmistakable look of hand-me-downs, and her nail polish had been picked at as if she had been nervously chewing.

"Is he . . . is that man a priest?"

I smiled awkwardly. "Sort of, I guess. He has a way with people."

"Do you think it's okay if I talk to him?"

Surprised, I hesitated, but when I looked toward him and found him watching me, I knew the answer. "Sure, sweetheart. Go pick his brain. It's full of useful tidbits in tons of languages."

She turned instantly and went to join him at the table. I took my time, selected more mustard and mayo than I needed, got a fork, just in case, and settled on a few more napkins for my glove compartment before I meandered back.

She had pulled a wadded up paper bag from a cargo pocket inside her jeans and had put it on the table in front of him. His hands were folded and he was looking at her face with that divine impartiality that amazed me. I had stolen a piece of candy once, and my mother had gone on like a harpy for almost two hours.

I set my tray down and took a seat quietly.

"That's everything," she said. "Should I give it back?"

"Will it erase what you did?"

She was ashamed and completely confused as to why she should be. Without his guidance, she would get frustrated and forget he had ever touched her. Anxiously, I tried to nudge him with my eyes, but he would not look anywhere but her face.

"No. So . . . do I keep it?"

"Will it make you feel worse, or better, do you think?"

She shrugged, but it was obvious she knew they would only be reminders of her crime.

He ignored the bag like it wasn't there. "I won't tell you what you should do. I believe you will figure it out."

She frowned and I almost lost the faith he kept instructing me to keep.

"If I try to give it back, they'll arrest me."

"Ah," he replied and leaned forward, "so the real issue is, do you believe that the punishment they will give you is deserved?"

She shrugged again in that all-purpose teenage answer, the refuge of someone who did not want to be caught against a wall unprepared.

Arthur crossed his arms. "If you do, then you must accept the punishment, but if you do not, then either you feel that you have done nothing wrong, or you believe that you have already learned the lesson. Which is true?"

Her head bowed and she shuffled her feet. "Learned my lesson."

He considered her through narrowing eyes. "Then what should you do with it?"

"Find a way to give it back so they don't catch me."

"Erasing a mistake with cunning is perhaps its own crime," he scolded and turned away in what appeared to her to be disappointment.

She looked around, adrift, remembered that I was there, and looked to me for help. As much respect as I had for his method, I had to help her; having been where she was, I had to.

"Mall security has an office. Tell them you found it on a bench and leave."

Arthur pretended I had not spoken and when he said nothing to her, she made a half-hearted escape attempt. Yet again, his hand snaked out and caught her. Afraid she had done something else wrong, she let him pull her back.

"This doesn't stop here," he murmured and retook her eyes with a docile glance. "There's a reason you did it and it's not the reason you tell yourself it is."

Her lips parted expectantly and she examined his face for signs of knowledge.

"You didn't want these things. You didn't really need to sell them. You weren't getting back at the people who hurt you. There was no one there to praise you for your stealth." There was a moment of softness, as if the room went quiet, as if the whole mall had suddenly ceased to be. She stared into his eyes and he looked right back at her, his hand on her far elbow, light but weighing her down. "So . . . did you get what you really wanted?"

She tried to speak but failed. A cough uncovered her tiny voice. "Yes."

"And what was that?"

I sat there motionless; transfixed by something that was the eerie contrast of Ursula's horrifying game. I knew what he wanted her to say, what she needed to say, but even if *I* had been asked to say it, I would have been too afraid. If she admitted it, it would be like stepping off a cliff into a raging river that was miles wide.

But sometimes, mercy was a more important lesson than the plunge of vulnerability, and no one understood that better than Arthur. "You were hoping, all this time," he breathed, "that someone would see you, the real you, and ask why. Why would someone as amazing as Anna not think more highly of herself?"

I sucked in air and the pit of my stomach tightened down.

Eva.

It wasn't just for Anna. It was to remind me what I never did, to show me back to the place where it had all begun, back to the question. Why did Eva do it when everything seemed to be going so well?

Anna nodded and I could see the little shards of light dancing around her eyes.

"Well," he sat back and carefully removed his hand, "I have asked it, but more importantly, *you* have asked it. When you can answer, then your lesson is truly learned, and not before. Do what you may to make amends, but remember that it is the source of the action that matters."

She sighed heavily and managed another nod.

Without saying anything, he reached into his pocket and pulled out a five dollar bill. He presented it to her and tucked it inside her sweater pocket.

"Go and spend that."

The moment was crowded by sound. She looked around vaguely and realized we were still in the eye of a capitalist hurricane. Taking out the money, she looked at it as if she recognized it, but couldn't figure out how it had gotten into her pocket. In that second, the slip of paper seemed to transform into a symbol of all the things she had used to conceal her own turmoil. As she looked at it in that glazed way, it seemed to become a foreign thing that she no longer understood.

"Katsu," Arthur whispered. I glanced at him, wondering if it was another one of those Sanskrit conundrums, but he was so focused upon her face, her blank stare and breathlessness, that it was as if he was waiting for something.

Like an automata, Anna slowly put the bill into her paper sack and with the decisiveness of presentation, dropped the bag onto the ground, turned around, and wandered away without ever glancing back.

Worried, I reached for the bag, but he stopped me.

"Leave it."

"Is she okay?" I demanded.

He smiled. "Yes. Eat your sandwich."

I obeyed, though it took me a few minutes to return to the routine of stuffing my face. I didn't eat because I was hungry; I had lost my appetite. I ate because I was stalling for time. If I asked too soon, he would not tell me, because it had been a lesson for me that I had not yet understood.

When I had eaten as much as I cared to, I sat back and took a deep breath. "Was that word Sanskrit too?"

Cradled in the hands that were bracing it, his head shook. "It originated in China. It means 'to shout'."

I looked at the paper bag in confusion and when a janitor picked it up and tossed it into the garbage he was emptying, marveled that Arthur let it happen.

"Why?" I demanded of the entire event in general.

Arthur watched the bag's progress from treasure to trash and closed his eyes peacefully.

"Because she walked into the river."

CHAPTER 13

After we left the mall, I dropped Arthur off at the coffee shop. I thought he might insist on staying with me until I had to face the monster, but he got out and said goodbye as amiably as usual. I assured him I'd meet everyone there, at our base of operations, when it was time. He leaned through my window and poked me in the third eye, which I had a feeling was wide open and staring at him in awe.

"Leave your katana in the car. Weapons are not permitted in the shop."

I watched him go, still too confused about what had happened with the girl to really laugh at his joke, though I wanted to. I sat there for a few moments before I made a decision. I had several hours until the club, and I would be damned if I'd go any longer without a means of doing some kind of research. The case and Arthur were both raising a lot of questions and I needed a way to stay on my toes, especially if I wanted to keep his cryptic friendship.

I drove to an electronics shop and made the salesman's day. I bought a state of the art laptop with wireless internet plan, and a cell phone, all picked out by him with the assurances that they were the best and that there was no assembly or setup required. By the time I left, I was sure that if I had asked him to scratch my back, he would have.

At the apartment, I sat in the happy face and plugged myself into the world wide web. I typed in the word and because I could see her face as he whispered it, added "Zen" to the search parameters. Within moments I had more information than I could possibly ever need.

"Katsu; a shout used to express one's own enlightened state, or induce another person to move beyond rational and logical thought to potentially achieve an initial experience of enlightenment."

Amazed, I read on. Time and again it spoke of the word as a guttural exclamation, but that was not how Arthur had used it. His voice had been so soft it had taken me several attempts to spell the word. I couldn't help but think there was a reason for that, and as I sloshed through links and descriptions, sorted ancient terminology from modern, I stumbled onto the Noble Eightfold Path, the rules set down by Buddha for his disciples to follow. Inherent in their wisdom was a very simple idea: no person wishing to alleviate suffering should ever do anything that was unnecessary, whether in speech, deed, or thought.

I considered Anna, her distant stare of uncanny peacefulness. She did not need to be shouted at, and indeed, that would have frightened her and forced her soul back into its shell. However, she was a child and like me, did not have words for such thoughts. He had supplied her with one.

"Katsu," I murmured, and sighed.

A few more taps and clicks carried me through the Buddha's teachings, his life as upheld by myth, his friends and companions, and finally, his demise. His last words echoed in my mind and heart and even brought a tear to my eye; how truly awesome would it have been to sit beside him and hear such a thing uttered for the first time *ever*, before mathematics or science, before the endless evolution of philosophy.

"All things are perishable. Through vigilance, awaken!"

As time ticked by, I researched, and at each turn encountered Arthur. With a smile, shaking my head every step of the way, I wondered why he had been so hesitant to call himself one of them, if they were certainly like him. Then I stumbled upon it and curiosity drove me to commit the word to memory and vow to tease him later.

"Srotapanna," I repeated, until it rolled off my tongue effortlessly.

I looked at the clock and realized that I only had a couple hours. I decided to test my new phone and called Unger. I expected him to be half-asleep, but he was wide awake and chewing something.

"Phone acquired, sir!" I saluted my reflection in the window.

"Good. Meet me at the diner down the street from the coffee shop."

"Huh, why?"

He slurped something. "Because I want to talk to you without them around."

I rummaged through my bags and got out my clothes, laid them out on the bed, and started the shower. "Again I say, why?"

"Because."

I sighed. "Give me twenty minutes."

"Twenty minutes," he complained, "what are you doing?"

I heaved a sigh grumpily. "Look, I'm only going to say this one more time. It's a disguise. If I don't blend in, there's no point!"

He backed down with a grumble. "I'm almost to dessert, so hurry up."

I hung up on him and wondered what had happened to the nice man who was so supportive. I was the one to blame though, since it was I who insisted he not treat me like a victim. I was also the one to involve myself in his investigation. I probably also got him in trouble. Truthfully, I liked this Unger better anyway, this was *my* Unger.

I showered off quickly, applied the makeup like someone who had done it once before, and this time, pulled back my hair in a tight bun. Rings and bracelets in place, cash, phone, and ID tucked into zipped pockets, I was ready physically, if not mentally. As I left, I found myself wishing I'd bought a stun gun or some pepper spray, though I doubted it would make any difference. I drove to the diner in an altered state, nervous, shaky, and desperate to hear Arthur's voice.

Unger was sitting at a booth drinking coffee and flipping through papers. He looked up as I got closer and froze in what seemed to be shock. I had to admit, I understood why. Thus far, he'd seen me only in ratty sweatshirts and a business suit, not in sleek black fashion with sultry façade in place.

I sat down and folded my hands. "What?"

Surprised and unhappy about it, he blinked. "You look . . . nice," he mumbled.

"Um, thanks?" I raised an eyebrow and shifted uncomfortably. "I always try to look my best when fighting crime."

He nodded. He was so dumbfounded by the fact that I cleaned up well that he didn't even think to question how *often* I fought crime.

"That was a joke."

He finally seemed to come to himself with a head jiggle. "Right. Sorry."

I leaned forward to give him a sweet smile. "You wanna make this a date, Detective?"

He snorted incredulously.

"What? I'm divorced and you don't wear a ring."

Unger could clearly not imagine me stooping to date him. "I'm old enough to be your father," he insisted.

"Yeah maybe, but if you do dishes and take out garbage, we'll make a great match," I laughed. "That's all I want, plus the occasional bouquet of roses." The waitress came over and offered me a cup of joe. I shook my head. It was Arthur's coffee or bust.

He sighed and swiped a crumb-speckled hand across his face. "I'm a lot older than I am."

"Do you mind if I ask when you're supposed to retire?"

His face fell in immediate, obvious dismay. "I've got a few years."

I eyed the manila folders in front of him and could see the edges of a few photographs. "After that?"

He laughed mirthlessly. "I'll probably end up getting a PI license." His eyes seemed to drift to the window, but he was seeing something else entirely, in some far off time. "It's either all or none. You can't go back and if you can't, you either move forward or don't go anywhere."

I rested my head on my hands thinking of Eva. "Yeah."

The fog cleared from his eyes as he glanced my way. "I was told to let this go. Your sister is an official Suicide. There is no case. Despite the oddities."

I nodded distantly and wondered why it was that some people could never push harder, even just a little bit, to get that much farther, to be that much more confident.

"But . . . I can't put it down."

"I was just thinking you would make a good P.I. and that I'd hire you," I mused.

He opened the folder and his expression became grave. "I took a few weeks off even though I have like, ten cases on the board right now. There is more to this than we thought."

In a blink, I was sitting upright, surreptitiously trying to catch a glimpse of the contents of his file. "Won't your partner be angry?"

"Naw. She won't be back for a few months. Our department just got two rookies in to replace those of us that might be leaving soon. We're covered," he assured, "or I should say, adequately staffed. I'm going to show this to you, because I think you can handle it."

"Flattery will get you everywhere, Detective."

A photo slid toward me on the table. It was a high contrast image of a white arm against black pavement, clean and unblemished except for a circular mark around one wrist that filleted bloodless skin wide open. It looked so clean that if I didn't know what a human arm was meant to look like, I might have supposed it grew that way.

"What is this?"

He was watching me closely, almost expectantly, as if waiting for a premonition. "This is the arm of a body that was discovered behind an abandoned house, almost one year ago. It had been drained of blood and washed clean of all evidence."

I picked up the picture and traced the slice marks with my fingertips. "Are these . . . like the ones on Eva's arm?"

"Yes, but your sister's were shallow. The M.E.'s report said that this man's hand was nearly severed."

"Do you think," I hesitated, after all, he had said that there was no case, "that they're connected?"

"He was stabbed in the neck."

"Could be a coincidence."

"Before he was chewed on by what the M.E. suspected was a person."

My mouth fell open. How many men had she killed? He saw the look on my face and nodded.

"After what you told me earlier, I did some more research and found this. I put the two together."

My heart was thumping again, restless to get out and away from a body that was about to walk right into the lair of the beast for what was essentially the second time, knowing full well what could happen.

"I guess this disproves the whole tree falling in a forest argument, huh?" I said quietly.

His expression wouldn't let up and that's when I knew there was more.

"Which leads me to my next point. How well do you know Arthur?"

I stopped myself before I could blurt out an answer that was completely subjective and unsupported. I *didn't* know him, no matter how good he was at making me feel like I knew him. The past few days had taught me nothing if not to be skeptical of all my senses at all times.

"I don't know him, but I *feel* him, Unger. He's a good guy."

Unger slid a sheet of paper to me. It was a photocopy of a land deed. "The coffee shop is in Sam's name, not his. Arthur Godard has no credit history, no bills, no bank accounts. As far as I can tell, he doesn't even have a Social Security number." He took a deep breath. "The man doesn't exist."

I stared at him. I could see from the look on his face that he desperately wanted me to prove myself his equal, but no matter how much I wanted to be the skeptic he needed. I couldn't. There was not a single thing about Arthur that made me suspicious, not even his lack of a background.

"I trust him."

"Because you had a vision or him helping you?" Unger demanded.

"Because he has made no demands, nor jeopardized my safety," I replied evenly, wondering just how many times I'd be caught paraphrasing Arthur. "When he does, then I'll think back."

He took back the papers and closed the folder impatiently. "By then, it may be too late."

"Why are you telling me this now, Unger?"

"I want you to be on your toes! We're walking a tightrope here, and I have no idea what's on the ground below."

I got to my feet and looked out the window, forcing myself to stay calm. "I get it, but right now, I have no choice. He was Eva's only friend, and that means something."

I waited for him at the door while he paid his bill and then we walked together to the coffee shop in silence. I wasn't sure what else could be said. I was winging it and nothing I tried to say to appease him would come out sounding authentic. Not only that, but with each step that took me closer to Arthur, the more I anticipated seeing him.

By the time we crossed the threshold. I was frantic with happiness and before Unger could protest, I had gone through the bindery and up to Arthur's apartment. I didn't even bother to knock, which was incredibly ridiculous of me, but when he didn't punish my misbehavior, it just made me more likely to barge in.

He looked up from his books and raised an eyebrow.

"Srotapanna," I stated triumphantly, "the stream-enterer."

The eyes seemed to glitter as he turned away, concealing his smirk from me. "That had been building a while. You could have asked before."

"I don't want a teacher, I want a friend," I countered as I came up behind him as quietly as possible to show off the ninja stealth of my cute new shoes. My hand wrapped around his head, but before I could tap him, he took hold of my fingers with gentle firmness and pulled me forward. With my face that close to his, I could almost imagine what it would be like to kiss him, if that wasn't a crime against everything sacred.

"Ah, so you draw a line between them?" he pondered as he looked askance at me. "I wonder why."

I shrugged and gave him a light hug. "Probably some kind of psychological hang-up about being outpaced by my peers." He let me go and I stepped back, feeling as shy and stupid as I ought to, but brave and forceful as a woman possessed.

"Knowing is the first step toward correction," he said with a chuckle.

"You sound like G.I. Joe." I tossed myself onto his sofa. "So Anna is a stream-enterer, one step closer to enlightenment, free from the first three taints: selfhood, skepticism, and ritual? *And* I've got a kickass outfit. Not bad for a day at the mall." I felt high, like I was in on some incredibly amazing truth that no one else would ever understand. "So what happens to her now?"

"I have no idea," he murmured and turned the page.

"Do you think she'll ever shoplift again?"

He picked up a separate book and laid it open. Stacks of discarded books littered his floor and the chair beside the desk, but just as I expected, Eva's book was at the center, still open. "I doubt it very much. She has no reason to."

"So you're okay with inducing enlightenment, but won't claim to be a Buddhist, why?"

He leaned back in his chair, his hands joining behind his head. "Ideas evolve, just like animals," he replied. "They play off one another, compete, and eventually are selected for their continued relevance. To group them all together under a name, to use that name as an explanation, a definition, is to confine those ideas and deny their complexity."

I wiggled farther into the cushions and sighed happily, able to, for at least a moment, pretend nothing was going to happen. "So you're saying that what the Buddha said was great, but that over time, the ideas change?"

"And to continue to ascribe to all of them is to deny the very truths at the heart of the Buddha's teachings," he finished.

"Which truths are those? And don't say anything about desire."

He clucked his tongue. "Shouldn't you be preparing?"

"I *am* preparing. Contrary to what you think, I go in for the shrewdness more than I do for the swords. I'm a spirit ninja."

He seemed to find that amusing. "I apologize."

"So which truths?"

"Do you know much about the context of the philosophy?" he asked and it sounded almost like a hypothetical.

I closed my eyes. "I know where he lived and whatnot."

"All faiths have a purpose, and that is to explain the aspects of reality most important to the culture in which they thrive. The Hindu faith was dominant in that part of the world," he explained, "and one of its chief ideas was to explain why men suffered. It reached the conclusion that they suffered because of something they had done, if not in this life, then in a past one."

"Karma, right?"

I could hear him moving books aside. "Yes. But the Buddha's experiences told him that even the wealthiest could suffer, that suffering was inevitable, and that there was not yet, any earthly way in existence to be rid of it. What he discovered during his meditations changed everything. The First Truth: to live is to suffer. The Second Truth: desire is the cause of suffering. The Third Truth: that suffering *can* be ended, and the Fourth . . ."

"The Eightfold Path," I interrupted "the means to end suffering. So what are you saying?"

He made a scolding sound at my enthusiasm. "Buddha's teachings were not simply what they said, but also what they *did*."

I thought about it while I listened to the smooth slipping of leather cover against leather cover. "You mean make revisions to Hinduism, to," I quoted with a smile, "make use of all the facts in evidence?"

He chuckled. "You are learning quickly. Soon there will be nothing for me to *not* teach you."

I opened my eyes and looked at him, thinking of Unger's revelations, trying to will him into that wonderful insightfulness so that he would clarify his identity or lack thereof without me having to ask. "And on that day you'll tell me your life story," I pressed, hoping he could hear the need in my voice.

If he did, he gave no sign. "You will learn everything you wish to know."

I sighed, my heart sinking just a bit. The truth was, I could no more imagine Arthur owning things than I could imagine him killing a man. It just wasn't him. However, there was that one tiny part of me, the one that had said Eva would never do something so stupid, constantly whispering to doubt him. But it had been wrong about Eva and I had learned that skepticism was in no way any more useful than belief.

"So the people who followed Buddha are only seeing half the message?" I mused.

"Freedom from ritual," he replied. "The third taint."

"Oh," I exclaimed, leaning forward, "they're falling back into the adherence to a dogma, instead of pondering the truths of the universe like you do all day."

He looked at me with an expression that was unmistakable. I was poking fun at him and it did nothing but reflect negatively on me, something he obviously did not want, or rather, did not want me to want.

"Sorry, I meant it as a compliment."

"Did you?"

I shrugged playfully, "Okay, you got me. It was more of a careless joke."

"Hmm."

He seemed to forget about me then as he became absorbed in his reading materials. I couldn't at that time, with all I was about to face, make room in my mind for what he was thinking. I would leave the detective work to him and Unger. I would slay the bad guys, but just recalling my mission planted a seed of nausea in my gut.

"You're going to make me feel better about this, right?"

He shook his head vaguely. "You do not have to do it, Lilith."

"True, but that would be dishonest. Someone told me that that kind of thing was bad."

"If they had to tell you, then perhaps you needed to hear it," he mumbled.

I folded my arms and tried to compress my abdomen. Much of my discomfort came down to having a plan. I had no idea what I was going to do to prevent Ursula from turning the contestant into a steak, but Arthur had sparked in me a notion that knowledge and tranquility were the most powerful of weapons. Time would tell if he was right, or if Unger's warning should have been heeded.

"Arthur?"

"Yes, Lilith?"

"Am I a stream-enterer?"

My forehead tingled as if he had touched me there, but not even his eyes shifted. "Do you know the word *dharma*?"

I dipped my head. "Duty."

"More specifically?" he prodded.

"To uphold the universe," I recalled, though I had no idea what that meant.

"You do not have to go to the club tonight, but you are choosing to act on what you saw. You are upholding the *dharma* to end suffering and keep the universe in balance." His voice softened and he shut the book in his hand. "If you must ask the question, then you are not ready. If you accept the *dharma without* question, then you are what you are."

I heaved a sigh of false annoyance. "Cryyyyyptic."

"But true."

"I suppose you're right," I said, though I know he heard the hesitation in my voice.

There was a perfunctory knock on the door and Unger poked his head inside. "It's time. We need to have a plan."

Arthur waved and both Unger and Sam nudged their way inside and leaned against the walls.

"Sam will tail you, Lilith," Unger declared with a suspicious look at Arthur's back. "When you go into the room, he'll get in somehow. Sam, keep an eye on her no matter what. If you need help or if something goes wrong," he hinted, avoiding using the words "henchmen" or "mind-reading", "call us. Arthur, you have a cell phone?"

Arthur was smiling. "No."

Unger scowled. "Then how are we supposed keep in touch?"

I looked back and forth between them. It was the old ritual of wolf versus wolf for alpha status, but I knew that Arthur was nothing if not free from ritual. He stood up and turned around with an apologetic look. "I'm sorry, Detective. I'm not very good with technology, but I'll bow to whatever orders you give most happily."

With a sigh and a brief pointed look at me, Unger reached into his pocket and tossed something black at Arthur. With the utmost grace, as if he expected it, Arthur caught the projectile and revealed it to be an older model phone.

"I've already entered our numbers into it and set them for the first three speed dial numbers. If it rings, answer it."

In deepest gratitude, Arthur smiled and examined the piece of machinery in amusement. "How auspicious that you had an extra."

"Lilith," Unger said, turning to me as if he was about to lecture me, "don't do anything heroic. You're there to do one thing, dissuade her with whatever she'll see in your head. That's it. Assuming of course that the woman can actually *do* what you say she can." He massaged his temples in what was definitely self-loathing. "When things get scary, call us immediately."

I gave a stoic nod, but I knew what was really going to happen. I was already experienced with thinking outside of a time loop. If Ursula saw what was in my head, I would be relieved of my telephone instantly. There was no way Sam would make it into the room. All the preparation was pointless except for the few words that made me feel better about what I was going to do. I looked at Arthur. He was examining my face, his blue eyes staring at mine meaningfully.

"We set?" Unger inquired.

The three of us nodded.

"Break," he muttered, and led the charge.

On the street, I took hold of Arthur's arm and slowed him to a stop. "Will you ride with me? I want to talk to you."

I didn't know exactly what I wanted to say to him, but I knew it had to be said, just in case I never came back.

He nodded. Unger tried to make me feel like the idiot I was with a glare, but could see that there was no choice.

"Make sure you let him off *before* you park, so that they don't see us together."

I gave a silent assent and dragged Arthur to my car. As we pulled away, I tried to organize my thoughts, but looming dread clouded my mind. We were mute the entire way until I pulled over several blocks away from the club and leaned my head against the steering wheel.

He reached out and placed his hand on my back. "Take a deep breath. Ground . . ."

"Myself in the physical," I finished. "Arthur, I know I said I wouldn't preface things, but I have to preface this."

His hand stopped at the back of my neck and cooled my heated skin.

"I know we only just met. I know that we don't know anything about each other, but I . . . I have this intense feeling . . ." I shook my head, blushing furiously, unable to decide which horrible conclusion was unnerving me more, "almost like . . . like we've always known each other."

He said nothing, but his hand slipped from me. I realized then that I would rather sit with him, invade his quiet life and set up camp, than ever go back to that apartment, or my empty house.

I squeezed my eyes shut and leapt off the cliff of trepidation into a deep chasm of uncertainty. "I want . . . I want to spend all my time with you. I know I sound insane, but there's something about you. I feel like I have to stay beside you. I feel like there's something missing in me that . . ." I let go of the wheel and held up my hands, "I don't know . . . that you fill in with all those things you say. I'm sorry."

It's official, I'm crazy.

I turned and looked at him, taking the step that Anna had been unable to take. I was opening up to someone, baring my soul, and standing before any and all consequences. In his eyes I saw that he understood, and would be mild as always. He was motionless and when he spoke, he affirmed all that I felt even as he tried to let me down gently.

"When it is light inside and dark without," he posited, "can you see past your window?"

I sucked in air and let it out in an embarrassed but happy laugh. "No."

"Why?"

"There's a glare."

"What you need is right before your eyes and blocks your view."

My eyes stung. I cleared my throat. "You're saying that because you can't feel about me the way I feel about you?"

He closed his eyes and dropped his chin. "What you envision, that perfect image your mother passed to you of two people growing into one another, cannot happen if there is only one person. What you love is a reflection of your own desires, not a reality."

"Then what is the reality," I argued, as if I had any right to demand that he feel anything, "that desire is the cause of suffering? Isn't the desire to rid one's self of suffering going to cause suffering?"

His lips turned upward in a sorrowful smile. "Yes, but it is a different type of suffering."

Exasperated and on edge, I clenched my fists. "What does that mean?"

Arthur turned and took hold of my wrist. "It means that I feel the same about everyone. There is no self here." I pursed my lips on the obscenities I wanted to shout, because I knew he was right. I was doing it again, reaching for the stability I lacked, just causing myself to fall farther into the illusion. "If you stay beside me," he continued, "you will be incomplete. If you reach for me, you will grasp at nothing. If you watch me, you will see only what you want."

"Unless I get rid of my 'self' and end my suffering." I nodded and collapsed back into the chair. He was an enigma and wanted to stay that way. Whatever his justification was, I had to respect it. "I get it. It hurts, but I get it."

"I don't want you to be in pain," Arthur reassured, "but that is the only solution I have. I can't go backward. Ideas only progress. I am sorry. I want to remain your friend."

"Then I can stay close to you?" I whispered.

"As long as what you seek is within you and what you become is of you."

He opened the car door and got out, but when I rolled down the window, he stooped and nodded his head in encouragement.

"Tell me what I'm about to do is what I'm supposed to do."

"Lilith, a river is unforgiving," he breathed. "If you can't hold your ground, you'll be swept away. There is no 'supposed to', only what is."

CHAPTER 14

As I waited in line, I watched Unger watch me from the same place where I had first laid eyes on Ursula. The dumpster was pushed back from the alley and the detective leaned against it smoking a cigarette. Sam got in line several people behind me and though he tried to give me a glance of support, the face I most wanted to see was Arthur's. Arthur, however, was nowhere to be found. I assumed he had been positioned in the place where he was least likely to encounter any fleeing villains he would refuse to harm, or any rats he might squish. The bouncer eyed me as before, though this time I was more afraid than nervous.

It was exactly as I remembered it, right down to the glowing ankh on my wrist, the garish lighting, and the stockyard. I squeezed through bodies that stank of sweat, was propelled onto the dance floor, and narrowly missed being elbowed in the head. On the stairwell, I pressed myself into the corner and waited. If the timing was right, any minute the security guard would appear.

He came up the stairs moments later, earpiece in and looking at me as if he were hearing any number of foul untruths from it. "Ms. Pierce?"

I nodded and let him lead me to the gallows. At the door, I gave a last backward glance at the powerless Sam, before I was swallowed whole by the darkness. Everything was as it had been. I came toward her and could already see the blood coagulating on the surface of her soul.

As if touched, she looked up and her emerald eyes narrowed. As the mouth twisted into a sneer, I knew that there was no strategy she could not break. There was only one solution and that was to ground myself in that moment and play from the hilt.

"It wouldn't do you any good," she laughed. One of her fingers depressed a piano key and a high C wavered in the air.

"Let's cut the crap. There's no point," I asserted somewhat shallowly. In truth my insides were churning.

Her laughter was so contrived it sounded mechanical. "What a pity. Tonight's game is ruined!"

"Wow, I'm *real* sorry about that. But I hear blood is really calorically dense, you should maybe see it as an opportunity to cut back."

She turned and glared at me, her smile affixed and unflinching. "You know nothing, no matter what you can do. You're weak and stupid, just like her."

As I looked at her, my imagination went mad. I could see Eva standing where I was, being bullied by this woman and her perfection, and it enraged me. Warmth flooded my face and a determination so vicious took hold of me that I might have punched a hole through steel.

"A bit defensive, are we?" I shot back. "What's wrong, Ursula, don't want to admit you have a problem?"

She stood up, one gloved hand trailing over the onyx surface of the piano as she moved closer to me. I was certain she'd respond, become furious, reach for her concealed dagger, but instead, she froze and looked at me bitterly.

Egged on by her sullenness, I grinned. A change was coming over me. All my life I had sacrificed real happiness for an efficient model of a happy life and I would not do it anymore. I was fighting back and if it had not been her, it would have been someone else.

"Vampirism wasn't all it was cracked up to be? Bet it gets pretty lame after a while. How long you been doing this?"

Her arms wrapped around her narrow body and I knew her weakness. For whatever reason, she hated what she was. It was on her face, in the mockery she made of pop culture, in the name of her club. It was a flaw and she loathed it.

"You have no idea the immense thing with which you toy so casually," she said softly. "You have no idea what a fool you are."

I shrugged, about ready to give up being me if it stopped people from saying that. "Beats being you."

Ursula's face writhed on her skull. "Does it? Alone and friendless, not even able to admit that you didn't care about your own sister enough to stop her! You and I are the exact same creature, Lilith."

I closed my eyes for a moment and knew that I couldn't run away. I would never get to say it to Eva, so why not scream it from the mountaintops?

"You're right. I fucked up, but here I am changing how I handle things. And no," I returned with a calm smile, "I'm not alone."

I thought of Arthur, my friend and teacher, and the notion calmed me. I could see the long dark hair, the full mouth, and most importantly, the blue eyes.

Ursula's face slackened and her mouth became a crimson O, just before it elongated into a manic, triumphant leer.

"Truly brainless," she hissed.

Before I could respond, the door opened. The contestants were entering to play the game, unaware that they were pawns in an even larger match. As before, I took a seat on the sidelines, but unlike the first time, I was waiting for an opportunity. When she focused her mind on them, I hoped she would be unable to stay with me. Brainless or not, I knew there had to be a way in. Nothing was perfect, not even superpowers.

I spotted the victim fated to nourish her craving and wondered if ever there had been a time when unseen forces had struggled over my future as Ursula and I were struggling for his. I was tempted to draw his attention and suggest he leave, but knew that if he got out, someone else would take his place.

The game played out as it had the first time, and though I thought she would at least have been flustered, whatever it was that Ursula had seen in my head pitched her voice higher, enlarged her gestures, and envenomed her with bravado. She was cruel to them, her subtle shrewdness forgotten for voracious grasping, and the magic began to seep from the entertainment. From beloved queen to tyrant, she transformed, and while it happened I could not help but smile.

Lie with gusto and confess with desperation; the game fed on their greatest fears and desires for belonging, but even as they thought of it as sport, it was really just a fix. It was a support group for shame-junkies, not a mea culpa. They wanted the consequences, masochists all. As I watched them, I understood and knew that the only way to truly win was to be fearless and need nothing.

Walk into the river.

The last round before finals was about to begin and with a serene surety, I got to my feet and took a place in line.

"You cannot play," she snarled, and was about to brush me aside when a great cry rose up from the audience. I looked directly into her flashing eyes and smiled as Arthur would have done.

"Let her play!" they chanted, unhappy with her oppression, writhing beneath her thumb, ravenous to hear one more secret. She had laid down the rules, but unless she planned on clearing the room, she would have to let me play or face a mutiny.

She met my placidity with ire. "You will regret this," she seethed.

I shook my head. "Desire is the cause of suffering and I can honestly say, Ursula, that I don't want to win."

Shaking with anger, her white skin looked almost bloodless. She stared at me, trying to find the outcome of my actions, but I had not foreseen them and she was no fortune teller. As the audience's fervor grew to fever-pitch, I closed my eyes and slowed my breathing. I reached for my toes with my thoughts and flexed them in my comfortable shoes.

Spirit Ninja, I thought happily. Arthur would be proud. Until he heard what I was thinking and informed me that even wanting to accomplish something was desire and would inevitably lead to suffering.

But it's a different kind of suffering.

The round carried on while I meditated, ignoring them completely. All that mattered was my turn, and if the game went according to my memory, then everyone before me was about to be eliminated. When I opened my eyes, she was standing in front of me, tossing my mind like a cat burglar looking for diamonds in the house of a pauper. The man beside me was waiting with baited breath to judge me and the rest of the room echoed with shouts and advice for him. The pause stretched into a minute and then two while Ursula glared at me and I smiled back blankly.

"No one is innocent," she whispered.

I bowed my head. "True, but not everyone keeps secrets."

Her eyes were almost snakelike in the low light.

"I do have one, though," I replied with the most pleasant expression I could manage.

She saw it just before I opened my mouth, but one hundred watchful eyes kept her at bay.

"You're going to kill the winner."

The audience quieted until disbelief set in. They hollered and hurled insults at me, but I was impervious, because I didn't have any pride to damage.

She laughed in my face, but her voice sounded tinny. Furiously, she slashed her gaze across the previous player's face. "Pass judgment," she spat.

"Sh . . . she's lying," he said quietly, "isn't she?"

I closed my eyes and shook my head slowly. "That would be dishonest."

"Get out!" she shrieked. I opened my eyes. Her breast was heaving. She reached out and shoved the man beside me. "Everyone, now! No game! Get out!"

The contestants stared around at each other and mumbled questions until Ursula took hold of the candelabra on the piano and hurled it at them.

"Out!"

In the wake of her spitting, raving lunacy, they cowered, and dissatisfied with her already, slumped off all too willingly. One by one, they passed through the door while I faced down her hatred with a tilted head and a smile.

"What's wrong, Ursula? Didn't you know the referee is as much a part of the game as the players?"

Before I could move or step back, she lunged at me. Startled, I tried to step out of her way, but as her body collided with mine, my foot lodged on the candlestick and with a heavy grunt, I crashed to the floor with her weight on top of me. Her green fingernails dug into the skin of my throat as she got her hands around my neck. I pushed at her arms, but she was determined. She wanted blood, and mine would do. Snarling, spittle falling from her mouth, she loomed over me, grinning like a jackal.

"Stupid girl," she laughed maniacally. With inhuman strength, she pinned me to the ground. Letting go of my throat with one hand, she caught my fist as it flew toward her face. Darkness began to shroud the edges of my eyes and with distant fuzziness I felt something cold slide from her wrist, across our hands, and onto my arm.

The pain brought me back to myself. It stabbed through my joint and radiated up my arm and through my hand. Her grip around my throat slackened and as sense returned to me, I looked over to find her greedy mouth sucking at the little trails of crimson trickling down my arm like sap. The gold bracelet was lodged in my flesh and her fingers were wrapped around my palm. Like a woman in the desert, she lapped at my blood and I looked on in horror, until something sparkled in the candles.

Without a thought, in the speed that minds near death are granted, I snatched at it and embedded it into her chest. With a shriek and an impotent gasp, she tumbled backward. I scrambled up holding my bleeding wrist carefully. Drops slid from my fingers onto the ground in time with the frantic pacing of my heart. I clamped my fingers across the veins and stared at her writhing body in disgust.

She rolled slowly and with the determination of a wounded lioness, pushed herself onto her knees. The knife stuck out of her chest just left of dead center. Hunched and bleeding, she panted up at me, her eyes burning with green fire.

Her laugh was almost inaudible, rattling in her broken chest. "We are . . . . the Sangha. We . . . are unstoppable."

Blood was pooling in my palm. I squeezed harder. "You look pretty stoppable to me, bitch."

She was losing strength, her smile slowly slackening, her eyes glazing over. "Pathetic," she slobbered. One hand wrapped around the hilt protruding from her blouse. "You will . . . end up . . . . just like her." She tipped forward and her free hand planted on the ground in an effort to keep her upright.

"What did you do to my sister?"

"Nothing . . ." she wheezed, laughing until the very end. "She did it . . . to herself."

I heard shouting at the door. My hand was going numb. I dropped to one knee and looked the witch in the eye.

"What did she do?"

The door thumped with what sounded like the weight of several people and protested with a crack. I reached out and grabbed her hair.

"Tell me what she did!" I demanded.

"Ask Arthur," she mumbled, then she slid out of my hand and died with a knowing red smile on her face.

With a smash, the doorframe gave out and Sam toppled through with Unger close behind. The two men looked around for me frantically and found me when I hit the floor. Sliding in the sticky blood, Sam skidded to a halt beside me and took hold of my arm. Unger's exhausted face appeared in front of me.

"Did you touch anything!" he shouted.

"Just the knife," I whispered feebly. "She jumped me."

His eyes were wide with alarm. He took one look at my wrist and pushed me bodily into Sam's embrace. "Get her out of here, now. Don't stop for anything."

CHAPTER 15

I woke up because a light was cascading through my eyelids as gracefully as a mack truck. My memory was jumbled and my mouth dry. While I tried to lick my lips, I worked hard to recall, but nothing came to me. I could see that I was in a hospital and when I tried to push the call button and my arm resisted, it came back in indistinct waves like a bad dream.

"Ah, you're awake," a voice said. "I'll get the doctor."

A few minutes later, the unmistakable sounds of expensive shoes clattered across the sterile tile floor and the rolling wheels of the low stool rattled closer.

A politely interested face leaned over me. "Been a long time since I've seen one of these," he smiled, holding up Ursula's gold bracelet. "They have a whole display of scarificators at this medical museum I visited when I was traveling through Europe."

I blinked at him and realized that he would be much less friendly if he knew what had happened. Something was going on.

"Scar . . . what?"

He lifted my arm and began to unwrap the bandages around my wrist. "Scarificators. They're devices circa Edwardian and Victorian England. Designed for bloodletting."

I frowned. "Yeah, I kinda figured that."

He chuckled. "Tough way to learn." Skin appeared, marred by a deep circular incision stitched shut. "People used to believe that bleeding was a good idea. They thought it drained the body of whatever disease or bad spirits might be living inside it. It was a real treatment for almost two thousand years."

I wiggled my fingers slowly and watched the tendons move. It hurt so bad I almost wept. My mouth wide open, I looked at him in sheer awe. "Oooow!"

Eyes glittering in what was obvious amusement and scientific curiosity, he poked my middle finger. "It'll hurt for a while, but that's good, it means that the nerves aren't damaged. It needs to be kept clean and bandaged and in a few weeks I'll remove the stitches. This thing," he tossed the bracelet up and caught it almost lovingly, "has a depth adjustment. It was set pretty deep."

"Right," I groaned and leaned back in the bed.

"It must have happened during the fight. The woman probably didn't even know she'd tweaked the setting," he mused aloud and set the shimmering cuff on the rollaway table.

I froze. So he knew about the fight. Which meant that either Unger had gotten me off on self-defense, or I was missing some information.

"Estate sales are lethal, huh?"

My stiffness slid away into the inflatable bed. "Ha ha," I offered, out of sheer relief.

"Well," he murmured, lowering himself until he could look at the bracelet at eye level, "I expect you'll be . . . a bit scarred . . ." his eyes flicked to mine in expectation. I gave him a gracious smile. "So you'll want to get rid of it, no?"

I lifted my eyebrows.

His tongue traced his lips in expectation. "What do you want for it?"

"Professional interest?" I chuckled.

He gave an embarrassed shrug.

"I'm afraid it's not for sale," said that gentle voice from the doorway in its unnamable accent.

I turned and there was Arthur, smiling as sympathetically as ever.

"Too bad," the doctor said with a sigh, "it's rare and in incredible condition. It's an antique!"

Arthur bowed his head. "If you're a collector, I have some rare books you could buy instead."

"Any copies of Grey's Anatomy?" he asked with a hungry stare. "My collection kind of has a theme."

"I could look around."

Happily, the doctor got to his feet and cast a friendly look at me. "I'm keeping you overnight, but I'll send you away with enough meds to last you forever and reschedule you to have the stitches out."

"Thanks, Doc."

He slid past Arthur with a wave and I was alone with the one person I couldn't face. He came and sat beside me and I tried to find a way to address what I felt, but I wasn't up to the task. After long moments of my silence, he bridged the gap with a sigh.

"I am sorry I was not there to save you. I fear you have again lost faith in me."

I looked into his eyes and saw the feeling there. For the first time, I wondered if it was real. Two people in one day had warned me about Arthur. Maybe it was time to confront the issue.

"Estate sale?" I asked, unable to say what I wanted to a face that seemed so honestly worried.

"Sam told them you got in a fight over the bracelet."

"At eleven o'clock at night?"

He shrugged. "They believed it. You were taken to emergency surgery."

"I got that," I said sitting up, "but what about Ursula?"

Arthur stood up and leaned over me to fluff my pillow. His scent filled my sinuses and made my lack of confidence hurt even worse. I felt like I was betraying him to doubt him, but what else could I do? Nothing made any sense and now I had to interrogate him, a person I had come to believe was above reproach.

"Detective Unger told his coworkers that he heard noises and broke down the door, that he saw a woman being choked by Ursula, and that the woman stabbed her in self-defense."

I covered my face, extending a thought of silent gratitude to the man for protecting me at the risk of his job and freedom. "Weren't there witnesses, cameras? Won't they know it was me? How did he explain being there in the first place?"

Arthur sat back down and leaned his chin on the guard rail. "He told them he was there to meet an informant on a case and as far as I know, the only cameras were over the bar."

"The cash registers," I muttered.

Arthur nodded. "At the risk of sounding insincere or cliché," he began, prefacing even though he had always told me not to, "are you alright?"

I sniffled and nodded my head even though in the back of my mind, I was trying to convince myself that the crazy bitch deserved it. I thought over her words and eventually became frustrated enough to turn to him for help.

"Arthur, what's a Sangha? Does it share the same root word as sanguine?" It would be just like Ursula to make such a pun.

He went still, looking at me in what appeared to be profound sorrow mingled with concern. "Yes," he said quietly. "The oldest word for 'stone' is the same as the word for 'blood', from it we get both 'sac', as in 'sacred, and 'sang', as in 'exsanguinate'."

"To bleed out." I shook my head. "What does Sangha mean, then?" I persisted.

"A gathering of people with a single goal, though it's usually a reference to a monastic group," he whispered and for the first time, looked away.

The time had come. I knew, and he knew from looking at me, that we had come as far as we could without a further exploration of the blank holes in our shared existences, in other words, Eva.

I swallowed hard and gripped the sheets in my good hand. "Why would she tell me to ask you about what Eva did to herself, Arthur?"

He refused to look at me, as if I was scolding him. "I am sorry, Lilith. I kept it from you as long as I could, but now I see that I have no choice."

A shiver went through me, though the room and everything in it was warm. "What are you saying?"

Arthur dropped his face. "She became obsessed and soon I realized that she was not . . . able to survive." He lifted his eyes, lashes sweeping upward beautifully. "Ursula is not human. None of them are, at least, not anymore."

I think my breathing stopped for a few moments until I felt the darkness pulling at me. "What are you saying?"

"It's complicated," he said.

I scowled at him. "How do you know?"

"I have been tracking their movements for a long while."

I stared at him in dumbfounded shock. Was he really going to reach into that magic bag and pull out such a ridiculous excuse? Then I thought about myself and realized it wasn't that farfetched when compared to my eerily perceptive dreamscapes.

"So what are they?"

"Perversions of a truth," he murmured distractedly.

"Meaning what?" I felt trapped, confined inside a stupid horror movie, unable to jump off the celluloid. How could this be happening to me, to Eva? "Vampires? Real . . . actual vampires?"

He tipped his head in an approximation of a nod. "Among other things. There are as many types as there are types of people."

"And the Sangha?"

"As you said," he confessed, "some of them crave blood and cannot help it. Perhaps it began with bleedings and evolved into the craving. I do not know."

"Ursula said Eva had done something to herself, was it . . ." I trailed off, unable to figure out if any words I might know actually applied to them.

After all, weren't they supposed to be immortal, unkillable, afraid of crosses and holy water, unable to walk in the sun?

"It is not as simple as that, I'm afraid," he replied. Slowly, his hand reached up and tentatively touched my forehead. "An omission is still a lie. Forgive me, but I wanted to keep you from it. Now I see that it is no longer safe, especially in your state."

"State?" I protested. "I'm fine! The cut didn't go *that* deep."

His dark head of long, shiny hair was already shaking. The azure eyes found me. "You do not understand, Lilith."

In one heartbeat, my world halted. "Understand what?"

"You are turning."

I think I retreated into the bed slightly and thankfully, he let me. "What? What are you talking about?"

He was still, and his face was so sad he almost looked as if he might weep. "The visions, Lilith, are a symptom."

"Of what?!" I shouted, trying to get away from him.

"Eva seems to have infected you."

My mouth fell open, but there was nothing to be said. He seemed so sure and when he was sure, he made me feel as if I had no business doubting. How could I question him, especially when his explanation, however preposterous, topped any I might have for the recently discovered psychic powers? Another shiver hit me, harder than an earthquake.

"This is crazy," I whispered.

"And serious," he insisted.

I punched the bed and the compressor clicked on, hissing angrily at me. "Are you trying to tell me that vampires *actually exist*?"

"They don't stand a chance," I heard her whisper and blinked my eyes against tears.

"The myth began somewhere," Arthur murmured.

"How?" My voice lifted to a dangerously high level. I was beginning to lose my cool. "How did it begin? This makes no sense! I didn't even my sister!"

He lifted his hand to quiet me and feeling overshadowed by his empathy, I deflated. "The mind is capable of many things. When it is given the permission, it can even stop death."

"Stop . . . death?" I repeated in a daze.

He took my hand, closed his long fingers around my palm. "I want to tell you a story. A story about a parrot."

My eyes darted to his face and bashed at his resolve. "A *parrot*?"

His smile was insistent. He knew how odd it sounded. "A parrot named Himsuka." I shook my head, but Arthur held sway with a glance.

"Himsuka was owned by a king and was so loved by him that often the king would seek his advice. One day, while flying through the jungle, Himsuka happened upon his father and decided to visit his home. He stayed with them for several weeks and because of this long absence from his friend, the king, Himsuka's family decided to send a gift back with their son. They thought hard about what to give and eventually remembered a tree that grew nearby and bore golden fruit. This fruit," Arthur revealed calmly, "was the fruit of immortality."

I thought of the Garden and the Tree of Knowledge, its shiny apples denounced by God.

"Himsuka took it home willingly," Arthur went on, "but the journey was long and soon, he had to rest. He hid the fruit within a tree and went to sleep on a branch, but this tree was the home of a serpent."

Frowning, I was thrown back again, to my youth, to my father reading me bedtime stories from the books in his mind or reciting the bible from memory, holding my hand and tucking me in despite my protests.

"The serpent was hungry and tried to eat the fruit, but it was not to his liking. The next day, Himsuka took the fruit to the king and presented it. Immediately, the king cut the fruit and was about to eat it, when someone suggested that he let the fruit be tested by a servant. He did so, and the man immediately fell down dead."

I let loose a soft laugh. "Damn snakes and their fruit."

Arthur bobbed his head. "The king was enraged and hacked Himsuka to pieces. Then he told the kingdom that the fruit was the fruit of death and threw it away, but even discarded, it grew into a tree. The king built a wall around it in fear, and no one went near it, until one day, an ailing, elderly couple ate the fruit, longing for death, and instead, awoke revived and youthful . . . and eternal."

I looked at him. The pause grew long. "Is that it? What does *that* tell me?"

He took my hand in both of his and began to play with my fingers. "The fruit is an idea, a truth, and the snake represents the many things that can sometimes twist the truth. Poor Himsuka was condemned due to a misunderstanding of the truth he shared, and therein lay the tragedy. But the fruit flourished and even now is eaten by those who do not know what it will really do to them."

I watched him splay my fingers and gently stroke the creases of my palm. "I'm confused."

He planted his index finger into the center of my hand. "It is an *idea,* Lilith. It changes, evolves, constantly. It spreads and for some, does nothing, but for others, unravels what they are. For them, the fruit is poison."

"An idea gave me superpowers?"

He chuckled and let go of my hand. "Ideas can give you dreams, change the world, why is it so difficult to believe that they can alter your body? Tibetan monks can slow their heartbeat to extraordinary lows. Olympic divers can go up to fifteen minutes without air. Japanese Zen masters died standing up, having written the last line of their jisei poems immediately before their deaths. Why are visions any different? Humans have been having them for years, tapping into the collective mind, so why can't that be concentrated in one mind changed by an idea?"

"But . . . but Eva didn't do anything to me!"

He looked through his brows at me in a prodding manner and the last conversation I had had with Eva came back to my mind. She had said a great deal that made almost no sense, could one of them have been *the* idea?

"Do you remember everything that happened when you spoke to her?" he asked quietly. "Every word she said?"

"Yes," I whispered.

"And the days that followed?"

I blinked, determined to turn the earth of my thoughts and find the seed, pluck it out, and show it to him. If I could do that, then I could deny it had ever happened, but to my misery, I could not recall. There were snippets, brief moments, faded and blurred recollections of standing vaguely in my house, looking around in confusion, but until I had shown up in the police station, there was nothing concise.

I shook my head in disbelief, my eyes stinging. What was going on?

"You were changing," he revealed. "It takes a little more than a month to finish for those that change fastest."

"My time is almost up," I breathed. "And the First Sangha? What happened to them?" I reached up and touched my damaged wrist gently. "Why was Ursula capable of seeing lies?"

He sighed and stood up, "The idea is meant to help, but like a fairy tale, people often regret what they desired. Their cravings cause them suffering. To Ursula, the most important thing was truth; it was so important that she lost sight of the one pure truth: that all truth is relative and mutable."

I looked up at him in consternation, "That's a paradox."

"Yes," he replied with a nod. "And so the misunderstanding begins."

"Then . . . my dream?"

"Prevention and the knowledge to facilitate it," Arthur interrupted, and I thanked him for taking the pressure of saying the word from me. "If you had known what would happen to your parents, you would never have let them leave. If you had known about Howard's wandering, you would never have chosen to involve yourself with him. If you had known about and understood Eva's hardships . . ."

My heart plummeted. "I could have stopped her."

I stared at his hands, gripping the rail easily.

"The fruit of knowledge."

My eyes slid up his arm to his shoulder and face. "Why the blood?"

He shrugged. "It represents life, all the physical things they lack. Perhaps they crave closeness. I cannot say and as I said, it's different for each one."

"Closeness," I whispered. Eva, all her young life, had wanted nothing but to be close to someone, to be listened to, to be loved completely, without resentment, without anger, without second thoughts. That was what she had craved and that was why she had fallen apart.

"She could be herself."

I fought to get out the words, "I'm going to be one of them?"

Arthur leaned over me and kissed my forehead. It was sudden, but reminded me that I was not alone. "You are not finished yet. That is why I am fighting so hard to get you to put down the fruit."

I laughed suddenly. "So that's why! All this skepticism, the way you reacted to me going to the club! You were trying to . . . . to . . . train me?"

He leaned back and looked into my eyes with an unbelievably kindhearted look. "I'm sorry. I did not mean to compromise your integrity, but I could see immediately what was happening and, though I could not stop her, I wanted to at least help you." Another kiss was placed on my sleeping third eye. "Forgive me, or I won't be happy."

"Well, desire is the cause of suffering, someone once told me."

His Adam's apple moved in a silent chuckle. "Indeed and you could rid me of some of mine by simply accepting my apology."

I don't know what possessed me. I reached up and tenderly pushed a strand of hair from his face. "I forgive you,' I murmured, "but only if you keep me from ending up like that bloodthirsty witch."

His stare hardened and I sensed the determination in his words. "I promise, I will do my best for you."

I leaned back against the pillow and closed my eyes. "I wonder," I said sleepily, "what happened to *their* Himsuka."

A phone rang, and surprised to find it in his pocket, Arthur withdrew Unger's old cell and opened it. As if from another era, he seemed delighted to find it worked.

"Yes, Detective."

He blinked at me as Unger's loud voice ricocheted around the room. After a few moments, he handed the phone to me.

"Hey Matthew, nice to hear your shouts!" I said in a monotone.

"Lilith?"

"Still with the living," I said, though my voice was catching every few words, "sort of."

He sighed in relief and took a few moments to collect himself. "I've been shitting myself for the last *four hours* wondering, and would have been fine if *either of them* had answered their *god damned* phones!" he snarled, accenting each piece of rage with a quieter version of the scathing speech he had given the pleasantly smiling man in front of me.

"I'm fine, Detective, relatively speaking."

"What's that mean? Is your arm okay?"

I think the sheer enormity of it had pulverized my ability to stay rational. I laughed outright. "Yeah . . . it's fine."

Though I'm not sure I am.

I waited for him to hurl another question at me, but it seemed he was finished.

"Tell me she's dead, Unger," I whispered desperately.

His voice dropped to the throaty whisper of gruff and unpolished sympathy, "She's dead."

"You sure?"

"Yeah, of course!"

I nodded.

"Moksha's here though," he divulged, "and raising bloody hell."

"Right," I muttered, because it couldn't ever be simple. I looked at the scarificator. "Fucking vampires."

Arthur raised an eyebrow, but said nothing.

"What?" Unger demanded.

"I'm . . . not even going to try and explain this one."

* * *

I carefully stacked the red volumes inside the box from my seat in the happy face.

"You shouldn't be lifting anything heavy with that hand," Sam warned. He picked up the box and looked down at me, his sleeves rolled up to expose the blurred black lines of his military tattoo.

"I'm being very careful," I replied with a smile.

"Did you take your antibiotics today?"

I raised my eyebrows. "Since when do you put two words together?" At his facial twitch, I waved away his offense. "I'll take it when we're done here."

He left the apartment to take the box down to the car, passing Arthur on the way in. I avoided looking at him. I still had so many questions and even though he made me feel comfortable, even happy, he also made my lack of knowledge apparent. In his company, whenever the footing was obviously unequal, I felt as if I had fallen behind the class and was fighting to catch up.

Tell the truth.

The truth was, I still felt bad about having doubted him and couldn't bear to ask him anything when in that state of mind. I couldn't make sense of my feelings, whether I was attracted to him because I saw him as stable, or had tapped some part of my missing sexuality.

He unloaded what little there was in the kitchenette and carefully put it into boxes for Goodwill. Unger had decided that it wasn't safe for me to stay there, especially if Moksha wondered what had really happened to Ursula. So while I was allowed to leave the hospital and go to and from the coffee shop, I was never alone. Sam had become my constant companion, and for the ninja mission of rescuing Eva's property, the entire Scooby Gang had been recruited.

I glanced back at Arthur and was surprised to find him gazing at me, leaning against the breakfast bar.

"What?" I laughed nervously, looking away.

"You've been very quiet."

"I have a lot to think about." I put a few more books into the empty box. Without any rational thoughts to rely upon, I somehow thought that if I put my back to him, he wouldn't be able to see what I was going through, but Arthur was the most astute person I had ever met. I should have known better.

"This is true," he murmured casually, "but are you not using that as an excuse to avoid dealing with the issues?"

"Truth getting in the way of truth?" I mumbled, closing the box. The shelves were almost empty, her closet was clean, and soon everything would be gone. I would be closing the door on Eva's life on a down note, wondering why she had done this to me.

"I'm sure there are a thousand questions in your mind," Arthur hinted.

"If you're trying to get me to ask you, I'm not going to. I don't want a teacher."

He laughed quietly, "Have you considered that perhaps it is a debriefing necessary for you to join an elite squad of vampire-hunting spirit ninjas?"

I stopped what I was doing and turned to look at him. He was smiling still and seemed so pleased with himself that I couldn't help but laugh.

"Alright, alright." I threw up my hands. "Go on then."

He sighed. I knew he could sense it, the distance I was putting between us, and I suppose I had just been waiting for him to try and cross it. I took a dust cloth to the shelves and wiped away the last pieces of my sister.

"How long have you been tracking *them*?"

"Them? You mean the Arhat."

"The Arhat?" I frowned, more Sanskrit.

"Those of the Sangha," he murmured, pulling the plates down and stacking them in a crate.

"I thought that's what they were called: the Sangha."

"The Sangha is an organization, but the people in it are Arhat."

"Oookay," I said, giving in. "So how long?"

"Would you believe if I said most of my life?"

I glanced at him. "Yes." It would certainly explain his lack of an identity, after all, how could a person hunt monsters when the monsters hired researchers like my sister, unless they obscured their existence in some way? "Why?"

He shrugged, but didn't look away from his task. "It's a duty. I've been watching them, but the older ones are almost impossible to find, let alone follow. They hide extremely well and are skeptical of all others. They and their underlings have such varied abilities, it is difficult to go into any circumstance feeling capable."

I walked over to the bar and lay my bandaged wrist on the counter. "What sort of abilities?"

"Premonitions," he replied with a pointed glance at me, "telepathy, the ability to control others with fear."

"You said older . . ." I hesitated,

"The closer to the source, the stronger they are."

"Immortal?" I whispered.

He pulled out a sponge and began scrubbing the tile, his face turned from mine. "I do not believe it is perfect immortality."

"How can you be sure?"

He went still, but did not turn. I watched his breathing, slow and calm. "Ursula was more than one hundred years old."

I gasped. "Shut up!" He turned to look at me finally, assessing my reaction. "You're not jerking me around?"

He looked confused by the slang. "No."

"Well, she died pretty easily."

"Clinical immortality," he explained. "When left to their own devices, the Arhat do not die, but if injured, if the systems of their bodies are disrupted, then they perish just like a normal person, if they are unable to heal fast enough."

I laid my head down on the counter and let the cool tile refresh me. He continued to work until the counter gleamed. When he was finished, he began emptying the refrigerator, dumping rotting takeout containers in the garbage.

"Where does it come from, Arthur?"

He narrowed his eyes at a Styrofoam container that smelled particularly awful and dropped it before looking up.

"It can be traced back to the very foundation of Buddhism, to the enlightenment," he said softly, his revelation contrasted by the mundane task he was performing. It made it even clearer to me that this was his everyday life, not the overwhelmingly strange event it was for me. Never mind that he had a coffee shop, or that he wore socks, or made sandwiches; he was a vampire hunter. All the normal stuff was window dressing. Then again, I mused, would I have liked him as much if he had been nothing *but* the normal stuff?

"You're not going to tell me that Buddha was a vampire."

He blinked. "No."

"Okay, so . . ."

"The Buddha traveled with a group of disciples, commonly called the First Circle, many of whom passed on eventually."

"Passed on, you mean died?"

"Yes. Though, in this case, we equate enlightenment with immortality, the outsiders had no knowledge of this. All those who followed the Buddha, dead or not, were accounted as enlightened by outsiders."

"Okay," I mumbled, bemused.

"The disciples were called 'Arhat' or 'worthy ones'."

"Ah, I see."

He crossed his arms and stared at the full bag in concern. At my glance he shook his head. "Your sister did not eat well."

I nodded imprecisely. "I was the cook."

Sam reappeared and picked up the last few boxes. He looked in Arthur's direction. "I'm going to take these over and come back."

"We'll be fine," Arthur dismissed. When Sam again vanished, he turned back to me, his work forgotten. "When Buddha died, he gave specific instructions that there was to be no leader, that after he was gone, they were to adhere to the teachings, the truth. However, after his death, many of his followers immediately organized an assembly to declare who would be the next leader of the faith. It was called the First Council, or Sangha of the Buddha."

"Then that's where it all went wrong," I mused. His hands were very close to mine, and I couldn't help but watch them and hope that they found mine. My wrist twinged, a reminder of Ursula's craving that brought me back to myself and my own failings. I pulled my eyes from his hands, determined not to want his touch, to finally stand on my own and be "of myself". "If the enlightenment led to this, then why would you have spread it to Anna?"

"A virus comes to three ends," he elaborated. "The body develops an immunity to become stronger, or the virus hides within the body and becomes a part of it, or the virus kills its host. What Anna received was just enough exposure to make her stronger, tailored for her specific needs, an inoculation."

I stood up and heaved a sigh, trying to reason through it. If his picture was accurate then Anna got over the virus, the Arhat were permanently afflicted with it, and Eva died because of it.

Just before she infected me.

"So I'm not a stream-enterer. I'm one of them . . . the Arhat."

"All Arhat were Stream-Enterers, until they passed into the change."

Disgruntled, I looked away. "How could you do this to me?" I mumbled, but if Arthur heard me, he said nothing.

"Have you heard the legend of the Bodhi Sattva?"

I shook my head, not really listening. Sullen and distraught, I laid my head back on the counter. His hand patted me gently.

"Three men wander into the desert. When they are at their weakest, they happen upon an enclosure encircled by a high wall with no doors. The first man climbs up on his friend's shoulders, discovers a garden and climbs over. The second man climbs up on the third man's shoulders, sees the garden and with a shout of joy, disappears over the wall. The third man, left to himself, climbs laboriously up the wall, but when he sees the garden, turns away and goes back into the desert to point other wanderers toward the oasis. The Bodhi Sattva are enlightened individuals who forgo the transcendence of Nirvana in order to help others find their way. Ins."

I lost myself in the sensation of his fingers moving through my hair, closed my eyes and drifted. "That's noble of them."

"Legend tells us that they are gifted."

"With what?"

"Uncanny insight," he answered.

I sat up sharply. "Who do we know with that affliction?"

His mouth was a beautifully curved line. "Another legend, based on truth, but not entirely truthful."

"Yeah," I muttered, almost angrily, "you'd think that the Buddha would've been a Bodhi Sattva if it was such a great idea."

"Many people argue that he is," Arthur said with another shrug, "In his first sermon, he said 'this is my last existence; now there is no rebirth.' Many believe that those words referred to reincarnation, but that doesn't mean anything. As with Elvis, I suppose some people cannot help but keep him alive in their minds, though his passing is documented."

"Well, the couple in the Himsuka story *did* get young again when they ate the fruit."

The smile grew. "True. The Theravada school, focused upon the word, believes that the Bodhi Sattva is an as yet, unenlightened individual working toward nirvana, because they have not yet died and transcended, but the Mahayana school believe that their generosity gains them a kind of honorary enlightenment called 'bodhicitta'."

"Hmm. I wonder which school the Sangha loves best."

"The Mahayana Buddhists are devotional. Such a faith allows the Sangha freedom and access to a group of humans."

"You mean that because they worship Buddha instead of revering him that the Sangha can use that to their advantage?"

"Yes."

"So it *is* a big conspiracy."

But even with his perfect recounting of an obscure history, I could not see how an idea could do so much. I knew that the brain took on the shape that was needed to hold the thoughts a person might have, and that some thoughts could become obsessions, and even that some obsessions could lead to chemical imbalances strong enough to compel a person to act. I wondered if that was what it felt like for the Sangha, if for them it was a never-ending torture of compulsions. It made the word "craving" take on whole new meanings for me.

Until that moment, I had hated Moksha, seen him as a representation of my sister's downfall. Now, all I felt was pity. I bowed my head and knew I should have reserved judgment, but how could I when I was acting within the real world? How could I have known that what happened to Eva, just as Ursula had said, was her own doing? More importantly, how could she have condemned me to that?

"I know you hate me. I've always known."

"How did they become clinically immortal?" I asked.

"Cravings are the root of suffering. To rid themselves of suffering, the Stream-Enterers meditated in hopes of curing themselves from within, to annihilate their attachment to the things they desired. But entering into the *jhana,* or that many-leveled perfect state of cognition, can cause a person to acquire, what the Buddha called right knowledge and right liberation."

"Right knowledge? You mean the uncanny insight?"

"It would seem so. Perfect knowledge of whatever they choose to focus upon."

"So what's 'right liberation'?"

"The heights to which mind and body may travel. The self-awakening."

"And you think that that is when they become immortal?"

"Yes."

"So the Arhat meditate, achieve the *jhana,* and become immortal. Well, obviously, the disciples who died were *not* enlightened. They were just *srotapanna*. Right?"

"So it is believed, but it depends entirely upon whether or not you believe the Buddha is dead."

"That must have sucked," I shook my head, feeling sorry for them even though I didn't want to, "suddenly being left alone at the head of a faith you have no ability to follow. But if they get there, to the perfect place, then how can they devolve?"

"Ideas do not ever move backward, for even with amnesia, the brain is the perfect shape to recall those memories. They achieved a height, but at the last step, fell short and are left in permanent suffering." He traced a circle on the table. "It is a wheel, moving forward, very much like the Karmic cycle . . ."

"Samsara."

He nodded and looked into my eyes. "You can understand now, why Moksha would choose such a name. It was meant to be ironic. With an eternity and right knowledge, what do you think would happen?"

I knew what he was hinting at. He was implying that they would eventually become frustrated with their state of being. "But if they got that far, then wouldn't that mean they were free from the taints? Wouldn't that make them free of selfhood?"

"Some would say there is no way that a man could achieve ultimate understanding only to devolve, they talk of *annica,* the understanding that all things are one and are impermanent, but when one has immortality, that is not such an easy thing to accept. They have come to believe, over time, that they went even farther than the Buddha, because they did not die. Now, they see no resolution."

He went back to his chores silently, scrubbing the appliances amicably. I half-expected him to whistle while he worked, he seemed so happy to be helping. It was probably penance for failing as the knight in shining armor.

As I pushed the beanbag toward the garbage bags by the door with my foot, I saw my sister, scrambling over that wall toward what she thought would save her. I saw her clambering up on my shoulders, reaching for the green blur of love and serenity, leaving me behind.

"How could you do this to me?" Another angry kick sent the bag into the door. I stood staring at its mouth, grinning at me no matter what I did, no matter how afraid and uncertain, conflicted and lost. What would happen to me? Would I end up craving something worse than blood? Would I end up high-diving into a concrete ocean?

I felt his hands on my shoulders and unable to suppress the urge, sobbed.

"You're wrong about her," he said into my ear. "Your life has been one ending after another. The last was your marriage. Eva knew that without your devotion to her, you would finally be free of all the desires that might tie you down and wanted to give you a chance at eternity. She leapt from that wall and helped you over. She was your Bodhi Sattva."

CHAPTER 16

I stared at Unger. He stared back, blinking like any good cynic. The waitress attempted to refill his coffee, but his hand guarded the top. With an annoyed look that obviously wanted him to take notice of her unbuttoned top button, she sauntered away.

"You're serious, aren't you?"

It was a formality. By this point, he was used to the absurd from me. I sighed and tilted my head. "What, Matty, don't believe me?"

He frowned at my wrist. "Oh, I believe you, and that's what's fucking with me."

I leaned back and chuckled. It had been his idea: a trip to the diner, a debriefing on my debriefing over the pie and greasy food that Arthur seemed to shun without a word. Two normal people bashing about disproportionately shaped strangenesses, like horribly deformed hot potatoes.

"Why do you believe it? I mean, you've been a detective *how long*?"

He shook his head. "*Too* long." He leaned his chin on his hand. "That's just it. Do it long enough and you come to the notion that it never ends, that somewhere, someone is fighting you, making sure it never goes away. The longer I do this, the more I believe in it."

"'It' being evil?"

He nodded.

"So what do we do about it? If Arthur's right, then . . . what?"

His disgruntled inner watchdog came to the fore. "What makes you think he's right?"

I shrugged.

"Yeah yeah, I know. I *feel* him too."

It was a begrudging agreement that promised further skepticism ahead. As I sat there looking at the poor man, I began to see Arthur in a new light. I knew that what I felt was somehow illusory, that without him, I would not necessarily be able to think as he did, with the kind of patience he employed, the kind of reasoning that was "not reasoning". In a way, that's what Unger and I shared. We were both trying to superimpose our world over Arthur's and make a 3D image in which we could exist.

He sat up straight. "I don't know what his method is," he mumbled, "but I know what I would do if I was a P.I. and this was a normal case."

"Pound the pavement, Mr. Gumshoe?"

He scowled. "I'm not Humphrey Bogart."

I smiled at him flirtatiously and noticed his blush. "You're *my* Humphrey Bogart. Can I be your Gretta Garbo?"

"Shut up."

"Okay, so what would you do?"

He shoved his coffee away in what looked like discomfort. "If we want to speculate that Moksha and Ursula were linked, then we have to believe that whatever Eva was doing was somehow tied into it."

I nodded, because it was what I had thought all along.

"No matter what *kind* of people they are," Unger specified, "they're still people. They'll have the same weaknesses as people would."

I looked at him dubiously. "Yeah, because most people go into blood-withdrawal."

"They'll have money, secrets stored in vaults, people they don't trust, et cetera."

"Ooooh," I grinned, "stool pigeons."

He growled. "Your sister was the head record keeper."

"Yeah."

He held out his hand. "So we go to the records."

I shook my head. "They'd never let us in. Hell, I don't even know where in the building they keep the records."

He massaged his face and leaned back, casting his eyes out the window to the twilight streets. I picked at his apple pie with a finger. After several moments, he looked back at me.

"Her journals."

I nodded, "Arthur's already got that covered."

He glared at me.

"And I'm sure he is doing a fine job, though you're welcome to investigate his 'methodology'."

"I'm more interested in letting him tell me what he finds and see if I believe him," Unger said quietly. "Meanwhile, I plan on cross-checking."

"Oh?"

"Ursula's club *was* owned by Moksha's company, just like you said," he explained. He opened his wallet and threw a few bills onto the table. "Because I was first on scene, it's my case, if I want it."

I watched him get to his feet.

"And I do," he offered me a hand.

"And here you were having such a great vacation!" I took it and stood up. "You're going to use it as an excuse to delve into her shady relationship with him?"

He smiled slyly, "Will I ever."

"And?" I hinted, smiling eagerly.

He held me at arms length and smiled at me. "You're bored with the ascetics, fancy that."

I pulled my hand away and crossed my arms in stubborn refusal to allow him to leave without assigning me my next mission. Looking at me, his face slowly changed from amused to false aggravation.

"Fine. Take Sam to the County Records Office. Find anything you can about the AMRTA building. All construction or building renovations go on file, because they have to apply for permits."

As we left the diner, I walked backwards before him. "You honestly think that those files would be above board? Wouldn't they keep things like that safe, if they had anything that needed hiding?"

He shrugged and took out a cigarette. "Possibly, but if they do, I'm thinking you'd know where the line got fudged."

I smiled. "You have such faith in me and my talents!"

He lit the cigarette and narrowed his eyes, looking exactly like Sam Spade, minus the hat.

"You like me don't you, just admit it!"

He shook his head, but despite the clinging lips, managed a smile. While he stood outside, I went into the shop and trotted up the stairs. As usual, Arthur looked like he'd been swallowed whole by a library. A portion of shelves had been cleared and all of Eva's books rested there exactly as they had in her apartment. He was staring at the first red volume, frowning in concentration the likes of which I'd never seen from him.

Without warning, I put my arms around him and hugged, but as usual, he did not flinch.

"Did you enjoy the pie?"

I laughed. The way he said "pie" made it sound like an unearthly delicacy. "Yes."

"Did Unger?"

Behind him, I crossed my arms. "Is 'pie' a euphemism for conversations pertaining to you, had behind your back?"

His head tilted. "Hmm."

"Are you irritated?" I teased.

He detached his eyes from the page and turned to look at me, expression soft and ambivalent. "It is his cautious nature that makes him strong and useful to you. I would no sooner have him change that, than I would have him quit his job."

"Then you know he doesn't trust you."

"Nor should he." He stood up and stretched happily.

I think my eyebrows got lost in my hair. "Can't you *be* trusted?"

He was looking at the ceiling vaguely, hands braided behind his head. "I can, but that would make things much more difficult for me, in many ways."

I frowned at this, wondering what a man did that was better accomplished in the *absence* of trust. "He's given me a mission. I need Sam."

He looked at me for a time and then gave a slow nod of his head. "He's a free agent. Just be careful."

I clicked my heels together and saluted, to his amusement. "What about the journals?"

My question brought back the recollection of whatever logical wall was damaging his handsome cranium; his brows drew closer together. "I think I might procure outside help with these."

"Wow," I marveled, "Arthur Godard claiming ignorance."

He smiled that perfect smile and lifted one shoulder casually. I sang inside. "It happens, but please don't let it color your opinion of me."

"It couldn't," I admitted with an honest gaze, "if anything, it convinces me of your humility."

His eyes slid shut and I knew it was his way of saying goodbye without coming any closer. I reached out and gingerly poked my stitches.

Of myself.

I went downstairs repeating the words in my mind, cursing myself again for finding Arthur irresistible, despite my better judgment. Sam was at a table, leafing through papers and adding numbers on a calculator, his military tattoo twitching as his fingers moved. When I sat down, he looked up.

"Ever been to the County Records Office?"

He blinked at me and shook his head.

"Wanna?"

One eyebrow dropped. "Okay."

After he cleaned up his books and put them behind the counter, we walked to the parking lot and got into his Honda. As he drove across town, I practiced clenching my fist, working the damaged parts of my arm to regain strength, channeling all my will into a speedy recovery.

He glanced at my clasping hand, "Did you take your meds?"

"Why are you always asking me that?"

He looked away. I went on flexing.

"What are we looking for?"

"Blueprints."

At a stoplight, he tapped the wheel with his thumbs and the tattoo twitched again.

"Sam, what branch of the service were you in?" I inquired, pretending that I didn't care, though I was dying to know.

"Army," he said tersely.

I watched him out of the corner of my eye, imagining pasts for him that Arthur would never be so ill-mannered to hint at. So demure and easy-going, how had someone like Arthur met him? How had they become friends if at all? From the several interactions I'd seen, I got the feeling that Arthur admired him and that in return, Sam felt strangely protective. Sam had invested money in the coffee shop project, whereas Arthur, to my knowledge, had not. Sam owned the building that housed Arthur's books and even the man himself, but rented a small flat nearby. Sam ran the business, did the shopping, and even the chores, and though I had never seen Arthur leave a trace of himself beyond the scattered pages of unbound books, there had to be a reason Sam put up with it.

At the office, I disarmed an older gentleman with a smile and was shown the records we required. It was a box filled with wilted sheets of large photosensitive drafts mixed in with reams of paperwork. The dust burned my eyes and I sneezed hard enough that I felt the stitches in my wrist pull.

"I'll do it," Sam offered.

We sat at a plastic card table, unfurling sheet after sheet in silence. I watched him all the while and could tell the scrutiny did not go unnoticed. I wanted him to tell me more. I was certain, and not just with the usual amount of certainty, that Sam had secrets to tell, and for some reason, I desperately wanted him to reveal them to me. I thought of Ursula's passion for the truth and for blood, and tried to put the desire out of my head, but it was impossible. I sat there watching my mostly mute companion, wondering if it was possible to catch the Arhat's gifts by association.

While I worked my fist, he glanced between me and the plans until it finally bothered him to distraction.

"What?"

I smiled and nudged my chin at his tattoo.

He looked back at the plans and as if he was uncomfortable, but had no choice, pushed the words out between breaths. . "Special Forces."

I said nothing. Letting Arthur's example guide me, I knew Sam would tell me about it only if he needed to, and that otherwise, it was none of my business. I had offered up my ear, and to do anything else would be an imposition. Even so, I couldn't help but ponder the raspy, damaged voice and what debt he owed to our mutual friend.

"I went to Iraq," he garbled.

I pressed my lips together, determined not to speak, and let my eyes be an open and convenient place to keep his secrets.

"I saw a lot of things," he went on, almost unable to look at me.

My fingers ached, I was clenching so hard, but something in the tone of his voice seemed to make the pain less significant. I continued to squeeze.

"I took a piece of shrapnel to my throat. They got most of it out, but I had to come back."

One ream of pages was set aside and another picked up. I glanced at the top page. It was a permit for construction on the empty lot that had preexisted AMRTA.

"Things were different. They told me I couldn't serve anymore. They said," he hesitated, as if saying it meant that it was true, even if he disagreed with their assessment, "they said I had PTSD."

I managed a compassionate nod. That was what the first therapist had said about Eva right after our parents had died, during the two years when she had refused to speak and her journals had become her only voice.

He sniffed and unrolled the plans dated as the most recent. "I got discharged. For a while, I was broke, wandering around like a damn fool, pissed off about everything. I got in fights, got drunk a lot. One night, I got into it bad with these three assholes in Atlanta," he shook his head, calloused hands spreading out the dark blue sheets veined with white lines. "They left me for dead."

My hand was cold. I relaxed and blood seeped back with the feeling.

"Arthur found me," he revealed, looking up at me. His usually guarded face had relaxed and his brown eyes were almost shimmering. "I was bloody and fucked up, lying in an alley. He . . . helped me," he said with a shrug. "We ended up here and he sort of said it was a good place for me to start again. After that, I got a loan for the shop and he helped me put everything together. If not for him, it would have been a stupid dream that I would never even have admitted having."

I smiled. Arthur *did* have a way of making sense of other people's dreams. "How did you find out about *them* . . . the Arhat?"

He looked over my shoulder with a sharp eye and then leaned closer. My fingers curled toward my palm again and tightened their grip on nothing; I felt no pain.

"One night, almost right after the grand opening, this man came to the shop right as I was closing." His expression hardened. "He looked like he'd been hit by a car, you know? Bashed all to hell. I've only seen that kind of stuff in combat."

My mouth opened on a silent question.

Sam shook his head. "Arthur said he knew the guy. They started talking in this other language, right, and then the guy just dies, right on the ground where the front table is."

"Did you call the police?" I whispered, focused intently on his face.

"Sure, but when they got there, Arthur disappeared. Wouldn't talk to them. I lied for him, because I didn't know what else to do. I left it for a long time, wouldn't ask about it. Not my business, you know?"

I looked away with a nod. Of course a man with as violent and painful a past would never even think to dive into areas that would have driven me mad with curiosity. Most of Sam's youth had probably been spent learning to never question, to watch every back, not just the ones he liked, and to come to a grudging acceptance of everything he could not change.

"But . . ." I looked up and it seemed the memory still haunted Sam, "he died on *my* floor. When I finally asked, and Arthur told me, I don't know . . ." he sat back winking in the low light, "I just believed him. Since then, I've seen it with my own eyes."

"Seen what?"

"All kinds of stuff, the abilities they have. When Eva started . . ."

My fist shook a bit, the tremble tugged on my mind until I let the hand fall limp. "How well did you know her?"

"Not well," he confessed, with a compassionate smile. "She came in all the time, to talk to Arthur, and we spoke a couple times. When I asked about her, he told me all about what was happening. He asked me to leave her to him."

I believed him. "So you're the muscle?"

He shrugged, "I guess, though so far, all I've done is a little surveillance. Arthur's kind of non-violent."

So he *was* the stalker, by accident. I chuckled. "Yeah, I got that. So, what was the dead guy's story?"

"That's just it," Sam mumbled, turning the plans in a quarter-circle, "he didn't say. Just told me that the guy was a friend, someone he'd known a while, someone who helped him with his dharma, and I let it go."

Wide-eyed, I squeezed again. "I guess the guy didn't have Special Forces training."

"That's what I thought," Sam agreed. He went back to the plans, narrowing his eyes as if he could slip his gaze between the lines and see things that weren't really there. Shaking my head in perplexity, I put my hands on the table and closed my eyes.

"Shit, Lilith," he hissed.

"What?" I looked at him. His face was pointed at my wrist.

Through the bandages, blood had seeped, but I had felt no soreness whatsoever. "Damn," I marveled.

"Let's go."

"Oh no," I protested, pulling my arm away from him, "we finish what we came here to do. You're a soldier, I'm a ninja. Deal."

He seemed taken aback. "What is it with you and ninjas?"

I shrugged and laid my injured arm in the crook of the opposite elbow, looking at him pointedly, "Black is slimming."

After a few minutes of staring, he sighed and jabbed the plans. "This is the area labeled 'file storage'," he indicated the basement substructure. "These were the final plans, but if you look here," he picked up an older set and lay them across the recent, "you see that the space is twice as big."

"So which do you think got built?"

"I don't know, but a lot of times groups that have secrets worth keeping," he cleared his throat and eyed me, "don't want anyone knowing that they planned to build that last cupboard."

"But it's in the original plans because the architect drew them up without knowing the intended use."

He nodded.

"I don't want to know how you know that."

He gave me a smile. "Wonder what they keep in there."

"Probably the records that Eva was organizing." I sat back and sighed, trying to see it from her eyes. "A place like that, a young, impressionable girl, she'd do what was asked and never wonder."

"Until she did."

I looked up at the drop-ceiling and fluorescent light fixture. "What would they have there that was worth four hundred thousand dollars?"

"If only she had left a note," Sam grumbled sarcastically and I knew what he was thinking. He was seeing a set of unreadable volumes bound in red leather, but there was no way of knowing if they had anything to do with her AMRTA assignment.

While he gathered our finds together and persuaded the clerk to aid him in photocopying them, I mused.

"If you had someone with that kind of power, would you make use of it?"

"Damn right, I would."

Sam may have Special Forces training, but I didn't. If I tried to go in physically, I would put myself and the search in jeopardy, and that was something I was sure Eva didn't want. Arthur would also scold me for being so caught up in my eagerness for answers that I didn't think about my circumstances. Club Trishna was enough of an experience with jumping in the deep end without a plan to know such risk-taking was a bad idea. So, why not make use of all the powers my unavoidable transformation made available? That had to be what Eva had intended, after all.

I closed my eyes and made a mental list. Both visions had foretold traumatic events, given me a heads up, almost like a defense mechanism. It was a long shot, but if I *knew* that a situation was risky, couldn't I purposely trigger one and use the information if I concentrated hard enough?

I clenched my fist and grounded myself in the physical. I pushed my thoughts from muscle to bone, to my blood vessels, and then into my own blood.

Spirit Ninja.

CHAPTER 17

Sam came back from the copy machine and put a hand on my shoulder. "Lilith?"

Caught in the middle of meditation when I had no business attempting it with my limited education, I leaned back and looked up at him. "Yo."

He nudged his head at the door.

"Wanna do some espionage?" I angled offhandedly.

He raised an eyebrow and stuffed the copies under his arm. "I want to bandage your wrist again."

I shook my head. "Nope. You're my bodyguard, and I say we make use of your training."

He halted and frowned at me. "Like how?"

Smiling wickedly, I opened the door for him and waved a goodbye at the clerk. "Oh, I thought we'd break into the AMRTA records room."

He snorted and coughed out a disbelieving laugh. "Yeah, right."

When I stopped following him and held my peace, he turned and examined my smug face. "What?"

"Trust me."

He took a deep breath and looked at the street as if standing uncertainly at a crossroads. "We should tell Arthur," he hesitated.

I rushed past him and grabbed his arm, dragging him behind me as if I was a tugboat. "That's why we have cell phones. Come on. I'm a psychic remember?"

He grumbled incoherently, but obeyed. With the plans stowed in the back, he drove toward the building. It was midday and the structure gleamed like a piece of black crystal shooting from the ground, as we parked around the corner. I jumped out before the car was even completely in the space and ran toward the building, uncertain how much time I'd have. He came after me, growling my name, but I didn't listen. I walked like I knew exactly where I was going, entered with a group of lunchbreakers on their way back, and managed to squeeze into an elevator while the security guard was turned. As the doors closed, I caught sight of Sam, unable to follow and not happy about it. He was reaching in his pocket for his phone. Behind him, the guard had spotted him.

I closed my eyes and counted seconds. Around me, the employees were shifting their weight. None of them recognized me, but I told them with glances that I had every right to be there, even though my attire was not within the dress code and I did not have an entrance badge. I rode the elevator up to the seventh floor and then back down. I rode until there was nobody on it with me and in a triumphant gesture, poked the B button. Cautiously, I squeezed myself into the corner next to the panel and waited. When at last the metal box came to rest in the bottom of the shaft and the door slid open, I leaned out and looked.

It was a long white hall, running from right to left, lined with doors and completely vacant. At one end I saw a glass wall, and since the other seemed to be a dead end, I rounded the bend and walked directly toward the glass. Tiptoeing in my ninja shoes, I crept past each door, until I saw the sign.

Eva Pierce, Records

It was just a placard on the white wall beside a door, but I couldn't move past it. My wrist twinged. I glanced down. The blood stain was larger. My veins were keeping time in heartbeats. I cast a look at the glass wall and saw that it was a large automatic sliding door with a key pad. Which was I meant to enter? If I went into the office, I could reach out to her, but to what end? She couldn't answer my questions.

Everything means something. She would have known.

I closed my eyes and turned away.

If they hadn't changed the nameplate, then they hadn't changed the code either, and if Eva had set the code, I knew what it would be. With a nod, I typed in my birthday. A green light blinked and the door hissed open. It was cold inside and sterile smelling, like a giant refrigerator.

I stepped past the threshold, my heart pounding in success, and immediately regretted it. A loud, screeching sound echoed around me. Swearing, I looked around in a rush. White walls, white drafting tables lit from beneath, white shelves filled with what looked like boxes of leather-encased scrolls. One sat open on a table, surrounded by the tools used to preserve it. Across it in lines was a variation on the Sanskrit I had seen before.

Something red blinked in my periphery. I glanced up and spotted the flashing red light of a security camera. They could see me.

"Clever."

I spun toward the elevator, and with only a tiny glance at the name plate, hurled myself at the button, but it was already engaged. Desperately, I looked around and realized that if there was an elevator, there had to be another way out in case of fire. Running full tilt, I threw open doors. Every room was for storage, except the last. In the blaring scream of the alarm, I heard nothing, but something in me knew that the elevator had opened. I looked back long enough to see several security guards tumbling out of the opening. They spotted me, and with a shout, gave chase, but I was already on my way up. I took the stairs in threes, thanking god for the hours spent on the stair-climber in my bedroom, a piece of equipment I would never have used if not for the feelings of inadequacy Howard had spawned in me.

I reached the ground floor and knew that there would most likely be someone waiting there for me, but as I opened the secure door, prepared to kick my way out if necessary, I instead found a body splayed out across the opening, its blue shirt smeared with blood. On the other side of the body, Sam relaxed his fist.

"Now!"

I leapt over the groaning man and with Sam pushing me from behind, raced toward our parked car. We jumped in and sped away, Sam glancing in his rearview mirror constantly.

It wasn't until I spotted the diner that I breathed a sigh of relief.

"I'm glad we didn't take your car," Sam laughed shakily.

I looked down at my wrist. "Yeah."

He pulled in and parked. We sat in the truck in silence.

"Did you find anything?"

I glanced over at him, he was gripping the steering wheel, staring into space. "Only what looked like some kind of viewing room, like a museum, or something. Hermetically sealed."

He nodded and swallowed. "You know, you suck as a ninja."

"Shut up, Special Forces."

We got out of the car and looked at each other over the roof, grinning like cats who'd dined on canary. It seemed like Sam thrived in battle and had been missing the rush.

"Hey, I kept up my part, distraction *and* cavalry."

"Yeah yeah." I waited for him at the back door while he pulled out our copies.

"What do we tell Arthur?" he asked, his face finally returning to a semi-normal serious state.

I smiled, "Trust me."

At the top of the stairs, I flexed my fingers and squeezed my fist before opening the door.

Beyond it sat a person, though that was not my first guess. It had its graffiti-tagged back to me, a shock of blue hair sticking up from a black hoody. It was sitting cross-legged, facing the bookshelf that now housed Eva's canon, seemingly involved in some meditation. I stepped inside and looked around for Arthur, but the person on the floor was the only one there.

"Um, who . . .?" I began.

"Am I?" The young man rolled backward and looked up at me from the ground. He had playful brown eyes that sparkled, several facial piercings, and a winning grin. "People call me Jinx."

I raised my eyebrows.

"Why do they call you that," we both said at the same time.

As I frowned, his smile grew. "You owe me a coke."

My mouth fell open.

"What the hell?" we chorused.

"That's another one," he laughed and pointed up at me with a black polished nail peeking out from fingerless gloves embossed with a skeleton pattern. There was an accent to his voice that was vaguely French.

Bemused and stubborn, I pinched my lips shut, determined not to speak until I had figured him out. How did he know what I was about to say? He couldn't have heard me, because as I examined him in silence, I realized he was wearing headphones turned up to full volume, buzzing in the air around his head with incessant house music. Then it hit me.

Duh.

"Yeah, you got me," he mumbled and rolled upward. Like an acrobat, he jumped to his feet and presented me with a gloved hand. He was almost a head shorter than me and couldn't have been more than fifteen, but looks were oft times, very, *very* deceiving. He was one of *them* and whatever allowed him to know what I was about to say, was his ability.

I put together a phrase and *fully* intended to say it.

He rolled his eyes. "There's no reason to be mean."

I blinked. "Then what . . ."

"Lily!" He shouted, a little louder than necessary, probably due to the music. He wiggled his fingers in midair insistently, as if trying to convince me that he was a friend. "I'm like Eva. I'm Art's friend."

So he was the "punk" Eva's neighbors told the police about.

I looked at his hand and reached for it, but it dropped as he set eager eyes on my wrist.

"Wicked accessory!" he shouted. "Does it hurt?"

I made to answer, but he interrupted.

"Sucks man! I woulda at least hit 'em up for some painkillers!"

I began a nod and prepared to say something about how it really hadn't hurt at all since the first time. I couldn't complain.

He waved my comments aside, "But it's like the only perk, right?!"

With a smile that was determined to be polite, I stared at him. He looked back at me in friendly anticipation. The moment stretched, until finally I couldn't stand it. I opened my mouth.

"I'm here to look at your sister's books," he yelled.

Suddenly I knew why Arthur was gone. Conversations with this kid were decidedly one-sided.

He shrugged guiltily, "I know, I'm sorry, but I can't help it. I'm trying really hard, I swear, but imagine how you'd feel if you had to hear everything twice!"

I'd probably . . .

"Yeah! The headphones make it easier! That way I can at least ignore the audio stuff and stick to the mental!"

What a horrible . . . I attempted to think.

"Totally!" He pushed his fingers between tousled blue spikes and pulled them toward the ceiling in an expression of exasperation. "I don't get it! I mean, why should I get this lame ass power, when spoonfed people like you get to see the future and shit?" he complained loudly.

Spoon . . .

"I mean infected." He pointed at himself proudly. "I didn't get infected! *I* infected *me*!"

I'm not talking . . .

He reached up and pulled out the earphones. "Sorry" he whispered. "Force of habit with people who don't get it. I'll be good if you do."

I walked over to the sofa and sat down, trying to figure out how much I had to think about saying before he could complete the thought.

"How . . .?" I got out.

"That much," he said with another grin and retook his seat on the floor.

Befuddled, I shook my head. How had a kid so young infected himself? For that matter how had Eva done it? I had supposed it happened by being friends with Ursula's warped concept of Zen, but even though Jinx seemed the type to hang out at Club Trishna, he looked like he wouldn't have made it past the door. So what was it that had burrowed inside their respective brains and forced them across the river?

I formed the question and he answered it with another rolling of his eyes. "Hell to the No. I don't do black and somber. I'm one hundred percent computer games and action figures."

Laughing, I thought about it.

"I'm not an Arhat. I'm a mathematician," he answered as he pulled a red book from the shelf and opened it. "Math's as much a 'killing word' as Zen, man."

I blinked.

"Sorry, obscure Dune reference," he mumbled, flipping through pages as if he'd discovered the next Superman comic. "I meant that I studied math. *Really* studied it, not like those posers who get degrees and then bitchfag out by working for Intell or the cocksucking NSA. If I wanted to blow shit up, I could do it in my garage and claim all the arch villain cred myself. Screw those asswipes."

I found I couldn't help but laugh as the words came to me.

He glanced up, "Seriously. One day I think I've got Unified Field Theory cold and the next day it's twice as much bullshit. I mean, I love it, don't get me wrong. It's way spooky in the right setting, but most of the time, it's just fucking annoying."

He began rocking back and forth like a kid on a sugar high, scanning the pages with a few darting looks.

You must drink . . .

"So true." He set the book down and pulled out another. "There's this whole diatribe against addictive substances in Buddhism, right? They think that part of the reason people can't get enlightenment is because they cling to desires like that. If they're right, I didn't make it, because I love the damn stuff so fucking much," his words sped up until I wondered if *I* might have to be a psychic just to understand *him*. "I mean I drink like fifteen cups of coffee a day, like five cans of Redbull, and if I meet new people who are cool, like a six pack of coke a day, right? I'm a speed freak. So you know I always figured it was impatience that was my *trishna* you know? I mean why else would I . . ."

I made to interrupt, but was shut down.

"Yeah. It's okay though, because whenever I get pulled over on my motorcycle, I can always say to the cop 'Yeah, five miles over', before he opens his donut-hole."

Fine with giving my swollen throat a break, I tried to stop smiling, but the boy was amusing to a fault, and as long as he was there to help, I couldn't be happier.

So . . .

"I'm here to find the code, if there is one." He pulled another red book out and lay the three side by side, shaking his head. "But this is just words. Is it like this all the way through?"

It was coming much more easily to me. I closed my eyes and squeezed my fist.

He made a humming noise. "Okay, okay. Have you looked through all of these?"

I squeezed again.

"Are there any numbers in any of them, in any of the other books?"

With what was a mental shout, I sat up and pointed at the green books.

He snatched one from the shelf, opened it, and after a few moments, a grin split his cute face nearly from ear to ear.

"I know what this is. It's gotta be! Fucking awesome!"

I leaned forward in interest. Without looking up, he slid his fingers down the columns of numbers. "It's the legend to the cyclic permutation! Fucking wicked shit from World War Two!"

He looked up at my confusion. "They used it to carry messages, because it's a one-time use code! It's unbreakable without the key!" He set the book down in response to another unspoken half-question and pointed to the first column, which to me looked like nothing more than a weight measurement.

125 lbs, October 22, 2008.

"Four numbers," he said, "one twenty-five, ten, twenty-two, and two thousand eight. Now cut 'em in half, so the four numbers are in two separate columns."

I kept nodding even after he'd already gone on.

"The first two," he pointed, "one twenty-five and ten. Does ten divide evenly into one twenty-five?"

I don't know why I even bothered.

"No. The nearest number into which ten can divide is one hundred twenty!" He smiled up at me expectantly.

I'm not a . . .

"Sorry," he pre-plied. "So that means that in order to get a number that can be divided by ten, we have to subtract five from one twenty-five."

He reached into his back pocket and pulled out a notepad and a pen that looked like a syringe filled with blood. I eyed it.

"I know, right, totally cool. Get 'em from the clinic, free like condoms but without the weird looks." He glanced up at me, "Well, *different* weird looks, but who cares, at least they don't wonder about my sexual activities." He turned back to the pad and wrote something down, then presented it to me as if looking for a golden star.

125≡5mod10

I stared at it and probably would have been happier if it was Sanskrit.

He shook his head, harassed. "Mortals," he grumbled, until I thought something at him and he blushed, "oh yeah, sorry. Anyway, so this gives us a number, see. We take that number, five, and count down on the first page in the red books five rows, then we take the second number, four, and count that many words into the row. Bam, first word of our message from Eva."

Stunned, I looked at the many volumes. *This will take . . .*

Jinx heaved a sigh, "Yeah, totally. I'm gonna need to take them . . ."

But Arthur had appeared in the doorway and had a pensive look on his face.

Jinx rolled backward again and stared up at Arthur like a child in his playroom. "You're shitting me."

Arthur crossed his arms.

"But the equipment I need is like super heavy and it's already all set up back home!"

Arthur turned away.

"Damn, Art, so not cool," Jinx complained, until Arthur tossed a look back at him and the boy perked up. "You mean it right?!" he shouted, smiling broadly.

"Of course," Arthur replied, his voice drowned out by Jinx's simultaneous mimicry.

Leaping to his feet and dancing in a happy circle, he pointed at Arthur and laughed. "Now Sam's gotta, cuz you *owe* me!"

Wha . . .?

"Espresso! Nectar of the Gods," he yelped and before I could think about saying anything, had disappeared out the door.

Arthur and I exchanged a look, and unable to stop myself, I laughed so hard I couldn't breathe.

"Where . . . on earth . . . did you . . . find him?" I wheezed.

Arthur shrugged. "He found me."

"What is he, like twelve?"

He raised a finely arched eyebrow. "Two hundred, I think."

"No . . . way."

CHAPTER 18

I opened my eyes. I was lying on the couch. The grin already in place, I sat bolt upright and looked at my wrist. It was freshly bandaged and I had not done it. My vision-quest was a success. At my feet, Jinx sat, five books out and open, at a loss without my excellent foreknowledge of the journals.

Our eyes met and I formed the thought.

In instantaneous awe, he pulled out his headphones. "Tight."

I rolled off the sofa and reached for the green legend. Opening it, I set it down and turned to the first page of the first red book. Then I reached into his jacket pocket without any kind of greeting and retrieved his pen and paper. Hurriedly, I scrawled the formula he'd shown me and triumphantly dropped the syringe before it could creep me out even more.

He looked at the formula, grinning, then looked up at me in wonder. "Cyclic permutation code! Fucking sweet!"

Arthur's not . . .

"Fuck, are you serious?" he whined.

I didn't even have to nod.

"God damn it!" He got up and looked at me. "Espresso? *Yes*!"

He turned around and jogged to the door, but at the threshold, waved. "Nice meeting you . . . again, I guess."

I bowed, because we both knew what it meant to experience things twice, but to his ten second sneak peek, I was a prophet.

"I owe you two cokes," we both said.

"Three," he specified gratefully, and disappeared.

Still pleased with myself, I turned and found Arthur standing in the hallway holding the beanbag chair. My smile faded.

"You passed out in the Records Office."

"On *purpose*," I clarified and pointed at the happy face. "What's that doing here?"

"Jinx needs it. I'm not sure what it meant, but when he saw it in the bed of the pickup truck, he shouted something about 'watching the watchmen' and demanded to keep it," he said quietly and put it on the floor. "Since you were going to throw it away, I assumed it would be fine. Is it?"

"Yeah, I guess." I got the reference to the graphic novel, but knew that Arthur never would. "I didn't think about it before, but since he's such a comic fan, it'll probably go well with his action figures."

"So you met. Where did he go?"

"Home, to get his computer, and yeah we met," I held up my hands, seeking recognition, *"in my head."*

Calm as ever, Arthur blinked. "You can control it?"

I dropped my arms in frustration. "Yes! I *used* it! I *am* the *ultimate* spirit ninja!" and I plopped myself down on the sofa, my chin tilted up in smugness that only drew an expression from him that seemed both a frown and a smile at once. "I've also had some sort of realization."

"Oh?"

"I think I can do what Ursula did."

His head came up and around so quickly, I thought he'd heard some hypersonic noise I hadn't, but the look on his face was not worried, it was peaceful, as if he'd been waiting for me to say that.

"I see. How can you be sure?"

"Sam told me his life story."

His eyebrows lifted. "Proof enough. Sam never speaks of his past, even to me. You were not hard on him?"

"No. I'm totally trained in how to be a super-*hero*," I pledged with a nod, "not a righteously vengeful bitch. You have taught me well."

"Taking pride in your flaw only reinforces it." He didn't have to say what came next. The pain in my wrist said it all.

"I learned something," I sulked. "Given my dearth of accomplishments in life, can't we just be pleased?"

He opened the refrigerator, hiding his face from me. "My pleasure means nothing if you are not safe."

Annoyed and feeling bad that I might have worried them, I pulled my hair back and tied it up. "Okay, I get it. Can you tell me *why* I can do it? How is it possible?"

I wanted him to tell me that that wasn't what happened to Eva, that she hadn't sat at Ursula's feet, in rapt attention.

He sighed. "Your transition is unique in my experience. You are very special, my dear."

I shook my head, blushing. "But I'm not supposed to take pride in that, right?"

"The question itself implies the answer."

After a minute, the door closed and a plastic container of food was brought to me on a tray. Inside it was a wonderful salad topped with cheese and cranberries, pasta, and a fruit tart. I suddenly realized I hadn't eaten in a long time and though I knew I should *want* to eat it, I didn't. Politely, I took the food from his hands and forced myself to eat it. When I finished, Arthur took a seat and crossed his arms.

"I broke into AMRTA. It wasn't hard. The security isn't as tight as I thought. A number keypad, motion sensors, and a camera, but I guess if no one can read your treasure and it falls apart at a wrong look, you don't need much security. Either that, or they just want the illusion of security. The code was my birthday, which means Eva spent her time in that room, doing whatever she was hired to do." I chewed another bite, avoiding his face. "It was like a museum, a sealed clean room, with all these moldy, old looking scrolls in plastic boxes. They were written in Sanskrit, I think. Did Eva know Sanskrit?"

"Yes."

I frowned. "Oh. Well . . . then I came here and we cracked the code. Jinx is going to input all the data into his computers and then we'll get our answers."

Arthur was silent for a long time. When I finally dared to look up at him, he seemed blank.

"You're not my father," I said, before I thought about the words, "I don't have to apologize to you."

He raised an eyebrow.

"I'm sorry," I immediately gasped. "That came out wrong! I know you're only trying to help me. I'm sorry! I just . . ." I shook my head.

His lips moved in a tender smile. "I know, Lilith. You do not have to apologize to anyone. Everything means something, right?"

I looked at my feet. There it was again, that subtle correction. He was reminding me without seeming to, that I was fixated on an idea that would spiral into darkness if I wasn't able to control my reaction to it.

Of myself.

I didn't need to apologize, we both knew, but if I didn't keep my grip, I'd end up like Ursula.

"Got it. No blood-drinking. Right."

In his almost silent way, Arthur chuckled. "How many cokes did he get out of *you*?"

"First or second time?" I replied with a smile.

"Both," he murmured in mild dismay.

"Two the first, one the second, but that one was a freebee."

He turned in his chair and struck some hash marks on a running tally he seemed to be keeping. In deference to my newest friend, I pointed at the slashes. "Um, you promised him espresso."

Turning back, he blinked at me.

"He'll be expecting it."

He wrote it in and pointed to my wrist without looking. "Don't do that again."

"Giving me orders?"

"Suggestions. You strained the stitches."

"It doesn't hurt. In my vision," I said without preamble. Now that I saw how he interacted with Jinx, I understood why he had a taste for a lack of prefacing. "Jinx said that he infected himself by studying math."

Arthur nodded. "Do you remember the invisible road to nowhere?"

I thought back to the mall. That trip seemed to have happened so many months ago, but it was only a few days. "Yes."

"He found it."

"Katsu."

"Yes."

"Ah," I rubbed my wrist carefully. "So, what did it for Eva? You never said."

He smiled and pointed to the red books. "I'm sure she told us."

"Do you think," I wondered aloud, "that the Sangha are planning a counter-strike?"

With a deep breath, he bowed his head. "They don't need to plan. They are opportunists with abilities like yours. They will let the pieces fall into place and eventually you will come to them."

"No I . . ." then I thought of the vision. If I hadn't been able to go spirit-stealth at that moment, would I have gone in physically? When I realized I couldn't answer my own question, I buried my face in my hands. "Crap."

He turned away knowingly.

"Sam told me about the man who died downstairs," I revealed, hoping my newfound talent would work on him, but when I put all my concentration into reading his face, feeling the air for the vibrations of a speeding heartbeat, I found nothing. "Who was he?"

"Stop, Lilith. You do not need to interrogate your friends."

My cheeks burned, and I looked at the floor in embarrassment.
"Okay, I won't experiment on you, but I still want to know who he was."

"An old friend," Arthur said quietly.

"Who . . . *found* you?"

"Yes."

"Like Jinx did."

His eyes met mine and searched them. "Yes."

"A two hundred year old immortal ubergeek walks into a coffee shop and you just say, 'wow, how lucky'? Come on," I demanded.

Arthur tilted his head. "He's a caffeine addict. It's not that unlikely."

* * *

The white glow of the computer screens was an eerily attractive compliment to Jinx's personal color scheme. He sat in the coveted beanbag in the dark, peering at the gibberish, scanning Eva's volumes into his hard drive, comparing and inputting all the numbers he'd derived from the legend. He was a tireless typing god and did not ever object to the uncomfortable happy face. I kept him supplied, running down to the café every couple of hours to refill his giant espresso, bound and determined to maintain his state of vibrating quickness. Headphones in, he only looked at me to smile in thanks, and it was in that focus, in the glances of understanding, that I saw his maturity.

He was average height for a grown person of nearly two centuries prior, which meant he was about shoulder height to me and seemed much younger than he actually had been, whenever it was he had achieved Right Liberation. That, combined with his demeanor and syntax, made the perfect camouflage. It was no wonder I could not perceive his true age, but grateful for the composure it gave him, I sat on pins and needles.

Finally, he sat forward and put down his two keyboards, one normal, one a plate of what looked like glass stuck with uniquely arranged preprogrammed keys.

"*Mon dieu*!" He flattened back his spikes like a hedgehog being petted, and then fluffed them forward again with a limp arm. He didn't seem tired, and indeed, I wasn't sure they ever really slept. I knew I did, but then again, as Arthur had said, I wasn't finished changing yet.

I blinked at Jinx. *Done?*

"Not even close," he muttered, sounding as if he had just uncovered, through painstaking, gentle excavation, the tip of a perfectly preserved pyramid of pure diamond. "Where's Art?"

I began the sentence and Jinx gave a nod.

"Yeah, okay. I need to stretch my legs anyway." He got to his feet and reached for the ceiling. When his arms fell, his face was pointed in my direction. Relaxed and seemingly enraptured, he smiled the smile of appreciation for greatness. "Your sister was a genius."

He turned around and went downstairs, leaving me to reason through what he said. I thought back to our youth together. I had been much older than Eva and even though I had just quitted her age, still found her bothersome. Before the accident, she was a sidekick I didn't really want, someone annoying who always seemed to get in my way: making it so that I couldn't go out with my friends, borrowing my clothes for dressup games, crying anytime I looked at her funny. After the accident, she was a stranger that I willingly tried not to think about, even as I grudgingly fulfilled my obligation to her. Had she been a genius all along, desperate for the incomprehensible qualities I possessed? Had she been reaching all along, only to finally give up?

I clenched my fist.

Had her last act been to foster in me the unavoidable compulsion to seek, where once I had been apathetic toward her?

Serves me right.

The two of them reappeared and with a glance at each other over my somber face, took their seats.

"Should we get Sam and Unger?" I asked aloud, for Arthur's benefit.

Jinx plucked the headphones from his ears. "I don't think you're going to wanna."

"Why?"

Arthur looked at Jinx and immediately the boy's eyes widened. "Sorry, didn't realize."

"What?" I insisted.

Arthur turned back to me slowly and with his hand extended, formed a smile on his face that surprised me. It was the kiss before a forceful blow, a look that told me something was coming, and for a moment, I feared what to expect.

"We can't risk exposing them to it," Arthur said quietly.

I looked at the open books, the shadows of code being deciphered slithering across them. "Exposing them to what changed her?"

He nodded and in the silence, the notion struck at my chest like a cobra.

"What about you?" I whispered.

The smile remained as an apology, even as he bowed his head in a plea for forgiveness. My lips moved, but I couldn't form the idea. Scores of conflicting emotions commanded a variety of responses from shouting, to hitting him, to sobbing, to sitting there in shock.

He, Arthur, my friend, was an Arhat.

Jinx was staring at my shaking hands, his childlike eyes round in the darkness. "Lily, it's not *that* surprising. You've known it all along."

I realized only then what he meant. The strange draw I felt toward Arthur, the unshakeable composure, the philosophical banter, and the strange way he seemed to separate himself from the world; they were all signs of his age and wisdom. But if he was one of us, he had to have an ability. As I looked away, my gaze unfocused, I was certain it had something to do with knowing exactly what I needed to hear and saying it in exactly the right way, at exactly the right time. I had thought ours was an immense connection that defied logic or physicality, but all along, it was magic.

I looked into his face in betrayal and the blue eyes looked back sorrowfully.

"Lilith, please don't lose faith in me. I *am* your friend. I swear to you that has always been real."

He seemed to mean it, but it could just as easily have been another enchantment. I looked at Jinx, partly to see what he thought of such a thing, and partly to ascertain if he was under the same spell.

He smiled in support. "He's one of the good guys, Lily."

I shook my head, about to ask him how I could be so sure of that.

"You can *feel* it."

"Does Sam know? Did you tell Eva?" I spat in accusation. "Is that why she . . ."

"Stop," Arthur reached out suddenly and took my hands, looking me in the eye as sternly as he could. It was what I needed to see and hear, but I could find no reason for it to be false. As far as I knew, there was no alternate plot. Arthur had, as he had said, made no demands of me and had only ever tried to keep me safe. He had *no reason* to use his magic on me then, if indeed, he could control it at all.

Uncanny insight, I took a deep breath, *that's why he pushed you away.*

I nodded, sure he was still my friend even if he was not the exotic thing I had needed to break free of my boring life of failures.

Of myself.

When he saw the comprehension and acceptance in my face, he nodded. "Sam knows, though he pretends not to. Eva knew. It was part of what drew her here." He sighed heavily and squeezed my hands. "It was what we talked about, in the alley, the last time I saw her."

"That was you," I breathed.

He nodded.

"Why aren't you insane like them?"

He bowed his head. "Insane is a relative term, I'm afraid. Forgive me. If I had told you everything all at once . . ."

"You would have shit a brick," Jinx paraphrased with a grin in place, ever the comic relief.

I knew they were right. Without seeing what we could be, without knowing what I *had* to be, I could never have embraced Arthur or his quest.

"What's your *trishna*?" I inquired, looking into his face boldly.

"What keeps me here is the *dharma*."

"Spirit ninja," I charged softly.

It was the perfect smile again, and he seemed grateful to give it.

I clenched my hands around his and without a thought, brought the backs of them to my forehead. "Ursula taught me one thing, that the only way to keep from lying is to never have a secret."

Jinx was already shaking his head. "It's not a lie, not if he already knew when and where you'd find out. Then it's just letting it unfold as it should have."

Arthur's face had relaxed. "I will never conceal the truth from you, Lilith. You will find what you need to as you need to. I have more than enough faith in your powers of perception."

I raised my eyebrows, because I could feel the old me reasserting dominance, and the old me couldn't handle too much strain before it attempted to withdraw. I knew it was a character flaw, not being able to set my character aside whenever necessary, but I was no Arthur.

"Not as much faith as I have in yours. I'm freaking out right now."

Jinx began giggling halfway through and crisis averted, turned back to his computer. "Can I pull the curtain off of this motherfucker, before I get lost in the wicked debates that could come from the unique interaction of our varied super powers?"

Chuckling, I nodded, but could not help looking askance at the man about whom I continually discovered I knew nothing.

"Great, so," Jinx launched into his explanation that to an observer, because of his abilities, would have seemed like a lecture, "the gloriousness of a cyclic permutation is that it's cyclic, right?" He turned the monitor toward us and pointed at his scan of the last page in the last book. One word on the page was highlighted in red. "See we could pick one word for each coordinate, in a repeating pattern, or we could go through the whole set of volumes with the first coordinates, right, until we get to the end. At the end, we find that we have three lines left, so we have two choices. We can do an 'aces high or low' and go back to the beginning, counting the first two lines and repeating," his finger dragged across the screen to the first page, and pointed out the word it would indicate, "or we can assume that she meant us to see this as another modulus problem and infer another number for later use."

He looked to us and as always, with his second or two time lapse, launched back in to answer our questions.

"I've done both and both yielded results. That's when I realized there was more to it and figured out which one she intended."

We looked at him. He wiggled in his seat. "We could go round and round and round with the same two numbers, but your sister knew that eventually, they would no longer yield sense. We'd go round until we came back with gibberish. From looking at it, I realized," he picked up the green book and pointed. "The number of commas in each set of numbers shows how many times we cycle through the books with these numbers, and a period indicates that we should stop when we reach gibberish and seek out no more complexity. It tells me to move onto the next set of modulus coordinates."

I blinked again. *So can you . . .* I began to ask.

"Yes, I can read it now, but that isn't the coolest thing," he continued, pounding his knees with his fists to impress his feelings upon me. "The coolest thing is that *any* set of coordinates yields something perfectly rational, but useless."

"That's . . ."

"I know! This code has infinite complexity and to someone who didn't know what they were looking for, it'd be a nightmare! She's hiding the real message in plain sight, because without the key and the right set of eyes, you have *no idea* what message is the one intended."

Everything means something.

He grinned at me. "Do you know how long it would take me to put something like this together with just my head and a bunch of paper and ink?"

My neck muscles tightened to shake my head.

"I don't even know," he anticipated. "I can do it with tech, but to do this old school . . ." he paused and looked at the book in his hand in bewilderment. "What did she study again?"

I wanted to answer, but as before, I couldn't recall.

"She wanted to take care of artifacts and translate pictographs. It was her dream," Arthur said, relieving me of a burden I couldn't possibly carry. "She double-majored in Art History and Linguistics and double-minored in Comparative Literature and Book Arts. That is why it took her so long to finish."

I sat back, utterly broken, two giant sets of misconceptions destroyed in one fifteen minute span of time. In that moment, I knew what a heinous, awful, horrible bitch I was. Eva was amazing, a beautiful person I should have showered with affection, and I had not seen it. I had been so caught up in my own suffering, I never even guessed that she was anything but a failure like me.

Jinx was already shaking his head. "No way she learned that in *any* of those fields," he stabbed the book with a finger. "This is *not* learned behavior. This is fucking *brilliance*. It's gotta be a *gift*!"

I frowned, forcing myself to think of that word, not by its first definition, but by the definition relevant to our world.

"You're saying it was her power?" I said, surprised that he let me get the sentence out.

He turned to his special keyboard and hit a button. The screen changed and in a new window, a document formed from the scattered words. "This is only the first segment of what I believe is the intended message, cycling through the books twice, as directed by the commas, using the first modulus coordinates." He turned to Arthur, "Look familiar?"

For the first time since we began our association, Arthur looked stunned. "The Buddhavacana Sutras," he disclosed quietly.

"It's different from the ones in circulation. These are the *lost* Buddhavacana Sutras," Jinx corrected.

"What?"

The boy already had an elucidation ready. "See, just like the Biblical scriptures of the Christian canon, all the Buddhist texts have been royally fucked by time and stupid assholes who want to include *their* two cents, not to mention interested 'Bodhi Sattva' or Arhat who wanted a piece of the action. Buddha predates Christ by like five hundred years, according to legend, but the oldest texts ever recovered about him weren't written until the first century."

"So, it was all by . . ."

"Oral tradition," he interrupted. "One of Buddha's sidekicks, Ananda, had an idenic memory and could recall all of the words the Buddha spoke. At the First Sangha of the Buddha, Ananda was asked to recite them, and did so from memory."

"*Srotapanna*," Arthur said in a tone of voice that was unreadable. In his perfect accent, the word sounded lovely. "Ananda was the first Stream-Enterer, so called by the Buddha himself. He did not achieve the *jhana*, and thus, right liberation until after the Buddha died."

I watched his face closely, but could find nothing. "You're saying . . ." I prompted the mathematician.

"Ananda recited them and someone from the First Sangha wrote the *Buddhavacara Sutras* down. Over time, the Sangha adapted, translated, altered, and tweaked them, until they were written down by humanity. The originals," he confirmed with a nod, "were kept by the Arhat of the Sangha. What your sister was reading, were the purest words of the Buddha. She infected herself from the source."

My mouth fell open so wide, they could probably see my molars.

"But without guidance . . . hell even *with* it," Jinx said with a whistle, "that's a memeplex that'd fuck *anyone* over. The Buddha should have kept his mouth shut."

"Mem . . ."

Jinx made an annoyed sound and glared at Arthur. "You haven't taught her about memetics? I mean that's from the seventies! Fuck Art, what the hell *do* you read?"

Arthur said nothing. He seemed to be rethinking all his interactions with Eva in blank silence.

Without an audience, Jinx turned back to me, shivering like an eager puppy. "Memetics is just one word for the study of how ideas compete and propagate. It's only become a study in the last thirty years or so, as we come to understand how genes work and the similarities between them and thought processes. Said simply, a memeplex is a group of ideas that work together as a unit, almost like an organism and its constituent molecules."

"Not sure I understand. You're saying ideas are alive?"

"No," he squinted at me. "I'm saying ideas are forced to obey the same rules that govern your immune system, DNA copying, and so on, just like electricity must follow the paths of wires. Thus, they function *like an* organism. If a memeplex can acquire more ideas, or interpretations, or versions of the truth, it grows, and can survive longer in a more hostile environment, can inoculate itself against invasion, can even copy itself into the min of another through association. It mimics the paths of organic life because it's based on the same substrate."

I understood finally, what Eva must have endured. Sitting in that white room, day after day, translating and reading those words over and over, uncovering the imaginary road to nowhere without anyone to point her in the right non-direction. What would it feel like, to be inundated with one rationality-shattering revelation after another? What would she have inferred? What would she have cast aside? And how could she be sure her filtration of the details was even close to accurate? It would have buried her.

Something in my thoughts triggered a memory. I leapt up and yanked the black journal out of its place among it fellows.

"It's a wall that stretches upward, constantly tipping over me like a wave. I see far from beneath it, but it rolls over and I'm blind again. I breathe in dust and drown. I am buried in a fat, breathing, sweating animal that churns as it eats me whole. I sink into its flesh and am incorporated. When I open my eyes again, I see the horizon through the gaze of a universe."

I read it aloud, wondering in the back of my mind how similar our voices sounded, if for Arthur, it was painful to hear. He sat with his gaze veiled, Jinx at his feet nodding in time with words yet to come, experiencing what had to be an epic-sounding echo.

He looked up just before I finished, but waited politely. "Hard core."

"But how could this be her gift?" I demanded, stooping down to caress one of the red volumes. "The gifts come from the desires that are most important to us, our cravings, so if she wanted to be understood, why would her gift be to . . ."

I stopped. Jinx was looking at me, allowing me to repeat myself so that I could work through the mystery. It had worked.

I flipped through the pages until I found what I was looking for. "Even though I never knew what she was thinking, I knew she hurt. Even though we were apart, we were together in sadness. Even though we were different, we were the same. She was tired of being seen. From therapists, to our aunt, to me, she was sick of being asked 'are you okay?' She wanted a mask to keep her feelings from affecting us," I whispered looking at the empty happy face, suddenly wanting to curl up in it for comfort.

"The soul is chipped," I read, *"the days are hammers. They find my weak spaces and pry. They look at me with nails and sharp tools. They chisel me raw. What am I now? They say, 'You are beautiful. You are perfect, faceted and sparkling.' But my beauty was my filth, my roughened splendor, my mystery. They stole it from me to make themselves richer and now, thousands strong, they smile as I reflect them. But my soul is a black stone, an obsidian mirror, and when they tire of deceiving themselves, they will see the darkness of their crude refinement. They will scry and find no future. I am a gateway to nothingness."*

"An obsidian mirror," I repeated. "Something even Ursula couldn't crack. Something they couldn't even break with torture," I wrapped my hand around my wrist. "A permanent mystery."

"That you had to solve," Jinx whispered. "Like the badass cryptographer she was, she built it into the meme she used to infect you. You were programmed to find something that could never be found."

"And uncover everything that could, by accident," I finished. I fell into the beanbag chair and laid the book down reverentially. "Katsu, Ev."

Arthur looked as if he wanted to speak, and Jinx was already smiling at him.

"Go ahead, Art. It's something I don't mind hearing twice."

He bowed his head. "Death is the final obfuscation and now," he looked at me, "you will never expose her mystery."

CHAPTER 19

With the books scanned into his hard drive, Jinx had no reason to stay, and I would soon be alone again amongst the three mature, grounded men. While Sam drove the computer and the bean bag back to wherever Jinx lived, I sat with the boy-like entity in the coffee shop, watching him suck down the last dregs of his payment.

As early morning patrons came and went, I leaned my head in my hand and sighed as obviously as possible. I felt utterly lost and entitled to any guidance that *anyone* might have. If there was no mystery, then what should I do, focus on my current *state*? Did knowing my weakness change it? I had so many questions and it appeared that no one, for whatever reason, wanted to answer them. Arthur seemed preoccupied; Unger was off on a wild goose chase and was not answering his phone; and Jinx, loveable, sweet, too-quick-for-his-own-good Jinx, gave clipped answers that were vague at best.

It was as if Eva had done something illegal in this secret society, and that I was being protected from a world in which I didn't belong. But with nothing to live for back home, I would have preferred being an outlaw instead of a burden.

"I just don't get it," I murmured at the ears deafened by house music. "How can you keep up your energy if you don't eat?"

Really, I was curious for selfish reasons. Since the salad the day before, I had not eaten, nor had any hunger pangs bothered me. It seemed that the change was like an avalanche, small at first, then a sudden, crushing wave of alterations. It was more than a bit petrifying.

Jinx was already smiling. As I leaned forward to tease him about having the shakes, I found myself marveling. In my experience, most people waited for any gap to spit out their own thoughts into a conversation without paying attention to the other person's, but Jinx was an entirely different animal. He may have seemed impatient, but in actuality was listening quite intently, he was just out of sync with my reality. It had to take a great deal of patience for him to communicate with anyone.

"I do eat. I eat this."

"But caffeine only goes so far. There's vitamins and stuff.

"Do you know anything about nanoscale robots?"

I raised my eyebrows and shook my head.

He flagged the girl working the bar and pointed at his cup. She frowned, probably certain that even though he was a guest, he was outstaying his welcome. Jinx rolled his eyes and began jiggling his knee impatiently until the girl nodded and turned away, then he launched in at full speed, going a million miles a minute as usual.

"The body has a natural homeostasis, okay, a balance."

I nodded.

"But it's inefficient at repairing itself. Humans take in nourishment and it gets deconstructed, broken down into its constituent blocks, which are then recombined into the proteins that make up their cells. The less work the body has to do, the more complete your nutrition. In other words, you are what you eat. Excess or broken pieces are discarded as waste, right? Any disruption of this balance results in a breakdown of that cycle. Meaning, that if you lack food, get hurt, or have a mutation in your genes, the whole system grinds to a halt."

"So . . ."

"What if you could recycle?"

I made a face, not wanting to think about recycling my own waste like one of Jinx's Fremin warriors minus his Still Suit.

"Imagine what would happen if you could inject a person with a robot that's only, say, three molecules big."

His eyes slid to the barrista and were watching her move behind the bar as if he was hunting beans. With a smile, I pretended not to notice.

"So because it's so tiny, it can find the pieces it needs to repair itself anywhere, pulling bits from broken pieces, recombining molecules at will. I mean it's only three molecules big, right? It would never break down or be disabled."

I didn't respond. I knew better.

"Now what if the function of the nanobot was to replicate and repair? It would make more of itself, like a virus, spread throughout the body because it's tiny enough to be absorbed through cell membranes. It would do this until every single cell had one like it, and then would forever repair that cell's DNA, thus preventing aging, injury, or any need for outside nourishment. In other words, it would freeze you where you were and make you invulnerable!"

"What does . . .?"

"The bots come from outside you, but," he set down the empty cup in anticipation of the full one and leaned forward, eyes wide, "what if you had such control over your own body that you could halt cellular breakdown by yourself? What if you could take all the broken pieces, break them down, and use them to repair your own anatomy? Fucking awesome, huh?"

I stared at him in consternation. Arthur had confessed that though right liberation could not be unattained, it was *not* true immortality that it could be thwarted, but Unger had confirmed that Ursula was dead. So if their kind . . . *my* kind, were so strong, then how could we be killed?

Jinx began shaking his head. "Got into a wreck on my bike last year. Had to go to the hospital, because I was unconscious. When you're unconscious, you can't focus on your state. Of course, when I woke up, I healed up just fine, so quick they weren't sure what the hell I was. If you had enough concentration, you couldn't be hurt ever, but hey, we've all got flaws." He grinned at me mischievously. "Heard you did a number on Ursula. About time someone wacked that bitch. Guess she didn't ask you if you were ready and able to kill someone. If she had, she would have called security when you told her about stabbing her in the fucking chest."

Surprised, I suddenly felt a pang of diffuse guilt. Surely, she was a murderer, but now that I was becoming like her, I wasn't sure my case was so clear-cut.

"I'm not a very good liar, but I'm pretty decent at not coming up with an idea until about two seconds before I'll need it."

He laughed. "Way to work with what you got."

"So you knew Ursula?"

He shrugged and glanced at the bar again, "Knew *of* her. Couldn't get me to do more than that, not even for all the coffee in Columbia."

"Why?"

Finally, the waitress appeared, holding his new cup on a tray as if she were aiming at his head. His eyes tracked her movements and as she put the thing down, he snatched it up. With an annoyed glance at me, she collected his empty cup and walked away. If Jinx hadn't had a tab, I was sure he could have singlehandedly paid her salary. It was no wonder she was bothered.

"So, Ursula . . ."

"Was *way* cursed," he mumbled, into his cup. "*Everyone* avoided her, except a select few."

"And by *everyone* . . .?"

"I mean all of *us*."

"*Us*, huh?" I muttered and polished off my own coffee.

"The many species of immortal, I mean," he replied, "including all the Arhat."

"Why? I should think you'd be used to freaks and crazies."

"Because she could see," he answered, "not just see the truth, but people's deepest fears and misconceptions. That's power, man, and it's a power that could level worlds."

I wanted to push harder, to get answers, to find out what her story had been. What was the source of her enmity toward Moksha? Had she been a liability? Was Moksha happy to be rid of her and thus had no quarrel with me? Would I hear from AMRTA again, or be forgotten? I hoped it was the latter, but a voice in the back of my mind was replaying my visions, and I knew that there was more to come.

The boy across from me would never say anything, I knew. After letting Arthur's secret slip, I was sure he had probably already cleared what would and would not be discussed. I could see it in the way his eyes kept flicking over my shoulder to the bindery, in the lack of specificity, in the way he kept trying to divert the conversation. But who was Arthur to dictate anything? I was grateful for his protection and guidance, but if what Eva had done to me was irreversible, then how long did he really think he had before I needed to know?

A gun in the hands of someone who didn't know how to use it was almost twice as lethal as a gun held by a sharpshooter. Not only that, but hadn't I shown myself completely capable of dealing with weird and extraordinary things?

He slurped at the coffee contentedly, his eyes half-lidded. "You shouldn't be so upset. Your *trishna* is knowing, so embrace ignorance and be free."

With a good-natured glare at his cup, I raised my eyebrow.

"I know," he grumbled. "I'm a huge hypocrite, right?"

"If I slit your wrist, will you bleed brown sludge?"

"I know, right? But hey, we gotta fuel ourselves with something."

"But," I began.

"Mitochonrdria gotta burn fuel! I'm just way more efficient. If I wasn't *this*," he gestured downward at his body, "I'd die of malnourishment, and happily too, I might add."

"So what happens to all the liquid?" I asked with a laugh.

He was chuckling. "Look I didn't say we didn't occasionally use the bathroom to rid ourselves of impurities."

"Psychic powers, clinical immortality, but still has to know where the nearest toilet is."

He made a face.

"So how do I jump on the anti-death bandwagon?" I prodded, holding out my damaged wrist in order to garner sympathy.

His eyes darted to the ditch door.

"Jinx," I scolded.

He grimaced in what looked like physical discomfort. "Aw come on, Lily. Don't!"

"You don't think I deserve to know?"

He fluffed his spikes and looked for Arthur, then dropped his voice, "You don't know *anything* do you?" At my fixed stare, a look of pity transformed his features. "Nothing? He hasn't told you . . .?"

"No!" I looked over my shoulder, determined to learn how to meditate as effectively as they did. "He didn't even tell me *he* was one of them, so what makes you think he'd be offering a tutorial on how to auto-heal? You're honor bound to help an injured fellow."

Skeptical, Jinx set down his cup, something he almost never did unless he was focused. He shook his head, mouth open, for once, unable to find words. After a few goldfish gulps, he reached up and took out his headphones.

"He has to have a reason," he whispered.

"Why does he have to have a reason, and why should his reason matter?" I lost him around the first "why"; he was staring into space. "I am so *over* . . ."

"Don't . . ." he interrupted, his eyes darting upward, "don't say it."

"Why?" I demanded, my arms crossed.

The dark eyes set in the youthful façade seemed to finally look their age.

"He's my friend."

"Mine . . ."

"So why are . . ." I tried to interrupt to explain that by keeping me in the dark, he was making a preposterous demand of me, and that violated the ideals of friendship as laid down by Arthur himself, but Jinx talked over me, already prepared, "with your limited knowledge, how can you possibly know what you should or should not understand?"

My mouth fell open. "It's *my* . . ."

"Do you want to end up like *her,*" he insisted, "torturing the truth out of people as if it mattered?"

"Well . . ."

"Then just chill!"

Stunned, I sat back and looked away. Suddenly, I didn't like Jinx so much. He reminded me of my first grade teacher and her quest to make me stop dotting my "I's" with hearts. Disgruntled and more than a little betrayed, I got up and snatched his coffee cup from the table. Before he could say anything, I had finished it and replaced it.

"You first!" I turned to walk away, but his gloved hand shot out and took hold of my unblemished wrist. When I looked back, I found him staring at the open window of the bindery in hesitation.

"Wait . . ." he heaved a sigh and stood up. "You're right. If he didn't want you to know, he'd never have left you with me. I'm shit for secrets. Not as if I wanted to keep them. They fall into my brain just before people's better judgment intervenes."

"And you can't keep them because your mouth runs faster th . . ."

He rolled his eyes, "Thanks, Lily, I feel better already."

I looked at his hand, still holding my wrist, and then back to his worried eyes. "You gonna do something, or just hold my hand, kid?"

He twitched in place like a child doing the potty dance. "Shit!" he hissed and without any further commentary, tugged me toward the front door. The bell rang above our heads as he cursed at me in a stream of expletives the likes of which I'd never heard. At the curb, he halted and rounded on me, gesticulating wildly. "He's gonna know! I mean it's not like we're anything more than allies, but fucking cockmongers, Lily, I want to *stay* allies!"

I blinked at him, taken aback. "Jinx, are you . . .?"

"No!" the boy denied with a huff. "Arthur's the nicest person ever. He'd never do anything to me."

"Yeah, but . . ."

He waved me silent. "There are some things you can't learn by listening, some things you have to figure out on your own. That's just the way it is!"

I nodded, willing to allow him whatever freedom he needed to make amends with the idea of defying Arthur's plans for me.

He was battering my face with glances, beginning phrases that he cast aside, moving his hands as if there was something he wanted to explain, but by the very attempt, would fail to express. Finally, he dropped his arms and stood looking at me.

"Fuck it," he grumbled. "Come on."

"Where are we going?"

"You'll see." He tossed a wave at a lime green and black motorcycle parked in the loading zone that looked like it could be *very* fast.

"Nice ride. Is it a Ninja?"

He smiled, but it was clear he was still upset. "Put this on." He threw me a helmet so sleek it almost looked like a giant Magic Eight Ball.

I shook it. *Am I going to die in a fiery crash?*

"No," he muttered as he straddled the seat. "I've had a motorcycle since 1956. The crash wasn't my fault."

Three weeks ago, I'd been standing in my living room, divorce papers in hand, looking around at my house and hating it for its stability, lamenting that I had never gone on some grand adventure. Now I was riding on motorcycles with immortal hackers and uncovering age old conspiracies. Shaking my head, I sat behind him, wrapped my arms around his tiny waist, and squeezed.

"Can't we take my car?"

With a lurch, we sped away from the curb and down the street. The cool, early morning air felt good to my skin. I'd been cooped up for days in a heightened state of stress, and it felt freeing to be flying through the city, a hair's breadth away from danger.

I expected him to drive us out to the older buildings, to a warehouse like Ursula's hovel by the meat packing plant, or to an abandoned building that he and some squatting friends had tagged up with neon, but he made for the heart of the residential district. The farther we got from the river, the nicer the houses seemed, until we found a golf course and a huge mansionette surrounded by a gate.

The iron grating rolled open as we neared and tiny black security cameras followed our progress. The long circular drive was full of motorbikes of varying ages, some antiques in mint condition. He stopped in front of the large wooden door, and the bike coughed politely into silence.

"So, this is my crib."

I took off the helmet. "Isn't this . . .?"

"Gouache and so not me? I didn't want to build here, but it was the only area with a new power grid. A total necessity."

I looked at the palatial, Spanish architecture and chuckled. "I expected modern, glass, and at least one life-sized replica of C3PO."

He blinked at me in shock. "Since when do you have geek cred?"

"I know, right? I keep it in my utility belt."

"And I keep the life-sized *R2D2* in my study," he snickered, leading the way inside. "It's a kickass trashcan."

We passed into the circular foyer, wrapped around by the large spiral staircase. At the very next doorway, the entire house changed. The common areas were filled with memorabilia, posters, and as he had claimed, action figures. From varying eras and canons, his collection lined walls and sat in mounted shadow boxes. It was like a science fiction museum, cooled down to mandatory temperatures and lit with funneled natural daylight from above.

I looked around, impressed. It was definitely the exact opposite of Arthur's monastic existence. It was obvious Jinx knew how to invest and indulge his every *trishna*. Something in me went all maternal and shook its head at him in adoration.

"How old are you again?"

He narrowed his eyes and put on his headphones. "Shut it."

"No, don't get me wrong, it's really . . ." I followed him through the living room that was really a home theater with a giant projector screen, "amazing."

Jinx looked over his shoulder at me in disbelief. "Yeah, right, and you're just dying to move in with me."

"Do you have friends over often? Lots of little D and D . . ."

"Kiss my ass."

The beanbag was sitting on the floor beside the coffee table, smiling up at me in what seemed like contentment.

You fit right in.

We walked through a darkened doorway and into what must have been a den. It was noticeably colder than the rest of the home and surrounded with free-floating glass shelves wide enough to house all of his electronics. The walls painted black with what seemed to be chalkboard paint, a shelving unit with innumerable CD cases, and the multicolored wires and cables stuck in bundles beneath the desks were all perfect accents.

"I don't know, I could see myself here, but my room would have to be a little more . . ."

"Why do people always use the word Zen to describe décor?" he grumbled. He collapsed into a rolling chair designed to look like the captain's chair from the Enterprise, and slid across the stone floor to a bank of monitors. The computer from Arthur's sat on the floor and while he reabsorbed it into his setup, I stood watching him. "A truly *Zen* house would be a dirt floor and a bohdi tree to sit under."

"Ha! I think they're talking about the Shinto-inspired rock . . ."

"Yeah, but what does that have to do with anything Zen?"

"Composure confining nature without breaking it or something like . . ."

"Yeah, but," he sat up and flipped several switches and the machine hummed back to life aside its fellows, "why limit, why edit your existence? What's the point of living forever if you can't immerse yourself in life?"

"True, but your bedroom is a place to . . ."

He looked up at me sardonically. "I don't sleep."

Laughing, I sat down on a cubical ottoman positioned right next to the robot trashcan. "Okay, yeah. I just thought that all of you enlightened . . ."

He was already scowling and held out his gloved hands. "Okay, let's just get this straight. I'm not a Buddhist, I'm a mathematician. Yes our memeplexes overlap, but we're not the same. We're totally different species. And secondly, there's no such thing as *enlightenment*, it's a myth."

I opened my mouth.

He smeared his face and spun away to turn on his vast array of monitors. "Wow, you're ignorant."

"Gee thanks, Jinx, I feel . . ."

"Do you know anything about oncology?"

"You . . ."

"So when a cell mutates, and then divides, the cell it creates will be mutated. Then that cell will make mutants and so on. Tumorgenesis is a domino effect of one mutation leading to further mutations until the cells have no utility whatsoever. Metastasis is when that mutation spreads, so that it's possible for you to have liver cancer in your lungs, or anywhere in your body."

I frowned and folded my hands in my lap. "What does that have to do with . . ."

"That's how it happens."

I looked at his face, suddenly the very picture of maturity, despite its odd framing of blue and the shiny smattering of metal studs.

"There's the source and then there's the mutations that come from it, because no matter how hard we try, we can't keep the ideas from changing." He perched on his captain's chair and stared into space. "It's because they're all different. No one thinks the same, no matter how similar. That's the curse; a good idea is only good for the person who thought it first, for everyone else, it's a knockoff."

I almost felt as if I should whisper, the air was suddenly so tense. The computers droned, the air vibrated, and in that audible silence, my nervousness grew.

"So . . ."

His little chin rested on his knees and his eyes slid to me. "I feel sorry for them, in a way."

I managed to look curious.

"The Arhat."

"Why?"

He opened whatever program he was using to decode Eva's books. The text yielded by the first set of modulus coordinates glowed on one of the flat screens. With a few quick taps, he set it to work picking out the sense from the noise. "They just don't get it."

"I wish I got it," I mumbled. "I have no idea why Arthur's protecting me. You all don't seem too bad off, so what's up?"

He shook his head seriously. "If I tell you what I know, you won't be much better off. In fact, you may be worse."

I raised my eyebrow comically as if to tell him that I was already quite sure of that fact. "Just tell me what it means to be infected?" I thought of the flaky scrolls in their hermetically sealed room. "Why would they let her read the Sutras if they knew she'd . . ."

"That's obvious," Jinx muttered. "I get it, why don't you?"

I glared in his general direction, intending to swear at him in exasperation. "Arthur . . ."

"Doesn't tell me anything," Jinx explained, still working over Eva's documents. "What I know, I've figured out while doing odd jobs for him or researching for myself. He's as much a mystery to me as he is to you."

My mouth fell open, but not in any unspoken phrase. I just stared at him in wonder. "But . . ."

"I said we were allies, but I didn't say we told each other everything. It's a mutually beneficial relationship. I do my thing, he does his, and sometimes those two overlap, because I agree with what he's doing. I mean, it isn't every day you meet someone who distrusts even their own kind."

"Then . . ."

His finger stabbed the keyboard as if to shut me up. "Five years ago, I was on my way south. I stopped in the coffee shop and there he was. I've been helping him off and on ever since."

"Why were you . . .?"

His eyes narrowed. "I had another thing I was doing."

"Thing?"

"I was heading toward a coven in . . ."

I snorted. "Coven? So what, now we're all Anne Rice fans or . . .?"

"Hey, that's what they call *themselves*; they're not Arhat, so whatever. They wanna be posers, it's they're business. I just hook them up with networks and shit. Do their webpages."

My snort evolved into chuckling that I tried to keep hidden. "You're the vampiric tech support department?"

"Fuck off." He glowered at the screen as if determined not to speak, but failed miserably. "I have skills. I'm unique."

"I'll say."

"I'm infamous. I've got a rep."

I refused to say what he knew I was going to. "So how many . . . memeplex . . . immortality cancer thingies . . .?"

"There's only a few." He began scrolling through her list of coordinates, as if trying to plan out how he'd attack her problem, jotting notes on a mechanical pad that scrawled onto the monitor at my right with whatever color he decided to use. "The Sangha are the largest, by far, but there are even a few smaller groups of Arhat, which is why we draw a distinction."

Amazed, I leaned even farther forward. "How many math-based . . .?"

"We're all self-infected. There's this other guy in Germany. Two dudes who travel around Asia. Probably a few more, but who can say? We're kind of solitary, asocial. Closest we get to a Sangha or coven is a comic book convention."

"Where are you from originally?"

"France."

"Like the Coneheads' France or . . ."

"I have blue hair because I like the way it complements my skin," he grumbled. "I'm not an alien."

"Have you," I hesitated and tried to come up with better verbiage, "*infected* anyone?"

He looked up at me, insulted. "Um, no. Duh."

"But you know each other when you meet?" I tucked my arms and legs up into a ball and peeked over my elbows at him. "Is it like the Highlander sense?"

He glanced at me skeptically, but it was obvious he wanted to laugh. "You're a closet nerd, right? The chick who dates the popular guy, but in the right company is always the first one to admit she Tivos anything starring Scott Bakula?"

I giggled. "I just liked the story. It was romantic."

He shook his head as if trying to dislodge his growing smile. "I bet, immortal man falls in love with woman, continues to love her after her death, is haunted by her memory, all set to the dulcet tones of Freddy Mercury. Who wouldn't? No wonder you're all over him."

"All over who?"

His childlike face smoothed into a wry askance.

"We haven't even done anything," I insisted like an eighth-grader.

His eyebrow ring jiggled.

"Did he say something to you?"

Jinx snorted. "You're totally smitten. It's *so* obvious."

"Jealous?" I shot back.

The boyish face scowled at me suddenly. "No!"

"What, don't swing that way, funny how you're blushing and fall right in line wh . . ."

"I'm a mathematician," he spat, "I don't swing *any* way. Art just . . . has a way . . ." as he trailed off in the vague confusion of a person trying to recall what had happened to them under hypnosis, I nodded, sympathizing completely.

"I think it's his gift," I said quietly.

"I know," the boy muttered, "but knowing that doesn't make me immune."

I sighed, in complete agreement. "Who says I want to be immune? I'd settle for a good . . ." he held up his hand to stop me, making a sickened face, "but he's celibate."

"That's common," Jinx said with a nod. "Doesn't have to be. We can have kids just like normal people, but most of us have seen how bad it is for others to associate with us."

I watched Eva's sentences line up like soldiers called to ranks on his monitor, turning from a jumble of stanzas into the alien tale of a man on a mission to attain perfection. In my periphery, Jinx sat, tapping keys, doing whatever it was that he did so uniquely. I wanted to just get it out there, line up all the facts like ducks to be shot down, but I had absolutely no idea if my assumptions meant anything. I opened my mouth and he glanced my way.

"I know you think that, but it really isn't glamorous or romantic in any way! Lily," he put his hands together as if he was about to pray and turned his chair toward me, "the meme the Buddha began destroyed the capacity for cogent thought. It made flaws in perception evident, which is something the human brain can't handle, since it works *because* of those perceptions. You shouldn't be surprised to find that the majority of the Arhat are completely bonkers."

I shook my head slightly, still not seeing it, and in desperation, he reached out and grabbed my hand.

"They attended a class, were told that the grade would change their lives, then the teacher disappeared and left the test behind. They are trapped there, always failing, missing the last answer, and will never find it."

I looked at his hand distantly, knowing exactly what it was like to feel an unavoidable sensation that something was missing. "Am I going to go nuts too?"

I lifted my gaze to his and was surprised to find the dubious expression. "I dunno," he whispered. "Hope not, but if Eva did, then . . ."

"Not much hope, I guess. When I get there, put two in my skull like I clawed my way out of a casket, okay?"

"No. You can be okay, if you try." He let go of me. "You just have to find it for yourself, or you'll be trapped too. They know that, that's why they hired Eva. That's why they haven't come for you."

He looked into my eyes until it was clear I was *not* going to look away, that I *wanted* to understand the meanings.

"Error correction," he said with a heavy breath, "that's what they want. They have tried to find the solution to the riddle, but I can track their failures, about forty years back. They've been trying for so long without success that I think they're going to employ another strategy, and given what they have to work with, it's no surprise."

"Trying what?" I rasped. I was sure that at any moment, he was going to clam up and return to the code of silence, but it seemed he was a species distant enough to not care about our laws.

He turned in his chair and brought another terminal to life. On the screen was a newspaper microfilm image dated several decades earlier. He swiveled the screen to me and anxious, I read. It was something of an obituary, annotating the young man's life, detailing his exceptional college career in languages and his strange downward spiral into depression and suicide. It told of his drinking, of the strange cuts on his wrist, and most importantly, of his stroll into traffic. My eyes fell to my lap.

"Detective Unger . .?"

"I've sent them all to him, on Art's orders" Jinx murmured, careful not to startle me. "There's about twenty in all, but based on the dates, I'm almost certain there's more that have been covered up."

My throat ached and suddenly it was a struggle to swallow. "I don't understand."

"They're manufacturing a cure," the creature across from me replied gently. "They hire a person to translate their supposed historical finds, in hopes that that person will incorporate the ideas therein. Inevitably, they do, and in each circumstance, they turn."

My wrist pulsed and with a careworn glance, I found it oozing again. "And then what? Why do they all commit suicide?"

"We don't know that they do, but it seems like quite a few have. The rest could have been the Sangha disposing of the evidence."

He brought up another article, this one from the turn of the century about a man who had apparently drowned, and while I sat in mute shock, staring at the picture, he receded into his chair.

"Whatever the Sangha does to their subjects in order to extract their cure, seems to scramble their minds. Either that, or their brains were already scrambled. That's all I can figure."

"So . . ." my eyes remained fixed on the image. His hair was different, his clothing like a slide from a stereoscope, but that wicked, apathetic smile was the same, "they put the source meme into a person's hands, wait and see what happens, swoop in like the fucking Gestapo to gain information, fail, and then torture them? It doesn't make sense."

"Sure it does."

He followed my gaze to the monitor and with a click, resurrected another picture from the past, but not just any past, *my* past. It was an image I'd been sickened by from the moment I first saw it. The car twisted like warm pretzel dough, the sparkling auto glass scattered on the pavement like rock candy, the splatter of blood over which the photographer had probably salivated, and in the background, a crowd of people. "Local historian and wife die in drunk driving accident," the headline read, and in the caption, "Robert and Susan Pierce are survived by two daughters." The mouse directed my attention to a grainy corner of the crowd and with a few waves of mechanical wind to ruffle the pixels into place, I saw what he wanted me to see.

That same fucking sleazy face.

"Lily," Jinx whispered, "Moksha killed your parents and brought your sister here. She was a lab experiment to fix them."

"That's impossible!" I exclaimed, even though I could see the proof myself. My experience with the careless hand of Death had taught me that destruction was random, that nothing was fair. Life was organization and death was a scattering of pieces. The very act of living made the chaos of death unacceptable to me, and the notion that such disorganization was according to someone's plan, was equally unacceptable. I couldn't believe in God for that very reason, so why should I grant the Sangha any power in my life?

"It's not impossible on our timescale," Jinx insisted politely, giving me enough time to say such a ridiculous thing, simply because he knew I needed to. "He made sure that all the therapists, advisors, and mentors she encountered were his agents, and when the time was right, and she was prepared, he snatched her up. He's just their recruiter, going around finding the right type of person. She was just one of many and he's gotten so good at it, I'm tempted to think she was the last."

"Last what?" I gasped. My skin crawled with uncanny awareness as I stared into the smug expression, frozen in time just like its owner. "What are they trying to achieve?"

"Another Buddha to teach them the final lesson."

Winded, I sucked air in great gasps like a bellows. My vision began to darken, and I knew that if I didn't get a hold of myself, I was going to pass out. It was all just words, surely. I could push them away and be objective, I was sure, but the feelings wouldn't let me. Like ghosts they swarmed around my mind, until the anxiety became the only calm place in the storm.

"How do you know this?"

He looked away from me. "Your sister had this article in one of her journals. Art found it. He asked me to research it."

"Why?" I demanded in a broken voice, fighting for consciousness. "Why didn't he tell me?"

"Eva figured it all out, and even though she believed she wasn't the cure, that doesn't mean she couldn't see who could be. You're pure, infected but unschooled, standing in the stream, finding your own way across just like the Buddha did. Art couldn't tell you anything, because any influence he has over you destroys whatever change you're capable of making. You're the cure, Lilith. It's you. At least, that's what *they* believe . . . I think."

I shook my head adamantly, unable to speak. His face tilted toward me as if he couldn't quite make out my thoughts for the first time and was trying to listen. In his eyes was the look of keen scientific interest tempered by his sympathy. It was obvious then, that whatever leap of logic I was meant to make, I hadn't.

"Arthur . . ." I attempted, "why would he . . .?"

"Lily," he replied soothingly, "he's one of them too, remember?"

CHAPTER 20

"Have you talked to him about it?" Unger asked me, and to my surprise, his voice sounded more like a mediator than a pessimistic cop close to retirement with nothing to lose.

Annoyed with him, I spun in Jinx's captain chair, wishing I could command that photon torpedoes be aimed at the coffee shop. "No! I don't want to talk to him! You were right and I didn't listen to you. I feel like such an ass!"

On the other end, his voice broke up in the bad reception.

"What?"

"I said, are you sure?"

"First you tell me not to trust him and now you're taking his side? What the hell, Unger, you leave your balls at his place?"

The man grumbled and I could hear the crackling of his police radio. "Well . . . maybe I was wrong. Lilith, this goes farther than I can see. The evidence in those cases Jinx gave me doesn't even exist anymore. I've done as much research as I can, but I'm stumped. Arthur is the only one who knows what he's talking about and . . . well . . . so what if he was using you?"

My mouth fell open in horrified shock. Was everyone losing their minds around me? Why was I the only sane one when I was the one who was supposed to be going nuts? Then again, like my mom had always said, when everyone around you seems nuts, maybe it was you.

"I mean . . . he's trying to save his . . . I don't know . . . people?"

I swiveled the chair again. Jinx came through the door, blue plastic glass with swirly straw in hand, sucking at what appeared to be another energy drink. I frowned at him and wiggled my fingers. With a petulant scowl, he did an about-face and disappeared to uncover a shiny cylindrical treasure with which he was willing to part.

"So what? I'm *so* not thinking of helping them out."

"Well, it's not like Arthur's going to hand you over to them," he replied in an aggravated tone of voice.

"What the hell?" I gasped. "Since when are you his best friend?"

"I'm not, but he already said you'd go to them. If he's in on their conspiracy, then maybe he's there to teach you to be more generous."

Insulted *and* shocked, I made faces at Jinx's monitors. "Are you trying to tell me something, Unger?"

"Just that you could try and see it from his perspective?"

"You know, I just remembered that my car's a rental and that my plane tickets are non-refundable."

He was on his way somewhere, his attention on his driving, either that, or he was thinking about what he would feel at my departure, though that hardly seemed the case.

"Huh," he said mirthlessly, "I forgot you live in California."

"Me too, but like I said, I'm starting to remember."

The car pulled into wherever it was going and the engine cut off. In the silence, his voice seemed much louder. "So you're going to drop all this? You're just going to leave when you're in this deep, when everything's this fucked up?"

I sighed. "No." Jinx reappeared as I spun in a lazy circle. A metal projectile was hurled at my face and a thumb jabbed me out of his seat. Instead of sitting sidecar, I got up with my energy drink and wandered toward the stairs. "I know I can't leave. I know he's the only one who can explain anything, it's just that . . . well . . . he's *not*. So far everything I've learned about what's really going on has been from Jinx and Eva, not Arthur."

"That's not true."

"Yes it is. He only told me things when it was inevitable that I would find out, when I absolutely had to know, or when he thought I might run away from him. I'm tempted to stay here and ignore him completely out of spite."

"Maybe go look up Moksha when you start sprouting fangs, and ask after their dental plan?" Unger muttered sarcastically, trying to show me how my logic would doom me to the fate Arthur had foretold.

I stormed up the stairs vengefully, thinking of that damn stair-climber in my bedroom back at the house, and marched down the hall in a rage. "Yeah, you know what? Maybe I will. I mean, what the hell? I know I'm not going to cure anyone, so why not just walk right in and say 'here's your next failure, jackasses'!"

I halted outside an open doorway. What lay beyond the threshold had to be an entire store of carefully sorted video games. Eyebrows raised, I backed away and with a shake of my head, found my nerves were cooling off in spite of me, thanks to Jinx's humorous influence. I popped open the can while Unger gathered his belongings, muttering curses under his breath at my rashness, and sipped at it, marveling that the stuff reminded me of Flintstone vitamins in a weird way.

"You don't want to do that, Lilith," he admonished. "They're not shy about killing people, in case you hadn't noticed. I've been learning all kinds of crap about these guys, thanks to Arthur's guidance."

"Like what? And when did he 'guide' you?"

"For your information, he called me on my cell."

"What the *hell* is going on? Am I in the twilight zone?"

He sighed. "AMRTA is just a front. There are so many shell corporations and false accounts here, that I'd need ten forensic accountants and Elliot Ness to even find where it begins. Whatever they're doing, it's a sure bet they're not just doing *one* thing, and I'm almost positive that they're not just doing it here."

I continued to shake my head and opened another door. It was a bathroom, a very nice, *large* bathroom that seemed cut from one giant slab of dark green rock. It was bigger than my bedroom back home and while I stood in the dry rain-shower, I momentarily pondered the adage that money couldn't buy happiness. It seemed to me that four hundred thousand dollars could definitely buy me *some* happiness, in the form of a giant Jacuzzi tub.

"Wow, Matthew, you almost sounded . . . I dunno, inspired. Getting back your detective lust? Gonna start ending your sentences with 'see?'?"

"Ha," he mumbled, "that was a gangster."

"Shut up. So, it's a big conspiracy, then? Jinx said there were more groups of Arhat than just the Sangha." I trotted down the corridor, opening doors at random, not entirely sure what I was looking for, feeling like a hero in a story, trying to locate that one magical item that would solve all my problems.

"It's amazing what a badge can get you, but honestly, Jinx probably knows more than I do. He's the hacker, after all." The car door opened and with a grunt, Unger got out. "Hang on." I heard the phone jostle, heard Unger turn off the speakerphone, heard the shuffling of papers as he juggled everything and kicked the door shut. At the slam, a car alarm blared right beside the mic.

Annoyed, I tugged the phone away from my ear. "Jesus, Unger, are you trying to make my headache worse?"

"Sorry." I heard his trunk open as the alarm continued to drone. "I didn't know about your parents until today either, before you bitch me out for that too. I called the Fresno County PD and had them fax me the reports, and by all accounts, there wasn't anything wrong with their car. It *was* an accident."

"Right, the same kind of accident that made me walk right into that fucking coffee shop! What about the drunk driver? Was he even drunk?" I growled, throwing open another door. It was dark beyond. I smoothed my hand over the wall, searching for a switch.

"According to the file his blood alcohol level was about twice the legal limit."

"Sure it was. Begs the question how he navigated the freeway onramp, huh?"

"With your kind of abilities, there's no way to know how much was planning and how much was chance, but honestly, I'd be tempted to believe the kid. I've learned recently to never take my own knowledge too seriously."

In the background, the alarm continued to grate on my last nerve.

"Where *are* you?" I demanded, finally touching the switch.

"Parking garage at the station. Marks always sets this damn alarm so low. Fucking kids think that having money means a new car every five fucking years."

Bright light temporarily blinded me and I blinked. In the fluorescence, I looked around and found an almost identical copy of AMRTA's records room, in miniature, but its white walls were stuck with thousands of pictures. Names were scrawled across thick, black lines drawn to connect the portraits, and each had a list of details beneath it. On the underlit drafting tables sat all kinds of documentation, an entire storehouse of knowledge organized into neat piles.

Something pulled me inside. My ear no longer heard the screaming car alarm or Unger's persistently logical voice. Instead, my thoughts were warped and twisted by a feeling. I knew where I was meant to go, because going anywhere else would not be right. I walked past the tables stacked with life stories, ignored all the evidence of their world, *my* world. I went straight for the photo and its place in the gridwork.

A stalwart me in tomboy fashion, seated on the fulcrum of a seesaw, my arm across her petite shoulders, her face toward me in a smile of admiration, framed by those pretty blonde swirls that had darkened somewhat with maturity. She wore a pink gingham summer dress and matching sandals. It had been hot that day in the park, and after that, we'd played on the Slip'N'Slide until the sun went down.

I reached out and ran my finger around her tiny face. "Hey there, munchkin."

I could still hear her giggle, feel that pride from knowing she looked to me for instruction. Now I was there, learning from her.

My, how the tables have turned.

"Huh?" he said, and with the word, the car alarm dropped back into my mind and flipped that metaphorical table upside down, jogging a memory of something that had never really happened. My heart jerked, trying to pull itself from me and rush to his aid.

"Unger, get back in your car."

"What?" he grumbled. "Why, you want me to pick you up?"

"No!" I shouted, the picture and room forgotten. "Just get in and lock the doors!"

His voice changed immediately. "Oh hell . . ."

I heard his feet scuffle, the key ring jingle, and then I heard the crashing sound. Hand to the wall, I shouted his name over and over, but no one answered.

This is my fault.

And then I opened my eyes. Jinx was sitting in front of me in the captain's chair, looking at me as if I had just done something *very* strange. Frantically, I fished in my pocket for my phone and pushed buttons, for some reason unable to focus my eyes on the amazingly difficult operations of my *convenient* cellular phone. Braced and tapping my foot impatiently, I heard myself demanding that the phone be answered, and when Sam finally greeted me, I had never been so happy to hear another voice in all my life.

"Lilith?"

"Sam, something's going to happen to Unger! It's them!"

He was silent.

"Please do something!"

"Where?"

"Garage at the police station!"

"I'm on my way."

He hung up without saying goodbye, and for that I was eternally grateful.

The boy tilted his head in awe and pulled out his headphones. "You just went . . . still."

I hid my face in my hands and knew what would happen next. The fun of having a unique ability had finally worn off and Arthur's admonishment sank into its place.

"Are you okay?"

"No," I mumbled. His fingertips brushed my shoulder and I lost my resolve. Tears fell into my hands and for a few minutes I allowed myself to crumble under the stress I had created by seeking the truth.

"What did you see?" he asked me quietly.

With a sniff and a tremor, I sat up and dried my face on the back of my sleeve. "The room upstairs, with all the photos, what is it?"

He sat back and heaved a sigh. "It's . . . all the information we've dug up." His fingers got tangled in his spikes for a moment as he debated how to say it. "We've been collecting it for the last year or so, piecing it all together."

"To take to the cops?"

"Oh yeah, cuz they'd believe it."

"Then why?"

He pursed his lips and stared at my wrist. "Call it staying organized."

I knew he wasn't telling me everything, but what could I do to make him? Not a damn thing.

"Where did you get our picture?"

Jinx turned back to the computers, plugged something in, and began moving files around. He was avoiding looking at me, busying himself. "I don't know. Art had it."

"He knew, didn't he? He knew what Moksha was planning to do before my sister came here, didn't he?"

He froze and swallowed hard. "I don't know, Lily. I swear."

I looked up at him skeptically and was about to say something rude, which I was sure he already knew, when the phone rang. The caller ID said it was Sam's phone and I answered it instantly, putting it on loudspeaker.

"Yes?"

"He's not here," Sam rasped. "His car is gone, but his phone and his briefcase are on the ground."

"But it's the Police Garage!" I shouted. "How can they let people just wander in and kidnap detectives?"

Sam chuckled darkly, sounding like a rock polisher over the speaker. "I guess they thought it was safe."

"Isn't there any security?"

"Cameras."

Jinx plopped into the captain chair and began typing furiously. Windows opened and closed, but the words on the screen were gibberish to me.

"Hang on." I hit mute. "What?"

"If they're up to date at all, then they'll have digital cameras uploading video footage to a server. If I can access it, then we might see something."

While he did battle with the police department's electronic databases, I went back to Sam.

"Does Arthur know?"

"Yes."

"About me," I pushed, "being gone?"

Sam cleared his perpetually congested throat. "He always knows."

"How?"

"I guess everything means something to him," he rasped. "He's always putting pieces together."

The response chilled me.

"I'll meet you at the shop," I said, and hung up.

"No luck," Jinx sighed in defeat. "You'd think they'd update as fast as the criminals, but I guess not. It's all old school." He stood up and turned to me. "You want me to take you back?"

I nodded dispassionately. It was time to face the music, time to ask Arthur outright to answer all my questions, time to be "of myself".

We rode back, my mind in a considerably different place than it had been on the previous trip. When it had just been my fate to consider, I was fine with giving Moksha and his cronies the finger, but now that Unger was an unwitting victim, I wasn't sure I had any choice.

Those crafty bastards. They had waited until the moment I found out about my parents, until I knew the full scope of their malice, before they acted. That told me several things: they were vicious and uncompromising *and* they had someone working for them who had the similar abilities to mine. Knowing that, should I just walk into AMRTA with my hands in the air? Was there any other option?

Jinx parked in the lot and ran inside ahead of me; I was in no hurry to confront Arthur and my rental car was a tantalizing sortie. I could run, right then, turn my back and walk away, but it did not escape me that Unger had been the one in my latest vision asking if that was such a good idea. I stared at the immaculate blue paint and chrome of my car and wondered what they were doing to Matthew, if there was torture involved, if they had another Ursula lying around handy when they had to interrogate someone. Would they kill him?

I turned to the doorway and found Arthur standing there, his handsome face unusually worried. He said nothing, just took the full weight of my angry askance.

"You should have told me everything," I whispered unevenly.

He bowed his head. "I was being careful for very good reasons, Lilith."

"What good reason would that be; me liking you enough to sit in the same room as you and eat your spoonfed bullshit?"

His eyes fell. "No."

"How long before Eva did a nose dive onto a street corner did you know she would be one of Moksha's experiments?" I spat.

He looked at me, not in surprise, but in sorrow. His voice was quiet, when usually, he said everything in a tone that denied all skepticism. "I tried to save her."

"Why should you be the only one?" I shouted. "Why couldn't you find me and tell me? Why did it have to get this far?"

He was silent, looking at the ground between us as if he wanted to walk toward me, but knew that at that moment, I would just push him away. He was right. At that moment, I was keenly aware that whatever attraction made me seek him out in search of comfort, was probably just a product of his craving to be well-liked or something equally selfish.

"I'm not their cure," I said shakily, "or yours."

He took my accusation without a word.

"They took Matthew because they knew him. They saw him with me twice, at the AMRTA building, at the club. They'll think we work together. If I don't show up, they'll kill him."

"You don't know that," he soothed.

"Yes, I do."

Arthur sighed and lifted his folded hands as if to begin an argument.

"Don't," I said with a wave. "I'm going. I've already decided."

He looked at me, but did not seem upset or worried for my safety. Instead the corners of his mouth were turned upward subtly and his skin was smoothed in complete resignation.

"Take this with you," he replied and with a toss, had lobbed a tiny object on a lanyard to me. "It contains all of Eva's work, translated and deciphered. I believe you will need it."

It was a flash drive the size of a piece of chalk, coated in a rubbery protective layer. It had to be something Jinx had contributed. I put the lanyard around my neck and took a deep breath.

"You're not going to stop me."

"No," he shook his head. "You are very stubborn, and the decision was yours to make."

"Where . . ." in my hand the keys were jingling as the fingers holding them shook, "where will they take me?"

"I don't know," he admitted.

"Will they . . ." I swallowed, "kill me?"

He shrugged, almost casually.

I wanted to be hurt or outraged, but I couldn't. I knew what he was telling me. He wanted me to walk across the river, know what I was doing and accept the consequences. He wanted me to see my own fate and desire to change it. He wanted me to suffer until I could face death and not be afraid.

Accept the dharma.

I blinked. Was it another lesson taught without teaching, or was it part of the plan all along? I couldn't say anymore. He had never asked me to *believe* in him, only to have faith. Faith was the belief in absence of fact, and every fact had pointed me away from him, though I still wanted to stay by his side. It was that desire that hurt the most.

I took another deep, steadying breath and walked to my car.

"Lilith," he called after me. When I turned back, he was smiling. "Do you remember the invisible road to nowhere?"

I think I nodded, because my voice wouldn't function.

"It doesn't really exist," he said with a nod, then turned his back and walked into the building.

I stared after him, hearing her voice again from that phone call so long ago. *"It doesn't exist, Lily, I know."*

I looked at the USB drive as it rested in my hand and wondered what it was I was going to do. There I was again, walking in without a plan, uncertain what to expect, but as bad as that seemed, it had worked once. In a world where the future seemed predetermined and monsters possessed the uncanny ability to know my fears, what point was there in having a plan anyway?

CHAPTER 21

I sat in the AMRTA parking lot as I had before, staring at the building, wondering how much I would never know about the Arhat. How did it happen? A phrase or two, specifically tailored to eat away at a person until the obsession drove them to such intense focus that they somehow managed to cheat death?

I had asked myself the question before, in moments of idle fancy: what would I do if I was immortal? With enough time, the world would run out of things to show me, surely. With enough time, art and evolution would be tainted by pessimism. Humans were all the same, in every era, they had to be, or history would cease to teach us valuable lessons. So with enough time, no matter how pacifistic the Arhat were, I could see them coming to loathe what they had been, even as they longed to be rid of their condition.

How much of what they did was forgivable?

If I walked in oozing hatred, then I would be as much in danger of their wrath as Unger. How had Arthur said it? Ignorance breeds incorrect behavior. Therefore, knowledge should lead to right behavior. Being one of them, I could surely understand their predicament.

I had never been the forgiving type. I held grudges like baseball bats and knowing this, had done as much as possible to never involve myself in disputes. Howard had always called me an impossible nag, the kind of wife that could drive a man crazy with bickering, nitpicking, and constant correction. Now I had nothing left. My rage had gotten me nowhere, my cynicism had been useless, and I could see it quite plainly. My flaws were evident.

This was the ultimate test of the person I had become. People could change, the mind could go back to an earlier state, the flaws or heights we'd achieved could be abandoned at any time. It had to be true, or I was on a long walk off a short pier.

I got out of my car and walked into the building where the security guard looked at me in mild shock. A few moments later, I was escorted by several men to Moksha's office, where he sat in his antique chair with the smug look on his deceitful face.

"Ms. Blake, wasn't it?" he said with a chuckle.

I thought back to the tenets of the Buddhist monks, to the principles of conservation. No matter how right I would be to call the man an unmitigated ass, I couldn't, because in this circumstance, it did absolutely no good and though he may not be diminished by it, I surely would be.

"It's Pierce, actually," I admitted.

His laugh grew a little. "Yes, I know."

"And I know what it is you're doing. I'll stay with you, go wherever you want, but let Unger go. Drop him off downtown." He raised an eyebrow, but I ignored it, kept my expressions from going wild, in spite of my shaky nerves, and held out my phone. "I want proof. He'll call me after you release him. Don't try anything else. I'll know."

The smile transformed into an almost malicious grin. "You're in no position to negotiate."

"I'm not negotiating," I said quietly. "I am asking you to do something kind for me. Put me in your debt. Do it, please."

The brow fell and the eyes narrowed. He looked at me as if confused and disgusted by the state. While he examined my face, I mimicked Arthur's calm, copied his benign way of commanding a room. Though I probably failed miserably, Moksha continued to stare.

"What will you do if I refuse?"

"Spend more time talking with you about the nature of generosity, I imagine."

Something was churning behind his eyes, some kind of outrage or dissatisfaction. The longer I looked into his face, the angrier he seemed.

"If we let him go, how can we be sure we have your cooperation?"

A division was growing in me as I looked at him, the little scheming man in his great tower of glass. The two halves of me, old and new were pulling apart. One side longed to point out, in a snide voice, that if I intended to be uncooperative, I would not be standing there with the flash drive around my neck. The other side of me knew a peculiar enjoyment, as if for the first time, I had stepped back and found the extremes of emotion to be quite amusing. A smile slowly tugged on my face and in my state of assumed calm, I was helpless to stop it.

"A man cannot conceal joy," I said, though I wasn't sure where it was coming from, "because joy undoes deceit. What I have, I will share, because I must. There is no other choice."

While he marveled at me, I did the same. The two halves of me were looking at each other, sizing each other up, and though the new one smiled, the old was not sure what to make of it. I looked down at my chest and saw the little charm around my neck.

I held it out. "This is everything I know, all the information Eva stole. I will give it to you. Now let Unger go, please."

Moksha shook his head, not in answer to my question, but in an emotion akin to disbelief. "I still fail to see how it would be in my best interests."

"If you're not going to let him go, then what was the point of bringing me here?" I asked. "If I am what you think, I would have come eventually. Doing this only pulls you farther from the path and makes you less able to hear what I have to say."

He turned in his chair and got to his feet. With slow, contemplative strides, he found his way to me and folded his hands behind his back. His face reverted back to its grin but his eyes were filled with malice. "What makes you think I care about what you have to say?"

I understood in that moment. I could see that whatever he *had* been, he was no longer a good, pacifistic individual. He liked what he had become, but then again, how could a person with no soul or conscience know what they were missing?

"How old are you?" I inquired softly, no emotion in my words. "You must be young."

He leaned forward, so that his face was only a few inches from mine, and glared into my eyes, trying to threaten me with his proximity, but I was done with being threatened.

"You don't want a cure, do you?" I said, closing my eyes. "You like it here, in your castle, mucking about with other peoples' lives. You're not even one of the real First Sangha, are you? You're just an Arhat, an nth level mutation. I bet I can guess what your *trishna* is, that little hurdle at the end of the race that you just couldn't quite make it over. It was power, wasn't it? Once you achieved your liberation, you fell in love with the power. What insight does it give you?" I opened my eyes to find him leaning back on his heels, stunned, his expression almost horrified. "Can you see people's weaknesses, I wonder? Is that why they chose you to do this?"

Eva wasn't crazy. She wasn't losing her mind because of some irresolvable equation, some unattainable grace. Sometimes when everyone but you was nuts, they were all just nuts.

The heart of Buddhist doctrine was to erase suffering, but in all their long lifetimes, they could not do it, because it was impossible. Like Arthur had said, even if you managed to shrug off attachment, you still suffered on behalf of all the others who had not. To live *at all*, immortal or otherwise, was to suffer, and that was something Eva had loved most about life. It was what reminded her of her flaws, made her work harder, made her fight to stay alive and cherish those few moments of happiness. By embracing misery she had defied them all and unafraid, had crossed the river.

Moksha had been too good for his own good.

"You can see weaknesses, Moksha, but can you see mine?"

I looked him in the eye, completely composed, certain, for no obvious reason, that he would not be able to find a crack in my resolve, that his eyes, however sharp, would never chip away at me. I was an obsidian mirror and he would see only his darkest self.

He took a step back, his throat working in a swallow, his mouth twisting in an approximation of disgust that his eyes could not support. Eventually, he turned away and walked to his phone. He spoke quietly into the receiver and then hung up, slightly put out. I spent almost twenty minutes in silence, watching him avoid my gaze, make excuses not to look at me, actively pretend I was not standing there, seeing right through him.

In my hand, my cell vibrated, and the ID was a number I did not recognize.

"Yes?" I answered.

The person on the other end coughed and when he spoke, he sounded out of breath. "It's me."

With a sigh of relief, I nodded. "Where are you?"

"The café. They dropped me off in the middle of the park. I ran here in case they followed me."

"Prove it," I said quietly.

He didn't ask for a reason. The phone jiggled and I could hear him speaking to someone. Eventually a woman's voice came on the line. I recognized it as the waitress who always tried to insist I have coffee. I asked her for her name, and though she was confused, she gave the right one. When he came back to the line, I was almost too choked to ask after his health.

"They hit me over the head, but I'm okay, I think."

"You know what to do?"

"Yes . . ." he hesitated, "Lilith, where are you?"

"I have to go now, Matthew."

"What? Tell me where you are!" His voice lifted in anxiety. I wondered what he must be feeling, sworn to protect the peace, but saved by a woman who didn't even know how to load a pistol. "Tell me what's going on!"

"I can't," I answered in a broken whisper. "Just stay safe, okay?"

He fell silent for a while and I could almost feel his sickened realization. "Lilith . . ."

"Thanks for being there," I said. "Thanks for having faith and for questioning the facts that got you there."

I hung up before he could protest again and lifted my face to the mastermind of all the tragedies that had plagued my life.

"I'm satisfied."

He had been watching me intently, but when I looked at him, his eyes shied away. He hit the intercom button. "She's ready."

The door opened and some men in dark suits entered. Their gaits were almost silent and they seemed alert. Nothing was said, but in one gesture, I knew I was meant to follow them. They surrounded me and tried to press me from the room, but something in me refused to move. I looked at Moksha, who was staring at my knees in wide-eyed confusion.

"Boredom will eventually set in," I said to him, "and one day you'll be standing still on an island, with no idea where to go, because all your bridges will have burned." His eyes flicked to me, and like Anna's had, unfocused. "The smaller you are, the larger and more terrifying the world. You should not be trying to reduce yourself so thoroughly."

One of the men reached out and pushed me with a glance. I left the room, but for some reason, with all the new things I was about to experience, Moksha's face stayed with me as I walked down the stairs to the side entrance of the lobby. He had seemed so stunned and lost. I wasn't sure why, but I almost wanted to reassure him.

At the doors of the building, the guard asked me very kindly for my belongings. I handed over my phone, my keys, and my driver's license. The man continued to stare at me, but when I saw his eyes flick to the drive, I shook my head.

"This stays on my body. I'll release it when the time comes."

I thought he might protest, but instead, he nodded to the door. Several black cars waited out front and I was directed into one of them. The door was opened for me, and to my surprise, only one man got in behind me.

As the cars pulled away and carried me toward the freeway, I locked the man in one of Arthur's patented faraway, inescapable stares. He looked right back, unbothered, perhaps even curious, and took out the earpiece that connected him to his fellows. What he wanted, I could not guess, but if he was willing to be polite, then so was I.

"Where are you taking me?"

"To the compound."

I nodded, though I had no idea what he meant. "And then?"

He shrugged.

"How far is it?"

"Several hours."

I leaned back and released him. Looking out the window, I thought again of Eva's brilliance and realized how unfair I had been with Arthur. Had my sister somehow infected me with a more sophisticated meme than the one she had experienced? It had taken years for the Arhat of the Sangha to achieve their right knowledge and liberation, but I was already able to force a vision, if I wanted to. Arthur had looked at me strangely when he realized that, and at the time, I had thought it was out of parental concern, but what if it was shock? Perhaps the reason he had not tried to train me in healing myself, was because he believed it was already possible for me to do so.

I looked down at my wrist and the stained bandage. It always seemed to bleed, but it never seemed to hurt. Gingerly, I unwrapped the bandage and looked at it closely. Flexing my hand, I watched the stitches shift and move, but still, felt no pain. An idea struck me. I held it out to my guard.

"Do you have a knife?"

He nodded, hesitantly.

"Cut these stitches," I commanded, and though I expected him to say no, he reached under his jacket, drew a collapsible hunting knife and carefully brushed it against my injury. The sharp blade severed their ties easily, and as they split open, I plucked them out of my skin as if removing worms from the earth. It bled, but much less than I expected and after all of the threads had been removed, I leaned back in my seat, holding the arm cautiously, and stared at the wound.

It could be unconscious, but if that was true, then Jinx would have recovered in his coma. It had to be something I could control, just like the visions. Perhaps, at first, it was just despising the pain that sent it away, and perhaps it was as simple as demanding that it heal for it to do so. I closed my eyes on the broken skin and focused. In my mind, I repeated the phrase over and over, insisting that the wound leave me, that the skin repair itself as it seemed the inside had. I did as I had done in my vision, as Arthur had told me; I grounded myself in the physical, heightened my mind until it saw every beat of my heart or twitch of my nerves. I felt my body completely, and in that state, found the jagged gash across the otherwise smooth arm.

I lost touch with the world, with the car and its softly flowing air conditioner, leather seats, and smooth suspension. I was carried away, deeper into myself, and it wasn't until the car stopped, that I realized something had changed. I opened my eyes.

My guard was blinking from my face to my arm, laying limp on the armrest. I looked down and found the skin as unblemished as it had ever been. There was not even the trace of a scar.

The stitches had been in the way.

The cars ahead of us were emptying. My guard slid across his seat and opened the door for me, but I wasn't paying attention. I was remembering that the M.E. had said Eva's wrist was cut antemortum, and showed signs of healing. If she could do what I just did, then the timeline for her last week was vastly different. What if she had only just left Ursula when she decided to kill herself? What if it was that encounter that told her all she needed to know and drove her to write in an appointment? I had always thought it was the phone call that was important, but what if she had been setting it up for weeks and had picked the date for a reason?

She hadn't given the year in her journal. It was two numbers, two numbers and a single period. August ninth; eight and nine; eighth line, ninth word, beginning on the page indicated by the *trishna* symbol, and terminating when it ceased to make sense.

A message.

"Ms. Pierce," he said.

I looked over. They were waiting, very calmly, and were not forcing me from the vehicle.

Gentlemen kidnappers.

I got out and looked around. We were in the grasslands, and as far as I could see in every direction there was nothing but farmland, yet in front of me stood a massive, modern building like a stack of smooth brown boxes of various sizes. There were other smaller buildings around the property, and it was enclosed by a perimeter fence, but there were almost no people about the premises.

I looked at my guard. "The compound?"

He nodded and held out his arm.

"What is it?"

"A vihara . . . monastery."

"And who lives here?"

"The Sangha," he said quietly. His companions were eyeing me in that same curious way, looking me over as if to assess my fitness. Finally, I was sure that if there was ever a place, aside from a football game, where a lack of makeup, old t-shirt, and torn jeans were acceptable, I had found it. They were probably all psychics, more entertained by my insides. With a nod and a more decisive stride than I felt, I wondered which end of the attractiveness spectrum I was on in that regard. My head was not mucked up by a collection of useless considerations, scattered hopes, or wasted gestures.

Aside from the corner shrine devoted to Eva, I was quite sure it was tidy and that while I was away, the appliances were unplugged, and the newspaper deliveries canceled.

Don't go nuts now, Lily.

I followed them inside and found an entry rather like a hotel's. There was a desk, a collection of ambiguous, inoffensive art, and surfaces that a person could eat off of. They walked me past all of it, their front for the rest of the world, and took me down a hallway to a large conference room. There were no windows, though, and as I entered the room, I felt a momentary stab of claustrophobia.

Alone, I sat in one of the chairs and tried to recall the specific journal page. I had stared at it for hours, read each line a dozen times. In my heyday, I had memorized so many things, the periodic table, pi to the one hundredth decimal, even the nations of the world, and her stanzas were just lists of words. I was certain I could recreate it without the record hanging around my neck, for surely they would never allow me to see it again, once it was given over.

I mouthed the words, wrote them with my finger on the table top, and reconstructed their positions in my head. The page ended at thirty-two lines, and I had not taken the time to memorize the following page. Thirty-two lines meant four words of whatever message was intended. I counted, eighth row, ninth word, and from there to the sixteenth line, ninth word, and to my surprise, when I put those words in order, it was a complete thought.

"He is among us."

Closing my eyes, I sat back, completely uncertain of how that might help me. Jinx had said any set of coordinates would yield something, but knowing her as I did, I couldn't believe it was an unintentional communication. Then I thought of so many other numbers that might mean something, her birthday, mine, our parents' crash, the day I got married, the day she graduated. Perhaps all of them would yield a result, and perhaps they would all lead me nowhere. Perhaps I should do as Jinx suggested and chill.

"*Trishna,*" I whispered. It was what she had written in the red ink to attract me to that page. Was it a joke at my expense, a warning, or was it an indicator? Was she telling me to seek, in this one case, for the knowledge she had encrypted?

"The cause of suffering," someone replied.

CHAPTER 22

I looked up at the man standing in the doorway, leaning against it as if he was completely comfortable with making me feel uncomfortable, and found someone who reminded me very much of Arthur. He was not as tall or handsome, was not at all charismatic or inviting, but he had that same caramel skin and vaguely Asian bone structure. His black hair, unlike Arthur's, was clipped short and smoothed back. Dark like coals, his eyes were untouched by his benevolent expression.

When he smiled at my perusal, he revealed a row of perfect, sparkling, white teeth, the canines just a bit too sharp.

"You have learned some Sanskrit!" he said happily, and in the lilt of his voice, there was the faintest trace of an accent. "Eva would be proud."

"Don't," I hissed, certain that like Moksha, this man was a villain. He had to be, or he would not have treated me so casually. With him, I had the same eerie feeling of recognition, the same vibe of immediate disgust. He was like me, but not like me. "Don't say her name."

His grin did not diminish. "You believe I have committed an offense against you."

"Moksha killed my parents on your orders."

His head tilted, almost exactly as Arthur's so often did when he was about to scold me in that playful way, but there was nothing playful about this man. He was nothing but sly. "You have proof of this?"

"Yes."

He sighed. "The man is a bit . . . shall we say, zealous?"

"He's sick."

The teeth appeared again. "Aren't we all."

Disgusted, I reached up and curled my fingers around the flash drive. "What do you want from me?"

He slid away from the wall and moved smoothly toward the table, his dark eyes drawn to my hand and the treasure it held. "Just . . . your thoughts."

I snorted and tapped my inner Jinx. "Yeah right, and I'm sure you've got a nice shiny penny to exchange for them, huh?"

He said nothing, but his smile hardened. He put his hands on the table and leaned over it slowly, staring down my resolution to refuse them. His gaze searched me hungrily, but blinked, having found nothing in my stoicism.

"Make jokes if you like, Lilith, but I promise you, I am not a person you want to antagonize."

"Antagonize? What makes you think *I'm* someone to antagonize?" I shot back. My heart was racing and adrenalin flooded my veins as if I were on a roller coaster. Each tiny movement of his hand or face, though there were few, felt like I was falling, like I had an ear infection and was reeling. "What happened to you? What about the Eightfold Path? What about right action, wisdom, liberation?"

He leaned back and looked down his nose at me. "He led us astray and then he abandoned us. He took the easy way, because he could. It did not affect him the way it affected us and he did not stay long enough to see it. If he could have, he would have condoned our search. If he was experiencing this, he would understand. We have no choice."

I sat up straight and glared at him. "If you're so pissed off about immortality, then why don't *you* jump off a building!"

"It isn't as simple as living or dying."

"Oh really, well everyone has issues and we all make do, somehow managing to *not* kill people while doing so!"

"Don't you dare lecture me!" he hissed, his features transforming just as Ursula's had. In a matter of moments, he turned from refinement to cruelty, and glared down at me as if he wanted to rip me apart with his bare hands. "You have no idea how it feels!"

"Yeah, right!" I snarled, gaining my feet, finally able to put a face to my outrage. "I'm sure endless time to see and do all that you might want to is horrible! I bet it's just miserable being completely invulnerable to sickness and that whole pesky aging thing! At least you have each other! You *stole* my family from me!"

My voice gave out into a sudden sob. Surprised by my own reaction, my abrupt loss of composure, my tears, I staggered back away from the table, still holding the drive like a talisman. My back hit the wall. I froze and looked around, but there was only one way out. Through him.

He watched me cry, seemed to be pondering my brush with a mental breakdown, and eventually rethought his method of approach. He raised a hand in a casual peace offering. A Rolex sparkled there.

"There is a great deal you do not know, but continue in this way, and eventually," he smiled grimly, "you will."

Even with the wall at my back and a table between us, I still felt threatened by him. Try as I might to take deep breaths or compose myself, I was unable to do so. His stare was eating a hole in my nerves, like a sound at the edges of the audible, squealing through my brain like an ice pick. The longer he stared, the more debilitating it was, motion sickness of the mind. Urgency grew in my breast, until all I wanted to do was hide.

Arthur had said there were Arhat who could make others obey. Could this man be one of them? If I knew he was, could I stop it?

"You really don't make sense," I gasped, and without intending to, held the drive up before my face.

"It's detachment," he said, in a surprisingly quiet voice. "We're set apart, surrounded by it but unable to love it. There's no joy, no happiness, just experience! Constant information with no purpose, because there is no purpose!" He turned and slowly walked along the table, preparing to come toward me. I cowered, terrified with no idea why I was so afraid. "There has to be another truth! There has to be a way of undoing this!"

"What," I slid along the wall, around the opposite side of the table, my limbs rebelling, "does it have to do with me?"

"In it, but not of it," he whispered and the hair on the back of my neck stood on end. His smile turned into a sudden snarl and with superhuman speed, he was before me, reached out, and unceremoniously took hold of my wrist.

Violently, He pulled my arm and almost wrenched it from the socket as he spun me toward the door. Thrown bodily, I let go of the drive and stumbled, catching the leg of a chair with my foot. It crashed to the floor and unable to catch myself, I followed, skidded on my knees, and felt a sharp pain in my ankle. I rolled onto my back, prepared to kick and scream, but he was already leaning over me, glaring into my eyes with that unnaturally vengeful leer. I froze beneath him, shivering as he reached out and unclipped the drive from the lanyard around my neck.

He leaned closer to me, until his mouth was beside my ear, the shiny white teeth beside my throbbing pulse point. "We began in the slime, came forth to dry land. We want you to begin on the land and take to the air. Carry us with you."

The door opened above my head and my friend from the car stuck his head into the room.

"Take her to the cell," my host growled.

"No!" I shrieked as he stood up and walked over me. I got to my knees, crawled after him, tried to regain my feet, and found that the damaged ankle would not obey me. I limped out into the hallway and jerked my arm away from the guard as he reached for it. "I'm not the cure!"

He stopped in his tracks and turned to look at me in the dim light, reminding me uncannily of my first meeting with Arthur.

"Not yet," he grinned.

The guard reached for me again, but ended up supporting me more than coercing me. I was "helped" back the way we had come and taken to an elevator. It carried us down, far into the depths of the apparently massive compound, and deposited us in a sterile-looking, metal corridor; an industrial intestine lined with doors, I was almost certain it digested people whole. Tiny windows set into the doors made certain spectators could peep in, though I could tell from my captors' lowered eyes that they didn't want to. They suddenly seemed to diminish in size and it was clear they did not like being at my side.

As I limped toward the first set of doors, the air became more and more oppressive with a smell and a sound. It was the metallic scent of blood carried on the air with shrieks of fear and moans of agony. A shudder wracked me, as the noise grew in volume. Something splattered against the window at my left with such high velocity that it startled me. It was blood.

I jumped back and fell against the opposite door. My head collided with the window and dizzy, I tried to steady myself. My eyes lifted to the portal and met a face that was almost unrecognizable as human. It had eye sockets, a nose, and even teeth, but it looked as if a wild animal had clawed at it. It oozed blood, and as its mandible dropped open, I realized it had bitten out its own tongue.

With a gasp, I lurched away from it and was caught by my escort. Shivering in his grasp, I was torn between revulsion and empathy. The grotesque visage remained in the window, leering at me with its empty eye sockets and soon, every window had a face in it too, all in various states of mutilation, all watching us.

"Wha . . . what's wrong w . . . with them!"

His hands pushed me gently toward the last door on the right. It stood open. "They're mad."

I planted my feet as best I could. "Why? What happened to them? Who are they!"

He pushed again and sent me into the door frame. I resisted, grabbed hold of the jamb, my fingers clawing at it. He plucked at them, but I continued to fight.

"They are the ones who cannot withstand," he said through gritted teeth, and with one last shove, hurled me through the door which was slammed behind me. I crashed into it, threw my weight behind my hands and punched at it futilely. His face appeared in the window, expressionless, but he reached up and removed his earpiece. "They are here for their protection."

"Why are you doing this to me?" I cried weakly.

"Withstand," he said quietly and walked away.

I slid to the ground and wept until my eyes were so swollen I could not see, and my throat burned. The wall beneath my face had warmed from the heat of my tears, my joints ached, and my ankle was stiff. Turning, I examined my cell and wondered just how long it would be mine.

Long enough for you to tear your own eyes out.

I fought for calm, leaned back and forced myself to breathe deeply. I tried to stay sensible, repeat those oh-so-helpful words of wisdom that they put on commercials for alarm companies or post on roadside billboards. I had to think rationally, reason, talk myself through it, but all those things seemed terrifyingly difficult.

In it, but not of it.

That was why they were doing this to me. I couldn't help but wonder if she had known all along that this would happen to me. If I was one of them, then logic dictated my fate would be the same, unless I found some other knowledge, some alternate source of confidence. Unless I could be one of them, but of myself. It was a test.

The thought frightened me back into weeping. For some reason, I began rocking back and forth, was chilled by the stale air, and could find no occupation that minimized my anguish. I sat on that cold floor for hours, perhaps days, flitting between emotional states like a hummingbird on crack. I chafed my limbs, tried to ignore the sounds, and waited for any sign that they were coming back to get me. Eventually, I knew they were never coming back, not even to bring me water. I had no choice but to solve the puzzle.

If it was inevitable that I decay in the same way as the creatures in the hall, then the answer was to find a way to remain the same. I stared at the drain hole in the floor and shook my head, knowing that my only option was the frozen meditative state of the *jhana*. After all, it was in the *jhana* that right knowledge and liberation were attained in the first place. Eva had pushed me into that state once, and the changes had begun, so perhaps in an exploration of that state, more changes would come, more strength attained. It could turn me into their cure, but it was also the only thing that would make me a fitting opposition to their plans.

I have no choice.

A new intent came to me. It was the lack of direction that unnerved me, but with this self-selected ninja mission, I could focus. To induce the peace of the *jhana*, I stretched and flexed, did yoga on the ground until I could feel all the tiny movements of my body, feel the muscles give and the tendons relax. Then, I lay down on the floor and closed my eyes.

No one had ever successfully cleared their mind and stayed conscious, I was sure. It couldn't happen. The conscious mind, by itself, is constantly moving, talking, pondering, and just to shut it up people practice chants for years, monotonous sounds that contain enough vowels and fricatives to make Henry Higgins go apeshit. They short-circuited their brains. Some went to therapists and allowed a gentle voice to soothe that endless banter and engage it in a conversation that did not rely upon the streaming video of their senses. The only catch was that their mind was putty in another mind's hands. Self-induced hypnosis seemed, as I lay on the cold rubber floor, feeling the pain in my ankle, like the most absurd, impossible, unreasonable thing to do, until it happened.

My thoughts went still. There was nothing. No sound, no movement, no sensation of any kind, as if my spinal cord had been severed, and then suddenly, I realized that even though I felt nothing, I could think about feeling nothing. My mind had started back up, but I was trapped inside it, because it had ditched my broken body and was keeping itself company. I wondered if I was sleeping, but convinced myself that if a person wondered about being asleep, that must mean they had achieved whatever it was I was meant to achieve and would either wake up or . . . what?

I tried to open my eyes, and the thought sent me reeling. In that moment, sight took on a whole new meaning, as I was floating at the ceiling, looking down at myself.

It was like seeing a stranger. I knew it was me, but I saw it as apart, and that realization alone was enough to persuade me of something profound: that I was not my body. Jinx would probably scold me, tell me something about the unique series of propriosceptors that were activated when a person was conscious, but were disabled in extreme relaxation. He would probably say something about brain waves, projection, or aural memory, but I was more than prepared to tell him to bite me, because in that moment, I was free.

But there was no such thing as freedom. To live, in any state, was to make plans, to have feelings, to yearn, strive, or hope. To live was to suffer when those hopes were cast aside.

". . . because you're the strongest person I know."

I had wondered *when* the change had happened. All this time, it nagged at me that there was a hole in my otherwise perfect memory, a chunk of my life that had either not been important enough to record, or transcended the operation, but in my higher plain of concentration, the memories could find me. The lost time pooled in my brain like cooling metal, warmed me through, and gave me a new shape.

The dial tone in my ear, buzzing. Something in her voice tugging on me like a lost child. In her words, she was dead already, and in my heart I was already suffering as much as any person ever could. I had known what would happen, not in the prescient sense, but in that aching, half-realized intuition tracking inevitabilities through time. To be so certain flattened my spirit completely.

If death existed, I had thought as the phone slid from my hand, then everything was pointless and temporary, and if that could be so, then all truth was equal, and there were no consequences. In that space of wasted moments, all that was false, illusory, conjectured, was as powerful as reality. Nothing meant anything, but if that was true, then everything meant something.

That had been the moment, that perfect liberation. My life, or the thing that was defined as my existence, had ended, but had brought new meaning to what was left.

It had not been minutes or even hours that I had sat there at my kitchen table, staring into nothing, my hand in the tepid water. I had lost about three full days to my trance. With my thoughts unfocused, I had watched Eva from that distance, my mind like a camera recording for later viewing. I had followed her to Ursula's lair. I had been with her as she withstood their questions and insults. I had watched her level Arthur with that stare that no one could refuse and ask him, point blank, what he thought he was doing.

I wanted her to demand an explanation for his betrayal, insist that he apologize for wanting the cure as much as they did, but I could tell that she was not angry with him. She was impatient.

"Something must be done."

"It will happen as it will," he had replied, his face cast downward like a scolded child.

There she stood, defiant, a mastermind in the making, her hazel eyes eerily clear. *"The Buddha, Jesus, all of those names, they're not just words. They're not just icons. They are our reminders."*

He shook his head and closed his eyes. *"No one should need such reminders."*

"Yet here we are."

Arthur looked up and a moment passed in silence.

"I agree with you!" she insisted, *"but something must give. They were able to unlock their bodies, but once physical suffering disappears, the promise of an afterlife and the figure of an enlightened man is not enough to sustain! All that has kept the Arhat struggling and learning, is gone. Without that, there's no hope for them."*

She lifted her hands, Ursula's mark patched with a bandage it did not need. It was almost as if she had kept the wound intentionally as a reminder of something she wanted Arthur to see. She reached for him, but he shied away, almost as if he could not allow her to touch him, and she looked after him in sorrow. It was an odd reaction that made me wonder about the dynamics of their friendship. I'd wondered if Eva had seen him as I did, but it was obvious that was not the case; if anything, she treated him like a judge she was petitioning.

"The transformation didn't make them gods or even monsters. It made them human forever," she said to herself, more than to him, *"but human isn't good enough. How we think, the things we feel, the way we perceive reality, are not meant for immortality. They know that and yet they strive to live, because they are certain that there is nothing else more important, that to give up life is the gravest of errors. They have no direction, Arthur! They will be here, forever, with no one to lead them, no icon above them, when that is all their human minds can manage!"*

Once again, I was in the shadow of her knowledge, uncertain about everything I thought I knew. Why did it seem as if she was holding him responsible?

"You do not have to say it," he said quietly.

"She's right!" she insisted. I wondered if she could have meant Ursula, and pictured the woman pontificating to her captive audience of one. The image troubled me. *"This is the tipping point. If we do not weight things in our favor, all that work will be undone. They are in the end stages. More and more are stored each year or disappear, never to be heard from again. Ursula has gone stark-raving mad and there are plenty of others like her. The end isn't coming. It's here."*

Arthur frowned at the gash on her wrist. *"Does it hurt?"*

"No." She covered the bandage with her other hand self-consciously. *"It's nothing I can't handle."*

"Are you sure?"

"Arthur, things have changed. You know how I see the world. You're the only one who really knows. They need something, anything, to give them a direction."

"It cannot be me and it cannot be you."

"No . . ." she sighed, *"it can't."* She looked away and seemed so lonely suddenly, I wanted to hold her. *"It all began that day. If I had . . . My parents . . ."* she whispered in confession, *"maybe I didn't love them enough? Maybe I was too young."*

This time, Arthur reached for *her*. *"Maybe Lilith took their place, kept them alive for you. You are not a bad person, Eva. No one is."*

She nodded, though it was a dubious nod at best. *"You're right. I should have listened to you. But I've always known what I had to do."*

Stunned, I almost forgot that I was haunting a memory and nearly shouted at her. Could she have known all along about our parents, about the Arhat? How long ago had she begun to change? Maybe reading the

Sutras was a final stage. Perhaps Eva was not the naïve little girl she had always seemed. She had walked into the fray with complete knowledge, but I could not imagine why. Was it to save Arthur or was it out of compassion for the Arhat? How had she come to learn so much?

"We are still missing pieces, Eva," Arthur whispered. *"Can you build upon what you do not fully understand?"*

"I can build on anything, Arthur. Have faith."

"But will it be fiction?"

"Is there really such a thing as false hope?" she countered, crossing her arms.

"Lying solves nothing."

"We planned it right. There is truth to every word and everything means something."

"We?" He waited in her silence, examining her, assessing her expression which seemed almost guilty.

After a long while, she chuckled and nodded her head. *"Yes, we."*

"Are they ready?" he whispered. *"They are terrified that this path is a suffering worse than what they endure, than what they knew before. They believe that on the other side, is not just a lack of joy, but a reality where joy is shown to be a false thing, Because they believe this, they will never progress, even with the perfect leader and the ideal set of values. A man cannot fly, if he cannot fall."*

I saw her smile and heard her whisper my name.

"Then I will push," she said.

He gave a slow blink and seemed to know exactly what she meant by that.

"The fruit is poison."

"Only the first bite."

"Who will take it?"

"Must you ask?"

She stared him down, trying to convince him with her gaze, but when he seemed withdrawn, she walked away.

Arthur stood in the alley for some time, looking up at the light that was her window, his face composed of that perfectly ambiguous expression that only he seemed capable of achieving. I found myself wondering what he was thinking. He had to suppose that she had already set into motion a series of events that would put me right in their hands. He was too wise not to. When he looked at me, did he see me as a person, or as the end result of her craft?

Ashamed, I was sorry that I had been so short with him, when it was quite probable I would never be able to apologize. My faith in him had wavered and I felt so stupid. All along he could see how little I knew her. The righteous quest for truth was pointless, because Eva had not needed saving.

My image of her was wrong, frozen at our parents' funeral; a snapshot of her eyes glistening, her hands curled into her skirt, gripping it tightly. She had always been vulnerable, someone I needed to protect, and that was why I couldn't see the lust for immortality that was born on that tragic day.

It seemed that their argument had convinced her she was right, because after witnessing it, the premonition of her death had swept over me, still sitting at my kitchen table, fingers turning to prunes. I had been with her on the roof's edge, even though she had not yet set foot upon it.

"Human is not good enough. Live better, or die as nothing more than this," she said to herself, or perhaps to the world. Then she spread her arms wide and leapt.

My flashback to the premonition ended, leaving me with a vague dizziness of time-displacement.

Back in the present, looking down at my body, I could see the resemblance it had to her corpse, though it was so much more neatly arranged. If I were going to end my life, I thought, I was much too neat to do it so haphazardly. If I had jumped from a building, I would probably just be wondering how I could land in the neatest possible way. It was perhaps her last way of thumbing her nose at the order I had always applied to her chaos. Limbs splayed, clothes askew, a wonderful Rorschach test of dark red and pin-striping.

What do you see?

Human wasn't good enough, but they were still trying to be human even though their perception of reality had changed drastically. They were still doing business, living lives, interacting in the old ways. From different to self-hating, from perfect knowledge to detachment, their very nature made eternity a dismal fate instead of a wondrous opportunity.

It was no wonder they come to hate the Buddha, felt abandoned by him, but could he really be blamed? Had he known about the death inside that golden fruit when he presented it to the kingdom?

CHAPTER 23

I don't know how long I was suspended above my motionless carcass. I saw no change, noticed no passage of time, but after a while, I realized I could still hear - if that was that right word - the screams of the other inmates. I knew the temperature of the room, though I had no sense of flesh or blood. I could still *discern,* but was completely unable to do anything about *what* I discerned.

Helpless.

Like I was standing on a mountain top, I looked out over a great horizon and had absolutely no idea what I was supposed to do now that I'd climbed up. Was I meant to observe, but do nothing, change nothing? Was I meant to float around forever, hovering above my own head, pondering the nature of all things? I mean that was great and all, being able to ditch the meat sack anytime, and I'm sure in the right circumstances it'd be tremendously enlightening about the nature of consciousness, but to me, it was shaping up to be a pretty boring eternity. And yet the Buddha had endured the *jhana* time and again, even charged his followers to embrace its seeming passivity.

What can this possibly teach me?

It occurred to me then, as I pondered all that I had seen, that surely, in this incorporeal state, I could escape not only my flesh, but the proximity to it. Could I, I wondered, stretch out my thoughts to my friends and . . .

I would have blinked, but as it was, I had no eyelids *to* blink. The blue, spiky beacon below me, however, banished all confusion. I was in Jinx's home, hovering above his shoulder, listening to him as he mumbled to himself in multilingual, expletive-rich outrage.

He was sitting in his records room. A haphazard pile of file folders had been pushed over in front of him. He was sifting through them with one hand and typing on a laptop with the other. I realized then, that I had never been so glad to see anyone. It was an entirely new experience for perfidious me, thinking of the self as separate from the body, the ghost in the machine, and it was nice to see that the contents of my life were constant.

"Why can't we just break down the door?" Unger growled from the head of one of the mountainous tables. Until he spoke, I had no idea he was present and wondered *why* he was there. Jinx: eternally youthful, quick to a fault and Unger: dragged through the muck of life, barely standing and ambiguous on his path; if any people could be more different, I'd never met them.

"Because it's not that simple," Jinx replied in a long-suffering voice and turned up his music.

"Why not?" Unger flipped over a few pages with an angry finger, as if the whole room offended him. I could certainly understand why it might. It was like he'd been swallowed whole by an entire case file and was realizing how detail-oriented his life had been, and how little it had actually accomplished.

"Because."

"That's easy for you to say; you're one of *them*."

"So's Lily, and for your information, I am an entirely different species of *them*, so shut it."

"I didn't come here to watch you do . . . whatever. I came here to plan a strategy."

"Which I could do much better without you, ironically," Jinx grumbled almost silently.

I read over his shoulder, scanned his laptop screen with my mind's eye, still slightly stunned that I was able to. The skeptical voice within was yammering something about manufacturing a reality when in dangerous and uncertain circumstances to appease the conscious mind, but I was much too busy putting two and two together to care about its advice. I *wanted* to believe that this was *actually* happening.

Jinx had somehow, due to his two centuries of acquired skills, hacked the banking records from my sister's account and was tracing the deposits. Marveling, I realized it had never occurred to me to do so. I had always just assumed the money was Moksha's, but now that I considered it, I wondered if it could be. After all, why would Moksha pay someone who might end up killing themselves like all the other experiments, knowing that money would come to her next of kin? I sincerely doubted that they'd feel such an expense was worth the time and effort.

Unfortunately, I couldn't raise those questions with the one person who would have investigated them. He was leaning on his hand just then, sighing in what I would have considered exhaustion, if not for the fact that he never slept; it was probably just caffeine withdrawal. I tried to think in his direction, repeat his name over and over until he heard me calling, but he registered not the slightest sensation of my existence.

Unger wandered over, slowly browsing the records as if shopping at a particularly odious fish market. Eventually, he found his way to Jinx's side and put himself directly in the way of my view.

No sooner had I touched upon the sensation of frustration, than my vantage changed, and I was facing them. Whatever was going on, it seemed that I was in the highest form of control, able to command merely by desiring, evade obstructions by *wanting* to know.

Unger whistled, impressed. "You know I could arrest you for this, right?"

Jinx raised an eyebrow stud before the detective even finished and I was mildly awed that the boy didn't cut him off. "Maybe, but I'm a hacker. By the time I was done, *you'd* be in prison instead."

Unger's face screwed up momentarily. "So what are you . . .?"

"Following a hunch."

"A hunch?" The detective leaned forward and glared at the screen. "One of *his* or one of your own?"

"I assume you mean Art," Jinx said, gently shoving the man back. "Things with Art don't work that way."

"So, how do they . . .?" Unger muttered, looking at the tiny hand in mild reproach.

The boy made a noise in his throat to interrupt. "You wouldn't understand. It's an *us* thing."

I watched Unger's expression tick. There was not the slightest chance he cared about what *we* were, because I saw the look on his face when he'd broken down Ursula's door. Unger cared about life. It was what drove him to exhaust himself, to fight for people in need, to discover. "Try me."

"Art never asks anyone to do anything. He just seems to attract exactly the type of people to fulfill whatever tasks might be waiting." Jinx frowned in concentration, obviously trying to put words to inexplicable feelings. "I'm pretty sure he knows what we're going to do and so he just lets it happen and only intervenes when he thinks we need it."

"So he *used* Lilith."

It was a very different tone of voice than the one Unger had used to suggest I be more patient with Arthur's *dharma,* but then again, that had been a vision. The *real* Matthew Unger probably never suggested anyone allow themselves to be compromised for *any* cause, noble or otherwise. If I had had more faith in him, I would have known it was a vision much earlier and would have been able to prevent all of this.

Some uncanny insight.

"Arthur *uses* you to get things done?"

The boy shook his head in perplexed denial, "No. I mean, it's more like, I dunno, outsourcing, or something. It's his ability, I think, like, a combination of the whole fortune telling thing and sooth saying."

The detective eyed his blue hair in disbelief. "So, *you* have a hunch that's really *his,* and then *you* do all the work, because it's *your* hunch. Then you take the work to *him* and *he* does *what* with it?"

Jinx shrugged.

"But they're *your* hunches. Don't *you* want to take them somewhere?"

"I do, but that's kind of the point. I take them somewhere and get back to him. I'm an independent contractor."

"Who isn't paid."

"Have you *had* Sam's coffee?"

Unger's brows drew together and though he was stoic, I could see the smile he was trying to hide. Their faces seemed so much clearer in the *jhana,* as my eyes did not get in the way of my sight. It was absolutely heady how much detail I could find. It would be easy to become reliant upon it.

"So he didn't ask you to do something illegal, but you did it anyway."

It was the demeanor of an investigator, acted out in tiny gestures and suggestions. Unger was interrogating an immortal without even seeming to, baiting him into answering questions, taking advantage of his weaknesses to gain information. It was almost supernatural, if not for the fact that I now had a very different perspective on the word.

"If I told him I was doing it, he would have told me to stop, for my own safety; which is why I *didn't* tell him." The boy looked up at him mischievously, completely oblivious to the manipulation, or obeying it without concern. "He also didn't ask me to find out who sent Eva the money. Nor did he ask me to find out that the corporation in question is a front for another group. And when I find out what I'm looking for, I probably won't tell him that either. I'll get back to him when I hit a wall, and *then* we'll plan something."

Unger's face blanked as he tried to sum up all he wanted to know in a single word that would make it past Jinx's impatient guard. "Group?"

Gloating, the boy turned away and gave a lazy shrug. "Yeah, but it's all real confusing, so you probably don't wanna hear about it. I mean, you'll probably end up investigating it, and then you'll find out all this secret stuff, and then you'll eventually end up needing help or wanting to tell someone, and then it will get back to *him,* and maybe turn out that it was all a part of *his* game plan anyway. Besides, you work for a government agency, which tends to breed suspicion against any large-scale conspiracy theory."

The scowl on Unger's face was almost comical. He crossed his arms and glowered down at the boy.

"What?" Jinx said lightly, still enjoying his strategic advantage. "It's a documented phenomenon. I mean you guys know how incompetent you are and how impossible it is for you to keep secrets, so you think you're in a position to know how unlikely a conspiracy is. Which is exactly how they keep a conspiracy a secret from the very people who are a part of it! I don't even want to go into . . ." he trailed off helpfully, just as Unger opened his mouth to interrupt.

"Jinx!"

Leaning back, the hacker tapped a few keys aimlessly. "I'm just saying . . ." but trailed off, anticipating Unger's hasty rejoinder.

"Well say something useful."

Jinx was already looking up at him speculatively, and considered him for a long while. Then the sparkle of revelation awoke in his eye and he launched himself forward in his chair to point at the screen of his computer.

"Okay, so, like, the money that was deposited into Eva's account originated in the Caiman Islands. It was a dummy account, a way of washing money."

"Laundering . . ."

"No 'washing'. They just wanted a few degrees of separation; they weren't even trying," the boy insisted. "It's almost like they wanted the Sangha to know."

"They?"

But Jinx was a snowball rolling downhill. "Normally, any inquiries into the money would end there, because it was just a number and was closed right after she died, but there is not a single safe that these hands cannot crack."

Just to accent this, he squeezed his fists and cracked his knuckles.

Unger rolled his eyes.

"I took it upon myself to follow the money backward, and you'll never guess where it ended."

"Where?"

Jinx's smile flashed. "You sure you want to know?"

"Just get to the . . ." Unger growled.

"Not easy to do, Sherlock." Jinx got up from the table and went to the wall of lines, to the branch on which Eva and I were both positioned. Without a word, he pointed at our photograph and then traced the line backward, past other photos, pages of biographic information, and old newspaper clippings. He walked slowly, Unger trailing behind in something akin to awe at the sheer size of the "family tree". When they came to the beginning, just to the left of the doorway, the boy's polished nail lifted and tapped a name. And that's when I understood.

There was the Buddha, a mounted bas relief sculpture, gilded in gold. From him sprang a list of names, written in both English and Sanskrit, but only one had "offspring" and it was a name I recognized.

Unger stared at it in bewilderment while Jinx smiled crookedly and continued to tap the wall.

"The Buddha didn't write anything down. Writing is antithetical to the 'live in the moment' ideology. It wasn't until *after* his death that his followers transcribed his sermons, but . . ."

They couldn't remember, I thought to myself, just as Jinx echoed my words.

"The disciple Ananda was graced with an idenic memory, so they wrote down what he told them to, but there's no guarantee that his reproduction was accurate."

In triumph, Jinx turned back to Unger and watched him follow the logic, which the man did like the expert he was, but concealed like the old curmudgeon I loved.

Hand crooked over his rough chin, he brooded. "So, what are . . .?"

"Well, I've been thinking about it for a long time; I mean, it's not like you hear about any of these guy," he pointed to the list of names beside the Buddha, "rampaging over earth, laying waste and shit. It's all the younger guys raising hell," Jinx's childlike eyes were glittering in fierce amusement and pent up excitement, "so what if it wasn't Buddha's fault? What if it was Ananda's? What if he did something, and every Arhat after that was fucked?"

I waited, desperately willing Unger to ask the question I longed to ask. After a few pensive moments, he did.

"Intentionally?"

"Well, that's the real question, isn't it?"

"What's that have to do with Eva's bank account?"

Deflated, Jinx threw up his hands. One of them collided with the list of names on the wall. "Look, the disciples of Buddha that were left after his death ended up forming the First Sangha. They told Ananda, still a Stream-Enterer, that he wasn't allowed to be a part of the meetings, unless he achieved the next 'stage' of enlightenment, unless he was liberated. The legend says that he studied hard, meditated for days to achieve the *jhana*, just so that he could recite the sutras. What if he was pissed enough to sabotage their efforts to spread Buddhism? The original Arhat go on, completely oblivious, passing around their pamphlets like Mormons, unaware that they're spreading a lethal disease!"

Unger stared at the wall. "You think that this *Ananda* guy formed a group too?" At Jinx's prodding look, he chewed his lip and continued to murmur, "And you think that that group might just be willing to keep their eye on the Sangha, approach one of their assets, and turn them."

Jinx almost exploded in a rush of air he fluffed and fanned with his hands. "That money originated in an account that was opened by a charity called 'The Guardians of the Dharma' which was Ananda's title! They paid her to recover information from *inside* AMRTA. And the payments began two weeks *before* she started work at AMRTA."

Something was missing. Why would the Guardians of the Dharma want to hand the Sangha a potential cure for the disease *their leader* created? Most importantly, why had Eva agreed? I could still see the determination in her face as she stood arguing with Arthur in the alley. She had seemed to want the cure as well, which meant that she was probably not an ideal informant for the Guardians.

"I'm not sure about this," Unger muttered. "There's a lot missing. Without facts, we can't be sure. You're the mathematician. I thought that was . . . your thing."

For a moment, it seemed that Unger had leveled the boy with the gravest of insults. Silently fuming, he turned on his heel and walked back to his computer. It was obvious he had come to like the astonished admiration with which I greeted his momentous disclosures and did not like being directly criticized. Something told me that was one reason why Arthur preferred him to research on his own.

"I've been wading through several thousand years of history. You didn't even know the Sangha existed before two weeks ago and you expect *me* to have proof? You go find proof! I've got stuff to do!"

Eyebrows raised, Unger leaned against the door and took out his cigarettes. Packing them as loudly as possible, he watched the boy ignore him. Soon rings of smoke encircled him and wafted toward the immortal. Sardonic smile in place, Unger tossed the butt on the floor and stepped on it, trying to get a rise out of my colorful friend.

The eyes slid to where Unger's brown leather shoe was squishing and narrowed. "Pick it up."

The unofficial winner of the stand-off grinned. "So what does *he* say about this hunch of yours?"

Obviously bothered, Jinx slammed the laptop closed. "*He* doesn't say *anything*, because *I* don't need the help! Unlike some people, I'm very good at figuring things out *and* I don't make it a habit of getting into trouble out of which other people have to rescue me!"

There I was, the third party to an argument that was about me, but unable to break it up. I hovered between them, longing to take their hands and force them to shake, to explain to Jinx that I did what I did because I liked Unger, and to explain to the detective that the immortal was not dangerous to me or anyone else.

Was this the point? I was flattered two people cared so much about me, but why was I seeing this when I could in no way change anything?

Unger glared at Jinx, who glared back.

"I didn't ask her to do it. I didn't want her to do it. I would gladly trade places, but something tells me they wouldn't offer."

I would have smiled if possible. If I didn't know any better, I'd have thought he had a crush on me. His protectiveness was almost sweet.

Jinx looked away, shaking his head, "Yeah, that's easy for *you* to say."

"I knew her longer than you did, so what's your problem? If anyone should want to help her, it'd be me."

"Right. You're going to rescue one of '*us*', huh? Why does *that* surprise me?"

Stepping away from the wall, Unger started toward him. "I don't care about any of that!"

"Could have fooled me."

"Look, you little . . ."

Just then, the door opened and Sam appeared holding a tray. He blinked in the uncomfortable silence and held up the tray as if it was a shield or a peace offering, or both.

"Um . . ." he whispered in his gravelly voice, "Art thought you guys might want some coffee."

At mention of the benevolent leader, the two combatants exchanged a glance and in an instant, came to a truce. It seemed Arthur was astute enough to put *both* of them in their places and remind them why they were there without ever stepping foot in the room.

Sam set the tray down across from Jinx, who snatched up a cup and slurped at it as if he was dying of thirst. "Sweet fucking Christ! If coffee was sex you'd be a motherfucking gigolo, you magnificent, growling bastard!"

With a sigh, Unger sat down next to them and I could feel his resignation. No, the world would not obey the rules he had spent his life upholding; it was a waste of time to hold out any longer. "So what are we going to do?"

Jinx looked up from his cup and glanced between the two humans. They looked back, deferring to the most experienced person in the room, a kid with blue hair and a lip piercing.

"Are you a pirate or a ninja, Unger?"

The detective frowned as Sam choked on his French roast. "What?"

"It's a serious question," Jinx insisted.

The man blinked.

"Can you be . . .?" Sam rumbled.

"No," Jinx looked horrified at the very thought of someone choosing to occupy two diametrically opposed worlds simultaneously.

"Look, a pirate would knock down the door with a cannonball. A ninja would find a ventilation shaft. Which is more tactically sound?"

Sam leaned forward in all seriousness, "Depends on what your enemies are."

A shiny, black nail rose. "And that is why we do our research ahead of time."

"We don't even know where . . .!"

Jinx sighed once again and got a hand tangled in his spikes. "Wow, you have a low opinion of me. As soon as I saw her face after the vision, I knew. She didn't walk in with nothing."

"The drive?" Unger demanded skeptically. "What's that . . .?"

"And whe' do we put da dwive when we wanna see da thtuff dat's on it?" Jinx carried on in a false voice, still trying to tug his fingers free from his eggwhite-coated head.

"Into the computer," Sam offered judiciously in place of whatever swearword was about to pop out of Matthew's mouth.

"Exactly," Jinx picked the cup back up and cradled it as if it was the holy graille. "If they so much as *try* to access that drive, I'll swoop in like a motherfucking pterodactyl and detach their fucking heads with my wicked awesome claws."

"Dinosaur techno ninja," Unger muttered, rolling his eyes again. "Now I see why she likes you."

Arthur picked that auspicious moment to enter the room. He had a faraway look on his face and was carrying one of Eva's red journals. It was as if my spirit jumped in response, and like a series of time-lapse photos, my vantage skipped to his face. Sharp focus made the perfection of his visage almost impossible and though I had no fingers, I wanted to touch him.

I knew he didn't care about the cure, wasn't responsible in any way for Eva's death, and wanted nothing but my best interests, but I could still feel my churning, conflicting emotions, permeated by that pervasive attraction I could not explain. The man was still a mystery, perhaps even more tantalizing than the sister I'd never known, but he was all I had. Locked in my rubber room, just seeing him was such a tremendous comfort.

Jinx turned to him, and before Arthur could say hello, leapt up. "Pirate or Ninja?"

Arthur blinked and glanced at the others.

"That's not a fair answer, Art! You can only pick the pirate or the ninja, not their accessories."

"Why?"

The boy gave a harassed sigh, beset on all sides. "Fine, whatever."

"What did he . . .?" Unger began.

But Jinx was already annoyed with the metaphor. "Never mind!"

I had a sneaking suspicion I knew what he had answered, though, and it probably flapped its colorful wings and asked after crackers.

The parrot.

"Sure shut you up," the detective laughed.

"Screw you, Dick." Jinx crammed his headphones deeper into his ears and out of apparent spite, turned up the volume again. "You know, you should probably indulge me, given our current circumstances!" Then the hacker went back to his computer in a mild sulk.

One of Arthur's dark eyebrows arched slowly. "I take it that he feels he is not appreciated."

Unger shrugged casually and leaned back in his chair, still holding out hope that the hierarchy was undecided. "I have a feeling he thrives under . . ."

"You wouldn't know, you bovine fucktard," Jinx grumbled under his breath.

"Jinx," Arthur murmured, coming up behind him to smooth his bristling, blue head, "I am positive whatever you are doing will benefit Lilith. Defensiveness will only slow us down."

I wanted to smile, to reassure the youthful immortal, even if his research was making things less clear for me. There were so many agendas being pushed, it was less like playing chess and more like Chinese Checkers. As rational as I was, I had never been much for playing games, they just seemed like wastes of time. It probably had something to do with being completely uncompetitive, something my life of sacrifice had beaten into me.

Jinx sighed. "I wish we could just be sure she's alright. It's been a week, and we have no new info!"

A week? I could have sworn my memories were recovered in the span of a few moments, that they were just behind a mental door I had opened. It now occurred to me that perhaps the *jhana* wasn't as simple as a nifty means of doing research. It did something to time, or it took a long while to achieve and slip from.

"If you could enter the *jhana,* it would be easy," Arthur admonished gently. "All things become clear if one knows what one wants to see."

Couldn't you be more specific for those of us in *it?*

He set down the journal and began flipping through the pages, leaning over the boy's shoulder. To the others in the room, it would seem as if he was trying to look up something for the boy to read, but I could tell from my ever-precise vantage, that his azure gaze was set on the screen.

"I can't help it if I'm not all aaahaaahaaahaaaaahhhhh," Jinx sang, waving his hands in the air around his head as if fighting off bees. "I'm a realist. I deal with facts. I zone out when I've had that perfect balance of speed and thumping bass and I lay shit down, hardcore. Though, I have to admit that Tibetan monks make excellent sample tracks."

Unger snickered. "So you can't do the out of body thing?"

"I spend enough time on the net," Jinx mumbled, tapping keys to pop open window after window for Arthur's inspection.

I watched Arthur's face, watched his eyes narrow imperceptibly, watched him glance up at the Buddha on the wall and arrange all the pieces, visible or not, into a nice, clear picture that only made sense to him. It was fascinating, and even though I could not hear his thoughts, I was happy to watch the gears of his mind turn for once.

"Sam," he interrupted quietly, "will you contact the monastery and inform them that I will be arriving there tomorrow? I need to meet with the head monk, immediately."

The man swallowed, and for the first time, I saw the scar across his neck as it pulled on the intact flesh surrounding it.

"What's up?" he growled.

"We have something to discuss."

His brow furrowed, but he got up from his chair and went out into the hall. Finally, Arthur's fingers stopped turning pages and formed a bridge across the red *trishna* symbol.

Jinx snapped to attention. "Done and done, Kimosabi."

The typing began, several more windows opened and closed and to my excitement, the numbers eight and nine were entered into the field for modulus coordinates.

He is among us.

"I am more interested in the rest of the message."

My consciousness did a metaphysical double-take.

You can hear me?

"Yes."

The boy tilted back and winked up at Arthur, while Unger's face paled.

How?

After a while, the answer arrived of its own accord. I could see it in his still demeanor, his comprehensive knowledge, his exotic features, and the deliberate, practiced way that he moved as if trying not to look as controlled as he truly was. It was as he had said; the older, the more accomplished they were in the art of self-discipline. The older, the stronger.

You're contemporary with the Buddha, aren't you? I marveled. *You're one of the oldest Arhat, a member of the First Circle.*

The dark head bowed as if expecting a reprimand for lying through omission, "Yes."

In awe, I held my peace, unable to imagine what it would be like to see the mythical man face to face. Would he smile, shake my hand, know me at a glance? Would he say something profound that transformed me into a happy deconstructed mess, or was I already immune to that?

Jinx continued to stare up at Arthur as the man mumbled softly to me, but impatient, could no longer stand it. "Is she okay? What have they done to her?"

Leaning forward, Unger scowled. "What are you two . . .?"

The boy waved his confusion aside. "Super powers at work. Butt out, newb."

I'm in their compound, in a cell, I told Arthur. *There's no food or water. I was injured. I thought I would go nuts if I . . .*

"Did not go into the *jhana*," he acknowledged.

Yes.

"They are trying to force you into the next phase, speed up your transition in hopes that you will have a revelation as the Buddha did. They believe that Eva has imparted some new information to you."

How could she have? I had contemplated it too, but if Jinx was right, then the source for her knowledge was the same as every other Arhat and would be equally as dangerous.

"You have only the barest exposure and yet already developed abilities. This means you are different."

Taken aback, I wondered what would come after. If my change was different, or accelerated, perhaps madness would come on more quickly too. Could I transcend it with my greater skills? When I had been on the other plain for a given period of time, were the Sangha going to send someone after me, remove me like a manmade diamond and torture me for information? It hardly seemed plausible, since I apparently no longer felt pain. It was as Eva had written, but I didn't want to be like her, I realized. I didn't want to be invisible, alone. I wanted to save everyone, even them, because . . .

I accepted the dharma.

"Yes," Arthur interrupted my dire thoughts in his quiet, non-invasive way. "Lilith, have you seen anyone else there?"

It's horrible, Arthur. There's these monsters in cells, tearing themselves into pieces. They scream constantly and there's so much blood. Why not let them die?

"Besides those, anyone else?"

I thought back upon my arrival, which had a dizzying effect on my perspective. *Only the guards and the man who took the flash drive from me.*

"What did he look like?" Arthur pressed, leaning forward with his eyes closed, as if he was trying to use his mind to peer into my memory.

He was just a man.

Arthur sighed again and opened his eyes, like he had discovered what he was looking for and found it not to his liking. "Be careful. He is a desperate man, even if he seems composed. He will be hard on you, because he is sure you are the end."

Why?

He blinked, somewhat startled. "Because you are everything he wished to be and more."

More?

His eyes closed and I knew he would say no more than that.

Would you like me to do some espionage? I am in complete *spirit form, after all.*

I could tell he appreciated my light humor. "Do as you will," he offered with a tight smile. "I have faith in your talents, but do not endanger yourself."

Aren't you going to rescue me? I replied, but knew, as Jinx had said, it wasn't as simple as that. *I might lose faith in you otherwise.*

"I do not believe you will need rescuing."

Jinx snorted and flipped off the world in general. "Kick ass, Lily, and take some names for me."

I'll try, but I kind of wish the whole vampire thing gave me super strength and speed.

"Where's nuclear waste when you need it?" Jinx chuckled after Arthur relayed my message, no doubt in more eloquent language.

"Such things are only necessary for those who put their trust in power," Arthur chided amicably. He crossed his arms and tilted his head. "Often, the most effective way of preventing injury is to evade detection altogether."

"Bend like a reed in the wind, right?" Jinx chuckled. "What happens if you're facing a lawnmower?"

Way to make me feel better.

There was a delay as Arthur intended to repeat my words, which meant that the exchange flowed at a normal pace for the first time, an irony that was not lost on the grinning hacker.

"It is what it is, baby," he shrugged.

Call me baby again and you'll have a date with my weedwacker.

"Here," he said and hit a key, "peace offering."

Eva's entire message arranged itself on screen. It was exactly the same: four words, but it was followed by a sequence of nonsense in a bold, red font.

"This program parses language, stops arranging after the first grammatical inconsistency. These four words *are* the full message, unless there's another set of coordinates we're meant to apply to the following randomized data."

I knew which set to try next, but I wasn't about to tell them. Instead, I stared at the screen and committed those words to memory as fast as possible. I was sure, for some reason, that it was not a message I wanted them to see, that it was intended for me alone. It could have just been wishful thinking, but that no longer mattered to me. Hope was hope, false or not.

"Who is 'he'," Unger wondered aloud.

Arthur looked away and slowly sank into a chair. For some reason, he seemed despondent. To the others, he probably seemed pensive, but I was sure it was the first time I had seen any kind of suffering carve itself onto his smooth, polished face.

What is it, Arthur?

He shook his head. "Eva, the fruit is poison."

The distant look in his eyes made me wonder if he was remembering the alley, but to everyone else in the room, it appeared as if Arthur had gotten us confused. In the uncomfortable silence that followed the seeming mistake, I could almost hear Unger macerating on his tongue in an effort not to hurt my feelings. Jinx fixed his eyes on the piles of folders and did not look away. Sam's low rumble came from outside, but had no effect on the tense moment.

Eva's dead, Arthur.

"Yes, so she is, but when she wrote this, she was not."

You can't warn her now.

He turned, and to my astonishment, looked right at the piece of me that watched him. "I *am* warning her then, no matter what will happen now."

Sam reentered the room and waded through the thick silence to a chair, obviously aware that he had missed something important.

"Sam, will you please explain how time works to Arthur?" Unger demanded. "It's bad enough that Eva's dead, but talking to her as if she's still around only makes it harder on Lilith."

"Lilith isn't here."

"Tell him that too."

The humans shared a moment.

"Wouldn't help," Sam finally declared.

Arthur's face returned to its usual emotional ambiguity. "Perception does not change the facts. She may be dead, but I may still want what is best for her."

"Should have stopped her from jumping then, huh?" Unger snapped.

I said nothing, but I felt it. His words echoed my own thoughts. Why hadn't Arthur stopped her, if he was so capable?

"I did all that I could," Arthur explained. "Eva had her reasons for doing what she did. I could not change them, for my own reasons."

"Her death was a coded message too," Jinx intervened. He shut the laptop and I was forced to give up my exercise, though I was fairly certain I would retain the jumble of words when I woke.

The *jhana* took away all unnecessary thoughts and concerns. It freed the onboard computer that was my self to think about things other than breathing, feeling, contemplating. It made everything immediate, instantaneous. It meshed past with present and presented the future with clarity. Perhaps that was why Arthur said what he said, because he walked around with one foot in the *jhana*.

"These modulus are the date of her jump," Jinx finished.

"She could have just written them down in a calendar and gone into hiding," Unger muttered.

"If she had, you would not be here," Arthur pointed out. "Would that be preferable to you, Detective?"

For a few moments, Unger bit his lip and glared at the space around Arthur's head, as if looking for me to convince me how untrue that was. "No," he said finally, "I like knowing the truth."

"There's only one truth," Jinx whispered. "There is no spoon."

He giggled to himself, but unfortunately for him, the only one to appreciate the reference was an invisible, disembodied spirit. Unger seemed as if he wanted to smack himself in the forehead, while Arthur smiled happily.

"So you have taken up philosophy!" he murmured, to which, Jinx rolled his eyes.

"You people suck. I wish Lily was here."

I am.

"I wish you were *here* here," he clarified.

An alarm went off, ringing like a telephone on Jinx's tiny computer speakers. Suddenly, he pitched himself forward, opened the machine, and began a furious round of tapping.

"What is it?" Unger demanded.

"They're accessing the drive."

No one spoke lest they disturb his fugue state. He reached, at one point, for the empty coffee cup and scowled at its lack of nourishment.

"Well, this is bogus. Lily, are you in Shanghai?"

What? I responded in surprise. *No. I'm only a few hours away by car. Somewhere where there's lots of grass, I think.*

He swore and went back to his mechanical communion. A few moments later, his battle ended, and he leaned back with a sigh, his face flushed. "Epic fail."

Arthur placed a hand on his back in encouragement.

"They assumed there might be a bug in the drive. They opened it on a system that wasn't connected to their mainframe, but my bug is a burrower, and like the cockroach, will survive the zombie apocalypse, right alongside the Twinkie."

"Then . . ." Sam hinted.

"They'll wait and see if anything happens. They'll scour the files, but when they don't find the bug, they'll think it's safe. If they ever link that system with the mainframe, I'll have a backdoor."

Unger blinked in what I knew was secret admiration.

"I need a Redbull," Jinx hissed and with a fluff of his spikes and a gesture at the breeze that was me, he wandered out of the room, leaving another uncomfortable dynamic in his wake.

Things were quiet for a time, all parties thinking about their next move while Unger smacked his cigarette pack against his opposite hand.

"So," he said finally, as he pulled out a cigarette and put it to his lips. He had a sly look in his eye. "What do you think of his Ananda theory?"

I waited to see if his direct question would have a more positive result than mine had, and remarkably, it seemed that Arthur was caught a bit off guard. Surprised, I waited.

"Which Ananda theory?" Arthur countered.

"The one that's really *yours*."

Sam looked between them and sensing the tension, got up and followed Jinx. "I guess I don't need to worry about your wrist anymore. Hang tough, Ninja Girl."

Unger opened his Zippo. The click click of the striker seemed to echo around the room. "Answer me this," he said around his habit, "are *you* Ananda?"

My vision skipped, agitated like a pool of water by the single drop of sincerity. I expected it to even out, smooth back into my looking glass, but it continued to distort and my concentration was lost. I was pulled through the cheese grater of space and sliver by sliver, returned to my body. Sensation began to come back to me; hands squeezing my limbs, the stomach-stealing momentum of being hoisted up.

My body was being moved.

CHAPTER 24

When I opened my eyes, I was lying on some kind of cushioned table covered in white leather. A soft, chenille throw was haphazardly rumpled at my feet, as if the one who had moved me had not thought it necessary to cover me. Next to me, was a tray table on wheels littered with instruments for what appeared to be a physical examination. It was almost as if I had been carried to a doctor's office, but I could see that the room was a more luxurious place.

It opened onto a terrace through French doors that stood wide. A gentle breeze lifted the sheer white curtains until they whipped around a massive dark wooden desk. The floor was covered in a natural fiber rug. Weird objects and wooden statuary stood around sparsely or in awkward groupings, as though the decorator simply got bored with arranging things and walked away. In all, it gave the impression of the elegant simplicity of an eclectic traveler, or at least, the attempt at it.

Outside, sunlight glared, blinding eyes that were accustomed to the dimmer interior. It was midday at least, but when I had been with Jinx, I was sure it had been evening. Had it taken me hours to awaken?

I wanted to sit and ponder all that I had learned, spend endless hours brooding over the likelihood of Arthur's secret identity, but the open door and the freedom it offered was too great a temptation. I began taking stock of myself, preparing for a daring escape that was probably exactly what they wanted, since they had been the ones to leave the door open.

Gingerly, I poked and prodded my own flesh, trying to tell what effects, if any, the *jhana* state had had on my body; after all, since my first exposure to it, I had gotten on a plane and flown half way across the country on a premonition. After the second, Ursula's gift had developed. Could it be cumulative? Would I acquire more abilities the more times I entered into meditation? There was no one to tell me. If Arthur was right about my transformation, it was happening in a way that no one could anticipate.

I cautiously moved my injured ankle surprised to not feel the slightest hint of pain or stiffness after my long sojourn. I wiggled the toes, stretched it hard, but the sprain had apparently vanished, and I hadn't even had to think about healing it the way I had for my wrist.

At least I've got that super power down cold.

In that moment, voices approached the French doors. I hastily leaned back and closed my eyes, trying to seem as lifeless as possible. Two men were talking in that long-dead language, arguing about something in tones that barely restrained whatever words were being held as weapons. One voice was my captor's: deep and controlled, a perfect, preternatural inflection seemingly designed to unnerve. The other voice was emotional, vacillating between pleading and force, and was somehow familiar.

"I said no," my nameless host finally growled in English. "Do you honestly want to risk the exposure? Think clearly, man."

There was a strangled sob and then a few loud breaths. "I know," the other voice panted hoarsely, "but I can't . . . stop thinking about it."

"Try harder. We had an agreement, an understanding; you can't just go back on that now. You were given power because we believed you to be capable of restraining yourself. Are you now going to disappoint?"

"I'm trying so hard, but I just feel like I would be alright if . . ."

There was a scuffle, as if the hysterical man were trying to get inside, and my host was attempting to keep him out. Then suddenly, the cart of tools was overturned in an echoing clatter.

"Get control of yourself!"

The familiar voice began to laugh and sob at once, sounding almost insane. My skin tingled with gooseflesh. It was like Ursula's cackle all over again.

"I'm trying, Karl, but it's . . . it's like a . . . a . . . drug. You know it is. I can see it on your face. You're not trying to keep me from seeing her! You just want it all for yourself."

Karl, hmm?

"If you don't calm down . . ." Karl's voice dropped to a terrifying depth as he leaned over his companion. "I'm running out of cells, but I'm sure we can find somewhere to put you."

The other man cackled and seemed to get roughly to his feet. "Just let me talk to her, once. Let me ask her what she meant! Just let me ask, one time, and I'll . . . I'll leave if you want. I'll vanish! Please!"

There was another thump of an object falling over, as if the stranger had grasped for Karl's hands and been shoved away. "You can't walk away from this, Moksha. It's too late. There's no going back. There is no vanishing."

"But . . ." and I finally recognized the voice, though it was much changed, "but what about the cure? I thought . . . I thought that . . ."

"There is no cure," Karl dismissed impatiently, to my shock. "The Arhat of the Sangha are damned and the only member of the First Circle that is still alive is Ananda."

I could almost picture the pompous CEO, fallen from high, shaking his head in confusion above the white collar of his pristine blazer. "No. I thought so too, but . . . but when she . . . you *can* see it, can't you? She had to have . . . to be that way, she had to have been exposed to . . . I'm not mad, Karl, I know what I saw!"

"Forget it."

"I can't!" Moksha cried. His voice sank to the floor and vanished within the folds of frantic weeping.

My heart jerked painfully in my chest as I lay there, trying to silence what I felt. I wanted to hate him. I wanted him to fall into a pit of black despair, just as my sister had fallen to that black street, but it felt wrong, somehow. It was Arthur's voice I heard in the back of my mind, reminding me of the *dharma.*

There is no going back.

I had no idea what Moksha had seen, what he needed to glean from further contact with me, but I had no choice.

I sat up suddenly and found him with my gaze.

Karl's back was to me. He was glaring down at the crumpled figure in disgust, fixing his collar and adjusting his expensive watch.

"I knew it was wrong to trust you with Ursula. It is obvious she has had a negative effect on your state of mind. It's not surprising with an attractive gift like hers, especially to someone like you." There was scorn in his voice, as if he found Moksha's imperfection particularly repulsive.

"Me? What about you? You drink blood just as we did."

"And yet I'm not a slavering lunatic like she was. I hate to say it, but I think the others were right."

Tears slipping down his face, Moksha looked up at him vaguely. "A black mirror," he whispered, "that's what Ursula saw. That's what we both saw."

Karl shook his head and walked to the desk, where he picked up the telephone and summoned assistance. I slid from the table and onto my knees in front of Moksha's unfocused gaze.

I want to save everyone, I thought.

Without knowing why, I reached out and touched his face, brushing blood and tears away. Life sparked back into his eyes and they found me with something like awe. I watched his expression change from loss to abundance, watched him smile weakly and relax back against the wall in what seemed like the bliss of a child.

"You asked me about weaknesses . . . you were hers and she was yours," he said quietly, putting his cold hands over mine. "Now you're perfect; alone, but surrounded."

"What do you know about the Guardians?" I asked.

I heard Karl spin and drop the phone at the sound of my voice, but I ignored it.

Moksha gave me a slack smile. "Do they want Ananda back now? They can have him. We won't need him anymore."

"Why were they paying Eva?"

Moksha shrugged, and lifted one of my hands to kiss. I was surprised to find that my skin did not crawl. The poor man, it seemed, had had some kind of break. He no longer seemed at all threatening. "Perhaps they wanted to be sure he was safe. Maybe they knew she was different. That you both were."

As if it was a delayed reaction, all the hairs on the back of my neck stood up.

"You didn't know until I mentioned the money," I pressed, cradling his moist face. "That was the first time, in your office."

He nodded happily, a shattered mess. "They knew we would be blinded by her. But how did they know? How could they see? They're just human, but they knew . . . I lost hope too soon. Now I'm too small to survive. I am so tired," he murmured, just before Karl shoved me back and pulled him to his feet. I stayed on my knees while they dragged the man who had once been my only enemy from the room. He didn't fight them, didn't look away from me, went to whatever imprisonment they had with a smile on his face.

Karl reappeared almost instantly, his face contorted in outrage. I had only a moment to stand up and compose myself. When our eyes met, my spine experienced a surging prickle that landed at the base of my skull and reverberated over the surface of my skin. A lethargic, medicated feeling dampened the urge to run even as goose flesh rose on my arms. I thought about how long I had been there, vulnerable to his unknowable perversions, and nearly jumped behind the examination table.

He smiled slyly. "Feeling rested?"

After a few moments of gathering my strength, I managed to summon a retort. "Why yes, I always find rubber floors so very comfortable. By the way, someone bit a hole in the wall, you might want to have it looked at."

His smile grew a bit, though his eyes maintained the voltage up my spine. It was clear that my delayed reaction was like patting him on the back for a job well-done.

"I apologize if the accommodations did not meet your expectations. None of our other guests have complained."

"I noticed that they don't have tongues."

His laugh was a staccato hiss. "Indeed. They seem to like keeping secrets."

I crossed my arms and tried to seem headstrong and independent, though I felt truly on my own for the first time. For once, Arthur's enigma and Eva's mystery were both preferable to this conundrum.

I looked away and thought about what Arthur had said about me being all that he desired. "You seem so sincere about wanting a cure, and yet you store your fellow Arhat in vaults. So, I suppose you understand why I'm confused. Who are you? What *exact* function do you serve in the Sangha? Are you a lackey, because I don't like dealing with underlings."

"I have lived for hundreds of years. Do you honestly think you can intimidate me?" he murmured in amusement.

"I don't care if I can or not. It's a simple question and the fact that you don't answer it tells me a great deal. So when do I get to see your bosses?"

He regarded me stoically for a time, then shook his head, obviously disappointed. "You are stubborn, just like her."

"Runs in the family. You think I'm a bitch, you should'a met my mom."

He snorted and propped open the dislodged patio door. The scent of lavender and mint wafted by me on a delicious draft. "I take it the *jhana* has had no effect."

I cocked my head to one side, "Actually, it's done me a world of good. Did you know that you can go wherever you want and *see* whatever you want?"

He froze and looked at me over his shoulder, watching me for signs of dishonesty. Apparently, he hadn't gotten that metaphysical memo. Ursula's gift tickled at my hindbrain. I could see that I had achieved a level of the *jhana* he had not. The thought was comforting. I sneered back, tempted to stick out my perfect tongue, and the perusal ended. He walked through the doors and waved a hand in beckon.

I followed him reluctantly, glancing at the solid objects on display, wondering how quickly he would respond if I picked one up and *intended* to bash him over the head with it. My fingers went out, but as if my arm was not my own, the numbing effects of his stare crippled me.

"I wouldn't, if I were you. It would be disastrous for your health. It usually is when the brain and the body go in separate directions."

Power over others.

It was his gift, and I had no means to escape it. Moksha had been so hysterical that Karl could not control him, and it had gotten him a cell in the bowels of the compound. Even if I had had a way to shrug off its effects, there was no guarantee that I would get any farther than him.

I curled my fingers back into my palm and looked after his unconcerned form as it left its back to me. I passed through the door and was immediately struck blind. I lifted a hand to shade my eyes, and slowly they began to adjust, though the light still hurt me.

It seemed that we were in a more private section of a garden. There was an elevated koi pond to my right and a waterfall trickled away from it, following a tiny path that wrapped around the dense shrubs. Trailing behind, I memorized as much detail as possible, creating a map in my mind that would be useful when I needed to "kick ass and take names".

Around the bend, the path widened. Fruit trees and flowering bushes buzzed with insect life, and it seemed that I had never before seen so many. They crawled on every surface, and for the first time, I could hear them, feel them, sense their existences as they went about their munching and pollinating.

Surprised, I stared around me, following some internal impulse to seek out the little distortions. A hummingbird fluttered around a beautiful lilac bush in full bloom. It hovered beside me for a moment at eye level, its body still, its wings a blur of movement. Almost as if it was acknowledging me, it stayed and only jaunted away when the jailor stopped and glared my way. It zigged and zagged to the air above the bush and turned back to see me. I found myself smiling, wondering what it saw.

Was this the true value of the *jhana*? Was it like a reset button, pulling me from my mind, so that I could reevaluate the world? It was incredible how detailed things were, and equally incredible that I had never noticed it before.

I was just beginning to think highly of the Arhat's aesthetic sense when the growth suddenly tapered off and the path turned to a thick green lawn. It was a large open space, a kind of manmade hill. Around its edges, other paths converged and at the top, a large tree reached toward the sun, casting speckles of light on the green slope, full of birds and bugs, swaying gently in the wind.

Around its thick trunk, there seemed to be a circle of large boulders, and beside one of the smaller rocks stood a man in a saffron colored robe that looped over one shoulder like a sari. He was bald, his muscled arms holding a platter, upon which sat a tea set. He seemed to be looking up into the branches of the tree, speaking to it.

My unsociable host led me up the hill toward the tree and as we crested the rise, I realized that the boulders were not in a circle. Indeed, they were in no discernible pattern at all. The entire base of the tree had been turned into a tiny desert and lines had been scored in the sand. They swirled without direction around the randomized rocks, like little whirlpools or ant trails; a massive fingerprint of soft, white powder. It was lovely, a contrast of life and dearth of life, a yin and yang that seemed so perfect it was impossible.

Zen.

As we reached the edge of the rock garden, the monk again spoke up into the tree, uttering a few smooth words that sounded almost coaxing. He glanced at me and at sight of my gender, instantly averted his gaze. As if desperate, he looked back up into the branches and pleaded with them.

To my surprise, there was a sudden motion and a person dropped out of the dense foliage. It was not really a drop, per say. It was as if they alighted on the ground, as if the air gently settled them there of its own free will. Movement utterly conserved, the yellow robe drifted into place and a long, beautiful, golden arm snaked out to touch the tree trunk as if in thanks.

Bewildered, I stood looking at the person with my mouth hanging open.

"I told you not to let him climb the tree," my captor snarled at the monk with the tray.

The tree-climber's eyes were wide and childlike. He had a playful mouth that might laugh at any time. He was perfectly striking, similar in coloring and bone structure to Arthur and the man beside me, but the longer I gazed at him, the less distinct he became. I could not tell his gender. If not for our host's convenient pronouns, I would have been at a loss, even with my new eyes.

As I looked at him and my eyes met his darker ones, it seemed all of my nervousness subsided. I began to feel fuzzy, as if nothing sounded better than taking a seat on the sand and sharing a cup of tea with him.

His smile widened.

"You *will* talk to this woman," my host said, and something in his tone told me that they had gone through a similar scenario before without success. "This ridiculous silence ends now! Do you understand?"

The robed man didn't even acknowledge Karl, or his perfect voice. He just stood there smiling at me as if we were long lost friends. Warmth began to replace the cold lack of feeling my guide had awakened. It was almost as if I could go back to the *jhana* while standing there and fly over the tree anytime I wanted.

The jailer then turned to the man with the tea set and barked some instructions at him in the dead language. As if annoyed that he had to listen when his real master preferred sitting in trees, the servant gave a shallow bow.

"You will sit with him and talk," the jailer then said to me.

Of course I would, I mused. Really I had no other choice, for nothing at that moment sounded as lovely. I was completely calm, staring into the man's eyes, and it was then that my *trishna* grumbled in protest.

Awakened to my senses, I turned to Karl. "Why should I?"

It was the first time I had questioned him. It didn't matter that there was nothing to gain from it, it was the fact that I *could* that impressed him. He stared at me as if astonished. Then, leaning close in greater threat, he dropped his deep voice even lower. It plumbed the depths of my ear canal and echoed off my resolve, and I could almost hear the machinations in it, the self-control it took to craft. "Because if you do not, you *will* regret it."

I crossed my arms stubbornly. "How? It's not as if you can torture me. I don't feel pain anymore and heal, dare I say, *super* fast. There's nothing you can do to harm me."

I watched as the tiny muscles in his face writhed. Each movement of his features seemed vast to my eyes, but resulted in only tiny differences of expression. I found that I could see his pores, detect the tiny blood vessels on the lids of his eyes. I was so lost in my newest ability that I barely heard him threaten me.

"Have you forgotten *how* you came to be here?"

I swallowed. They wouldn't hurt me; they would go for my human friends, Unger, Sam, possibly my aunt in Ohio, or my two cousins in New York. It was just one more reminder, as if I needed it, that I was not on an adventure or safari among new species of animal. I was among enemies.

I wanted to hurl an insult at him, but I couldn't. The tree-climber was watching, and try as I might, I could not avoid the sensation of accountability, as if I should know better. It reminded me of my mother, of the times when I was small and would get it into my head to do something naughty. She would glance at me with that look that said "I know what you're thinking and though I am not going to stop you, you should really consider that I am far wiser." That one look at him recalled for me the desperation of the Arhat, the terror they must be enduring. One look inspired pity in me, and again, calmed me completely.

"If you say so, but the harder you squeeze, the more it will slip through your fingers," I said lightly, glancing up at the wide limb where my new friend had been sitting.

"Advise me when you contemplate chewing a hole in a rubber wall and we will see how blithe are your replies," Karl spat at me. Then he turned back to the other man and dropped his arms to his sides where he clenched his fists. "Everything has an end!"

Turning on his heel, he stormed off to perpetrate some villainy, and for the first time, I thought I could see the impatience bubbling at the surface of his character. Where Arthur was a peaceful lake on a summer day, that man was a simmering volcano about to blow, and the mute man in front of me was . . .

I blinked at him. He stared back comfortably.

Still waters run deep.

He was tall and thin, but by no means skeletal. Long, dark hair was tied firmly at the very top of his head like a plume, but fell down his back without a strand out of place. His skin seemed to glow with a kind of bronze shimmer and was taut and smooth. Long, thick lashes brushed against finely arched brows and perfect lips curved into an almost ethereal smile of welcome. He looked exactly like statues from Thai temples, but seemed so much more inviting.

"My name is Lilith," I said, knowing it was completely unnecessary. Like Arthur, this person exuded an aura of omniscience, or perhaps an aura of acceptance. Maybe he didn't know everything, but what he didn't know would come to *him*, not the other way around; he was so inviting, I could imagine knowledge flooding toward him like unloved animals, wiggling up to his fingers to be stroked and coddled.

Shaking my head in confusion, I looked at the careful lines in the sand and wondered where it was I was supposed to sit. I tried, with slow, deliberate movements, to leap to a rock and not disturb the patterns, but the rock was too far to make it a clean landing. My companion watched me politely, saying nothing of my manners, nor any other topic. At the edge of the garden, the man with the tea tray seemed put out that I had ruined the wonderful effect.

"Sorry," I mumbled. "I hope you can fix it."

No one spoke. Shielding my eyes against the sunlight that streamed through the branches, I looked up at my companion. His head was tilted to the side and he was still smiling.

"I get the feeling you don't talk much and that maybe he should have just left me in the cell," I said nervously.

Instantly, his posture changed. He dipped at the knee and took a seat in the sand. Like a graceful stork, he folded his legs and slid into the lotus position as if born to it. Then he looked up at me through his eyelashes and seemed so sweet that I found myself laughing. He was an empath, I was sure. He had known how strange I felt staring up at a man I had never met.

The servant came over, pointedly tip-toeing to keep from mussing the lines.

"The lady wants tea?" he asked in a thick accent.

If the timeline was accurate, then I hadn't eaten in a couple of weeks, and stubborn, I refused to go beyond the point of no return. "Yes, the lady does."

He obliged, setting the tea tray on a large flat rock beside his master, though he refused to look at me. When I held out my hand for my teacup, he shied away from it deftly, and instead, left the cup on the tray for me to take. I at once recalled the things I had read about modern Buddhist monasteries and their practices. Monks avoided women, so as to cleanse their mind of impure thoughts, but somehow, I still got the impression he didn't like me very much.

He poured a second cup from a separate pot and carefully handed that to my silent companion. When he retrieved a lemon wedge and dropped it into the cup, I realized that the liquid was just hot water. I eyed my tea and swished it around, suddenly feeling like an extravagant heathen.

Finished with his chore, the monk stepped cautiously off the sand, again trying to make as tiny an imprint as possible, and then arranged himself at the edge of the little oasis of sand like a sitting hen.

My friend watched him go and as soon as the man found a comfortable position and was paying attention, he shoved his hands into the sand and dug a great hole. With youthful glee, he swirled his fingers through the lines, upset mounds and furrows, and in one final flurry of movement that sent sand into my clothes and hair, smoothed the entire plain around himself as if making a snow angel. Then he glanced at the monk and smiled.

I take it he doesn't make mandalas.

I giggled, thinking that he seemed like a large child, playing in a sand box in his best clothes, just to spite his parents. The monk bowed, but I could see the frown on his face. It occurred to me then that he must have just raked the lines, for there had been no footprints of the tree-climber's trek to his perch.

I tried to blink an apology, but got nowhere.

My friend looked at my cup and nudged his head, so I sipped it politely. It was a creamy green, with earthy back notes and just a hint of a floral nose, and it rolled around in my stomach warmly. It was also very strong, and before I had even finished drinking it, I felt the kick of the caffeine. Jinx would be glowing happily.

As I swirled it around my tongue, I thought of the 'nanobot' metaphor. If it was accurate, Jinx could probably manufacture caffeine in his own body like a cocoa plant, but I had no idea if that would have some kind of effect on the homeostasis he talked of. I wondered then, if I could interrupt the drug, stop its effects by convincing my body to ignore it. If I could, then poison would be one less thing I'd have to worry about in that horrible place, at least. I made a mental note to try it later, if the near future allowed me another opportunity to go into the *jhana,* which it most certainly would.

My companion was sitting amicably, awaiting my attention without intruding upon my thoughts. I tossed a casual smile at him and he responded, the bright yellow lemon wedge covering his teeth completely.

I laughed, surprising myself and our chaperone, but could not stop. I kept laughing until long after he took the rind out of his mouth and set it on the saucer. It seemed that all my pent up emotions saw the tide, and like drowning rats, clung to debris in hopes of finding dry land. I laughed until I was empty, until my sides hurt, and finally, I caught my breath.

"Thanks for that," I said, wiping my eyes.

He put his hands together and bowed over them.

I set the cup aside and leaned forward, dropping my voice. Ursula's gift might not work on him, but I had to try and get some truth out of this meeting. I watched him closely and asked my test question. "Is this a vow of silence, or are you just a quiet person?"

He blinked, tilted into my confidence, and held up a finger, then leaned back looking satisfied, as if he'd just uttered an entire soliloquy and been applauded.

Amused, I took the hint. He avoided gifts by simply not participating. It was like Arthur's Zen, all done in silence, each meaning unique to the individual watching.

"If I didn't know any better, I'd assume you weren't speaking out of spite."

He frowned delicately, for obvious comedic effect.

"That's what he'll think, you know."

He gave a minute shrug, as if he had absolutely no control over anything that our jailer chose to feel.

"How long will he leave me here with you?"

He shrugged again. His robe dislodged and slid down his shoulder.

"Will it be a while, do you think?"

The little monk sitting on the rock came to life suddenly. "Hours sometimes. Long time. Last girl here for whole day."

My heart skipped a beat. The last girl. He must have meant Eva.

"Was she blonde?" I asked, trying to sound casual. "Her hair, was it blonde?"

The man nodded, though it was clear he did not want to talk about it anymore, and perhaps should not have mentioned it in the first place. I nodded stiffly and lay back on the warm sand, hoping he wouldn't bury me and make designs over my body while I slept, as revenge.

"I hope you won't mind if I pop out for a bit," I said to my companion.

He shook his head, and made a hand sign that to me plainly said he was comparing me to a bird flying to freedom. I grinned and closed my eyes.

If they weren't going to give me an opportunity to escape bodily, well, then, I would just wander around in the astral plain. Short of killing me, they could not stop me.

Part of me was anxious to get back to Arthur, to reveal what I had seen, ask him if he knew my silent conversationalist, tell him about Moksha's strange nervous breakdown, and Eva's vistis to the Vihara. The other part of me wanted to see if, in this round of concentration, I'd somehow manifest Karl's or Moksha's gifts. I wasn't sure if it was possible, but I might as well try. It might come in handy, especially if I wanted to teach that asshole a lesson in humility.

I went straight to Arthur like a bee to honey, and found him, not at Jinx's side, but standing in a darkened room. The tiny auras of hundreds of lit candles flickered, illuminating a large, golden sculpture on a low platform. It sat in contentment and utter acceptance, one hand nestled in its lap, the other raised in the semblance of a wave.

It was a temple and Arthur was looking the Buddha right in the eye.

In the background, monks went about their business, cleaning, praying, watching Arthur without watching him. In tiny glances, they took in his seemingly disrespectful demeanor and said nothing.

Arthur, I murmured to his psyche.

His chin dipped in welcome, but his eyes remained fixed on the Buddha's face.

Shouldn't you kneel or something?

"This is not my religion," he said, almost surprising me right out of my meditation.

Oh?

"It was never meant to *be* a religion." The look in his eye seemed almost confrontational, and I could imagine why. It was not the Buddha he disliked; it was the existence of the statue that upset him. Arthur was against the entire idea of a messianic leader, and I could see it in the cold blue stare he gave the golden face.

Freedom from ritual.

He nodded.

A withered old man in a pumpkin-colored robe tottered toward Arthur from a door at the side of the platform. Beside him walked a younger monk, who occasionally put a hand out to assist him.

They're going to kick you out if you keep glaring at their icon and talking to yourself.

"They know what I am," he said quietly as they neared him.

So this is the monastery you told Sam to call?

"Yes."

The old man said something in what sounded like Cantonese and bowed as low as his crooked back would let him. I wondered how old he was, to look so gnarled with age, for it seemed to me that men of Asian descent did not show the effects of time until there were so many years tallied behind their name that it dwindled in significance.

Arthur spoke to him for several moments, his smooth tongue making easy work of strange syllables. Truly, it was astonishing how many languages he spoke, but then again, if I had forever, I could probably pick up a few things too.

Jt's not a hypothetical anymore.

If I had been a slave to my own neurochemistry, I might have felt uneasy at the notion of suddenly facing eternity. As it was, in the *jhana,* I was fine with the idea. If the Sangha were not there to constantly perplex and endanger me, I could see myself considering the many hobbies I would eventually master, like knitting, acrobatics, or playing competitive backgammon.

"Is there such a thing?" Arthur mumbled, while the old man conferred with his companion.

You know, I really have no idea. What's that Japanese game with the white and black chips?

"Go."

Huh? Where?

"It is called Go."

Oh. Do you know how to play it?

"I lived in ancient Japan," he said quietly, as if I could forget that he was so "well-traveled", "where it was very popular. Someday I will teach you."

No thanks. Knowing you, you'd probably be trying to make a pretty design and win totally by accident.

He continued to converse with the monk while I waited to reveal my newest information to him. It seemed that they were hashing out a difficult arrangement of some kind. The younger man's brows were furrowed in concern and he periodically glanced at his elder to gauge the old man's reaction to whatever news Arthur was disclosing.

What are you to them?

"Nothing," he said. To my amusement, the little old man seemed not to mind Arthur's spontaneous bouts of English directed at the air. Indeed, he would wait patiently and look around as if searching for signs of me.

So how do they know you?

"They . . ."

Let me guess. They found *you.*

"Yes."

Is there a metaphysical website that you all leave personal ads in, because I need to get rid of an old freezer and the futon in my attic.

Suddenly, the old man turned at looked directly at me, as if he could plainly find my outline in space. It unnerved me, because somehow, instinctively, I knew he was just a plain, old, garden variety human being.

"You're the one they need to speak to," Arthur replied.

What? Me? How . . . can he see me?

"He is very insightful. They're waiting, Lilith. Tell them what you have to say."

What do I have to say? I mused, suddenly, completely, and joyfully confused.

"Tell them about the man in the tree," he prodded.

If I had been standing there, I would probably have choked on my own swallow, but in the *jhana,* it seemed like a perfectly normal leap of understanding for Arhtur to make, even though it did surprise me a bit.

I can't keep any secrets from you, can I?

Arthur smiled. "No, but knowing you, that is probably fortunate."

Are you calling me a trouble-maker?

Arthur shrugged and gestured to the old man, who was still staring fixedly at my lack of a position. He said something. Arthur treanslated.

"Have you seen him?"

I am in a place they call the Vihara. I think it's out in the grasslands. They just introduced me to a man who doesn't speak. He's wearing a golden robe.

What the old man said next, needed no translation. "Ananda!" he cried happily and placed his hands in a prayerful position. I would have chuckled if I could. I wondered if Unger had felt deflated when Arthur told him sincerely that he was not Ananda.

I got the impression Eva had seen him before too. Do you know anything about that?

Arthur nodded. "Yes, the Sangha arranged meetings between your sister and Ananda, but always at a different location, and until now, we had no idea where they kept him."

I thought of Arthur's questions to me the last time I had spied on him. He had asked me if I had met anyone else, because he had known Ananda was there somewhere, waiting to be found. *And you came here, knowing I would be able to tell them what they wanted to know, because the Sangha would try the same thing with me!*

"Yes," he replied unabashedly. The conversation with the old man continued until their business seemed to be concluded. Happy and supported on both sides, the old man puttered away, too excited to bother with an immortal and his imaginary friend.

Arthur turned back to the statue with a tiny shake of his head.

What?

"He will not get what he wants."

What's that?

Arthur sighed. "To see Ananda again, before he dies. We both know this is not a possibility."

Again? And how do you know the old man won't see Ananda again? I protested, thinking that if a man had lived that long, he at least deserved the benefit of the doubt.

"Because we both know when he will die," Arthur disclosed, glancing my way.

What? You can tell *like the exact date and time?*

"Yes," he said, matter-of-factly.

Oh. Well, that sucks.

His left brow twitched. "It *is* unfortunate. He loves Ananda very much."

I scanned the room. *So these are the Guardians who paid Eva?*

"Yes."

Was she hired to find Ananda? And why are they so obsessed with him? Is he their leader? A sudden thought came to me. Ananda had sat, in fervid meditation, concentrating on the single purpose: to attain enlightenment so that he could recite. Had he, like Ursula, gotten *exactly* what he'd wished for? And if Jinx was right, about it all being Ananda's fault, then how could he too possess a coping mechanism? If the idea that triggered such horrible transformations was built into the sutras Ananda created, how could he be affected by it?

Could even holding the thought in your head be enough? It was concerning, especially since I had no idea what the thought was. Imagining it worming its way through my personality, eating away at the core of me, was terrifying. My pity for the Sangha grew.

His memory, I said to Arthur, *it wasn't just an idenic memory. It wasn't human.*

"You are becoming quite wise in your immortality, my dear," Arthur murmured. "It is true. Ananda has been cursed with a perfect memory that he cannot escape, as the human mind can only hold so much. When the Sangha kidnapped him, they endangered him in a way they cannot imagine."

Kidnapped?

"The man who died in Sam's shop was one of his handlers," he explained. "After Ananda recited the sutras, he saw how things had changed. Eventually, he went out on his own. He lived in monasteries and such, but was always followed by those who knew who he was. When he decided to attain the *parinirvana* . . ."

What's parinirvana? I asked.

"Some would say it is the final level of the *jhana,*" Arthur clarified with a shrug, as if he did not necessarily believe it. "The final Nirvana where death and life entangle. A stage beyond death."

Beyond death? How can an immortal go beyond death? Isn't he already?

He crossed his arms. "It is perhaps not real death, but simply seems like it to all those watching. It is said to be impossible to return from, that the body lays in a deathlike state for many days, immune to decay. And then the person moves on. If Ananda achieved it and returned, he would be the only one. In any case, Ananda began a new life. Only to be surrounded once more by those who came to revere him for his harmonious character."

How ironic.

"Indeed. Eventually, a group formed around him, his own circle of followers, and they set about taking care of him, just as the Sangha had done for the Buddha. Eventually, as these enterprises do, the circle grew, organized, laid out goals. However, their mission is one of watchfulness, they are record keepers, an entire society of rememberers, and because Ananda believes the Buddha did not desire followers, he refuses to aid their enlightenment."

I could see then, why Arthur was waiting. The little old man was returning, making his slow way across the lovely garden, over a tiny decorative bridge that arched over a small stream. The poor gentleman; as much as he loved Ananda, did not merit being saved. It was heartbreaking. I realized then, how blessed I was not to sit at Death's table and challenge him to a game of backgammon.

So they're all *still human? They're not like the Sangha?*

"They live and die, and over time, have come to revere Ananda's immortality to such a degree, that he was ensconced in their shrines and temples. He is a saint to them and cannot ever be free of it."

Why?

"If he were to go into the world, he would be confronted with a great many things it would be impossible for him to forget."

They protect him from himself.

"Yes. To this day, Ananda is moved to safe houses every lifetime or so, the latest being a vihara in the Texas desert. The monastery is always the same in every way, and because of this there is nothing new for him to remember, thus he is not buried by the weight of time."

Why did they have to move him? Why not keep him in the same monastery?

"At first, to benefit from his teachings. However, most recently, he was moved for his safety. He was being tracked."

There were other monks trailing behind the elder, obviously anxious to speak to Arthur, but out of respect, were matching their pace to his slower one.

Tracked by the Sangha.

The old man lifted a hand and swatted at the air, shoving a greeting at Arthur as if it was too much of a burden. Arthur gave a graceful reply. "Yes."

Then they knew what he had done?

"Sometime in the last century, the man who imprisoned you came to believe that Ananda held the key."

Karl? Who is he? Did you know him?

"Not well. He was a *srotapanna,* of the outer circle, but he is not the same man he once was. He achieved right liberation long after the Sangha was already formed."

Through the course of their quest to find to reverse engineer their cure, the Sangha had begun testing the sutras, seeing what they did to regular people. It was only *after* those people kept leaping into traffic that it was the sutras themselves that were tainted. They must have realized it was not the Buddha's fault, it was Ananda's. If they had found out Ananda was still alive, what would they do?

"After the Sangha targeted Ananda, he was brought to the United States, sometime in the seventies."

I tried to picture him waiting in line for passport photos but couldn't. *And you followed to see what would happen.*

The group of men had reached the door and Arthur turned away from me. Words were exchanged and I realized that I was being introduced when they all turned toward my position in space and bowed as a group.

They're awfully friendly, I mused.

"You are very important to them."

Ah. There was a lot of that going around.

The escort extended his hand. In it was a stack of bedding and a key. Arthur took the items, turned back to the men, and bowed. I heard him say thank you in their language and then he turned and walked away, pulling me in his wake. The monks watched him go, and though he did not turn to see their faces, I could tell that the older they were, the sadder they seemed.

"Ananda was moved from place to place each time he was found, and for a time, that was enough. But the Sangha is persistent," Arthur went on, saying nothing of the arrangement that had been reached, "they did not act until they knew Eva was ready."

Ready . . . I felt the shimmer of anger distort my focus.

"Do you remember, several years ago, when a Buddhist temple in Texas was burned down by what the police suspected were neonazis?"

Of course, it was in every paper and news program. I could still see the spire flaming like a giant torch, and the news woman's face as she detailed that all the monks had been lined up against a wall and executed. Graffiti had been discovered on several unburned walls and a group of local hatemongers had been rounded up and convicted, though they denied their guilt. It was one of the cases that helped instantiate the Federal Hate Crime laws, ensuring that people who committed such racially motivated offenses in the future, were held accountable in the highest of courts.

Then the Nazis were *innocent!*

"In many ways, desiring a death is the same as committing a murder," Arthur explained. I watched him walk through the buildings, giant sparse rooms without doors, on his way to some place within. "The man who died in the shop was not at the temple when it was destroyed. He returned in time to see them taking Ananda away. He followed them here, but being one man, he had no recourse against their powers."

They got to him before he could save Ananda.

"And when he needed help the most, he found me."

The knight in shining armor, I finished.

As he passed several groups of monks, doing chores or yoga, they bowed to him, moved out of his way, seemed almost to clear his path. It was how I imagined kings being greeted, but Arthur paid no attention to it. It was as if their genuflection meant nothing to him. I understood why, but his gentle correction was belied by the unyielding blue shards in his eyes. It was obvious to me that he disliked the attention paid to him. I knew he preferred me and my careless humor.

"You see me perfectly, my dear," he said quietly.

Which one of the names on the Jinx's list had been Arthur's? I found myself wondering what his real name might have been, the first words uttered over his head as his mother cradled him in her arms. What would it sound like, if he said it? I wondered if my constant affection bothered him, if it made him uncomfortable.

"It does not," he whispered.

Good, because I will never stop displaying it even if it does, I tossed at him flirtatiously.

"I will allow it," was his gentle reply.

My body was blushing, slumped against the massive metal door that sealed me into my charnel house, but there was no time for silly things like that. I had to figure out what I should do, and it all came back to the silent man in the tree.

I pictured Ananda, one long, lithe leg dangling from a branch, a carefree smile on his pretty face. Memory, when I considered it in light of Ananda's gift, truly seemed a curse. Humans, blessedly ignorant of so much, spent a great deal of time chunking data together, linking miniscule thoughts to larger ones. They busied themselves, creating rafts for ideas, rather than allow them all to slosh around between their ears. If a person could not ever forget, if when they closed their eyes, they could see every face and name, every moment of time, every single pang of regret, what would it be like? Tiny moments, stacked like cordwood, crushing him flat, it was no wonder Ananda liked to hang upside down and play in sand.

What was he like; Ananda, I mean?

Arthur's mouth split into a grin. "Delightful. His name means 'Bliss', after all."

What did the Buddha think of him?

"The Buddha loved him dearly."

Weren't they relatives?

"Cousins, and later, Ananda became the Buddha's personal attendant. They were always together, and often the Buddha allowed him to handle his personal business, even teach for him."

He picked his way through the men in prayer in another, stepping carefully so as not to disturb them, making his way to a door. I hovered beside him, like a balloon on a string.

"Ananda was the storyteller," he continued, "always amusing us with his humor and ease. He had a way of making anyone feel comfortable, and a method of correcting faults that never caused a person to feel mocked. He was gentle and always brought a smile to my face. There was never a person as charismatic as he."

It was the first time I had ever heard Arthur speak of those days, when the *dharma* had not been his alone. I supposed it to be part of Ananda's lingering charm that he could sweep away such troubles, with just the memory of him. I recalled the way his gaze caused a chain reaction of warmth and relaxation through my anxious body, making it that much easier to control myself and defy Karl's gift. Ananda was a healer of the first order, and no doubt, it sprang from his natural amiability and love.

So why had he done this to the Arhat? Why had he made it impossible for them to ever use the sutras to create a cure? Why had he made it impossible for them to go back to the word and see their own error?

I made to ask Arthur, but he was already shaking his head. He opened a door. Beyond it was a tiny room devoid of artwork or personality. There was a low table and a sleeping mat folded up in the corner.

You're staying here? I said in mild shock.

"For a time. Thanks to your excellent compensation." He took a seat on the floor and set the money on the table.

Trapped in a cell and I still have to do all the work. But shouldn't you be with the others? I would have crossed my arms and sighed playfully at him if possible, but I knew he would infer that quite clearly.

"It is for Sam's sake that I stay away from the shop. Hopefully," he looked up at me, "in a few days, we will have Ananda's exact location, for, as I said, I have ultimate faith in you and Jinx."

Finally, he had answered me in less cryptic words. It was the first time in our relationship that I felt I knew him, and I was glad that I had known exactly which questions to ask to unlock his trust. With what he had given me, I felt that I could finally make sense of the bigger picture.

Jinx had called it error correction. The Sangha needed the key in order to unravel the cipher, just as the hacker had for Eva's journals. They hoped, that if they had Ananda, he would reveal the changes he had made, but in his wisdom, for whatever reason, he had refused to speak.

That's why Ursula was here, I directed at Arthur thoughtfully. *I knew she seemed a bit too much of a diva to be shacked up in a warehouse. They used her to interrogate Ananda, and when she failed, they tried to use Eva to get to him.* My sister had been nothing more than a bargaining chip and the sugar in their medicine. *They thought if they let her meet him, showed him someone that he came to like, then forced him to watch her fall apart because of what he had done, he would change his mind. They thought he would cure my sister and that she would cure them. But why doesn't Ananda escape?*

"You met him. Do you believe he needs to be elsewhere?"

I take your point. I thought about the fate that awaited me when I woke. Stuck again behind high walls, unable to do anything, bereft of the acceptance that kept Ananda sitting in a tree as calm as the day was long. *What do you think will happen to me, Arthur?*

"The answer is, whatever you want. You are bound by nothing."

I felt the tug, the restless jerking on my consciousness. My body was being prodded. They were calling me back to endure more anguish on their behalf. I wondered what would happen if I ignored them, if I stayed with him and curled around him like smoke, but the pull was unavoidable. I had no choice but to return.

I welled myself in the hollow of his ear, trying to stay as long as possible. *Am I the leader of her revolution?*

"It comes down to a choice," he whispered. "Do you wish to be? Be careful, though. Leadership comes with a price."

CHAPTER 25

Ananda was sitting beside me, burying my right leg in the sand as if we were at the beach. At the sight of him, my sympathy converted into a sense of purpose. I sat up calmly and considered the Arhat, wondering if his silence would hold out. I picked up my tea cup from the flat rock and took a sip, the liquid was cold. Ananda blinked at me innocently, and though he seemed perplexed, I knew he saw everything he needed to see.

I lie back on the sand and let the sunshine soak into me. Closing my eyes, I refused to ruminate on the horrible uncertainty. I felt the past like chains around me, choking me, condemning me, and I was tired of struggling. The Sangha, my friends, Eva, they all were waiting on me to do something, *become* something. But at that moment, all I wanted was to slide into the *jhana* and stay there forever.

When the hand shadowed my vision and warmed my forehead, I said nothing. If anyone could understand, it was Ananda, and yet, he was the one I should hate the most.

"Why do you stay here? A prisoner of the people who killed your friends?" I did not expect an answer. If Arthur was correct, Ananda would never say a word.

A voice came out of nowhere, drifting on the wind like a feather, "No man is ever a prisoner unless he chooses to be."

Caught off guard by his words, I nodded. His voice was softer even than Arthur's and had a more pronounced accent. I imagined him living in a monastery for centuries, happily raking up sand only to smoosh it with a bare toe.

"So you choose to be a prisoner?"

He stared down at me like a man who did not speak my language and was trying to understand. "Who would *choose* to be a prisoner?"

"I . . . I don't really know."

I looked at him stupidly, realizing how completely foolish I had sounded. He had, in one fell swoop eliminated my need to ask the question. The answer was plain: there was no such thing as imprisonment.

"If you're not a prisoner, then what are you doing here?"

"Sitting in the garden with you."

"Right. I should have realized."

Cheerfully, he dug his fingers into the sand beside me and lifted a handful upward. Like an hourglass, he let the grains slip through his fingers, and when they were empty, reached down and repeated the process.

"Ananda, why did you do it?"

"Does it matter?"

I shrugged, making a small mountain, poking a hole in it turning it into a volcano I could later smash. "Kind of. Do you know the Sangha sort of ruined my life to get to the truth?"

"Kind of . . . sort of . . . you should have greater conviction, shouldn't you?"

"I need to know the truth," I replied, but when I looked up at his face, realized that I was not dealing with the same type of people Unger questioned every day.

"What purpose would it serve to know anything?"

"I don't really know."

His fingers were longer than Arthur's and as they swept sand away from mine, their grace charmed me. I stopped what I was doing to watch him work.

"If you do not know what you should know, or why you should know, or even how you should know it best, then what makes you think there is anything *to* know?"

Our eyes met.

"Someone told me that everything meant something."

"Someone you trust?"

"Yes."

He nodded as if it decided the issue. I closed my eyes.

"Did the ambition bother you," I said weakly. "Was it because they wanted to be better?"

"It was because they did not," he replied, much to my surprise.

I opened my eyes and followed the arm to the tilted shoulder, followed the shoulder to the sorrowful face. The old Lilith would demand answers, but my *trishna* was finally too weak to control me. I stared at him and when my eyes began to spin with the perfection they found there, I covered them with my arm.

"A child cannot ever know the true wisdom of his father, nor can *his* son ever guess at *his*," Ananda murmured in that same, airy voice. "It is impossible to become better than the tools you use, without tossing those tools aside completely. That is the heart of the Buddha's teachings."

For some reason, I began to laugh, but the laugh swung dangerously out of my control, until I was sobbing just like Moksha. Smoothly, Ananda's hand slid from my forehead to my eyes, and dropping my arms to my sides, I let him hide me from the world.

"Was it to punish them?"

"Punishment has no purpose," he replied evenly, taking the accusation in stride. "It will never bring back the things lost, undo the suffering caused. Indeed, there is no way to ever undo suffering. It is a natural byproduct of life."

I reached up and covered his hand with my own. "Tell me the story, Ananda. Make me see."

He let out a soft sound in his throat as if to laugh, and it was the first useless utterance he had ever made.

"We were children together, he and I, friends from the very beginning. I followed him everywhere and would gladly have suffered anything to preserve him."

I sniffled. "The Buddha?"

"Yes." The hand retracted gently and I was left feeling almost abandoned, but when I sat up and faced him, it was replaced. Long fingers curved around my own and anchored me to the sea of sand. "Many times, when we traveled, we were invited to stay in the houses of rich men, and though many of his followers did not understand why he was so willing to include them in his teachings, when they would never give up what they had to join our cause, the Buddha stayed with them."

"I read about them," I added unhelpfully.

Ananda smiled and carefully smoothed the hair from my face, much to the veiled chagrin of his chaperone.

"Lord Buddha wanted all to hear what he had to say, and innocently, I believed it was out of compassion."

"Wasn't it?"

His ponytail brushed from side to side as he shook his head. "It was the first step, a way of sorting the flock, of pulling reason from the noise."

"You mean, he was searching for people that could be turned into Arhat?" I sat up taller, gripped the hands in mine more tightly, lest the man suddenly get bored and try to escape into the tree.

But he did not go anywhere. "I believe so."

"Go on," I encouraged, though my stomach was churning apprehensively.

"While we slept, he would walk. At times I would wake to see that he was not there and it would worry me. The last time, I went to find him, feeling something stir in me that called me to his side."

I watched his gaze push aside endless years so deftly it was astounding. I was sure it was like yesterday for him, that in that moment, he was still standing beside his master, worrying after him, wondering if their midnight trek was another lesson. His eyes were glassy, focused somewhere in the air between us.

"He was beneath the tree," Ananda whispered, "staring at it. 'What vexes you, my lord?' I asked him, and he turned to me in what seemed like the gravest sorrow, a sorrow I had never seen from him before. 'When the seed becomes a tree, it ceases to be a seed. I am not a man anymore, I am this,' and he pointed at the tree. "It could never be any other way. I knew it from the start,' he said to me," Ananda blinked slowly, and a single tear dropped to the thirsty ground. "It frightened me."

"Why?"

"To know him was to be certain of the falseness of certainty. We were safe in that, because it gave us only the responsibility we took instead of the responsibility we could manage."

Confused, I slid my hand from his and placed it on the smooth coppery skin of his forehead. His eyes closed easily.

"From my cousin to my leader, from my friend to my instructor. He was changing right before my eyes. 'I love you, lord,' I said to him, afraid that he might be suffering. 'That is the poison,' he whispered, and then walked away from me."

I tried to reason through what he was saying, but something about him would forever be lost in translation to me. "He believed they were fixated on him?"

Ananda nodded. "He became a tree, not a seed. As he walked away from me, I understood his final lesson to me, that I must cast my tools aside in order to be strong enough. Within the week, he was dead and they were talking of the Sangha, their glorious organization. Then they built the wall around their tree and lied to the world."

I thought of Himsuka and the fearful king. "It was just a misunderstanding. Innocent people are dying."

"Those are the tools with which they were born. Weapons, all."

"Only because you made it impossible for them," I insisted, but he shook his head and pulled my hand away.

"That is the secret, my dear," he replied sadly, then he tipped forward and put his mouth to my ear. "I changed nothing. The truth of the Buddha is completely intact."

My mouth fell open. My head swept backward and I stared into his face. I wanted to call him a liar, accuse him of continuing to perpetrate the worst crime imaginable, but I knew, unequivocally, with absolute certainty, that he was telling the truth. As if I was in the *jhana* and was gazing at his memories the way I had perused my own, I could clearly see the Buddha's back as he walked away, his message ringing in my ears.

"All is perishable. Through vigilance, awaken."

Ananda bowed his head. "There were no perfect transformations, not even for the First Circle, just fruit, falling from the tree. All of us have our weaknesses, and our ways of protecting ourselves form them. With the Buddha gone, there was no focus, no direction. Leaders came and went, and as each member of the First Circle rose to the fore, they found themselves lacking. They sought *parinirvana,* and never returned. I believe the Buddha intended them to be as seeds for new trees, but instead, they rot in the ground."

"Then . . . they can't ever . . ."

"There is no cure, because there is no disease."

I said nothing. The wind danced through the branches, shifting light across the sand. I heard the last few weeks again, as if I was dying, and finally Arthur's warnings made sense. He had cautioned Eva to stay away, because he had seen her weakness: me. She would have done anything to help me, to keep me safe, to stave off death for as long as possible. In the alley she had fought, not with him, but with his quiet insistence that nothing good could come of such experiments. He had warned me to be of myself, less like a tree, more like a seed.

I let go of Ananda's hands and pressed my palms to my eye sockets, trying to dam up tears that would come regardless. I thought of my parents, killed for no reason. I thought of the monks in Texas, slain as a means to an end. How many others had there been? How many others had died, never to come back, because of a stupid, errant piece of reasoning?

I thought of Ursula's green eyes and grinning red mouth.

"Why stay here, in silence, letting them believe you had the answers?" I sobbed.

"If a man is responsible for all, then he is accountable to none. It is the *dharma* and I will not apologize for it." He took my shoulders in his hands and pulled me into an embrace, though I remained stiff. "The longer I am silent, the worse it gets for them, not because I am holding the medicine they need in my hands and hiding it, but because they *believe* I am. I have become their newest focus; they *chose* to look to me for the lesson of independence, and to reach it, I am silent."

I understood it, though it left a sour taste in my mouth and a cold lump in my throat. It was a complicated manipulation, all of it, and the Buddha was behind it.

"You're the second Buddha, though you are not a Buddha."

"And so it is."

The disease was just a choice. The fixation was the weakness. The first and only Buddha set a standard they believed impossible without him, something he expected. Ananda became the focus of their shame, probably the mission Buddha had given him. Now the Arhat were looking to me with the full weight of all their expectations, when I had not the slightest clue.

His arms tightened and I felt the moist pressure of his lips between my eyes. It sent a shiver through me and reminded me of Arthur in a warm way. "Do not be afraid, dear one. You are what you need to be."

"To what?"

"To be yourself."

"What about them?" I gasped, pulling away.

He head tilted to the side. "What about them?"

I shook my head, but denied nothing.

"We believe in *annica,* but if all is one, then one is all. Be what you are, independent of them, and perhaps they will come around. There is no way to teach what the Buddha learned. It must simply be accepted."

"You're telling me to give up?"

But he was already smiling. "Give up what?"

I realized my fists were clenched and my limbs were so tense, I might fall over from exhaustion if I relaxed even the slightest bit. I was angry that I was not the leader. I was angry, because there was nothing I could do to help the people that had destroyed my sister's life. I was angry because her life had meant nothing. I was angry because I could not govern the universe.

But to live was to suffer, and fairness was an illusion. I was clinging to something that did not exist, fixating on something that was impossible. By doing that, was I not contributing to the disease?

I let go, took one great breath and pushed all the sickening emotions from me. Limply, I pitched forward into Ananda's arms, where I lay for some time in silence.

I could still hear her voice, if I tried hard enough, asking me what happened to people who died. I was about fourteen, which made her eight. At the time, I was an angry teenager, free from all earthly concerns beyond curfews, proms, and why my mother wouldn't let me wear makeup. I had shrugged off her too-serious concern.

"They go to heaven," I had said, knowing it was simplistic. I realized then, how irresponsible it was of me to make such declarations. Looking back on it, it almost made me hate my father for saying the same to me.

"How do you know that's right?"

I could remember putting my hands on my hips and feeling a preposterous amount of annoyance. *"Who cares if it's right? When you're dead, you don't feel anything anyway."*

That gave her pause. Her eyes widened in that innocent way and she cradled her chin in her hand. *"Do people really see their whole lives before they die?"*

I was waiting for a phone call, and as it rang, I tried to push her out the door. *"How should I know? Why don't you jump off a building and find out, Munchkin?"*

I remember her frown as I slammed the door in her face. It was the same frown she had had at the funeral. It was the same frown from the alley.

What had she been thinking? What unanswerable question had driven her? Had her final act been to follow my stupid, inflexible instructions?

I realized that my eyes were looking in the direction of the monk. He was watching the two of us as we lay curled up in each others' arms, and he was judging us.

"All men deceive, see what will befall them and do nothing, are cowards at their core, but all men desire better. The desire, ironically, is the one thing holding them back, because they cannot think about *how* they think, *why* they desire. They cannot believe that the desire to be better is hiding the method to achieve it."

"Then what else is there? What can I do?"

"The way is to trick them into finding the way," Ananda whispered to me.

"How?"

"Block every other path, but the one that leads them back to themselves."

I was still shaky, but I sat forward and couldn't help but chuckle. "You sound like Arthur. I bet all you First Circle guys probably talk exactly the same. Remind me to never *ever* hang out with a group of you. I have a feeling I would pick up a thesaurus and beat someone to death with it."

Ananda blinked at me. "You know a member of the First Circle?"

I pushed myself up onto my knees. "He was Eva's friend too, or something. Actually, I'm not sure what to think of him, but I'm sure he's *my* friend. I get the feeling he's blocking every way but the one that leads me to myself, the jerk." Ananda helped me to my feet, braced me when I tottered in place. "He told me about you. Said you were delightful."

"That is kind of him. I wish I could say the same, though I am sure he is also delightful, if he is your friend."

"I'm sure you'd know him if you saw him and not just because of your memory. He kind of stands out."

"Really?"

"He's like, well . . ." I glanced at the Arhat, "he has blue eyes, for starters. He said that was common when he was born. Something about intermarrying tribes. You're the historian," I shook my head indistinctly.

Ananda's face transformed so suddenly, I nearly laughed, his mouth splitting into a happy and surprised grin. It was his first expression that acknowledged how old he was, that he understood the passage of time and the division between then and now. "Ah," he breathed, "yes, I know him well. He *is* very delightful."

"You guys were friends?"

"Oh, yes."

"Was he always so cryptic?"

Ananda chuckled happily, "I am afraid so."

"You have to tell me, just so I can hassle him," I insisted, pulling free from his arm, "what's his real name?"

He jumped up, took a few spry steps back, and without even the slightest effort, leapt back up into the tree, a sly look in his eye. "I am sorry. I have no head for names."

I laughed, certain it was some kind of conspiracy; that he had bought into Arthur's desire for anonymity.

"You have a perfect memory, but have no head for names?" I looked up at his jovial face and sighed. "How is that even possible?"

"Many different people have the same name, is that not odd?"

"Ah," I replied, though I wasn't sure I knew what he meant. I turned, expecting to see Karl gliding across the grass on a vicious wind, but there was no one to escort me back to my cage. I had time to think.

I took a seat on the flat rock and faced the monk. If there was no cure, no disease, if there was no such thing as enlightenment or higher wisdom, if nirvana was a lie, if the Arhat were all victims of their own assumptions, then the Buddha must have known. Surely it was not a realization he had suddenly while standing beneath a tree. He had spoken to his followers of other Buddhas, and yet had talked of himself as the only Buddha. I had thought it a mistranslation, but what if it was a reference to their flaw? What if he had always known that he was the first, the seed, but that a second would be chosen and that a third might come to be because of their followership?

It all led to the same question: why bother at all? Either this was the most pointless endgame ever, or it wasn't the end game.

I sucked in air and blinked at the monk. He looked back at me, perplexed.

The first lesson: describe the tools, the second lesson: toss them aside, the third lesson: how to build a world without them. The enlightenment was an unfinished progression, not a moment. Katsu was not an instant of understanding. Katsu was the slamming of a door, and if enough doors could be locked, then the student would eventually wander in the right direction.

But what's the right direction?

That was the deepest riddle of them all. What was at the heart of the struggle, the ultimate goal of all mankind? Why did we rise each day, work hard all our lives, and die with our wills drawn up? Why did we live?

Because life happens, and why not?

We lived to continue to live. That was the destination, but the Arhat were immortal already, so what was their destination? To live *better*, as Eva had said. Each leader of each successive era of Arhat had to trick them into evolution, herd them like cattle to the complete control of their desires. That was Eva's mission. She had believed that now was the time for the next phase.

It comes to a choice.

My captor was sitting in front of a computer when I found him, leaning over it as if he wanted to dive into what he saw, the fingers of his right hand rolling the little wheel on the mouse in a frenzy. Suddenly, he pounded the desk and leaned back, frustrated. On the screen in front of him, Jinx's program was parsing language, sorting through random words, decoding Eva's journals. It would have been unsettling, watching that man run his claws through her vulnerable thoughts, if not for the success it signified.

Whoever had checked Jinx's drive for bugs, had reconnected their computer to the system and sent the files on the drive to Karl; which meant that Jinx could, at that moment, be rifling through their mainframe, adding to his knowledge base, constructing doom for their unsuspecting machines.

A heavy crystal wine glass sat before his left shoulder, and as Karl scrolled through the sutras, his hand shot out, much as Jinx's for a coffee mug, and grasped the prismatic stem. A dark red liquid sloshed around in the perfect lead-lined goblet, viscous and slowly congealing. It was blood, and not the kind that resulted from the tinkering of a few bartenders in a dark dance club. I watched him gulp it down, roll it around in his mouth lustfully, watched him close his eyes in contentment as he consumed a piece of someone else.

I found myself wondering whose blood it was, and realized that I already knew. My thoughts went back to Eva's autopsy and the puncture marks on her arm.

My calm fractured and then collapsed.

"Is Ananda finished with you, then?" he asked as he fingered the glass idly.

I swallowed. I had to maintain that state of utter complacency, that was neither interested in, nor attached to any answers that might be found. I had to be aloof.

"*I* left *him*."

There was a moment of pause as he wondered if I knew the truth, if Ananda had revealed the secrets to me that would undo their terrible condition. Staring at the dark red of the glass as it sloshed around like liquid gelatin, however, I would never have cured them if it *were* possible.

"And why would you do that? He is, after all, such a marvelous conversationalist."

"I've learned all I can from him."

"Really?" He sat forward and turned toward me, trying to seem casual, though I could see the ravenous glint in his eye and the tension of every sinew. "So he finally spoke to someone? I suppose that means you will soon have outlived your usefulness!"

I watched him, refusing to rise to his bait. In the back of my mind, I was contemplating strategy, thinking of how difficult it was to remember what my mother had always told me about the bullies at school.

It's not about them. It's about you. Who do you *want to be? Don't let them change you.*

I was trying to be compassionate, but I mostly just wanted to crush his larynx.

"My, the look on your face! You'd think I was going to toss you in with the undead right away!"

I thought of the hidden ones, forgotten, rotting underground like so many corpses, and marveled at the strange patterns people obeyed. From epiphany, to devotion, from devotion to myth, from myth to superstition and ritual, and from those to this final stage: whatever it took for the mind to obey when the heart could not. It was pathetic.

I felt strange, then. In a moment of disassociation much like seeing my own body from a distance, I stood, critically analyzing what I was. I was meta-thinking, thoughts about thoughts, and it was almost chilling. Had I obeyed that same path? If not for Arthur's intervention, wouldn't I have seen my fate as inevitable? What if it was the perception of the map, the physical map, that determined how a person traveled? What if the real destination was a place with no roads?

Suddenly, I no longer felt anxiety or disgust, as if my mind had shut off sensation and was simply analyzing data. It was colder than the jhana, but as seconds drifted by with me lost in its murky depths, I found it was not such a terrible state to occupy.

"You'd have at least a few weeks before Moksha began gnawing off his limbs, anyway," Karl chuckled.

He was testing me, sampling my personality for any drastic shifts. Detached as I was, I was unaffected by his bullying and callousness, but knew I could not allow him to see that. If I was going to paint myself a messiah, escape through acceptance, then I could not seem as emotionally isolated as he.

"I do not believe he will," I said softly.

"Why is that?"

"Because we have crossed paths."

His chuckle turned to outright mirth. "And something about you makes a difference?"

"Starving men do not beg for salt. I am what I needed to be."

He leaned back in the chair and raised an eyebrow, looking me up and down in mockery. "You are certainly arrogant for a prisoner."

I bowed my head, "A man is only a prisoner if he wishes to be."

"The biometric lock on the steel security door thinks otherwise," he shot back with a smug grin. "You enjoy parroting adages, don't you?"

Parroting. Ha.

These were the tiny arrows that cut us to ribbons, these pointless witticisms at each others' expense. If the larger portions of meaning in our lives were constructed of these brittle seconds, what fragile and hollow things they were.

"Believe what you want. It will not change anything. And I will not give weakness a place to form."

I turned away and my eyes caught the glass.

The cold, metallic casement of that eerie peacefulness began to melt and transform into ire. I clenched my fists and could feel my flesh warming. In a tremendous backlash, I suddenly saw it as my one responsibility to prove all that he said wrong. Every day people gave in, bit by bit, to insurmountable odds, or disproportionately huge circumstances. I no longer could, because I no longer wanted to. I had seen how false it really was. Someone had to do it, and that was me, even if escape was not in the picture.

It was a more powerful emotion than any I had ever felt, yet strangely, did not impel me to act. Instead it calmed me, taught me to be still, and laid his feelings at my feet, as transparent as glass.

I wonder if this is what Arthur feels.

He followed my gaze to his drink and swirled the particles around in their plasma like a sommelier about to sample. "You're wondering why, aren't you? Why blood, of all things?"

"No," I replied calmly. "I know why."

It wasn't just about closeness. The doctor had said bleeding was medicinal. At some point in their past, perhaps consuming blood had been the best medicine they could find.

Karl's aloof smile faltered. I think that for a moment, he thought my intensity was caused by a hunger like his own. He picked up the glass and proffered it to me. "Would you like some? She really was the closest we've ever come. You can taste the way her body was adapting to our conditioning. Amazing that the biology so closely follows the mind."

When I did not reach for it, he took another sip and sighed happily, "We kept a close eye on it, much as you would a wine. It started as drug tests, but after a while, there was no point in that ruse anymore. Eventually she relinquished it willingly, though now I realize that it was only her way of making sure that she could continue her visits with our mute friend. I think she got a great deal more from him than we wished her to. She was very clever, your sister."

My eyes narrowed, as I made use of the tricks my friend Moksha had taught me which I only now realized I could imitate. In the tiny muscular contractions of Karl's face, I read a hint of bitterness and shame. Whatever utility Eva had had, she was a personal benchmark for him. Karl had wanted my sister and had been unable to possess her. His ego still ached from the bashing.

He looked up at me, still swirling. "It makes me wonder what you'd taste like . . ."

My stomach plummeted. A piece of her, a living piece, above ground, outside the opalescent shell.

My hand shot out and in a sidelong swipe, I knocked the glass from his hand. Crimson fluid spattered his white linen shirt, spilled a pattern across the rug. The glass hit the ground with a hollow ring and rolled toward the door.

We stared at each other, he in surprise, and I in condign fury.

"Drink it now," I commanded.

He attempted a snort, but it ended in something of a growl. "You've ruined it."

"You were desperate for it before; why not lap it off the ground like a dog?"

His eyes went wide, the fine lines around them gone. He looked almost awed, until the slack skin around his mouth tightened and the shadows darkened. An insignificant alteration of expression, but to my more acute vision, it was as if he scowled.

He was up and diving toward me before I had any time to anticipate. I was unprepared for a physical fight, and even though I could defend myself, I was smaller, weaker, and seriously lacking in the psychic powers department. Tackling me to the ground, he crushed me to the floor. His hands clenched down around my throat, and his fingers began to squeeze like a steel vice. Darkness set in. There was a dull cracking sensation as he lifted my head off the ground and slammed it down again and again. I clawed at his hands, fighting desperately to breathe, but could not even budge his littlest finger. Losing coherence quickly, I realized I could no longer struggle; that each kick was using valuable resources, and taking me even closer to the end.

Can I die? I found myself wondering, as I began to black out.

Suddenly, the pressure lessened. A man was pulling Karl off of me. The two of them struggled about the room, furniture overturned. A grouping of statues landed all around me like tipped bowling pins as I struggled to pull even the tiniest breath through my swollen and collapsed throat. By the time my vision had begun to return, and my body had begun to heal, the fight was almost over. Karl seemed to have wounded the other man. He lay on the ground near the French doors, blood oozing from a gruesome head wound.

"William?" Karl raged. In his hand was a figurine that had been turned into a cudgel. "You betray me? After what the Sangha has done for you? The others, surely, but you?"

"Don't hurt her," the man on the ground slurred. I recognized him. He had been the security guard to throw me in the cell, the one whose knife I had borrowed to cut my stitches. His nose was broken and a large lump of detached tissue was hanging over his eye, exposing a massive skull fracture. "Please."

Karl lifted the statue and with a growl, smashed it down on the man's head. There was a sound like a watermelon being dropped from on high.

I realized only as it echoed into the silence, that I had screamed. Slowly, the maniac turned and dropped his weapon. He was disheveled, spattered with blood, cut and scraped, but somehow still managed to look businesslike. He stood up straight, fixed his collar, took a moment to make sure his shirt was tucked just so, and I sat on the floor, staring at the dead body in paralysis.

He had just killed a man in front of me. A sudden thought of Ursula laughing, licking blood off her fingers blasted through my brain as Karl, very calmly, did the same.

See what they're willing to do?

Karl took a deep breath. "Well, now that we've gotten that out of our system."

I sat, completely unable to breathe, or move, or think, and watched the pulp that had been William's head splotch the floor. I saw what seemed to be brain tissue and felt sure I would vomit, but nothing came. I bent over, coughing, when suddenly Karl grabbed hold of my hair and began dragging me. I tried to hold back, tried to tug free, but somewhere near William, I slid in the blood and lost my balance. My face smacked into the door frame.

Furious, Karl twisted my arm and bodily, hefted me onto my feet. With a massive shove, he sent me out the door a few steps, just far enough away from him that he could get over the threshold and recapture me. I managed to stomp on his insole, but that only angered him. With a single, massive punch, he hit me across the face. Sparks flew across my vision. I lost motor control. Then he grabbed me by the elbow and began to drag me again.

No amount of struggle seemed enough. I screamed, kicked, and punched. I even bit him, but each time, he would just hit me and send me flying. Finally, he tired of the whole process, and flagged down a few suited security men who had come running.

They picked me up, still thrashing as violently as my injuries would let me, and wove their way through the compound. Eventually, I was thrown into a chair. The click and snap of handcuffs woke me from my fear induced hysteria. I sat panting, looking around me in terror.

It was a large, cold room, and upon every wall surface were monitors. In a long bank on either wall, computer terminals were manned by dutiful techies, with none of Jinx's style or flare. They sat staring at their work with dull expressions, as if they had been medicated. Only the one over whom Karl loomed had any hint of emotion on his face, which had turned a greenish color as Karl continued to issue commands into his ear.

When he stood up straight, the computer tech snapped into action like a drone, typing out code and accessing data.

"You fucking pig," I sarled at Karl.

The man ignored me.

"Is this where the Buddha's grand message has gone? You just bashed a man's skull in! He was one of you!"

Karl's vicious eye rose over the hill of his shoulder and glared at me. "So grand even he could not bear to witness it?"

"What is that supposed to mean?" My voice was raw, garbled with pain, but I would be damned if I'd let him silence me, even if I had to whisper. "You're crazy!"

Karl smiled. "I am what my maker designed." I began to shake my head, but he would not hear it. "What did Ananda say to you, Lilith?"

"I'm never going to tell you."

"If you don't there will be serious consequences." He leaned forward smoothly, displacing the clone in his rolling chair, and tapped a single key. A monitor divided into four tiny screens. In horror, I recognized the coffee shop, buzzing with thirsty patrons and Jinx's home, its yard littered with motorcycles. The other two screens depicted places I did not recognize: a ranch-style home set back from the street and surrounded by an iron fence, and a large multi-storied building. In each window, inky shapes moved, gliding through the terrain in the familiar pose of sharp-shooters wielding AK's. They swarmed the sites, hand-signals and all, and prepared for their entrance.

Delighted in his brutal way, Karl snatched the headset from the operator and brought the mic to his lips.

"Get it over with."

With mechanical precision, the four teams kicked or rammed in doors, disabled Jinx's motion-sensitive cameras and repelled over his tall security gate.

I gasped. How did they know Jinx even existed? They must have followed me. I lurched forward and clung to Karl's arm with my free hand. "Don't, please! This isn't necessary! I'll tell you whatever you want to know!"

"Too late. These three have outlived their usefulness, but I'm sure you have other people you care about," he said, trying to shake me off.

I grappled for the mic, but with one momentous shove, he hurled me back. The chair I was chained to, flipped end over end, taking me with it. I smashed into the floor with a dizzying impact that knocked the wind from me, but then the pain vanished and I felt the warmth of the tissues repairing themselves. The arm of the chair to which the handcuff was attached had broken. I crawled slowly on my knees as the two computer nerds flanking me looked on in vague dismay. On the screens, the SWAT teams were converging on their unsuspecting targets.

I looked on, powerless, as the team in the upper right screen smashed in the front door of the house and marched through its hall and carpeted living area. The camera jiggled, mounted on one of their dark shoulders, and found the body of a man, sitting in a chair with a half-empty glass of Scotch beside his slack hand. It was Matthew.

He leapt up, reaching for his sidearm on the table beside his recliner. He got off one shot, just as the men came from behind. As they tackled him to the ground and restrained him, the team in the lower left screen broke through the window of Jinx's French doors and scattered through the mansion.

Breathless, I prayed that he was off somewhere else, but then I recalled that the green and black ninja had been parked in his driveway, which meant he had to be there.

The coffee shop emptied quickly, as customers screamed and dropped to their knees. The barrista reached for the telephone but was unceremoniously hit across the face with the butt of a gun and dragged outside. While I panted and tried to get back to my feet, the camera was carried through the shop to the upstairs apartment, I thanked Arthur's prescience for teaching him to hide out at the monastery. His immaculate white bathroom and bed were empty. All that existed to show anyone lived there at all were my sister's color-coded journals.

A gloved hand shot out from beneath the camera and disrespectfully shoved a few onto the floor. They rifled through her soul, looking for clues, and then tossed them aside.

"There's nothing here," a garbled voice said.

"Burn it," Karl demanded.

"Roger."

"Stop!" I shrieked, pulling my disobedient body upward. They were about to destroy Sam's well-deserved dream, and for some reason, that hurt more than anything else. I could see Arthur's face as he stood in his kitchen and told me that if the coffee shop burned to the ground, and all of his books were destroyed, he would be content doing something else, somewhere else.

"I have very little to miss."

"Tell them to stop!"

As the coffee crew stuck devices around the apartment, and Matthew was pushed, bleeding, into a black, windowless van, the team at Jinx's house got a mean surprise. The speakers echoed with a metallically shrill version of Jinx's smart mouth.

"Redundant security systems are bitches, huh? You fuckers really need to work on the ninja stealth. So not impressed."

My laugh squelched out beneath my sobs.

"Sir, it appears he saw us coming."

"I don't care if he did or not," Karl seethed, "Find out where . . ."

"It's called a panic room," Jinx chuckled, "and it's designed to be impenetrable."

Karl's face contorted. "Is it designed to be fire-proof?"

There was a moment of silence that was twice as long for Jinx, and unaccustomed to such things from him, I knew he was realizing the one flaw in the design.

"Prolly not," he said finally, "but I am."

"Hmm," Karl growled. "Smoke him out."

Images of carefully catalogued collections flickered through my mind, but oddly enough, the thing it lodged upon was that damned bean bag chair, grinning up at me emotionlessly. It was all I had left of her.

"You can't . . ." I murmured, "please." My face was damp with tears and though I was now standing, my hip would not function.

In two of the four screens, fires began, while in the last remaining screen, I saw them scale the stairs of an apartment building and turn a thin door to mere splinters. Sam was just inside, attempting to jump out a window. He was dragged back and before his training could kick in, they had outmatched him and shoved a black bag down over his head.

"Stop!" I cried, but no one was listening. I looked around at the others, those people who seemed to worship individuality, yet could not divide their mind from Karl's long enough to protest the destruction of one of their fellows. "How can you allow this to happen? When did it turn from seeing life as sacrosanct, to destroying everything you touch?"

They refused to look at me, their heads bowed in shame, while Karl continued to give orders to his crews. Jinx's house exploded in flashes of smoke. The camera was jostled as its operator ran from the building to a predetermined position. They surrounded the home and waited. Long minutes ticked by. As the Spanish architecture buckled beneath the growing inferno, a tiny figure staggered from the rubble, on fire. Before it could even stop, drop, and roll, it was hurled to the grass, put out by the sheer weight of bodies. It struggled only slightly, and as the camera shifted, a scorched, but never tarnished boy was hoisted up, still hurling obscenities.

The final screen was cleared by the team leader and heedless of the other occupants of the building, the fires were set. Smoke detectors went off from every side, and while the team fled, Sam in tow, families began emptying into the halls in various states of undress and fear.

I closed my eyes against the tears. Kicking and screaming, my companions were all black-bagged and restrained in the back of identical tactical vehicles. It was all because of me.

CHAPTER 26

As I sat bolt upright, soft arms released me. I turned, dizzy, frantic, overwhelmed, and found Ananda staring at me with a knowing glint in his doe eye. Reaching up, he placed a soft hand on my forehead. As if it was rain, all my misery slid off me into the sand and was forgotten.

"I . . ." I began, trying to find dry land in the ocean that had become my reality, full of undercurrents and crushing upheavals. "You . . ."

In one smooth motion, he held his finger up to his lips.

And I knew.

The fight with Karl had never taken place. Nor had my conversation with Ananda. The Guardian had remained true to his vow, silent until . . . until what?

He grinned and got to his feet, shaking clouds of sand out of delicate folds. Before I could say anything, he was back in the tree, staring down at me like a bemused squirrel.

I had time. If I could just get somewhere and figure this all out, I could get us both out, and maybe even end this fight. I had to find a place that was safe.

I jumped to my feet and looked around, trying to recall the map I'd been building in my mind, but my thoughts were so horribly confused. Ignoring Ananda's attendant as he tried to stop me without touching me, I made a dash for a door I had spotted off the courtyard. It appeared to be unguarded, until suddenly there was a man standing in front of it. I nearly collided with him, I was moving so quickly, but he caught me around the waist easily.

"Lilith," he said into my ear. He spun me around and gently shook some sense into me. I recognized him instantly as my gentleman kidnapper. His hair was tousled, his tie gone, and his earpiece unhooked from his ear. "Lilith," he repeated.

I held up my hands in instant submission. "You got me.""Come with me. The cells are full. It should be easy to find you somewhere else."

I frowned and held very still, feeling his chest move against my back as if every breath were labored. "When Karl sees that I'm gone . . ."

"I'm head of security," the man said. "I've already been given permission to put you in the main quarters if need be. But I can't leave you alone."

The way he said it sounded almost apologetic, and my fears were instantly at ease. Something about him told me that if there was a friend to be found in this place, he was that man.

I turned to attempt a smile of gratitude, and found the face of my gentleman kidnapper, a man I had, but moments before, witnessed gurgling in his own blood.

"William!" I gasped.

Surprised that I knew his name, he blinked at me. "How . . ."

I shook my head. "Just get me some place safe."

He nodded and took my arm chivalrously. He said nothing as he led me from the garden to one of the residential wings, though he closed his hand over mine as it rested in the crook of his elbow. I tried not to show my anxiousness as I mulled over how much time I had left, if the visions could be trusted.

Only once, when Mathew was kidnapped, had they ever proven linear, warning of things that would come immediately, and even then, I had been warned once before, far in advance. They seemed to hold snippets of information, designed to guide my choices or more often than not, events that proceeded from a choice I had made, showing me the negative impact that choice would have, before I'd even finished making it.

How could I know which rule this particular vision obeyed? What if, as my abilities grew and refined, they would all become instantaneous warnings?

I turned and looked at my escort. He was quiet, subdued, and yet he watched me as if waiting for something. If I trusted him, would he prove worthy? I had come to rely upon my visions, but maybe it was time to try Ursula's methods on for size.

I knew then, inexplicably, that though it was not necessary for the magic to work, it did help to be in physical contact. Something about his skin and the warmth that emanated from it, the transference of energy, told me that if I asked, I would know the truth. I thought back on all I now knew, on Karl's little speech about his choice of beverage and knew why Ursula had been so able to read me, even though she had never touched me.

Eva's blood was my blood.

"Can I trust you, William?" I asked, just as we entered the hall.

He halted in his tracks and blinked at me. "Yes," he said finally.

I smiled my most glowing smile and gave him an approving nod, because I was positive he was honest to his core.

He walked to a door and using a magnetic pass card, opened a set of double doors. On the other side, was a large room that reminded me of the honeymoon suite that Howard had booked for us.

My spirits instantly sank.

There was a large King-sized bed packed with pillows, a fabulous set of mahogany furniture, fine fabrics, soft carpeting, and above all, that same haphazard faux-elegance. I felt as if I was trapped in Las Vegas, minus the views of a garish strip of neon lights that turned the darkest shadows into cheerful, hope-filled day.

From the balcony, there was a view of the garden and Ananda's tree, though the legend was no longer inhabiting it and the lines in the sand were being redrawn.

On the other side of a regal archway was a bathroom the size of Eva's apartment, tiled entirely out of rose-veined marble. I wandered around it aimlessly, trying to phrase my question just right, with William in tow.

"You should clean up a bit," he suggested, "since you have the time."

I gazed at him. His had a look of gentility on his broad, masculine face. Cocking my head to the side, I realized that I could clearly picture him as a man in uniform. He had the spine of a Devil Dog and the deportment of a Naval Academy grad. Never once had he been disrespectful toward me, even though he had no reason to be polite. Sure, he'd shoved me into a cell, but who wouldn't with Karl giving the orders?

"William," I took a deep breath and glanced around, "if I needed to know something important, would you tell me?"

His brow furrowed slightly. "What do you need to know?"

"Are my friends in danger?" I sat on the edge of the mammoth tub that was almost like a pool. "Is Karl planning on sending a SWAT team to capture them?"

"Friendzzzzz . . .?" he commented on the plural. I stared back emotionlessly until he sighed and looked away. "Not that I know of."

It was my turn to frown. I put my face into my hands and wondered what I was meant to do. Had the vision been warning me against attempting to control Karl with his own power? Had it been trying to show me the outcome of Jinx's hack? Was it some eventuality that might come to pass if my actions had proceeded from that point?

Most importantly, could it now be avoided?

"I don't understand," I whispered.

William said nothing. He reached inside a closet and pulled out a towel and bathrobe, and hung them from the hooks just inside the archway.

"You should . . ."

"Not now," I cut in, realizing how abrasive I sounded just in time to correct my tone, "I don't need to bathe, I need to meditate."

It was a phrase I never thought I would say.

"Your friends are fine. Karl doesn't care about them as long as they don't interfere."

I shot to my feet and began pacing. "How can you be sure?"

"I just am. Detective Unger was released, remember?"

I didn't want to mention my other friends, the ones that they might *not* know about, namely Arthur. I could still see Ursula's ravenous death-grin as she ripped the image of him from my mind.

I turned away from William and wandered toward a makeup desk and lighted mirror.

"Forgive me if I don't trust you entirely." I plopped onto the stool and was about to rifle through the contents of the drawers, an activity that usually perked my spirits, but I caught sight of my face, and froze.

At first confused, I turned and looked behind me, but the room was normal. William stood a few feet away beside the foot of the tub, gazing at me with his passive keenness. Suddenly uneasy, I turned back to the mirror and realized that it wasn't the room's fault, it was mine.

My face was completely different, or more appropriately, looked like it was a mask being worn by someone with better and more pronounced bone structure. My skin was flawless, all fine lines and minor bothersome spots gone. It looked as if my complexion had transformed into beautifully pale sandstone, supple yet still stony, struck through with the pink stria of my lips. My dark hair, usually a rat's nest of wave and frizz had smoothed to a shimmering Pantene commercial. My dark eyes seemed to refract more light than usual, from obsidian to star sapphire. My expressions were so precise that my look of abject shock might have been used in a CIA handbook of what to look for during interrogations.

"Amazing, isn't it?" William murmured with a smile in his voice. He didn't care if I showered; he wanted me to see myself.

I stood up and looked at my reflection in a full length mirror to my right. Gone was my protective layer of whale-fat I had convinced myself was the epitome of feminine virtue. My well-maintained muscles seemed to jut from beneath my flesh. Sliding my hand under my t-shirt, I found that my stomach had completely smoothed into the washboard Howard had always wanted. My mouth hanging open, I looked for the scar on my hip, where a nail had torn through my skin during a friendly wrestling match with a neighbor boy, only to find that it too, had vanished.

"What . . .?" I gasped. "What the hell is going on?"

"You have control," William explained a little too happily for my state of mind. I dropped my hands and glanced his way, dumbfounded. "It means there are no more DNA copying errors. Right now you're regressing to the point at which you stopped maturing and began decaying. You're twenty-five again."

Twenty -five was not the best of years. "Is that supposed to make me feel better?"

His lips parted, but he said nothing.

I did a twirl and looked at all of my other womanly attributes, to find them all exactly where they should have been, which was *not* where I had left them.

"Fucking cockmongers . . . ."

He made a noise in his throat, as if he could no longer stand seeing me in distress and nearly lunged for me. With a determined expression, he took hold of my wrist and pulled me back into the bedroom. Without preamble, he pulled out one of the comfy chairs surrounding a round game table and pushed me into it. Sitting across from me, he put his elbows on his knees and took my hands in his.

His earpiece dangled from the collar of his coat, forgotten completely.

For a few moments, he tried to form words, his eyes sometimes pleading, sometimes ashamed. As distracted as I was, I couldn't help but feel curious and compassionate. Something about his face and the tiny looks he gave me piqued the interest of Moksha's little gift to me.

"What?" I coaxed gently.

"I want to tell you how it happened for me. I've been wanting to, all this time. I need you to know," he said, but the words seemed to tumble out, colliding with each other chaotically, leaving him looking a bit confused at his own need. "I'm not sure why."

Feeling as if I was party to some sort of dire confession, I leaned in and gave him a tender smile. "It would really help, thanks."

He cleared his throat and bowed his head over our joined hands. "I enlisted in 1942. I was young and had been itching to do my part. When I turned eighteen, I signed my name and was more than happy to do anything that would pay the Japs back."

He blushed and glanced up at me, "I mean . . ."

"I get it," I reassured.

"I didn't have any special skills. I grew up on a farm in Kentucky. I was just a dumb kid, but I had fantastic luck. Pretty soon, they started calling me "Clover" and making jokes about how if I was in a unit, everyone else was going to die."

I chuckled, "The unkillable man? That's ironic."

He shrugged, his face still obscured. "It was just dumb luck that I lived so long, but during the worst parts, like D-day, that's how you got promoted. You were just the longest lived." He sighed heavily. "I never realized how dark this world really was. At the time, I thought that there must be real evil in the universe, for things like . . . what I saw . . . to happen. Either there was evil, or there was nothing at all."

For a moment, I was back in my grandfather's lap, his first grandchild. I was listening contentedly while he told his old war stories to my father, an untouched pitcher of iced tea and a tape recorder between them.

"I can't even imagine," I breathed.

"I was at Auschwitz."

My soul frosted over. Nothing else needed to be said, no extra description given.

He let go of me long enough to push his hands through his sandy colored hair, then he anchored himself to me once again.

"After it was over, I . . . I just couldn't go back to the same old farm. Lots of the guys went back, talked about home like it was heaven, but for me, having been there . . . I couldn't go back to thinking the world was supposed to make sense. I traveled instead. Went to Asia for a while, wandered around there. When I was nearly forty, I sort of found myself in Tibet."

I perked up slightly; Tibet was reputed to be the Buddha's homeland.

"I started going to this temple. The head monk spoke a few languages, and we could sort of communicate. Before long, I was studying there. They gave me a place to live, food to eat, something to focus on besides my memories."

Jinx would laugh and ask him about Raz Al Gould, but something he said struck a chord with me. "It was a temple run by the Sangha, wasn't it?"

With an almost guilty nod, he looked up. "They seemed so wise, and maybe they are. Or maybe there's no such thing as wisdom."

"Someone once said wisdom is knowing what you do not know."

William granted me a smile. "When they gave me the sutras to read, I thought they were entrusting me with the greatest knowledge on earth. I read them obsessively, but at first, saw nothing. It all seemed too far removed, lost in translation, obscured by time and changing meaning."

That was exactly how it had always felt to me, and though I had read them, I just could not see how they had done so much to people like Eva, and apparently, William.

"But the more I read them, the more my mind seemed to trace back through definitions. I began to *understand* the meanings intuitively. Before too long, I *felt* them more than read them, and I saw how different they were from my reality. You're young," he said to me with a nod, "and your generation has seen such an influx of foreign culture that you can't possibly understand. To you, all this mind-without-mind stuff makes perfect sense . . ."

"No," I interrupted with a smile, "I think it's just been repeated so often that we *think* it makes sense, but really," I thought of Jinx's tirade on interior decorating, "we have not the slightest idea."

"It outraged me at first, being told that there was no such thing as evil, nor any such thing as good, that both were the same, just choices we made because of the desires we have. More than once, I threw the damn things across my room." He chuckled, "but I always went back, wanting to make sense of them, wanting to see what everyone before me had seen, what every person for so many centuries had found of value.

"When I realized it finally, I was sitting on my mat, staring into the night. It just hit me." He leaned back and his hands slid from mine. I missed the warmth instantly. "There were only choices, only thoughts. The walls we draw between opposites were illusory, only significant to us. The universe does not distinguish between the sack of atoms that is my body and that red dwarf star. It cannot tell me from another human. The values, the meanings we place on other people are false. So what, then, separates me from the Nazis, the Kamikazis, the Italians? What made me different?"

I shook my head, unable to speak. My throat was clamped shut preventing me from puncturing the invigorating bubble surrounding us with words that were too precise.

"Nothing," he said quietly, his bloodshot eyes glittering, "not a damn thing. There was no difference except the choices I made. Which then begged the question, that if I had been in their shoes, would I have made the same choices? I would like to say no, but I couldn't be sure. That eagerness and drive I had to help my country may still have been there if that country had been Germany.

"But then I knew that was not true. If all our decisions are based on that first, initial assumption, that axiom, I had come to believe life was a sacred thing that must not be disturbed. That was the core of my character, and all of my later decisions proceeded from that. I killed soldiers who killed innocent people and that was a truth I could live with."

"But it wasn't the only truth?" I asked in a hoarse whisper.

He shook his head, smile already in place. "It was just enough to get me by, but the longer I studied, the more I realized how shallow that reassurance was. I sank into depression, wondering if that was all there was. I didn't want to *function* in the world, I wanted to rise above it, get out of it, make something of it. To just fall in line with axioms, what a way to live."

I sat back, frowning, knowing that was exactly what I had felt while sitting in my kitchen, the dead phone in my limp hand.

"Everything means something."

"I knew it all had to be important, until it happened."

"What?"

"*It.* I was sitting there and it washed over me. I sat for a week, staring off into space, *feeling* the answer in my very bones."

"Right liberation."

He nodded and folded his hands in his lap. "Its effects lasted for a few weeks. I was euphoric, everything made such marvelous sense. But the more sense it made, the more I wanted to share it. I knew there had to be a way to explain it to other people of divergent and opposed cultures. I knew that if we could do that, there would never be another war."

I shook my head sadly, "And that was your first mistake."

His chin dipped. "I became obsessed with understanding cultures, seeing the tiny doorways I might be able to open into their minds. I was fanatical about it, and completely forgot the lesson. The Sangha encouraged me, and now I know why."

I sat up straighter. Was he about to denounce his leaders? "They were cultivating your talent."

"As long as I was of use to them, they allowed me to believe I was on the right path. When I began to notice my vision improving, they told me it was just the natural effects of being healthy. When I became certain I was seeing through things, around things, inside things, they said I was one with all things. But when I began to dream of things far away, experience the world from my bed at the monastery, I knew that they were horribly mistaken." He propped his elbows upon the table and buried his face in his hands. His fingers massaged his hairline, and his breathing quickened. "I can see whatever I want, but since I wanted to see it all, discover the root of human evil, all I see is . . ."

"The darkest of things." I put a hand on his shoulder and smoothed the wrinkles in his coat.

"I tried to cut out my own eyes, just like they did," I knew who he was talking about, the zombies in the cellar, slowly dismantling their own bodies, "but I saw it even then. When the eyes grew back, I nearly went mad, and it was then that they told me I couldn't die." He began to chuckle, but there was no happiness in it, only crazed sadness. "I went to them to escape those things, but they just keep happening. Now, because they did not stop it, I can't *stop* seeing them!"

My hand fell and dejected, I sat back again. "Which is why you are the head of security." And how, in my vision, he had been so timely with his attempted rescue.

He nodded, though he was still hiding in his hands from my judgments.

"William, how do you cope with it?" I thought of Ursula's thirst and found myself retreating from him into my chair, wondering if he would pounce upon me.

He reached into his pocket and tossed a bottle onto the table. "I go through six a day now and it's not enough. I can't go on like this much longer." His voice broke, and he fell silent.

The prescription was for an antipsychotic at a dosage my outdated pharmaceutical knowledge told me would fell a rhino.

"Oh, Will," I sighed.

He was looking for a cure, urging me to be kind, to free him. For the first time, it broke my heart that I had nothing to offer.

"Help me," he said almost too quietly to be heard. "I'll do whatever you want."

My limbs flooded with adrenalin, a sensation I now felt with a detached interest that allowed me to ignore it with no consequences. In my current state, that chemical indication of life or death lost much of its impact.

If not for the vision, I would not be speaking to William. If not for the vision, I would not have asked him about my friends and discovered his tactical importance. If not for my vision, I would never have heard those words, "whatever you want."

Evidently, it wasn't just the content of the vision, it was the timing. Could it be that some part of me was herding me toward an outcome it already knew about?

"If you do not go, there is proof she will do anything."

Arthur had understood the mechanics of my ability all along. The thought of him made me smile. When at last I learned what Arthur's gift had been, I would torment him without mercy.

"Please help me," William whispered again. I could hear the tremendous effort it took him, even years after the fact, to admit that he still could not numb himself to the horrors only humans could accomplish.

I reached out gently and pried his face from his fingers and cradled it lovingly. What would he think of me, I wondered, if I told him there was no end to this that was not a crushed skull?

"William, listen carefully to me," I insisted, uncertain I could even claim to be such an expert. His eyes sharpened, however, and he looked convinced. "Why are you still alive? Why not end it? I know you know how. Why do you and Karl struggle on, why do those creatures in the cells waste away so laboriously? What's the point?"

"We don't want to die."

"You don't want it all to be for nothing," I corrected, "but if the purpose of the struggle is to struggle, then we are as free as dust."

The look on his face turned from desperation to attentive stillness.

"The decision to see was your own. You asked for the responsibility, not fully understanding what might happen, but should that naiveté free you from the obligation? What drives you mad is that you have chosen a fate you do not want."

"You're saying that I should want it?" He tugged on my loose hands, and I clenched.

"I am saying the *dharma* is all you have. You did not ask to be born, but at some point you made peace with the idea of living. Make peace with this idea and accept your obligation. Be better than you are now."

"What is the *dharma*? I don't even know anymore."

"To uphold the truth of the universe."

"Which is?"

I could not help it, I could think of no better explanation. "The *dharma* is that very question. We know the answer, it's the question and that fact that we still ask it that drives us."

For a moment only, he stared into space, and then his face slackened into a smile. "You remind me of him."

"Whom?"

"Brother Ananda. When he looks at me, he always holds up his finger. I don't know why, but it's like he's never going to answer the question that he sees, and that that's the point."

"I'm afraid he just thinks it's amusing."

Chuckling, William ran his hand over his forehead. "You're telling me to embrace the things I see and act on them?"

"I'm telling you not to shy away from something. You have tried that. Try something else. The visions will never go away, because the part of you that asked for them will never allow it. What seems like pointless knowledge being piled onto your shoulders, means something. You just have to figure out what you are trying to tell yourself."

"That isn't something that the Arhat are willing to hear. They were told that their suffering would end, but they were just made to suffer more acutely because they see so much more deeply into the human heart."

"Well," I shrugged, "I'm afraid I don't have the answers they're looking for. I am glad you are at least willing and able to listen."

"True. They're all losing it," he revealed. "Ursula was the last straw. The other Sangha cells don't even correspond with us anymore, but they're just as bad, if not worse. They look down their noses on the addictions we've cultivated, but they have their own perversions." He tugged on the earpiece almost angrily, "Karl is slipping too. Every day he gets more impatient and paranoid."

"With good reason, it seems. You should put that back in, or he'll think you've turned too."

"He already knows I have. When he sent me away last, he used his gift. He made it so I could not disobey when he told me to watch you."

"Why?"

He blinked at me in surprise. "You scare him. He can't control you and he knows you possess Ursula's and Eva's gifts, not to mention your own. You have powers, but you don't act like an Arhat. You're a loose cannon."

"That's about to blow some shit up."

"What do you mean?"

I huffed and set my jaw. "Can they see us?"

William's brows shot up. "There's a camera system on each floor."

"Are the camera feeds dumped onto an online server?" I asked expertly. Since when had Jinx's voice taken over my thoughts? I found myself asking. I knew the answer though, it was the moment he became the one thing in my life that made me laugh. As it was, I could not help but see him furiously trying to hack the police station cameras.

William nodded. "What do you want me to do?"

"Close your eyes."

His smile reflected my own. He knew that whatever shadows he saw lurking in through the Vihara's halls, he should say nothing.

I sat back in the chair. My breathing slowed. The ground eroded beneath me, and when I was there, floating above, I went to work.

The visions, I realized, took no time at all. It was possible that a great number of consecutive decisions could be made and followed to their conclusions without even a single moment passing by. I could split up, overlap progressions, and in the end, it would be as if I had walked every possible path. I wasn't just one Spirit Ninja, I was an army.

It felt like staring at a 3-D image, or drawing with my left hand and right hand at the same time. It felt like playing two-handed Tetris. It was a Zen fugue and in it, there was no time for thinking. Knowledge came to me and I accepted it passively: the layout of the building, the positions of the security personnel, the locations of the cameras and their perspectives. With each time I was captured, I learned more. With each avenue closed, door slammed, and conversation overheard, I became more dangerous to them, and eventually, all the visions terminated with the exception of three.

In one, I had snuck down the corridor, in the opposite direction from the way I had come. I passed door after door, avoided the cameras I had seen as they panned from side to side. I snuck past pacing suits, overheard conversations, and slipped down a flight of stairs. They put me in the lobby, right beside the elevator to the horror-filled cellar. I could have turned and walked outside, but I already knew there was a group of minions on the other side, taking an addiction break.

I stared at the elevator and found my reflection, gilded by the brass doors, to be almost serene. I knew the look on my face and without hesitation, pushed the down button.

The doors closed around me, but even before they opened, the undead prisoners had assembled like a grim army. I walked slowly, looking each death mask in the metaphorical eye. Their faces tracked me to the center of the hallway, and when I spoke, their ears pricked.

"If I free you, will you be free?"

There was not even the whisper of a moan.

"I know you want an end to this, but what if I said that there was no end? Would that be unbearable, or could you learn to make use of your gifts? You chose this path for a reason, just because the path is dark, doesn't mean the reason isn't valid."

A raw, jagged stump tapped the window a few feet away as the monster that had devoured it seemed to knock. They wanted out, that much was obvious, but could I trust them to understand, or were they too far gone?

"If I open these doors, you can do as you wish. You can leave, you can run into traffic, you can jump into a bonfire, but if I ask you to join me instead, will you? If I ask you to help me continue on, will you?"

As one, they seemed to nod, and knowing it was all a dream, I put my hand over my heart.

"I'll send someone for you."

I walked down to the last door on the right. Moksha's smiling face waited for me in the window that had been mine.

"I don't deserve it," he murmured.

"Mercy is for those who deserve it the least. Just wait for me."

He shook his head and without another word, he sank to the floor and curled up in the corner. I closed my eyes and the vision terminated.

The knowledge I retained spread to my remaining selves, wandering the halls in search of an exit strategy. In one, I stumbled onto another suite like my own, and in the other, I walked headlong into Karl with a security detail in tow.

"Well well," he said, and in the echo, I heard another voice say the same.

It was Ananda, seated at the circular table in his room. He smiled up at me, comfortable in his jail.

"The old monk at the monastery is dying," I said urgently to him. "wouldn't it be nice to see him again, to say goodbye?"

His doe-like eyes slowly widened and the eternal smile grew. "Where there are no roads . . ." he replied.

"There you are," Karl grunted. "And here I was about to send for you."

Where there are no roads, there you are.

It was a Zen koan, a katsu moment that my own psyche had handed to me.

I didn't realize, before that moment, the truth behind the things I had told William. Perhaps the point of the visions was not to see the future so that I may change it. Perhaps it was to see what I needed to know, to see where I should be, to see the value of each step. Maybe the best way to escape was to walk right into the middle of war and survive on dumb luck alone.

Both visions collapsed. My divided mind was reunified.

"If you accept the Dharma without question, then you are what you are."

I jumped to the monastery and swept through the connected room like a fierce wind, but Arthur was not there. I felt the mental equivalent of a stunned gasp. For the first time, it seemed, the jhana had failed me. I had sought out someone, and the astral plain had not delivered. Arthur was no longer "findable".

Where is he?

I went room by room, but there was not the slightest trace of him. His room was vacant, the golden Buddha went unconfronted, and it seemed that all of the monks were either praying or sitting by their elder's bedside.

How was I to contact Jinx for help without an intermediary?

The withered monk stirred and immediately, the other monks offered him water and replaced the cool cloth on his forehead.

The man who had been his attendant leaned forward and whispered something in his ear, but to my surprise, the old man swiped the words from the air. His glassy eyes searched the room and even though he was standing on the brink of death, he found me.

Nihao.

Wrinkles shifted into a toothless grin. He could hear me, but then again, there was a language barrier. But why should language hold me back, if even space and time could not?

"How many languages do you speak?"

"As many as I need to."

Thoughts and memories were nothing more than electrical signals interpreted by our onboard software. If I inserted myself into his mind, could I take over his body, or learn how to speak to him?

I drifted to him and somewhat uncomfortably, settled in. It was almost like a dream. I was certain I was myself, but at the same time, that I was him. I saw his youth, not on a rural farm as I had expected, but in a city. I witnessed his life in a flurry of broken memories that reflected one another. I watched him grow old, saw Ananda through his eyes, and most importantly, learned Cantonese.

With a jolt, I pulled free of him to find him half out of bed, the other monks restraining him gently as he pitched forward in shock.

"You should not get up, Father," said the young man and if I could have, I would have smiled, because I could understand him.

"She's here," was his throaty reply.

They condescended, thinking it nothing more than a death rattle.

Tell him to call Sam. Say "Turn off the cameras at the Vihara", I insisted, *and I'll get Ananda to you.*

"Sam," the old man whispered.

The attendant frowned and bowed his head close to his leader's mouth. "What is it?"

"Sam . . . turn off cameras at Vihara."

He sat back and stared down at the glazed expression, then glanced around. "Bring me the telephone."

I leapt back to my body and to William's shock, threw a fist into the air.

"是性交!"

He jumped. "Huh?"

"Translation: Fuck yes!"

He cleared his throat. "Ah. Then you found a way out?"

"No."

The furrows formed between his eyebrows. "Oh."

"When I leave, find Ananda. Then go to the cellars and loose the zombie horde. Stay with Ananda until it's all over, and when the time comes, take him wherever he wants to go. Ok?"

"Yes."

"Now," I stood up and smiled down at him, "look the other way."

"Where are you going?"

"To accept the *dharma*."

CHAPTER 27

What Eva had said in the alley made that much more sense to me now. There was no such thing as false hope. Desire and suffering were balanced with each other, integral to one another, unavoidable, no negative, no positive. Eva's understanding of this was what put her at odds with the Buddha, the man who had discarded all earthly desire.

Or had he?

The Dharma was a desire, wasn't it?

A different kind of desire.

I now gave Eva the benefit of the doubt above all others. What if she had realized something profound about the nature of the Sangha's wayward thinking? As I looked at William, now happy to think that there was probably a way to get rid of misery by embracing it, I trusted her. Even though she was dead and gone, she was guiding me.

I took a deep breath at the door and turned the handle, certain that Jinx had lived up to his awesomeness. Indeed, no alarms blared, no guards stampeded down the hall. All was silence.

I trotted down the corridor and concealed myself in a corner. A few moments later, William came out to perform his mission. Assured that he and Ananda would be safe, I turned and made my way to the exact place where Karl had been, to show him exactly how dangerous I was.

The door was a large, thick one, the type you'd expect to have bolt locks. As anticipated, he was standing in it, holding an ipad, reviewing the details with a man in a white lab coat.

"The PCR increased the sample size enough to examine," the man was saying. "In comparison with the base sample and Subject One's last sample, there are incredible differences."

"Such as?"

He scowled indignantly, "I hope you realize the complexity of what you're casually asking us to sum up. This is incredible stuff."

"I don't have time for one of your biology lectures, Doctor."

Karl glanced at his watch, seemingly in a hurry, but Ursula's gifts overlapped Moksha's, and I knew him through and through. What had begun as a quest, a fixation, had lost its meaning and as he sat in his office, pondering the effectiveness of his machinations, swirling platelets in a goblet, he had begun to question all of it. He had begun accepting his fate and seeing the bright side. To him, I was not a means to an end anymore; I was just in the way. For him, there was no purpose to any of it.

And men who were hopeless were the most dangerous kind of monster even *without* super powers.

"One would think this would cause you to pay close attention, given how many resources you've poured into this project."

"I care; I just don't care how fascinating it is for you. Get to the point."

The man rolled his eyes subtly. "There are two overlapping evolutionary models. Your standard Darwinian binary phylogeny theorizes that speciation, or the division of new species from old ones, resembles branching limbs, as of a tree. One animal has an altered offspring and because of changing circumstances, that animal survives. Following in this way, speciation is a painfully slow process and it cannot explain the incredible variety we've amassed in the tiny lifespan of earth."

Karl's body language reflected an even greater boredom, though it was the posturing of a vividly depressed soul, "And the other phylogenic model?"

"It's called a star phylogeny. Basically, if we take samples of all the DNA from planet earth and sequence them, they demonstrate conserved traces of the same retroviruses. The theory postulates that large speciation of a population, where hundreds of new species come from one single ancestor, extends from the attack of these retroviruses."

Karl sighed and in response, the man's speech sped up. "Basically, a virus hits and scrambles the DNA of a population. Their offspring are mutated in thoroughly different ways, some survive, and thus begins several new species, like hundreds of fruit falling from the tree, all different."

I raised an eyebrow at the metaphor.

"What does this have to do with Lilith Pierce?"

I was beginning to wonder the same thing. It sounded like a subject that Jinx would love, but would probably bore me to tears, without his helpful presentations with colorful lines and nifty graphics. The vision however, I thought I ought to know, so there I was.

"I'm getting to it," the man grumbled. I knew then, that he was like Jinx, of another species, concerned only with his "art". It was in the irreverent way he spoke to Karl. "These viruses, like Herpes for example, folded themselves into the heterochromatin, hid themselves in the genome. Millions of years later, pretty much all mammalian life on earth has the trace of those bygone events . . . except Subject Two."

I blinked and like Karl, pricked my ears a little more sharply.

"What does that *mean*?"

"Her DNA is being refined. Most of that conserved DNA is extraneous, not integral to the final human phenotype at all, but some of it is subfunctionalized. Her body is determining which is integral and which isn't and is shedding the extraneous material. She's not just incorporating new characteristics, she's erasing mistakes, reverse engineering the roots of the tree from the fruit alone. This is spectacular!"

Karl became still, so still he looked petrified. Then with a slow, deliberate hand, he smoothed the nonexistent wrinkles on his brow. "What does this mean for her?"

"Well, she'll be sterile with anyone but her own kind," he snorted inelegantly, "so effectively, just sterile in general."

"Besides that."

"Well . . ." he shrugged lightly, "I guess it means she's not human anymore. She's not an Arhat either."

I might have expected to feel my blood freeze over, or rush from my core to my limbs to spur me to action, but nothing happened. The full weight of all the changes I had endured had not yet impacted my psyche. Either that, or I was comfortable with the idea of not being something I had never asked to be in the first place. Instead of scowling or staring at them in awe, I smiled.

Human isn't good enough.

"Extrapolate from this. What will it mean for us?"

"I'm not qualified for that," the man abdicated. "She's out of my league now. When she's done refining, it makes me wonder if she'll start building new." He turned and looked at the door. "I'll want more samples to examine over time."

"Eva passed this to her?"

"Unlikely, since Subject One was not similar in any way."

"Then . . . could Eva have passed the ability to encode? To incorporate all that she encountered in order to create a new memetic disease?"

"What do you mean?"

Karl's face became stony. "Could Subject Two absorb all she needs to undo our immortality? Did her sister turn her into a weapon?"

The man looked uncomfortable. "It's possible, but then again, so is the sudden and spontaneous generation of a third arm."

Stunned and confused, Karl turned from the man and caught sight of me. His eyes narrowed and like never before, seemed to contain the very fires of hell.

"Well, well."

Trapped and unwilling to run, I bowed my head.

"Here I am," I said gently.

His face twisting cruelly, he gestured to the scientist. "You wanted more samples," then he turned back to me, already sneering, "take as much as you like."

His newest bodyguard approached me almost cautiously, but I was not going to run.

"Where's William?" he growled.

I bobbed one shoulder prettily. "I'm not his keeper; our relationship was kind of the opposite, actually."

He reached for my arm, as if to grab me, but ever the clairvoyant, I stepped aside lithely and wandered toward the man in the white coat. Nonplussed, the goon trudged after me closely.

"Tell me, Doctor," I said with a smile, "does that conserved DNA mumbo jumbo explain why my ass looks so fantastic?"

His mouth dropped open and the lips worked futilely. "Hu uhh . . . um . . . well . . . no, not exactly, that's all due to copying errors in the tissues that produce collagen and elastin." In a quick askance, I caught him taking in my amazing behind.

I raised an eyebrow. "Would you like to examine it?"

He cleared his throat and it seemed as if his mouth had gone dry. "No, no it's fine."

Karl stared after me, his eyes boring little holes in my spinal column. "Where is William?" he demanded.

"I told you, I have no idea. Maybe your voice isn't what it used to be."

At that very moment, the security guard's hand flew to his earpiece, and he began heatedly whispering into his cuff. He halted beside me and spun on his heel.

"Sir, HQ says the cameras went down almost five minutes ago. They tried to reboot, but they're locked out. They can't figure out why."

I was almost inside the door, one toe on the other side of the threshold when Karl's hand tangled itself with the hair at the nape of my neck and yanked me backward. My first impulse was to fight back and it was hell to override it. I tipped backward against him, a limp captive. His other arm snaked up around my throat and squeezed, ever so lightly, but just enough to cut off circulation to my brain.

Calm, I relaxed against him.

"What have you done?"

"You're the lord of the manor aren't you, assisted by hordes of psychic henchmen?"

"Is this a game to you?" he seethed in my ear through clenched teeth. "Is this funny? Well, for me, it is about survival." With a sudden thrust, he shoved me away from him. I staggered a few feet and collided with the wall. I lost my balance and toppled to the floor. Without a moment's hesitation, he took hold of my hair again and coolly slammed my face into the wall.

I felt the plaster give, felt the concrete beneath it crumble into dust, felt my skin burst and my skull split, then the world went black.

I came to slowly and found I was sitting in a chair. I made to reach up and touch my scalp, but my hands were restrained with thick metal bands.

"She's too dangerous," someone was saying.

"Can she be reasoned with?" a woman answered, and from the tinny quality, I realized that it was a conference call. I tried to open my eyes, but my miraculous healing abilities seemed to have worried about the gaping head wound first and hadn't yet gotten to my swollen lids.

"She isn't one of us," Karl said. "The doctor says she is a completely different species now."

"Perhaps you could convin . . ."

Karl growled. "I will not be at her mercy."

"You say this now, when you cannot go back?" another voice cut in, in an almost gloating tone, "You created this Frankenstein's monster. It's your business. You handle it. We will not be a part of it, just as we said we would not from the very beginning, and you will not bargain your way back into the fold by admitting defeat."

"I don't think that's fair," the female voice said. "He did it for all of us, without any help."

"From the report, it would seem that he didn't *do* anything. We have a pack of Ananda's Guardians and a girl to thank, or despise, however you look at it."

"But if there is a chance that we could be free . . ."

"We both know there is no chance, and I for one would rather be immortal and tormented, than dead."

Karl took a slow breath that ended in a low growl. "Is this bickering how we are to solve problems? I now remember why I parted company with you before. You disgust me. We have become nothing more than petty women, sniping over vegetables. At least with a cure, we would benefit from our wisdom instead of running from it."

I could feel it then, the force of his character. While before I had seen him as a villain straight out of a gothic fiction novel, slave to a bloodthirsty and invisible master, I now understood him fully. He was ruthless, without morality, true, but among his own kind, he was the responsible guy. He looked for a cure while the others sat back and waited, causing whatever trouble they were causing. For that, he was condemned as being idealistic, and out-maneuvered when his attempts failed. Yet still he had persisted, stubborn to the end.

But having failed, he seemed to have forgotten his integrity. He no longer had anything to lose.

I sighed and he heard me. "She's awake. I'm going and when this is over, you can consider our communication finished."

"I thought we had already decided that, Karl."

"We can't just ignore each other," the sympathetic voice objected. "We agreed upon the rules at the beginning! We cannot afford division, but must remain . . ."

"We went separate ways years ago."

The call terminated. There were a few moments of silence as he collected his thoughts and transitioned from one amongst many to a master in his own house.

"What do we do, I wonder?" he said with false lightheartedness.

"About what?"

"I have pushed farther into this than any of them, and you are all we have to show for it: a Trojan horse, a bomb in our midst. For all your utility, you are harmful to us as long as you live."

"How are your cameras coming along? They figure out how to turn them back on yet?"

He chuckled sardonically, as if he finally faced a worthy adversary and appreciated it. "Was that your doing?"

"No," I said honestly.

"Hmm."

"You don't believe me?" The skin on my forehead stung as it reknitted into smooth flesh. As the puffiness began to dissipate, I winked at him innocently from one eye.

"I do, actually, but it makes me wonder who did it for you."

I sat up and flexed my forearms. "Is this really necessary?" I nodded toward the restraints. "I would have just sat down for you."

He smiled and turned to his right. My left eye not yet fully functional, I rotated my head and followed his glance. The scientist was standing there, holding a plastic tube. A few others stood behind him, all wearing similar coats and hesitant expressions.

"Do it," Karl ordered.

Powerless to disobey him, they came toward me slowly. I could see the discomfort in their eyes, but it was stifled by the dulling magic of Karl's voice. At the end of the plastic tube, a needle was uncapped and pushed into my vein. Without a word to me, they connected the tube to a machine and turned it on.

"What is this? Jonesing for a snack?"

The smile didn't falter. It almost seemed plastic on his dark face. "An outcome that is completely unintentional, I assure you."

The tube turned an inky red as my blood flowed away from me and was collected neatly in a sterile container. I tried not to be anxious, knowing that my heart rate would only make it easier for him.

"So what's the deal?"

"Deal?" He crossed his arms and lifted his eyebrows. "No deal. We're finished with you. You're too dangerous to keep around. Dangerous, unpredictable, and completely oblivious to your own nature." He brought a thumb to his bottom lip. "You should know, I never believed this would come to anything."

"That's not true, and we both know it. Now you're just trying to make failure hurt less."

He stroked his lip with the pad of his thumb, considering me. "No. I gave up long ago. It was Moksha and his pet witch. They kept sending me subjects, and as long as the project took no effort, we continued. Soon the Guardians were knocking and I knew that if they knew our weakness, they would send an agent. They chose well. Your sister was endearing, truly . . ." he paused and seemed to be thinking of her fondly, "genuine. I knew what they were up to, but I allowed her the little victory, because they are not strong enough to ever win against us. When they hear of your death, they will appear again and we will snap our trap around their necks. So, you are of more use dead and dissected. To that end, farewell."

I glanced around the large room. Computer monitors lined one wall and several men in dark suits were standing idly by, as if they had nothing better to do until the security system was rebooted. There were numerous doors, openings for escape, but there was no way I could break the metal bands, at least, not without progressing a little farther into the pit of perfection. No wonder he was so amused.

"I happen to know for a fact that they won't fall for your trap."

"Oh?"

I shrugged, "Let's just say that the guy who's tracking Ananda is a righteous badass. You're up shit creek, my friend."

He stared at me skeptically for some time before dropping his hand. "I daresay, I won't miss your foul mouth."

"In many cultures, visceral is synonymous with truth."

"Regrettably," he replied sarcastically. "Your charms may have afforded you some mercy, but you are in every way her inferior."

I glared at him, not out of jealousy, but because he would dare to mention how well he liked the girl he drove off a ledge. "We also both know that's a lie. I'm better because of her sacrifice, but because I am better, you cannot tolerate me. You see the light at the end of the tunnel, the possibility to evolve out of what you are, but you are terrified of it. You're scared shitless."

To my surprise, he slowly smiled in acquiescence. "All too true, but regrettably, I am the one with my hand on the button, as it were, which means my flaws are yours too."

"Only if I let you control me, which you never will. It's your *trishna,* and there's no way I'm going to be your enabler," I said bravely.

The smile grew. "Did you know that human blood keeps for several years on ice? I intend to enjoy your company for at least that long."

My humor failed me. I stared back at him unmoved.

"How did you say it . . ." he murmured, "sick?"

"Aren't we all," I sighed. My thoughts were beginning to feel fuzzy, and my heart skipped a beat. My vascular system would soon shut down, and unable to compensate fast enough, my body would die. Would they bury me, I wondered, or would they just dump the meat in a ditch like they had Ursula's victims?

He came close enough to stand over me in triumph, the smug look almost flattering on the smooth, regal face. "You should know something."

"Oh?"

He tilted forward and put his lips to my ear. "It may be that you are as ten of us put together, but we work as a group. I already have men tracking down your friend, the cyclist, and dealing with him."

I closed my eyes.

"Where did you find that freak?"

Even though my skin had begun to go cold and numb, I frowned. It took some effort, but the question warranted it. Could it be that they had no idea whatsoever that Arthur existed and that it was he who found Jinx?

"He found me."

He leaned back to take in my expression hungrily. "You didn't think we were oblivious, did you? He is talented, just as you are. Dare I say it, *super* talented, but there is one surefire way of undoing the damage he has caused."

"He'll see you coming, you know."

Karl tilted his head, "I'll be sure to remember that."

My muscles began to slacken. I could feel myself slumping, my pulse skipping like a perpetual motion stone in a never-ending pond. The room was suddenly chilly and shivers wracked me.

I felt as if I were pulling out of such mundane concerns as living. He was the only tangible thing for me then, because I could *feel* as Ursula had my desperation, the disgust and self-loathing within him. He was grinning, but deep down, I knew another little piece of him was starving to death.

"Karl," I whispered. His hair brushed my temple as he came close again. "I could have loved you. You and I share a sense of humor and . . . you seem like . . . you used to be a nice person. I don't think I . . . would mind being your cure."

I don't know if he responded. The room seemed to fade from me, and I floated in the blackest of places. I was clinging to life, fighting as Nature intended, but why should I bother? At the end, was it really necessary? There was such beauty in stillness. It was like the womb again, insulated and peaceful. The struggle took all of that away.

"A stage beyond death."

The darkness began to pulse until the strength of that rhythm shattered into pinpoints of light like stars. The lights grew and danced until at last, I was somewhere real.

She was facing me, standing on the ledge, smiling at me sweetly, but it wasn't really me she saw. It was her fate that brought her such happiness.

My soul ached and I wanted so badly to touch her, to reach out to her and take her hand. Why at the end, was I forced to relive this, to see her final moments all over again?

I'm sorry I wasn't there for you, Eva.

"But you *are*, Lily."

For an instant, I was overwhelmed.

You can hear me?

"We are sharing this moment," she said softly. "Time is only a perception, when the mind no longer holds onto it, all events are simultaneous."

So we do see our lives before we die?

"Only the event most important to us."

She glanced down and slid her bare feet to the very edge, curling her cute little toes over the brink. When she was born, I had played with her tiny feet, dictating which piggy received roast beef over and over, never thinking those moments would be my most prized possessions.

Eva . . . please don't jump. You don't have to help me.

She smiled, her eyes swimming in tears.

"I'm sorry, Lily . . . but I'm not doing this for you. This is the way it has to be for all of us."

If I could have, I would have screamed. I would have wrapped my arms around her ankles and begged, but I was a spirit, about to join her on the other side of nothing.

I'm dying, Eva. Don't jump. One of us should survive. Your revolution failed.

She shook her head.

You don't need me to be strong, I insisted. *You are strong enough on your own!*

"Lily," she reached out as if for me and I came closer, pulled to her by love. "I'm not afraid. I'm not sad. I'm not giving up. Just trust me like I trust you."

I wanted to, but when that meant losing her, I wasn't sure I could.

I need you to stay.

"No you don't. You are in the place with no roads, Lily. This is the time to become what you must be. I haven't done anything. It is all up to you and has been. You are the architect of this mutiny."

If that were true, I wouldn't be where I am now.

"Everything means something. There is a reason you are here, were here, and will be here again, in this moment."

Her toes wiggled in the air and she was already sighing happily.

Please . . . I love you. Don't do this.

"I was your weakness, and you were mine. Let go of me, Lily. I am letting go of you."

I can't! I don't know what to do now. All the time you've shown me the way, but what do I do now?

"You've always known the way. It is a part of what you are."

I'm just a human.

"Human isn't good enough. Live better or die as nothing more than this."

I extended myself toward her, but it was a futile gesture. Her arms wide, she tilted forward, and fell right through me.

CHAPTER 28

Hollow, I hovered, refusing to look for her broken body. Around the rooftop, the city I had come to hate glittered ambivalently in the sunlight, never knowing an angel had just plummeted to earth.

It was the same scene as the one from my memory. Nothing I had done could stop her. I *was* useless.

I looked at the place on the rooftop where I had been in my vision, when I had watched passively as she tipped herself over the side. Was I still there? Was *that* me still sitting at my kitchen table with my mind floating beside an air conditioning unit?

This was the crossroads of my life, where all paths intersected. As Eva had said, it would be the scar on my thoughts that may fade, but never disappear completely. I would come back to it in my dreams, flit through time to return and visit that moment, the point at which my new life began. It was just too painful to ignore. I had made her a victim, a prophetess, a villain, but were any of those real? If she had never been what she seemed, was she really responsible for any of it?

As I looked past the finite at my own reflection, I came to understand, and my soul was still.

Arthur, you sly old . . . whatever you are.

Time now seemed so malleable to me, so utterly illusory. With my abilities, it was possible to imagine whole lifetimes condensing down to a few moments. Perhaps this had already happened several times, for years even! I could have been lifting myself up by own bootstraps through the folds of time, gaining new abilities with each repetition. Perhaps Eva had never given me the gifts, but had instead passed to me the ability to condense and refine our world, as Karl had suggested. If that had been her only gift, then everything else was mine and all of my visions . . .

"The Sam I know is very kind."

The visions were not visions at all, but echoes of things that might have happened, but now never would. In some dimensions I might have only Ursula's power, while in another I possessed both Ursula's and Moksha's. Now I was complete and this was the final time, the *only* time that would ever resonate, the *only* ripple that would not rebound upon itself.

This was the moment, the only moment.

I flickered from my place near the "Old River Motel" sign to the position where the past me should have been, vulnerable and sick with grief. As I aligned my two selves, the world around me shifted. It seemed I had found a snag in reality and tugged upon it, and my vantage point was tossed about. In an instant, Lilith Pierce knew all she needed to know to put her on a plane and her futuristic counterpart awoke in a chair, her arm numb and cold and prickling around the spike of insensate metal.

The ground was shaking violently. Glass shattered around me and blew past my face. I could hear moans from all sides and finally there was a terrified scream. My addled brain retreated for a moment, convinced it had been hurled into a fiery lake, but the room was cold and dark, and when no demons came to torment me, I knew that I was alive.

Somewhere at my right, there was a thud, as what sounded like a soft, breakable body rammed into something more concrete and was then dragged across the shards. To my left there was the sickening slurp of sticky fluids being trod upon. Dull, secondary lighting flooded the room as apparently, a backup generator kicked on.

The scene was chaos. It seemed everything that could have been broken, had been. Spattered and smeared over the whole sorry mess of crushed wood and busted televisions were the thick contents of the pump, which lay on its side, empty. Bare footprints tracked through the sludge, and as I followed them with my veiled eyes, I found where they led.

The security staff and lab technicians had been corralled in the corner by a horde of the walking dead, groaning incoherently. Karl had vanished and had been replaced with the pleasant face of my tree-climbing friend and his ninja cohort.

"Are you alright?" William hissed. His hands fumbled urgently with the tape that adhered my IV to the skin of my forearm. As if propelled by my body, the needle slid out and the wound closed. He leaned over me and punched a few keys on a numbered keypad. The metal locks popped open. "Lilith?"

I blinked up at him, not sure what was real anymore. If I dared to believe in it, the pain of disappointment would be so much worse. Ananda was smiling at me, and like a drowning rat, I clung to that promise of safety.

"I'm not dead?"

"Do you feel dead?" he asked with a chuckle.

"What does dead feel like?"

"That is an excellent question that I fear will never be answered. Perhaps the *only* question like it."

I couldn't help it; the absurdity and emotional shock were too much. I laughed, but my face was moist with loosed tears.

William put a hand on my shoulder. "I would love to let you sit here and collect yourself, but we have a problem."

"What?" I looked to the corner of the room where my horde was holding my enemies at bay. "What's happened? Where's Moksha?"

William glanced at Ananda, but the Arhat was busy staring at the blood as if he were looking for fluffy animal shapes in the clouds. His sandals and feet were red with it, but he did not seem to mind.

"We don't know."

"And Karl?"

"He's the problem." He reached out and took hold of my wrist, pulling me to my feet, though my legs were shaky. "I fully intended to do what you asked me to, but . . ."

"We are not finished yet," Ananda whispered airily, "and neither is he."

William frowned and turned back to me, with a wave at Ananda. "He refused to leave. Then he said we should come to you, that you were in need of our help. I'm not sure how he knew, when even I couldn't see it."

"Why couldn't you see it?"

"I can't see you," he revealed with a guilt-riddled blink. "Not anymore. I tried."

Ananda reached up and smoothed his long skein of dark hair. "You could not see it, because she is unknowable."

"Then how did you know?"

"The earth spoke."

His companion frowned, but I understood. Those of us beyond the Crossroads, were no longer a part of this reality. Neither alive, nor dead, we were as silent as the hum of electrical energy to human ears.

Parinirvana.

That was the secret of Arthur's invisibility. "Are you unknowable too, Ananda?"

He closed his eyes and seemed to be listening to the strains of faraway music that no one else could hear. "I have never wished to be, but desire is the cause of suffering."

William turned to the door. It clanged as he opened it and an unconscious body tipped toward him through the opening. "We have to get out of here. If what he saw is real, then we're running late."

I stepped around the machinery, trying to ignore the tangy smell of my own blood staining the ground. "What did you see, Ananda?"

"A storm."

Without warning, the ground lurched again. My foot slipped and I collided with William's squared back. The walls shivered under the strain, dust shook free from the concrete ceiling, and one of the large monitors fell from its mount and smashed to pieces. I threw myself into the doorway where William was bracing himself, but Ananda and the assembly of hostage-takers seemed to be completely unmoved.

"Ananda, it's not safe!" William shouted over the rumble of the angry ground, but even as he said it, I realized how silly he was to do so. With our strength, insight, and longevity, we were indestructible. There was nothing to fear.

I relaxed and as if the tectonic plate had ears, its thunderous voice fell silent. I leaned away from the jamb. "Where is Karl?"

William looked around hesitantly, his steps careful and light. "I don't know! The whole system is down. All their cell doors were already open, and the elevator wasn't working."

A loose piece of the ceiling broke free suddenly, and crashed to the floor in front of us, announcing that even if the ground was safe, the danger had not vanished. I turned to find that Ananda was immediately behind me, still hearing commands I could not. At his heels were a few eyeless monsters, wandering after him like sheep.

I don't know why, but I reached for his hand and was calmed by the feel of his fingers twisting through mine. "How did you get them out?"

"We didn't," William grunted as he stepped over the giant chunk of concrete. "They were climbing out of the elevator shaft when we got to it. When they saw him, they just sort of stopped and followed after us."

Ahead of us, I heard a shout and instantly, William had flattened himself to the wall and was inching toward the corner. There was no way of knowing what sort of people were left inside the compound, but I was finished with them. I wanted out safely. My friends depended on it.

Suddenly, in a loud roar, an aftershock jerked the building's foundation to the left viciously. Ananda's fingers squeezed mine gently.

"What the hell is going on?" I whispered. "This part of the country never gets earthquakes."

"Nature itself rises up in defense of him," Ananda breathed in my ear. "You must calm yourself."

I spun to face him. "How can I? Karl knew about Jinx. He's probably on his way there now!"

"Do not be afraid," he replied. "They are in good hands."

I wanted to believe him, but knowing the cryptic Arhat as I did, I could not trust that those hands were not my own. I freed myself from him and without regard for consequences, walked determinately around the corner at top speed.

Two men lay crushed beneath slabs of concrete. One was dead, nothing more than a pulp leaking from the roughened edges. The other was pinned at the legs, already leaving red finger strokes on the ground where he clawed to pull himself free.

It would have been easy to leave him there to bleed out, but it was also easy to save him. I squatted down, a woman possessed, and grasped the edge of the slab. I cannot imagine how it must have looked, my tiny, feminine frame hoisting thousands of pounds in the air, but I did it casually, and without another thought, then left the man to heal among the rubble. I could think of only one thing and that was getting to Jinx before Karl could punish him for his own flaws.

As we ran through the labyrinthine halls toward our escape, it seemed as if the entire complex had been deserted just before it was picked up in the air and smashed to the ground. We encountered only a few souls, all of whom were trapped inside rooms, buried in debris, or injured in some way. By the time we reached the entrance, we had nearly ten people in tow, ten people I might have considered enemies. In dire circumstances, however, I could now clearly see that there were no differences between us.

William slid across the hood of a four door sedan, unlocking it with the touch of a button on his keychain. I didn't want to leave the others there, but when I turned and saw them looking after each other, I reluctantly got into the car.

Adjusting the mirror, William shot Ananda a speculative look in it. "Where to?"

"Head south."

The tires kicked up dust and pebbles as he tore out of the long drive. The security gates stood stubbornly closed, and as he gunned the engine, I made sure to buckle my seatbelt. Immortal or not, I didn't relish the thought of anymore physical trauma. Behind me, Ananda did the same, though he seemed almost amused by the cloth strap meant to protect him from metal.

We slammed into the gate going top speed. One panel flew outward from us, but the other twisted itself over the hood of the car, tearing metal and paint as it scraped away.

I watched the Vihara shrink away in the mirror and when it was gone, sank back into my seat with a relatively relieved sigh.

At the crown of my head, Ananda placed his hand, warming my soul. "It is a shame our vehicle was not large enough for them."

My mind went back to Moksha. I was surprised to find that I felt almost guilty.

"He is free," Ananda said quietly in my ear.

I turned and caught his eye. "Dead?"

He said nothing, but I could see the truth. I turned back to the road, and wiped a hand across my face.

"He murdered your family," William said in wonder. "I'm stunned you're not more vengeful."

"Nothing lasts forever,' Ananda replied, "and the end is always soon enough. There is no need to hurry anyone."

My t-shirt was covered with several weeks' worth of gore. It stank of earth, blood, and whatever wastes my body had secreted on its way to perfection. I pulled it off over my head and leaned back against the cool leather in my bra.

"I promised him I'd save him."

"You promised you would free him," Ananda corrected, "and you did."

The car was speeding toward the freeway. It would be a few hours before I could do anything for my impatient friend. There was no point in worrying.

"As gifted as I am, an earthquake is not something I can pull off," I grumbled. "He's not free because of me."

"Then perhaps it was unbelievable luck," he breathed in my ear.

"Yeah." I reached out and tapped the touch screen on the center console. It had a GPS function. I entered the approximate address of Jinx's villa and closed my eyes.

Behind me, I heard the sound of cloth being torn. "Do you believe in unbelievable luck?" Ananda persisted.

"No, unfortunately, but can we not talk about it now?"

He chuckled. Before long, a length of golden fabric was passed between the seats to me. It was a piece of Ananda's beautiful robe. I took it with a grateful blink and wrapped it around my neck and torso, tying it with a knot like a halter top.

My modesty preserved, I returned to meditation. The jhana dilated time, which to me sounded like the best medicine. I looked for Arthur, but again, could not find him. He was not at the coffee shop, or either Sam or Matthew's homes. I jumped to Jinx, but the mathematician was, as yet, unharmed, slurping down a caffeinated Icee as if it was manna from heaven, his attention wholly on his work. Matthew and Sam were upstairs in the records room, running the paperwork through a scanner as if they expected the worst.

Jinx's voice came over the home's internal speaker system. "I'm blind, guys. The whole fucking Vihara just blinked off the grid."

With a frown, Matthew walked over to the speaker and pushed the button. "Good . . ."

"Wasn't me. Dunno what happened. I was tearin' shit up and all of a sudden it went offline."

"Did you . . .?"

"No." The boy sounded harassed. "Could'a been the quake, but when I started jerkin' 'em around, they stopped uploading their activities into the mainframe. It's like they knew it had been infiltrated and didn't want us to figure out what they'd done with her. They're fucking obnoxiously prepared."

The two men exchanged dark looks.

"Anything from Art?"

Sam shook his head dismally.

Matthew pulled a cigarette out of his pocket and lit it as if annoyed with the whole world in general. "Does he do this a lot? Disappear when you need him the most?"

"No," Sam rasped. "If he's flying under radar, it's because he has to."

"That's very comforting. I'm sure we don't need to know what threatens an immortal. I mean, we're only his fucking coconspirators. *Human* coconspirators, I might add."

I flicked to the monastery, to the old man's bedside, but he was gone. With a sick feeling, I returned to the car. The city lay before us, sprawling across the gentle curve of the hills like tiny gems stitched to the black gown of night.

"The old monk is dead." I lowered my visor and found Ananda's face with the mirror.

He let out a sigh. "Yes, I know."

"Arthur was right. He said the man wouldn't get to see you again." I smoothed my tangled hair from my face. "It's my fault. I shocked his system when I used him to communicate with Sam."

"He was happy to be of use to you."

"Doesn't make me feel any better about it."

He tilted his lovely head to one side as his eager gaze took in the intricacies of the encroaching metropolis. "That is the price of leadership, I have learned."

The rest of the ride was silent except for the false voice of the GPS directing us to the fray. Ananda stroked and smoothed my hair, pulling it back and with my scrunchie, plaiting and twisting it into a sleek topknot. When we entered Jinx's golf course community, William cut the headlights and practically coasted to the nearest corner. We sat in the car as the engine rumbled into silence.

"What's the plan?"

"Stay in the car," I replied, opening my door.

William's hand shot out and captured my wrist. His face had gone pale, anxiousness building in his eyes with each second. "What kind of plan is that? I'm supposed to protect you."

I covered his hand with my own and tried to give him a heartening smile. "I'm stronger than you. If you come, I might end up having to protect *you*."

His brows tugged together sharply. "What should I do?"

I took my hand back carefully. "You're backup. Stay here and watch."

To my surprise, Ananda opened his door and got out. Even though he was as brightly colored as a traffic light, on the asphalt, his leather sandals were silent.

"Are you up for this?" I asked doubtfully. "Aren't you a pacifist?"

He smiled and patted my head. "There are other ways to win a battle."

Reminded of Arthur's question about the ability of a warrior to prepare for peace, I stood up and got my bearings. With one last glance at William, I pointed to the corner. "His house is around there. The one with all the motorcycles."

Within five strides, there was the sharp report of gunfire. We turned the corner to find that the entire street had been blocked off with black vans. The SWAT team had already assembled at the gate and was in the process of dismantling it. The security camera hung by its cord in pieces, a jagged hole in its lens.

I stepped back into the shadow of an ivy vine that climbed the stony wall, but Ananda stood, as bold as day, watching their activities with curiosity.

"The overseer is here," he said.

I glanced around the corner. Karl was jumping from the back of a van in a flurry of rage. As he ran to the gate, the men destroyed the electronic keypad and pried the door open at the hinges. Within seconds, they were swarming like carpenter ants, headed straight for the building's foundations.

"They're setting up explosive charges," I whispered. "They're going to burn down the house."

"Old habits," he replied gently, but he did not seem to be worried. He smiled at me and with another pat to my head, wandered toward the gate as if he merely had an interest in the horticulture. Baffled, I followed behind him.

The SWAT teams had closed in on the house leaving only one posted guard at the gate, but as Ananda waltzed past him, it was not the man in the orange robe that caught the guard's attention, it was the woman walking behind him.

Ananda was invisible.

"Freeze!" He pointed the gun at me.

But as his hand went to his radio to alert them I had arrived, Ananda leaned toward him and whispered in his ear. Without warning, the man took a seat on the ground and closed his eyes. His weapon lay beside him with the safety on.

As we continued past him toward the circular drive, I glanced back in awe. "How did you do that? No, *what* did you just do?"

Ananda stopped and turned to me. "Your focus is too narrow. You desire to save your friends, and because his aim is to destroy them, your energy disrupts his."

"You mean, if I *want* something, then they can see me?" I thought back to my practice session on Karl, to the agreement I made with the air. "So how can I possibly get past them if we don't agree on anything?"

He tilted his head. "You cannot choose which life is valuable. Either all life is sacred, or none of it is."

I dropped my eyes to the ground and understood. If I walked into this situation discriminating against them, their heckles would go up and I would be in much more danger than necessary. Really, the more I thought about it, the less I saw the value in discriminating anyway. I wanted to save everyone, after all.

"The night is very beautiful," Ananda breathed, his eyes cast upward. Overhead, the sky was darkening with thick, rolling clouds, threatening the world below.

"Yes," I murmured, watching the shadows twist over each other, hearing them clash and growl, "it is."

Things seemed brighter then, and for the first time since the rock garden, the little life forces around me began to buzz and hum within my soul, vibrating in my chest like sound from a subwoofer. The air glowed, each tiny insect and animal shining like twinkle lights in mist, little halos circling them as they wandered through the foliage.

"Can you see them?"

"Yes," I whispered. "They're so beautiful!"

"Each in its own way."

I stood there for a long time, looking around me with my eyes unfocused, delighting in the glitter and sparkle. When I found the house with my gaze, the distant forms of crouching men shimmered in a rainbow of colors, beckoning me. I turned to ask Ananda if he could see them too, but he was gone.

For some reason, I wasn't bothered by this. I ambled toward the house, wondering if I would cross paths with him, but perfectly fine with my fate if in fact, we never met again. I found a red aura standing in the side yard and out of sheer curiosity, moved toward it. When I was close enough to reach out and pass my hand through the auroral shards of light, I realized it was a person and that that person was afraid.

On impulse, I leaned forward and found its ear. "Be at ease," I whispered. Before I could lean away, the tension drained from his form. The colors shifted and changed, turning from red, to orange, to gold, and the man sank to the ground with a deep sigh.

Completely oblivious to any danger, I made a slow and meandering path toward the back door of the family room. It did not disturb me that the glass was broken; the blinking light of the explosive charge on the load-bearing wall did not seem out of place. I met another man on the stairs, he was angry, arguing with his shoulder radio.

"We don't have schematics, sir."

"Then smoke him out!" the radio grated, but I was too content to worry.

I put my hand on the man's arm, disrupting the rays of light only slightly. "Anger is a symptom, to be rid of it, you must remove the cause."

He undid his helmet with an uncoordinated hand and dropped it to the floor. His expression almost sickened, he looked back to the patio door and suddenly became interested in the fresh air. Like a marionette, he walked toward the door in a disjointed fashion, and went back outside.

I continued to the landing and then up to the records room. I don't know how I knew where I was going, or what was motivating me, but it seemed as good a path as any I could hope to walk. I met two more mercenaries on my way and in absolute compassion gave them helpful advice that somehow convinced them they would be better off outside on the grass, looking at the sky or watching the fireflies dance.

With the floor completely vacant, I found my way to the disarray of Jinx's file room. I looked around in mild interest, but it was the golden Buddha that caught my attention. I stared at it and could feel such a familiarity, that if someone had called us relatives, I might have agreed. I reached out and touched the Bindhi on his forehead, not at all surprised to hear a click and the harsh clang of metal locks opening.

I turned to find that a portion of the wall had slid aside and that my beloved friends were suddenly standing beside me.

Happy in a way I cannot ever remember being, I reached out and hugged the tiny blue-haired genius. "Ah, here you are! I'm glad to see you. You should see the sky, it's so lovely."

His mouth fell open. "Lily, are you okay? Whose blood is this?" He pulled his hands away from the waistband of my jeans, where the blood from the pump had spattered.

I kissed the corner of his mouth. "Don't worry silly, I'm not hurt."

"Where did they go? It's like they just left!"

"It's going to rain soon," I replied lightly. "We should all go play in the puddles."

Matthew reached out and pulled my lower lid down, unceremoniously examining my eyes like any police officer would. "She could be drugged, but her pupils aren't dilated."

I laughed.

"Lily, what's wrong with you? You're acting like a crackhead!"

My hands were on his shoulders and his glow was surrounding me. I felt an imperative, as if there was a sore spot in him that I should soothe. I pulled him to me and snuggled him, heedless of blood, or dirt, or anything else. The sweet scent of his hair gel was more beautiful than any flower.

"Did you know, Jinx, that all that may ever happen in the universe is happening right now? If you're still enough, you can see it all. You don't need to search. It will come to you."

He pushed me away carefully and looked up into my face. "Lily, come on, we can't stand around talking metaphysics. We've gotta . . ."

"She's high or something," Sam wondered in his strangled purr.

In my arms, the boy stiffened.

"No, she's just . . . maybe she's having some kind of PTSD episode?" Matthew diagnosed.

Jinx wriggled away from me, his hands out in front of him, swiping through the fog of colors as they shifted violently.

"Jinx?" Sam reached for the boy, but he tumbled backward into the wall over a stack of files and stood there breathing heavily, his hands pressed to his ears.

"What did she do to him?"

"I can't . . ." the immortal stammered, "I can't hear you!"

Sam and Matthew exchanged looks. "You mean you're deaf?" Matthew whispered, to test the theory.

"No . . . I can't . . . There's no echo." His hands fell, the fingers peeking from his gloves twitching. His face had turned an ashen grey, but was very quickly returning to its normal cherubian glow. "What did you do to me?"

I could feel the giddiness bubbling up from deep inside me. It erupted in a giggle that continued for some time, until finally, Sam reached out and took my hand.

"Lilith, we should go outside and play in the puddles."

"Yes, we should." I turned away and wandered out of the room, the three of them in tow. "May I go first?"

"Of course," he rasped in my ear. "You lead the way."

I led them back through the house, down the stairs to the theater room, and toward the shattered outline of the patio door, but the way was blocked by a sudden darkness that seemed to suck the light away. It was Karl and in his hand was a nine millimeter.

CHAPTER 29

I wasn't afraid, standing before him with a stupid grin on my face, until he took aim at Sam and pulled the trigger.

I saw the explosion in slow motion, the shower of sparks and the backlash of gunpowder seeming like a plume. As if a cloud had passed over my eyes, the colors dimmed and my focus was thrown back to darker parts of reality. Sam lay crumpled on the ground, moaning in agony.

I had not seen it coming.

Gasping, I dropped to his side and touched his shoulder. "Sam! Sam!" He rolled slightly, his hands clasped to the bloody opening in his side. Jinx leapt to his aid, adding pressure to the wound, while Matthew had already reacted and was staring down the barrel of his own weapon.

"Drop it!" he shouted, but it was pointless.

"Shoot me all you like, Detective," Karl spat. "You'll just be putting holes in you and your friend." He turned and looked at me, his face glowing in a layer of feverish sweat. "Stand up!"

I got to my feet shakily, and stepped into his line of fire. "Karl . . ."

"I killed you! You're dead!"

Confused, I held my hands out to him. "It was Parinirvana, Karl. I stepped back from the edge."

"You can't do that!" he shrieked, his arm shaking with the pressure of his grasp on the grip of his gun. "That's impossible! No one has done that!"

"But," I glanced back at Matthew. He was beginning to hesitate, his arm falling. "But Karl, it's what Ananda did, isn't it?"

"Ananda never died! He pretended! We have machines now! I saw you flatline! I saw you die! You were dead for almost an hour!"

"But here I am. I'm not like you anymore, remember?"

"Damn you!" he growled. The gun exploded again, but this time, I was prepared. I leaned into it and stumbled backward at the impact. My shoulder went numb, the trickle of blood reached my hand before I felt it. I looked down in shock and saw the gaping wound. Pressure built within it until it was almost uncomfortable, then the bullet slid out and clattered to the floor. The skin and muscle folded together and in less than twenty seconds, the wound was gone.

I raised my eyes to him. "Karl, put the gun down."

"No! No, I won't!" He waved it around haphazardly, and with his other hand pulled out a tiny black object with an antenna. "It is bad enough we live in misery, but to constantly fight for something we can't ever have is worse! I should have listened to them! I should have never allowed this to go on so long!"

He flipped a red switch cover, but before he could touch the trigger, the ground undulated in the throws of an aftershock. The cabinet doors of the nearby kitchen shattered as their frames warped. Glasses and plates fell from shelves and smashed to pieces. Matthew was thrown to his knees, the gun yanked from his grasp to skitter across the floor that split with a loud, tearing sound.

Karl stumbled, but instead of letting go, touched the button in vindictive pleasure. Percussive bangs resounded throughout the building, and the device sitting on the credenza exploded in flame, blowing an entire chunk of wall toward us. I ducked, but felt the large bodies of stone and wood slice past me and slam into the kitchen appliances.

Fire licked up the walls and it was clear that if we did not leave soon, immortality would be a moot point, but there was only one way out, and Karl was standing in it. He was hunched over, eyes glittering in rage, his face so flushed he looked sunburned. The veins on his neck were throbbing, and I could see the hurt and anger, built up over hundreds of years, oozing off him.

"Karl, please. Let them go!" I begged. The temperature was rising; moisture began to drip from my face.

"No! You will suffer just as I have, watching those I care about fall around me!"

I looked around for another means of escape, but every way was blocked by rubble and a growing inferno. I could hear the plaster upstairs beginning to bake and fall away, the wooden beams splitting in the heat.

"Why, Karl? Why are you so angry? Did you think that once you achieved liberation it would all be easy? There's no such thing as peace. It doesn't exist!"

"He lied to us! He promised us freedom and all we got was a new set of chains!"

A portion of the living room ceiling fell in and a roaring conflagration melted all of Jinx's precious plastic creatures, turning them to colored streaks down charring walls. The beanbag began to brown, the fabric curling like a rotting lemon peel, the happy face scorching away.

"*Did* he lie to you?" I shouted back. "He said that you should obey the dharma, heed the words, but instead you people turned him into a deity and organized a faith! What did it give you? What fears were you hiding and cultivating beneath that protective shield?"

"Shut *up*!" he roared, waving the gun at me like a talisman. We were fairly matched in strength and speed, and though I had more gifts, they meant nothing in these circumstances. All he had to ward me off were the remaining bullets in that gun.

"I won't listen to you anymore! Why would he show us this and then leave us here? Why did . . ." his voice fell as anger boiled away and left the sorrow behind, "did he hate us?"

Beyond him, the grass glowed a vibrant orange, tempting us with its cool softness, when a sudden flash of lightning left a smoking black mark in its wake. Without warning, the sky tore open and thousands of gallons were dumped upon us, as if Nature too, upheld the dharma.

Nature is the dharma. It began with the Buddha's sermons and was carried through time and space to the first Katsu, to the place with no roads. Like mathematics, Zen created nothing, it only uncovered the way it actually was.

Karl turned and let out an incoherent cry of rage, as his plans were thwarted yet again, and his weaknesses were laid bare.

Black smoke filled the room. At once, the air was acrid, a cloud of ash hot enough to burn. Steam and moisture dripped from the walls, and puddles began to form beside flashpoints.

Spinning in all directions, finally as mad as the creatures he had imprisoned, Karl leveled the weapon at me and pulled the trigger. Shot after shot ripped through me, a series of blows that winded, but did no real harm. One bullet clipped the side of my neck, another hit me in the stomach, and a third pierced my bicep. Arterial blood spurted down my front, crimson against the shimmering gold of my makeshift top, but it was not nearly so painful as watching Eva fall.

My joints and frame compromised, I collapsed to the floor to the sound of futile clicks. The gun was empty and no one else had been harmed. Throwing it aside, Karl made to lunge at me, to tear at my flesh with his bare hands, but suddenly, he stopped and his features slackened.

Ananda materialized in a cloud of smoke beside him like a magician, one graceful hand atop his head. The ravening spittle that clotted at the corners of Karl's mouth dripped free, and as if faint, his knees buckled. He tumbled to the ground, but as soon as the contact was broken, he began to regress. Like a child, he crawled away from Ananda, until he could put his back to the security of the partially destroyed kitchen island.

He was sobbing, his breathing ragged. He put his hands up in front of his face as if to push the peaceful man away, but Ananda was not pursuing him. Instead, he sighed in sympathy and shook his head.

"Have you lost sight of the goal? Or has the goal lost sight of you? Where have you gone, Karl?"

Karl coughed and pummeled the air with his fist. "This was not how it was meant to be! It was supposed to end! We were going to change the world, but there was no way to change, there was just this . . ."

Ananda sighed heavily, "You have changed the world, Karl. But is it more or less the world you envisioned, do you think?"

"No! No!" He shuddered and wrapped his arms around himself. I could sense the crackling energy building within him and feared that soon, if nothing broke, he would leap up and rip the heads off my friends and that I, a novice, would be unable to stop him.

"We would have followed him anywhere . . ." he whispered.

"You would have followed, you tried to lead, but I tell you, neither are required," said a voice I recognized immediately.

"Arthur!" I gasped. I turned, expecting him to be the knight he was, to rush in and save us, but Arthur's face was focused on Karl, and Karl looked as if he had been punched in the gut.

He had frozen, his face contorted in a look of horror. His limbs, like waxen prosthetics, fell to his sides. For a moment, I was confused, until I saw Ananda smile in a warm greeting.

"Cousin," he said happily, and the world seemed to shift beneath my shaking limbs.

Cousin?

Tinier concerns melted, all my anxiety vanished before the most obvious of truths.

Siddhartha Gautama.

In the alley, it had not been an argument, it had been an accord, a bargain struck between two partners. Arthur had tried to tell Eva exactly the sacrifice she was going to make, warn her off it, but she had accepted the dharma and put him in his place. In turn, he had accepted her and vowed to hold up his end. Together they had guided me to the Crossroads, through careful manipulation and friendship. I was of myself, because of them.

"Art!" Matthew yelped. I snapped back to reality and found Matthew pointing to his gun resting near to the slack hand of our foe.

My heart was pounding, bones and sinew straining to make me whole again. Stunned, but responsible to the last, I began the slow crawl that would take me to the gun, as Arthur, the first and last real Buddha, stepped farther into the room.

His hair was down, rivulets of water dripping from it to the thirsty ground. Lakes had formed in the hollows of his throat and collarbone, and his clothes clung to him. The smoke and steam swirled in the gusts of wind from outside, obscuring him for a moment while my mind sought out the distortion that was Karl's fractured reasoning.

Centuries eroded before my eyes. There he was as he had been in his middle years, a prince and a philosopher, wrapped in a saffron robe, his body thin and wiry. Kingdoms and thrones refused, he had wandered the earth for generations. He was nothing as I had imagined him, and yet, was everything he should have been.

Karl's mind became stuck in a loop of reasoning. From why, to how, and back again, his thoughts swirled. "It isn't so," he murmured almost inaudibly.

My limbs revolting, I pulled and pushed myself forward inch by inch. A bullet worked itself out of my chest like a sliver and one less tear hindered my progress. I was within arm's length of him, my bloody hand reaching for the gun.

"You aged! You withered away in front of us!" he cried out. "You were not like us!"

"Are you so certain? As certain as you have been about every other thing in your long life, my friend?"

My chest clamped down on his sadness and abandonment. It was a pain I understood, losing the one who guided you, to find that you could neither join them, nor claim the sweet release of death. My crawl came to a jerking stop, his feelings washing over me, putting out tiny fires that had been smoldering for weeks and even years.

"Lord, why would you leave us?"

Arthur's tone was so musical, with no aims for power or desires for progress. It fell into our heads and let the words be absorbed in due time. "If I had lived, the seeming miracle would obscure the lesson. It was a choice and I do not regret it. The Buddha died that day. My name is Arthur now."

"But . . ." Karl's senses seemed to return. He looked around vaguely at the chaos, to find me close by. "We spent so long searching . . . if you could die, while we remained . . . but you . . . just like us . . ."

I couldn't look away from him. The gun and its threat seemed so small then. I fell to one side and leaned a shoulder against the island, and either from shock or his affinity for the similarity I shared with my sister, he did not turn away from me.

"Nothing in this world is perfect," I said gently. "Everything is perishable. No plan, no greater cause, just this moment. And if we have only this moment, to forget ourselves even once is to commit the most unspeakable of crimes."

I dragged my lower body along until I could tip myself into Karl's lap. I thought he might strike me, but he just looked at me, dumbfounded, seeing her smile in my face.

"The curses seemed so real," he moaned.

"They are," another bullet pushed through to the outside and dropped into a fold of his shirt, "but they are by no means impossible to overcome. Nothing is, when you have forever."

Beneath my ear, his skin was throbbing with the pressure of his pulse, but was cold as marble. I gripped his shoulders pitilessly and climbed up his torso, huffing and wheezing, until we were at eye level. With a deep breath, I closed my eyes and settled my mind over his. The images and flashes of meaning shuffled through my brain and were filed away in my now perfect memory.

I rested my chin on his shoulder, as the bullet began to squirm to the surface of my neck. "Desire is the cause of joy," I said with a smile.

I twisted my fingers through his hair and pulled his mouth to the open wound. His lips closed around it and his hands clamped onto the small of my back. The tug of suction was almost sweet, and I found myself thinking that there was no sense in wasting it, if it was going to leak out of me anyway. His tongue touched the ragged skin, tickling it, sending a shiver through my spine that rebounded in my pelvic bone. Time obeyed a different rhythm, until weak and content, I fell away.

I did not look away from his dazed expression even as my friends tugged and lifted me. Even with the heat, fumes, and rain, my smile did not wilt. We left him there among the rubble, to confront his future the way we all entered and left the world: alone.

Spend this, I thought, seeing Anna in his glassy gaze.

"Katsu," I whispered.

CHAPTER 30

I lay wrapped in a blanket in Arthur's arms, healing bit by bit, watching through the car window as the fire trucks finished what the storm could not. The others had gone on ahead in the other two cars to care for Sam, granting me this opportunity to finally learn the truth. But resting there, listening to his slow, strong heartbeat, I realized I didn't really need it.

I knew then that I loved him dearly, in as many ways as there were people to feel it, and because I loved him, I had to trust him. It was a huge responsibility, to know that he would always rely on me to be my best, to withstand torment, to push for the success of others, but then again, responsibility was my middle name.

He brushed a strand of hair from my face. "Shall I tell you a story?"

I nodded shallowly.

"The bodhi tree was my Crossroads. Like you, at my death, I returned to it. Our scientific friend would talk of tachyons, non-locality, and time loops, I am sure, but . . ."

The chuckle shook loose the final bullet, and as the hole began to close, he covered it with his fingers.

"I withered, like a person, because sitting under that tree, I saw all I needed to. I could have stayed with them, tried to lead them by the hand, but . . ."

"They wouldn't have done it for themselves."

His chest rose and fell in a sigh.

"Have you gone back to the tree recently? Can you see your future too?

"Always, and yes."

I frowned slightly. I was certain that the visions were my unique gift, the result of my fixation upon preventing the horrible outcomes that plagued my life, but if Arthur could see too, then something was not right.

"But . . . then it's not . . ."

"Lilith, you are overlooking the *method* by which you may prevent things. Your fixation is the ability to have all the weapons you require to survive and protect your loved ones."

Each other's weaknesses. If she was alive, I couldn't focus.

"You can build yourself to be unstoppable against any attack. You are made to constantly improve."

"How? How do I do it? Sometimes it seemed I had a grasp of them, sometimes they slipped away. How does it happen?"

He smiled. "Perhaps we will never know. You are unique, as I said once."

"And Eva knew that is what would happen?"

"Your sister," he chuckled. "She was so very clever, and compassionate. She came and went from the shop, confiding in me about your parents, your life together, she had plans for Moksha, until AMRTA gave her her assignment. When she began to translate the sutras, I could see the change in her personality. She became more guarded, and soon I realized that . . . she had figured me out."

"She did. I've only just decoded it now . . . consciously, that is," I said quietly, "but she left me a list of characteristics. 'Abhi nila netto', blue eyes like storm clouds. I know Sanskrit now, by the way."

His laughter was a low rumble that vibrated through me. "I could never be sure of her though. She was exactly as she wished to be, you see."

"A blank space."

"Yes."

Outside the window, the rain drew lines in the spectacle of the fire engines, and bled light into light.

"And the alley?"

He shook his damp head. "I had come to tell her not to do what I suspected she might, but she had ideas of her own. There was no Crossroads for her," he sighed, "nothing in her life that impacted her severely enough, not even your parents. She could not cross the river. Something stood in her way."

I closed my eyes, thinking of her face when she'd asked him if that made her a bad person.

"She knew that even though she had no way to change her life, she could change yours, and by changing you, change everything else. She seemed to think you would understand what she was trying to do and would readily take up her slack."

"Stubborn, just like me," I said proudly. "I absorb powers. Ananda has his memory . . . do you . . . are you endowed with some talent at being in the right place at the right time?"

"What I am . . ." he hesitated, but in the span of a few breaths, trusted me in return, "I do not know if anyone else *can* be. Perhaps I am unique, because even though Ananda and you exist . . ."

"We wouldn't have, without you."

We rested there in silence for a time, as I pulled reason from seeming noise. It was a scant illustration of his state, but I knew it was all I would get from him.

I was sure he was waiting for my reaction, afraid I was hurt that he had not included me, and I was, but not enough to let it overpower the rational majority of voices in my mind. People were so easily pulled away, seduced by the idea of divinity that they lost track of the words spoken. Alive, the Buddha would have become a messiah even sooner, at least dead, he could bide his time. But what was he waiting for? What would the next evolution look like?

"I envision many things," he whispered.

"Global psychic networks, no more disease, peace on earth?"

"As you said, there can never be peace or perfection, but there can be success, triumph over circumstance. I envision a world where no one settles."

I thought of Karl, a man so buried in dismay that anger seemed the only tangible thing. "I don't understand him. He seemed so . . . powerful."

Arthur removed his fingers from the bullet wound and as if it were a magic trick, smooth skin was revealed. "Only because he had more knowledge than you. He had many years to cultivate new abilities, acquire new cravings and satisfy them in unique ways. But once you began outpacing him, he was left feeling inadequate, and in that state, could not react and evolve quickly enough."

"But why try to fight me? Shouldn't he feel success, having made me, having finally done what he set out to do?"

"You didn't attend your sister's graduation," he replied as gently as possible.

"Good point." My mother had always said that by the time she was finished making Thanksgiving dinner, she was too tired to eat it. When Eva called to tell me she was going to walk the line, what I felt was exhaustion, not freedom. I made some lame excuse and she convinced herself that college graduations didn't mean much, and that some people didn't even participate in them.

God, I sucked.

"Will he be alright now?"

"I believe so. All he lacked was a Crossroads, something you were kind enough to give him."

"And now?"

"His life will go on," Arthur whispered, "and some day, when it is possible, when he stares death in the face, he will return to that moment and decide to either live or die."

"Technically, that's already happened."

"True," he shifted his weight.

"Then . . ." I sat forward and watched as he pulled himself free and opened the car door, "is he technically . . . one of us?"

Arthur hugged the car roof and leaned in. "I suppose he might be."

My mouth fell open. "All those poems. You wrote them. You were the one wandering around, spreading and changing the faith into a philosophy once again! You've been doing this for years, haven't you?"

He gave a guilty smile, "Not doing, but preparing to do, absolutely. You were the only missing piece."

As he climbed into the driver's seat, I frowned after him. By the time we got to the shop, I had completely forgiven him. Everything had to be as it had been, or I would not be sitting there, contemplating the future.

Thanks, Ev.

He helped me out, and just to show him that I had no hard feelings, I took hold of his hand and turned it palm up. "Let's see the wheels or spirals, or whatever they're supposed to be."

He gave in and running the pad of my thumb over the shadows my new eyes could not penetrate, I sighed. All the creases of his hand ran outward from a central point, just like the spokes of a wheel.

"They look just like my father's," he clarified. "There's nothing mystical about it."

I brought the central point to my lips, "Says you."

At the top of the stairs, we discovered Jinx curled up on the sofa, dazed and out-of-sorts, mourning the loss of his dearly departed action figures. Matthew had apparently raided the coffee bar for a bottle of bourbon, and sat at Arthur's desk fixedly putting the sharper things in his life out of focus. William was washing his hands in the bathroom, the blood standing out almost prettily against the porcelain.

"He'll be fine. It was just a flesh wound, and that man's as thick a side of beef as I've ever seen. Good thing you had that first aid kit. If we'd called the EMT's, they wouldn't have needed their duffel bags."

"Always be prepared," Arthur advised quietly.

Sam was well-bandaged and propped up against the brass headboard, using Ananda as a pillow. My unused bottles of pain pills and antibiotics were already open on the bedside table.

I leaned over him and kissed his damp cheek. "Did you take *my* medication?"

He opened one eye. "Somebody ought to."

I left him there with a smile and went back out to the living room. As if he were Arthur, I slid my arms down over Matthew's shoulders and hugged him tightly.

"I'm retiring," he announced shakily. "I can't go back after all this. Not when there's real . . . monsters running around . . . no offense."

"None taken."

"What a coincidence," Arthur said, coming up behind us. "William, too, is looking for a new occupation. And with me gone, the back room will be vacant, the upstairs empty."

"Yes," I added with a repressed smile, "and 'Unger Investigation' just has such a witty ring to it."

The heavy-lidded eyes took me in distantly over his shoulder, then wheeled to Arthur. It was obvious an internal battle was raging. I knew though, that Matthew was a man who went by his instincts and that trust in Arthur would win. "What does William *do*, again, besides patch up bullet wounds?"

"He sees bad things."

There was a pause.

"He's got a military background," I pressed. "M1's and trenches, but it's still military."

Another glass was poured and bottomed out, "That might be useful," Matthew mumbled, "especially with Sam's training." He fished out a wilted cigarette. "Yeah, okay, but stuff like that costs money."

"I would be happy to invest."

He took in my smile, and after lighting his damp cigarette, sighed in gratitude.

"Say it."

He growled, then worked his vocal cords into an approximation of Humphrey Bogart, "You're *some* dame."

My giggle was cut short, as suddenly, Jinx seemed to come back to life with a shiver. It was as if he was only just catching up to the conversation, as if the lack of repetition made it more difficult to internalize information.

"Hang on a minute, *gone*?" It was when he was angriest, that the French seemed strongest, turning I's to e's and th's to z's. It was almost cute. "What do you fucking mean *gone*? Where the fuck are you going, Art?"

Arthur turned and smiled at the boy, "I have other places to be."

"You can't just fucking ditch!" He jumped up, flapping his arms. "What am I supposed to do? My god damned house burned down, all my shit is ash, I've lost my power, and now you're taking off? You bastard!"

"I could just say everything twice if it would make you feel better," I offered. Then I produced the shiny silver can I'd stolen from the refrigerator next to the coffee bar and set it on the edge of the desk next to Matthew's bottle.

Jinx stared at it, narrowed his eyes as if afraid he was looking at a mirage, then joined the rest of us a little too eagerly. After he had sucked the can dry like a starved calf, he crushed it with a single quick movement.

"I just wish that you'd brought the rains *before* my priceless keepsakes were crushed by flaming rubble."

I chuckled. "Do your possessions make you feel better about yourself?"

"I don't think that's possible. But they were so *cool*!"

I slicked back his spikes with a tender hand. "I especially liked the beanbag."

EPILOGUE

I set the tiny statue on top of the box with a miniscule, choked laugh. I tried, but could not remember having acquired it. It must have been Eva's and somehow ended up in the attic when she moved out of her room.

It was an Amitabha Buddha, sitting in as close to an elegant lotus position as mass-production could replicate, crowned with a spire, and made of a translucent, milky green plastic gilded with gold paint. It was everything the Buddha was not: gaudy, ugly, and poorly put together.

I sensed him behind me and moved aside, presenting the horrible artifact to him with an ostentatious wave.

He raised an eyebrow.

"You know, it doesn't look a thing like you."

"True. It's green."

I crooked my finger around my chin in false consternation, "I like the chubby ones better. They're jolly."

He smiled *that* smile. "I'm jolly."

"So then if I rub your stomach will you give me luck in my new life?"

"No." He shook his head lovingly, "but I *will* be beside you in your new life."

"Can I still rub your stomach?"

"I suppose." He took the box from me.

"These are the last two."

"Lilith, are you sure this is what you want?"

"I've never been surer about anything."

I stacked the last box on his already full arms and set the statue on top. Illustrious philosophical mind, incarnation of a living god, immortal super-hero: my butler.

Outside on the front porch, the family stood in the disarray of all their meager belongings. I had found them sleeping in their car, a single woman and her two daughters, victims of a recent foreclosure. Their faces were confused, eyes wide in disbelief. When I had invited them to my house for a meal, I didn't say that I'd be leaving it in their hands.

I took the keys out of my pocket and dropped them into the woman's palm. "The papers are inside, all signed. It has no mortgage. It's been in my family for a while."

Her mouth fell open and her fingers did not close. "Sh . . . shouldn't it *stay* in your family?"

"I'm all that's left and I don't need it."

Her eyes welled with tears, "But . . ."

I held up my finger. "One condition."

Her brows furrowed and for the first time, the skeptic appeared, "Yes?"

I reached out and snatched the green Buddha from its seat in front of Arthur's face. I presented it to the oldest daughter, who took it with a stern frown. Beside her, her younger sister shyly peeked out from behind their mother.

"This has to stay in the house, even if you sell it. Stick a note to it or bury it. Do whatever you want, but it must stay here."

Arthur made a noise. I shot an askance at him.

"A bit superstitious, isn't it?"

"Why, is it fighting a curse?" the girl asked.

I couldn't help my grin, "No, but it is very precious. My friend just doesn't think I should be granting objects a metaphysical importance they don't deserve."

She frowned even deeper. "So . . . why don't you take it?"

I poked her third eye amiably. "Because I have the real thing." I jabbed a thumb over my shoulder. "He's more handsome, isn't he?"

She blinked at me in bewilderment and then up at Arthur, who stood beside me, courteously shading her from the sun like a tree.

"I guess so," she shrugged.

With a wave, I excused my footman and as he loaded the box into the Goodwill van, I squatted down and took one of the girls' hands in each of mine.

"Whatever happens, no matter how mad you get at each other, please always remember one thing."

"What?" the older girl asked.

"You may sometimes not like each other, but you're made of the same stuff. No matter how bossy she gets," I said to the little one, "look up to her, because she learns from that. And no matter how silly she is," I said to the elder, "smile back, because she will remind you how wise you should be."

The two girls shared a look and shrugged.

I stood up. "Deal?" I held out my hand.

The woman looked at her girls and then to the house. She hesitated, mulled over the pros and cons in her mind.

"Deal," she whispered, and took my hand, "and thank you so much. I . . . don't know what to say."

"Don't say anything, just turn it back into the home it used to be."

I waved my goodbye and wandered over to the pickup. Arthur was leaning against it, his arms crossed.

"Well Sid, where are we . . .?"

"San Francisco," Jinx shouted from inside. "The Sangha have a temple there."

I raised my eyebrow at him.

"No, I'm not back to normal," he glowered. "I was just being rude."

"Normal?" I smirked in Arthur's direction as I walked to the driver's side. "Weren't you the one who said it was annoying?"

"Two hundred years and now I have to pay attention to people. Ugh."

I clucked my tongue. "Look at it this way, you can listen to your electronica music without constant interruption now."

He squirmed in his seat uncomfortably. "It turns out I really don't like it that much."

"Two hundred years, and you finally have to learn to like *real* music," I grinned.

He was sulking. "Lay off. Elecrtonica is very complex."

I shook my head. "Did you *go*? We're not taking bathroom breaks once we start."

"Kiss my ass," he grumbled, tapping some keys on his ever-present laptop. "I shut off my kidneys hours ago."

With a false sigh of harassment, I slid behind the wheel and shut the door. The technocrat had set up camp in the minicab, complete with a cooler of Redbull, a fleece blanket depicting the Transformers, and a suction-cupped Batman bobble-head, a scant remnant of his vast collection. The computer was plugged into the cigarette lighter and in return was powering several other apparatuses.

Beside him sat an enthusiastically focused Ananda, wearing jeans and watching an iPad as if entranced. We had tried to send him back to the Guardians, but in his typical way, he had just smiled and said he would rather learn more stories to tell. Really, I was sure he just wanted to be back at Arthur's side, to have one last chance of proving himself a friend, not a follower. I hoped for his sake, that his mind could withstand the trauma.

With a long finger, he turned and poked Jinx in the shoulder lightly.

"This Yoda person seems very wise," he said too loudly. "Why then does he insist that Skywalker avoid the dark side? With Jedi knowledge, they should be able to remain objective. For them, there would be no such thing as a Darth Vadar."

The boy snorted. "We're not talking about Chi, we're talking about space bacteria."

Ananda's exotic features seemed to sharpen in intense thought. "Can bacteria live in space?"

Jinx rolled his eyes, "You have much to learn my young Padowan." He leaned between the front seats. "I got our GPS position, Art; do you know which road you wanna take?"

"Roads?" Arthur murmured, shutting his door. "Where we're going, we don't need *roads*."

I pulled away from the curb and glanced up in the rearview mirror, amused. The boy's mouth was hanging open in abject shock. I could tell he was angry he hadn't seen it coming so that he could snicker in superiority.

"Art . . . did you just quote *Back to the* . . .?"

"Future," he anticipated in chorus with the boy. "Yes, and you owe me a coke."

With a giggle, I shook my head and reset the trip odometer. "That'll teach you to go on a road trip with three living Buddhas."

Deflated and flabbergasted, Jinx sank back and shot a glare in innocent Ananda's direction.

"Are we there yet?"

The End